The warrior whirled , for battle. The light from winding, narrow passage. He saw no sign of Lyrelee. Then, something moved at the limit of his vision, a shadowy flicker partially concealed by the curving walls of the naturally eroded cavern. Ariakas leapt forward, feet pounding along the floor as he raced to investigate.

He didn't see the net until it had fallen from the ceiling, wrapping him from the tip of his sword to the soles of his boots. Ariakas tumbled to the floor, and then something jerked on a line, contracting the strands around him. His helmet toppled off of his head, tipping in the net so that the gleaming gem shone directly in his eyes. Everything beyond the tight enclosure was pure blackness.

And silence.

His attackers moved with uncanny stealth, passing through the darkness like a soft breeze.

Saga

From the Creators of the DRAGONLANCE® Saga

VILLAINS

Before the Mask

Volume One—Verminaard
Michael and Teri Williams

The Black Wing

Volume Two—Khisanth
Mary Kirchoff

Emperor of Ansalon

Volume Three—Ariakas
Douglas Niles

Hederick, the Theocrat

Volume Four—Seeker Hederick
Ellen Dodge Severson
Available Winter 1994

Lord Toede

Volume Five—Fewmaster Toede
Jeff Grubb
Available Summer 1994

DragonLance® Saga

VILLAINS
Volume Three

EMPEROR OF ANSALON

Douglas Niles

TSR Inc.

DRAGONLANCE® VILLAINS SERIES

Volume Three

EMPEROR OF ANSALON

Cover art by Jeff Easley.

Interior art by Karl Waller.

First Printing: December 1993
Printed in the United States of America
Library of Congress Catalog Card Number: 92-61106

9 8 7 6 5 4 3 2 1

ISBN: 1-56076-680-8

TSR, Inc.	TSR Ltd.
P.O. Box 756	120 Church End, Cherry Hinton
Lake Geneva, WI 53147	Cambridge CB1 3LB
United States of America	United Kingdom

**For Christine,
always**

Prologue

The great bazaar of Khuri-Khan remained as Ariakas had remembered it, a dense throng of humans and kender mingling with more occasional elves and even a rare minotaur or domesticated ogre. A maelstrom of noise surrounded him: persuasive, singsong arguments of merchants, loud cries of outrage from overcharged customers, background cacophonies from minstrels and flutists, even sporadic clangs of daggers against shields or gauntlets. Each sound added to the unique and energetic character of the grand marketplace.

The warrior strode among the teeming crowds, and those in his path intuitively stepped aside to give passage. Perhaps it was his height that inspired fear—for he stood a handspan taller than most other men—or his bearing, which was erect and apparently imperturbable. Broad shoulders supported his solid neck, and his head rose like a lion's, his dark eyes studying the crowd from beneath a mane of long, windblown hair.

Ariakas paused a moment at the central fountain, where water arced upward and then spattered across a sun-drenched basin of mosaic. He hadn't visited the shop of Habbar-Akuk for many years, but he was certain he could still find the place.

There, to the left of the fountain, he recognized the narrow alley. A colorful stall, draped in bright fabrics gathered from across Ansalon, marked the alley entrance. Countless varieties of incense fogged the air around the canopy, triggering an olfactory memory that could not be mistaken. Beyond the scent-merchant, he saw a corral where short-legged mountain ponies were bought and sold, and he knew for certain he was in the right place.

He found the unpretentious facade of Habbar-Akuk's shop against the wall at the back of the alley. It was hard to imagine from the weather-beaten planks and the worn string-beads hanging across the entrance that this was the establishment of the wealthiest moneylender in all Khur. Perhaps, Ariakas thought with a tight smile, that's why Habbar has remained in business for so long.

Parting the colorful beads, Ariakas ducked his head in order to pass through the low doorway. The tall warrior remembered that in the past he'd always felt claustrophobic in these chambers, but perhaps that, too, was part of Habbar-Akuk's success. In any event, he knew that on this visit he wouldn't be staying long.

"High-Captain Ariakas! This is *indeed* a pleasure!" Habbar-Akuk himself, bowing deeply, emerged from behind his small desk to take the warrior's hand.

"Ah, you old crook," Ariakas replied, with affection. "All you see is my money walking through the door!"

"My lord, you do me injustice!" protested the plump

moneychanger, his pointed beard quivering in indignation. "I extend to you a welcome, a welcome most warm —and yet you wound me with your tongue!"

"Not so badly as I wounded the bandits that used to plague your southbound wagons," Ariakas noted, amused at the merchant's protestations.

"Ah, so you did. Never did I have a guard captain so capable, so diligent in his duties! I should never have let the warlords hire you away."

"Don't waste your regrets," Ariakas replied. "There was too much money to be made in the ogre campaigns —even if they were doomed from the start."

"Ah, ogres!" Habbar-Akuk made a great show of spitting into one corner of his office—a corner that had seen a great deal of expectoration in its time. "Even if Bloten still stands, your men gave the brutes an accounting they won't soon forget!

"In fact," continued the merchant, his eyes narrowing, "I had heard that the warlords intend to mount another expedition. I should think you'd be their first choice for command." His eyes asked the question for which his words were too discreet.

"Of course they want me—they're no fools," Ariakas noted without bragging. "I'm the only reason even a few of us returned from the last invasion."

Habbar-Akuk remained silent, knowing that he would receive further information. His instincts proved correct.

"I was promised full command of the invasion. They reminded me that it was ogres who killed my father—as if I could forget! But that reason only worked so long as Red Tusk was alive—naturally, that was a score that could not remain unavenged. Now that slate is clean— the killer of my father is dead by my own hand."

"Well said," murmured the moneychanger. "A man who does not pursue revenge is no man at all."

"Still, the warlords tried to kindle the old blood-lust, sure that I'd leap at the chance to continue these campaigns. And once, of course, I would have done so.

"But I tell you, good Habbar," continued the warrior, "I have no stomach to make war for fighting's sake. I've done too much of that, and where has it got me? Lucky to be alive, I'd say. And so I told the warlords as well."

The moneychanger nodded sagely, his eyes narrowing.

"They offered me more money, then," said Ariakas. "Enough to make me rich beyond my dreams. But I asked myself, what good is money to a man who lies in the dust, his skull crushed by an ogre club?"

"Say not—surely no such fate awaited the great Duulket Ariakas!"

"Such a fate awaits *every* man who invades Bloten, sooner or later," replied the mercenary captain. "These continuing campaigns are madness! It will take nothing less than a full-scale army to bring the ogre nation to its knees, and the warlords have no wish to spend that kind of money—even if there were such an army to be hired. I decided that I will remove myself from the risk."

"And I may play a small role to help?" Now Habbar-Akuk allowed his eyes to drift to the obviously heavy saddlebags the warrior carried over his shoulder.

"I have decided to try my fortunes across the mountains, in Sanction," Ariakas explained.

Habbar-Akuk nodded thoughtfully, as though the arduous mountain crossing were a thing attempted every day. "There are perils enough in the Khalkists, wherever you go. The savages of Zhakar block passage to the east, while the fortress of the bandit lord Oberon stands to the north of Bloten. Why to Sanction?"

"I have heard there are comforts there for a man who has money. That a gold piece from Khur can buy its equal in pure steel from the merchants of Sanction."

"Of course . . . and, too, you will be a man with money?" inquired Habbar-Akuk with a guileless look of curiosity.

Smiling tightly, Ariakas heaved the two satchels onto

the heavy counter. Despite its sturdy construction, the platform shuddered under the weight of clinking metal, and Habbar-Akuk's eyes sharpened in avaricious appraisal.

"It would seem that the warlords have already paid you well for your services," the merchant allowed with a pleased nod.

"Five years of my life should be worth something," Ariakas snapped. "Now, what I want is this: to convert these coins into valuables I can carry comfortably in my pack, something I can take on a long journey."

"Naturally," Habbar murmured. He touched the satchels. "Steel pieces, of course."

"For the most part, though there's gold and platinum too. Tell me, do you have something suitable?"

"These matters cannot be hurried," explained the moneychanger, opening each of the saddlebags and allowing his pudgy fingers to run through the metal coins. "Still, I think that I shall be able to accommodate you."

"I suspected as much. A fat diamond, perhaps—or a string of pearls?"

Habbar-Akuk held up his hands in mock horror. "*Please*, my lord. Nothing so mundane for one such as yourself! An occasion like this calls for a unique treasure, a thing suitable for yourself alone!"

"What's the matter with gemstones?" demanded Ariakas. "I don't want you loading me down with some statue, or a supposedly enchanted mirror that'll break the first time I take a rough fall!"

"No, no—nothing of the sort," disputed the merchant. "But, it's true, I have *just* the thing for you."

The pudgy merchant disappeared into his tiny back room and was gone for several minutes. Ariakas suspected that Habbar had a secret trapdoor connecting to underground treasuries, but he had never tried to find out. Habbar-Akuk had been a grateful employer to the man who had won safe passage for his merchant wagons all the way to Flotsam. The moneychanger had seen to it that the warrior benefitted from glowing recommendations to some of the most influential warlords in Khur. Ariakas, in turn, had converted those recommendations into several successful campaigns, and this small fortune. Thus, the two men had a relationship of mutual, if businesslike, respect.

At last Habbar-Akuk returned, and he looked at Ariakas appraisingly, as if deciding whether or not the warrior was worthy of the splendid deal he was about to offer.

"Well, what is it? Do you have something?"

"I have more than *something*," retorted the moneychanger. "I have the *perfect* thing."

He extended a small locket toward Ariakas. The tiny box, connected to a platinum chain, was studded with brilliant gemstones—rubies, diamonds, and emeralds. Even a cursory examination suggested to Ariakas that it was worth far more than the money he offered in exchange.

Turning it over in his hands, Ariakas flicked a switch, and the locket flipped open. The warrior caught his breath as he saw the perfectly etched image of a woman's face and shoulders. Despite the size of the picture, he sensed immediately that she was a person of exceptional—even breathtaking—beauty.

This locket would buy him a small palace, he knew, or a grand house, or a pastureful of horses . . . or whatever he wanted. As he held the locket he noticed the gentle curve of its frame, which swept inward at the waist like a woman's voluptuous body. He found the image enticing, and as the seconds passed, a more vivid picture of the lady began to materialize in his mind.

She would be tall, of course—that much he could tell from the shape. He believed—he *knew*—that she had flashing black eyes that would hold a man spellbound with their cool appraisal. Her waist was tiny, her body beautiful beyond compare, beyond imagination. His heart tore at his chest when his mind conjured the image of that perfection.

"Who—who is she?" he finally brought himself to ask.

Habbar-Akuk shrugged. "A lady of Sanction, as a matter of fact. Rich as a queen, I was told. Her beloved had that locket made before he died."

Oddly, the thought of the pictured woman's lover brought a surge of jealous rage to Ariakas, and it was with some satisfaction that he absorbed the news of the fellow's demise. "Sanction, you say?" The news was far from displeasing to him. "Do you wish to count the money?" He gestured to the saddlebags, holding his breath. Surely Habbar-Akuk would want more for such a rare treasure.

Surprisingly, the merchant shrugged. "It's right and proper, I know," was all he said.

Ariakas stared at the picture in the locket. That long neck drew his eyes with hypnotic power, and the clean sweep of her shoulders filled his imagination with alluring images of the body below.

"It's right," repeated Habbar-Akuk. He pulled the saddlebags onto the floor of the shop.

Ariakas nodded distantly, turning toward the door and its bead curtain. He still held the locket and stared at the picture, the jeweled treasure tightly clutched in his hand.

"Farewell, Lord Ariakas," murmured Habbar-Akuk before adding once more: "It is as it should be."

Ariakas passed through the door into the sun-dappled marketplace. Somehow, the frantic crowd seemed to have lost much of its intensity. The merchant's words rang in his memory, and he felt beyond a doubt that Habbar-Akuk had been correct.

It was right that Ariakas hold this locket, and right that he set out with it for Sanction.

PART ONE

SEDUCTION

Chapter 1
A Thief in the Khalkists

Ariakas woke in the night, roused by some unknown disturbance, a subtle shift in the rhythms of the darkness. Dry mountain crags soared to the sky all around him, outlined only in starlight, and the stillness allowed him to hear the distant rumble of surf against the shore. Close beside him, gray ash masked the dying remnant of his fire, a small collection of embers gleaming in crimson contrast to the dark night.

Sitting up, he shrugged off his bedroll. The certainty crystalized: something or some*one* had been through his camp. He felt equally certain that the encroacher was gone. The warrior took his own fresh awakening as sign that the intruder had intended him no harm.

Still, a sense of violation persisted, growing into a cold outrage as he touched the hilt of his sword, reassuring himself of its presence. The weapon was old, but sturdy and sharp—he felt a strong measure of relief feeling the weathered hand guard and grip.

Silently he rose to a crouch, allowing the fur blanket to tumble to the ground. Chill air tingled across his naked back as he stepped to his pack. A quick check showed that his rations of dried meat and hardtack remained untouched. In a sense the discovery disappointed him, for it meant that the visitor had not been merely a hungry animal.

Next he reached through the pack for his flask of lavarum, finding it immediately. He moved the bottle as he continued his one-handed search, and then he froze. Carefully he raised the flask, hefting it gently to gauge its weight. His lips curled into an involuntary grimace— fully a third of the precious liquor was gone!

Setting the silver container to the side then, he plunged his hand into the depths of the pack. He felt his long dagger, secure in its doeskin sheath. Moving the weapon, he reached farther—and a sickening sense of worry rose in him. Frantically clawing around, he felt nothing but the hard ground through the leather bottom. The locket! It was gone—stolen from his pack while he slept!

His anxiety and rage immediately flamed into powerful determination, like a banked fire welcoming the first breath of the bellows. Yet he forced himself to be calm as he looked at the stars. He had another hour until sunrise. There would be no finding the thief's trail without light, he knew. At the same time, when he began the pursuit, he wanted all of his endurance, all his speed and agility for the chase.

At issue was far more than the worth of a tiny, however precious, object. More important was the fact that this thief had entered camp in the dark of night—had stood over his sleeping form!—and then had proceeded to rob him and disappear. To Ariakas, the insult weighed as heavily on his mind as the loss of treasure. He would regain his locket, and at the same time deal a proper measure of retribution to the thief.

With this purpose in mind, he pulled his fur across his goose-pimpled flesh, once again resting his head on the cloak-wrapped pillow of his boots. A single star had winked out behind the looming crest of the mountain before he was asleep.

* * * * *

On one side of the camp, the Khalkist Mountains plunged toward the surging shore of the Newsea. A series of steplike granite ledges climbed away from the angry surf, each mountainous shoulder strewn with a patchwork blanket of wiry grass, chiseled bedrock, and loose, sharp-cornered scree.

Now, in the pale blue light filtering through the layer of dawn clouds, Ariakas awakened with a sense of purpose. The pounding of the surf was a lonely accompaniment to his solitude, penetrating coastal mists even though the Newsea itself lay partly concealed behind dissipating fog. Tendrils of that same fog cloaked the rugged heights, shrouding the summits in a gray overcast and slipping through the valleys and gorges like the thief through his camp.

He let his fire lie, taking a piece of hardtack for his breakfast, distracted into hurrying by a sense of urgency. In fact, his rage had been filtered into nothing more than a dire purpose, and vengeance was a purpose that compelled immediate and forceful action. As Habbar-Akuk had noted, a man who did not pursue revenge was no man at all.

When he hoisted his pack to his back, he thought of the locket, the picture of the woman. He was aware of an acute sense of loss, astonished to realize that he *missed* her! In the weeks since leaving Khuri-Khan, he had passed through the most rugged, inhospitable country on Krynn, and always *she* had been his companion. She helped him overcome his pronounced vertigo as he negotiated cliff-bracketed passes, or steep, treacherous glaciers. She had shared his frigid camp in rocky swales, where the nearest firewood was a thousand feet away—straight down. Always she had helped him ford streams, avoid avalanches.

Ariakas even wondered to himself if it had been the lady who had warned him about the ogre patrol two days earlier. He had always before taken for granted his innate ability to sense danger. It had been key to successful campaigns, enabling him and his men to escape deadly ambushes. Yet when he had encountered the ogres, the lady's presence articulated the alarm with peculiar urgency, precision . . . and care.

It had been the day before yesterday. Drizzling rain obscured vision, and Ariakas was chilled and uncomfortable as he trudged across lowland terrain. A strong premonition, which seemed to him like the lady's voice, warned him of danger. Taking shelter in a thicket of willows beside his trail, he silently watched a half dozen ogres march into view, passing within a few paces. Each of the beasts was a Basher, dressed in the crude loincloths of sentinels of Bloten. Bashers passionately hated humans, dwarves, and elves. Eight feet in height, with weight nearly double Ariakas's, each of the long-armed monsters wielded an assortment of clubs, axes, and swords. One of them alone was a threat to the most capable warrior—a band such as this, if alerted to his presence, would inevitably track him down and kill him.

As he watched the monsters disappear, it was hard for Ariakas to suppress his desire to attack. Remembering years of campaigns, of friends slain and villages razed, all his old hatreds threatened to surge into life. Curiously, then, he found cold solace in the fact that now he had no such obligations, no responsibilities beyond himself. The ogres vanished into the rain, and without further interruption or worry, Ariakas had resumed his trek to Sanction.

His attention returned to the matter before him. His eyes scanned the dry, brittle grass around his camp, and he pondered evidence that the thief was a very capable individual. At first glance he could see no sign of the intruder. His own bootprints from the day before stood out clearly, showing his course through the narrow valley below, following the pattern of switchbacks up to this high ledge.

Perhaps that's how he followed me, Ariakas mused. The trail was little-used, and the previous week's rain had ensured that his tracks were the only marks in the mud.

But why would the thief have scrambled up to such a height, and then only stolen the locket? Sure, it was the most valuable item he possessed, but his purse of coins held several valuable steel pieces, and no self-respecting cutpurse would have left them behind. Perhaps the fellow was shrewd, and only went for the easily transportable item of high value.

Too, the intruder must be a person of remarkable stealth. He had passed within a few feet of Ariakas, and the mercenary captain was a *very* light sleeper. The thief had opened the pack, taken a drink from the flask of lavarum, and removed the locket—all without attracting the man's attention.

Then the final question—why had the pilferer left him alive and armed? Above all things, Ariakas was a practical man. He disdained thievery—it was the desperate act of a weakling, he believed with conviction. And, too, it was impractical. A thief could not help but make enemies, and odds indicated that sooner or later one of those enemies would catch up with him and exact vengeance. Therefore, in his life Ariakas had only taken those things he earned, or whose owners stood no chance of ambushing him at some unknown moment in the future.

Yet in stealing this locket and leaving Ariakas alive, this thief seemed to be *asking* for trouble! Perhaps the fellow had supposed the theft would not be noticed for a day or two, but that seemed a farfetched explanation. Certainly Ariakas never would have taken such a risk.

As he continued to search for signs of a spoor, he began to seriously question his prospects for success. For long minutes he scrutinized the ground, circling his camp in an ever-widening spiral, without success. Surely the culprit hadn't *flown* from the scene of his crime!

Again the curl of fury twisted his lip, unnoticed by the warrior as he grunted and muttered his frustration. He was no woodsman, but neither was he a novice in the ways of the wild. Certainly the wet ground would yield *some* clue as to his thief's route of departure!

He considered the possibility of a blind pursuit—simply making a guess as to which way the fellow had gone. His chances of success were slim, but without a spoor it seemed the best he could do.

A tiny rock, flipped so that its muddy side faced the sky, caught his eye. Freezing in place, Ariakas studied the slope rising away from the stone. The snarl disappeared from his lips, replaced by a thin, taut-lipped smile. The footprint was so faint as to be almost invisible—merely a place where toes had pressed into the mountainside in an effort to gain secure purchase. Only the dislodged stone, streaked with mud where all the other stones had been washed clean by constant drizzle, told him that this was the place. Squinting, he looked upward, and found another obscure print a dozen paces away.

The trail! Without hesitation he secured the pack to his shoulders and made sure that his sword rested lightly in its scabbard. His own boots gouged deep, muddy wounds in the soil as he followed the faint track, long strides carrying him quickly up the hillside.

Throughout the day he followed the spoor across the tumbled landscape of the Khalkists. The rocky soil yielded precious few clues, but each time the path threatened to peter out before him, another subtle indication appeared.

Gradually he became aware that his quarry made no particular efforts to disguise his route. Ariakas followed a winding series of valleys away from the shoreline, but not once did the thief attempt to double back, or select a surprising turn in his path. Instead, he followed the course of the valleys, generally working his way toward a high pass that Ariakas could see above and before him.

By late afternoon the warrior had entered the flat valley before that pass, growing increasingly certain that the mountainous gap must have been his quarry's destination. For one thing, the vale he now traversed was a steep-sided gorge, with sheer rock walls climbing to the right and left. The only points of access seemed to be the slope he had climbed, which led from the coast of the Newsea to the narrow gash in the stony ridge before him.

Here, in this narrow valley, Ariakas found solid confirmation that he was on the right trail—and that the thief took no precautions to avoid pursuit. The left wall of the gorge, which the trail had followed below, suddenly veered inward, jutting to the very shore of the narrow stream that trickled along the valley floor. Low, muddy banks bracketed the tiny flowage, and the rock wall before him forced Ariakas to cross.

There in the mud he found his proof: a pair of footprints, where the thief had tiptoed through the muck and then either forded the stream or skipped across on the tops of several slick rocks rising from the placid water. Ariakas waded quickly through—the water didn't even reach the top of his boots—and on the other side, as he looked for confirmation, he received a surprise.

Two sets of prints led away from the stream, turning, as he had guessed, toward the looming pass in the high ridge. The information momentarily puzzled him, throwing a number of his assumptions into doubt. Could it be that a *pair* of intruders had slipped through his camp without awakening him? The odds of that stretched credulity to the snapping point. And, too, why had they let him live, and not even tried to take his sword!

The prints in the mud were small and indistinct, for the soft earth had already settled back to erase much of the detail. In any event, Ariakas took less note of the size of the footprints than in the quantity. It was with renewed vigilance that he moved away from the stream, angling up a long, grassy slope toward the narrow notch above.

As he climbed, another thought occurred to him. He had suspected all day that he followed a thief of remarkable, but innate, stealth. Judging from the lack of trail sign, the fellow had moved with an almost uncanny ability to leave the ground undisturbed. Now, with the knowledge that the scant spoor had been left by two thieves, Ariakas further revised his estimate of his quarry's stealth.

Yet at the same time, the two thieves had trekked through the mud of the streambank and left a plain spoor, when a little bit of wet-walking up the creek would have allowed them to emerge onto a cluster of boulders, leaving no footprints at all! It was clear they didn't care whether they were followed or not.

The latter suspicion heightened the warrior's sense of readiness. Was he walking into an ambush? It seemed like more than a faint possibility.

All these concerns focused in his brain as he approached the narrow gap. A tiny path cut back and forth across the steep slope, and every once in a while he saw the telltale smudges of footprints in the loose dirt.

He lacked the tracking skill to guess how long ago his quarry had passed, so he made the cautious assumption that they were close before him. Perhaps they'd even watched his long traverse up the bare mountainside.

At last the trail veered into the notch. A quick glance at the approach showed Ariakas that cover for himself was nonexistent, while any number of splintered cracks yawned within the pass, offering ample concealment to anyone who awaited him. Drawing his sword, he quickly scrambled up the last twenty feet of the trail and found himself standing between two weather-beaten shoulders of rock.

Every sense tingled alertly. He looked to the right and the left, trying to penetrate the shadows with his eyes. Nothing moved there. No sound disturbed him except for the growing howl of the wind. Indeed, the light breeze had risen into a steady gust as he crested the ridge, and it now blew his long hair back from his face, chilling his clean-shaven cheeks and chin. When he tried to stare into the distance, the biting force of the wind brought tears to his eyes.

Yet he was finally certain that no ambush awaited him within the narrow gap. As he stared into the distance, he tried to shrug off the eerie feeling that no other life existed in these rugged mountains—no life beyond the warm pulse of his own blood, his own rasping breath and growling determination.

He turned his back to the wind, giving respite to his eyes. His back-trail fell away below him. In the distance, between barren humps of low mountains, the gray waters of the Newsea surged relentlessly against the rocky shore. Far to the right, along the mist-screened coast, he saw a low-hanging bank of dark cloud—Sanction.

There the volcanic Lords of Doom spumed their smoke and ash into the air. The pall of darkness remained a constant fixture over that racked city, he knew. Though he had never been to Sanction, many of his mercenaries had seen that gods-bereft place, and had described it in excruciating detail. He unconsciously marked distance and direction for his future march. But then he turned back into the wind, back to the trail and the quarry before him. He would not travel to Sanction without the locket, and he would not regain the locket without confronting the thieves.

Only now did he begin to feel his weariness. The tension of the pursuit, the determination of the long climb, had sapped his energy more than he had realized. The trail before him led down an equally steep expanse of grassy shale. Before continuing, he slumped to the ground, placed his back against a flat rock, and tried to catch his breath.

His gaze swept across the vista before him, as his mind carefully appraised each challenge, each difficulty facing him.

First, the geographical: he now faced the most tortuous terrain he had ever seen. Sheer pinnacles of rock rose upward in a dozen locations, each of them culminating in a soaring peak that had surely never felt the footfall of a landbound creature. Rock-walled gorges plummeted out of sight between these heights, and if any trail scraped along those cliffs, he saw no sign of it from here.

Neither did he see sign of water, though dirty patches of snow clung to several shaded gullies on the southern faces of the peaks. A series of twisting ridges snaked their way around the gorges, skirting the greatest heights, but it seemed that every mile of forward progress would require an equal amount of ascent and descent. By contrast, the steep climb to reach this pass had been an amiable stroll.

Next, the quarry. Where had the two thieves gone? He noticed with growing frustration that the ground below him was rocky and dry. The moisture-laden clouds had expended their rain on the sea side of this soaring ridge, retaining no water for the barren heights before him. Here he would find no tracks in the mud. Too, the slope was primarily bare stone, with very small patches of hardy grass tufting upward here and there. Anyone who traveled with the stealth of those thieves would surely leave no sign of their path.

And finally, he saw *nothing* that looked like a logical trail. Wherever his quarry had gone, they had followed an improbable and dangerous route—and a dozen such possible paths currently presented themselves.

His fingers clenched into fists as he wrestled with the quandary. Did he dare to make a guess from so many possibilities, each of which offered inherent threats to his life just by making the attempt to follow? Or should he waste precious daylight—his best estimate placed sunset less than two hours away—by searching for signs that might not even exist?

The two courses of action wrestled in his mind as he caught his breath. Within a few minutes he was physically ready to move again, but he had not decided how to proceed, and he knew that he had to do *something*. Ariakas rose to his feet, hoisted his pack to his back and, knowing that he'd need both hands on the steep mountainside, slid his sword back into the scabbard. Stepping to the edge of the pass, he began to look for the best way down—but once more he allowed his eyes to drift across the barren, rugged terrain.

He froze, his breath quickening in tension. Something had caught his eye, near the summit of a neighboring ridge. *There!*

Ariakas couldn't believe his luck. Two figures, tiny in the distance, came into view. Slowly the pair worked across a steep slope, carefully grasping for handholds as they traversed a jagged ledge of rock.

Instinctively he dropped behind the blocking boulders of the pass. He could see the two clearly now, and there was no doubt in his mind that these were the thieves.

They moved with precision and care, but also with surprising speed. He calculated the course that had taken them from this pass to that ridge, and imagined the dizzying descent, followed by an exhausting climb, which had brought the culprits high onto the next mountain. Unconsciously Ariakas acknowledged that the thieves were at home in these mountains, and utterly fearless.

He could discern few details about the two figures. They wore earth-colored clothes—it was only their movement that had drawn his attention—and they climbed with careful grace. Within a few minutes they disappeared from his view, but now at least he knew which way to go.

Renewed energy surged through his veins, and he started down the slope with almost reckless enthusiasm. A small rockslide of loose scree tumbled around him as his long strides sought purchase on the slope. In this fashion he half ran, half slid all the way to the bottom of the pass. His heart pounded with excitement, and he felt steady endurance solidify his muscles as he splashed through the narrow stream and started up the opposite incline.

The place where the thieves had disappeared was chiseled in his mind, and he wasted no effort looking upward. Instead, his reaching steps carried him along the rising slope of the rocky massif. Gradually he gained altitude, but only when he arrived at the foot of the rocky column did he begin to work his way straight upward.

Now sweat beaded across his forehead. His pulse pounded in his temples, and he drew lungfuls of air in deep, rejuvenating breaths. Ever upward he moved, instinctively seeking handholds and secure footing, pulling himself through a steady ascent.

Finally he reached the place where he had seen the two thieves. During his rapid pursuit, the sun had slipped behind the western peaks, and a shroud of darkness had begun to draw across the sky. Ariakas ceased his climb and began a careful, sideways traverse. Stars twinkled in the east as he came around the shoulder, moving with extreme care. A single misstep would send him sliding hundreds, perhaps thousands, of feet down the rocky slope, yet he felt the image of the lady calling him on. Focused on his objective, Ariakas sensed only a vague awareness of the dizzying height.

Soon he reached a gentler slope, and he started forward without pausing for rest. Yet even here he couldn't spare a hand to draw his sword—he could only hope that the thieves remained as blithely oblivious to pursuit as they had appeared throughout the day.

Finally he felt dirt below his feet, and with a measure of gratitude he left the rocky promontory behind. Darkness closed about him now, but he could discern a low valley before him, and an even darker patch that could only be a grove of hardy cedars—the first trees he had seen all day.

Fierce triumph surged through his veins; full proof of his quarry rose before him. Who would believe the thieves could be so arrogant, so careless, as to build for themselves a fire?

Chapter 2
A Fight Without Fear

Ariakas crouched behind the shelter of a densely needled cedar
and studied the layout of the thieves' camp. He saw one
slender figure working over the fire, puttering with a
pan. The unmistakable scent of frying bacon reached his
nostrils, drawing an involuntary growl from his stomach.

He ignored the discomfort, pleased with the fact that
the night vision of at least one of his enemies would be
destroyed by looking into the bright coals. Ariakas
shrugged out of his pack, looked around, and picked an
approach route that led between several small, stunted
pines.

Taking pains to keep the thief between himself and
the fire, Ariakas ensured that his own eyes remained

sensitive to the subtleties of darkness. The warrior could not see the cook's companion, but knew from snatches of conversation drifting on the breeze that the fellow remained near the fire. As yet he could not identify any words, though the voices struck him as cheerful and chatty—certainly not the sounds made by someone expecting trouble.

Carefully he crept closer, moving with stealth and patience, making sure that not a twig cracked under his heavy boots. It took him some time just to reach the next tree, but he felt certain that his quarry had no plans to move any farther tonight. As if in confirmation, the second thief emerged into view and tossed several dry cedar branches onto the fire.

Ariakas ducked away, covering his eyes before the bright flames crackled upward to wash the entire grove in cheery illumination. The blaze sizzled and popped, giving him an idea. He reached out and touched several brittle branches of a dead cedar, snapping them off while the noise of the fire camouflaged the sound of his own activity.

Again he moved forward, worming his way on his hands and knees, carefully feeling for obstacles before him. Within a few minutes he reached the ring of trees closest to the fire. Here he settled down to spy.

The cook still poked at the fire. As the second thief turned from rummaging in a pack, Ariakas got a look at his face and body. With a jolt of surprise he realized that he had been robbed by a *kender*, and the knowledge brought a grimace of disgust to his face. The fellow wore the supple traveling clothes of the diminutive folk, with his long hair in the characteristic pony tail hanging over his left shoulder. His walk was almost a skip, and Ariakas was reminded of the inherent grace he had seen as the pair had moved across the mountainside that afternoon.

A quick glance showed him that the cook was also a kender, with even longer hair than the first. With a wry shake of his head Ariakas ducked back to consider his course of action.

Naturally, this explained a lot. The stealthy movement and faint trail coupled with the childlike clumsiness of the footprints by the stream . . . the locket stolen, the swig of lavarum, all while he had slumbered a few feet away . . . and the decision to leave him alive. No decision at all, really—surely it had never occurred to the kender to do anything else. None of this changed the central fact, of course: they had stolen his treasure, and he had caught them.

His objectives were still the same. Only the approach had changed. His original plan had been straightforward: frighten the thieves into producing the gem-studded object and then kill the leader in retribution and as an object lesson to the accomplice. However, he knew kender were utterly fearless—no intimidation, no bluff would produce the locket, or even an apology. Still, the little folk tended to be far more naive than the typical human thief. Perhaps he could trick them. If worse came to worst, he could kill them and find the treasure himself.

His decision made, Ariakas stepped around the tree and walked up to the fire as if his appearance here were perfectly natural. His sword remained in its scabbard, while his left hand held the clump of dry pine branches behind his back.

"Oh, hello there," said the first kender, who had just joined the cook by the fire. "You're almost in time for supper!"

The second turned with no visible expression of surprise. Ariakas felt another jolt as he saw that this was a female. Delicate lines scored her slender face—a face that might have belonged to a young girl except for its creases of maturity. "Did you bring that lavarum?" she chirped. "That'll be the perfect thing with this bacon-potato goulash!"

Despite his preparation, the directness of her remark took Ariakas by surprise. "Yes—yes I did," he blurted after a moment.

"Say, that was good stuff!" agreed the male, amiably indicating a place by the fire for Ariakas to sit. "I'm Cornsilk Tethersmeet—and this is my friend, Keppli." The female bobbed her head, a welcoming smile on her face.

Suddenly the ridiculousness of the situation infuriated Ariakas. Disgust rose like bile in his throat. He cast away the brittle branches—he saw no need to night-blind the kender.

"Look," he declared, his voice dropping to a menacing growl. "I've come to get my locket back—which one of you will get it for me?" His hand dropped to the hilt of his sword in none-too-subtle accent.

"Your *locket*?" Cornsilk Tethersmeet squeaked in surprise. "What makes you think *we* have it?"

"I *know* you have it," replied the human grimly. "Now, one of you get it for me!"

"I'm beginning to think we'll just keep this supper for ourselves," challenged Keppli, huffily. "You can just build your *own* fire, if that's the way you're going to be!"

Ariakas refused to alter his course. Carefully watching the pair, he sidestepped over to their packs and flipped open the flap of the first one.

"Hey! You can't do that—that's mine!" shrilled the female kender, jumping to her feet.

Ignoring her protests, he rummaged inside the leather satchel, pulling out a horseshoe, a blacksmith's hammer, a gem-studded brooch in the ornate platinum image of an eagle, and several bottles and flasks that apparently contained food and drink.

"Stop it!" protested Cornsilk, stepping toward him.

Ariakas drew his sword with his free hand and raised the blade. The little fellow stopped, a scowl of concentration wrinkling his face.

Plunging his hand into the second backpack, Ariakas pulled out a variety of boots—many of them too large for kender feet, and none with an obvious match—as well as a plush robe of soft brown fur. Finally his fingers touched a familiar leather-covered bundle.

"This!" he declared, pulling forth the chain. He allowed the gleaming locket to swing in the firelight, dangling before the startled kender. Orange glimmers danced across the platinum, and the rubies at the locket's corners glowed in reflection like baleful, accusing eyes.

"That's not *yours!*" declared Cornsilk Tethersmeet with a determined shake of his head.

"Do you remember where you got it?" challenged Ariakas.

"Sure—I found it!"

"*Where?*"

"In the mountains—last night," explained the kender patiently, as if he believed that he could change the human's mind.

"You stole this from my pack while I slept!" Ariakas barked.

The kender's eyes widened in shock and indignation. "I did no such thing! Why, if it had been in your pack, then *you* stole it—and I found it there!"

Growling in irritation, the warrior shook off the barrage of objections. Sword raised, he advanced on Cornsilk Tethersmeet. The final measure of justice remained, and to him it mattered not whether the thief was human or kender. The little fellow's next words stopped him in his tracks, however.

"That locket belongs to the lady in the tower," the kender protested, vexed by Ariakas's lack of understanding. "It's even got her picture in it! Why, I might even have remembered to give it back to her," he concluded with injured dignity.

"What lady?" inquired the human, intrigued in spite of himself.

"Why, the lady that the ogres of Oberon caught," explained the kender in exasperation. "They keep her in the tower over there." He gestured vaguely to the east.

"Who is she?" demanded Ariakas. He remembered the name Oberon, a bandit lord reputed to command a band of ogres to the north of Bloten. "And how do you know the locket's hers?"

"I *told* you who she is—the lady held prisoner by ogres! And I know it's her locket because she told me about it. She lost it before—or maybe it was stolen. She told me about those four big rubies in the corners, and the little clasp. Even that raven carved into the back. Plus, it's got her picture in it—right there! There can't be *two* lockets like that, can there?"

Ariakas resisted the urge to answer. "Tell me more about the lady."

"She's a princess, or a queen, or something," Keppli piped up. "I know that she's *rich*—or she was before the ogres got her and put her up in that tower!"

"Where does she come from?" the warrior pressed.

The two kender looked at each other and shrugged. "Go and ask her," Cornsilk Tethersmeet said, impatience registering in his voice. "Now, if you'll be kind enough to be on your way. . . ."

"One more question," stalled Ariakas, the hilt of his sword nestling comfortably in his palm. "Where is this tower, this place where the lady is imprisoned?"

"Over there," declared the kender. "About three days travel, I should say. It's on the border of Bloten, but I think the ogres who live there are just some kind of renegade band. They have their own warlord—the one they call Oberon."

"How is it that you know so much about them?" inquired Ariakas. He remembered Oberon's name with growing interest since Habbar-Akuk had mentioned the same brutal monster.

"Oh, we stayed there for a week last winter. They gave

us a nice room, up near the lady's, where we could see for miles—all the way to the Lords of Doom, on a clear day."

"But then," Keppli interjected, "we heard them talking about us and, well, it wasn't very pleasant—"

"And we never *did* get to meet Oberon!" asserted the male.

". . . not very pleasant at all," Keppli continued with a firm shake of her head.

"So we left," concluded Cornsilk. "As if those locks could hold anyone!"

"They hold the lady?" pressed Ariakas.

"Well, yes," admitted the kender, though he seemed prepared to argue the point. Then he shook his head. "So you see, you can't have her locket. If you'll just put it down—"

"I'm taking it. Nothing you've told me changes the fact that you're a thief—the worst kind of pilfering rogue, to sneak through the darkness and threaten a man while he sleeps!"

"Why, I—"

"Quiet!" Ariakas's voice became a roar, and the kender's mouth clamped shut in surprise. Cornsilk's dark, surprisingly mature eyes studied the warrior appraisingly—and with a total absence of fear. For some reason the kender's refusal to be afraid enraged the human. "Here's your justice, thief!" he barked, thrusting sharply with the sword.

Cornsilk was prepared for the move, but he hadn't anticipated the warrior's speed. The kender dropped and rolled to the side, but not before the tip of the sword ripped into the exposed side of his neck.

"Hey!" shouted Cornsilk, clapping a hand to the wound and staring in confusion at the bright, arterial blood spurting between his fingers. Then his eyes closed, and he sprawled to the ground.

"I will spare you," Ariakas said to Keppli, clasping the locket in his left hand as he held his sword at the ready.

Warily he eyed the female kender. "But pray remember this lesson before you steal again."

The fury in Keppli's eyes astonished him. She could not have blasted him harder by unleashing bolts of fire. In a steady, uncompromising voice, she taunted him. "Hail the human warrior, brave enough to murder! The goat who was his father would be proud! The sow that gave birth to him would squeal in delight!"

"Would you face your companion's fate?" he demanded, flushing angrily.

"It's nothing beside the fate in store for you!" she cried, her voice tinged with an edge of laughter. "Before the gods are done with you, raven wings will beat around your bones—lizards will crawl between your legs!"

"You're mad!" he snarled, slashing wildly at her, furious as she skipped beyond range of his sword.

"Madness is a thing *you* should know!" she sang, fierce triumph ringing in every word, biting into Ariakas like the sting of a poisoned blade. "Blood of insanity flows through your veins—only the shade of a heart beats within you. Oh, yes—madness is a thing you know too well!"

Ariakas lost all vestige of control. He lunged through the dying campfire, hacking at the nimble form. Somewhere in the back of his mind a voice of reason, of caution, told him that this was dangerous.

Even so, he dived after Keppli, darting the tip of his blade across her heel, drawing a squeak of pain as she tumbled to the ground. He leapt, but she rolled away from him, and as he skidded to one knee, she bounced to her feet.

Cold steel gleamed in her hand.

Raw instinct took hold of the warrior's arm, bringing his blade through a desperate arc as he toppled backward, striving to avoid the blade that snicked past his throat. Somehow he raised his sword.

Thrusting, he drove the weapon through the kender's body, cursing as her dagger sliced his chin and lip. Keppli spoke no words—she simply collapsed and died. Ariakas let his blade fall with its victim, clasping both hands to the blood that jetted from the long wound across his face.

Chapter 3
Fortress Oberon

It took nearly a week to find the tower, but when he did, no doubt lingered: before him loomed the dour keep where the lady pictured in the locket was held prisoner.

The lofty structure rose into the sky like a massive, weather-beaten tree trunk. Upthrust from a craggy summit of dark stone, the high, cylindrical tower seemed to defy gravity, to defy all worldly constraint as it soared above the peaks of the Khalkists. Clouds whipped past the parapets of its upper ramparts while mist shrouded the valleys—gorges actually—that lay a long plummet to all sides.

The fortress itself was taller than it was wide, and it seemed to perch like some serene vulture on its lofty pinnacle. Its black stone walls rose flush with the cliffs, soaring to narrow parapets. Near the top, six flanking spires jutted outward from the central tower and encircled the upper ramparts. A cone-shaped roof capped the main structure, though the surrounding spires were topped with the notched rims of stone parapets.

For the most part, the keep and its unassailable summit stood apart from other mountains, separated from them by wide chasms and gorges. Yet one mountain, equally lofty, rose close beside the fortress. A steep, treacherous pathway led to the summit of this adjoining peak. A drawbridge raised almost flush with the tower's wall could be lowered to span the gap between the pinnacles, giving the winding trail access to the keep's only door. Still, with the drawbridge raised, it seemed to the warrior that the fortress was as well protected as a castle floating on a cloud.

Groaning in weariness, Ariakas slumped against a boulder. The stone was hard, angular in shape, and so cold that it sapped the heat from his body despite the fur cloak he had made from the kender bedroll. Yet even now, in the shadow of an obstacle that loomed as impregnable as anything he had ever faced, he hadn't considered turning away. The temperature continued to drop, and an icy wind drove bits of snow like stinging needles against the exposed skin of his face. But no notion to seek a lower elevation entered his mind.

Instead, he looked about for a place to make his camp. The primary attribute of this camp, he knew, would not be shelter, though of course that was desirable. More importantly, however, he looked for a place from which he could observe the tower while remaining concealed. In time, he found a narrow niche in a steep slope, a dozen feet above the winding trail that approached the drawbridge. Here he was protected from the wind, and two large boulders screened his tiny camp from the tower's observation. He could lie prone, exposing just the top of his head between those two stones, and gain a good view of the lofty fortress—from its low gate to the soaring pinnacles of its six spires.

Making himself as comfortable as possible, Ariakas settled onto the ground to study his objective. In the hours since he had discovered the tower, he had seen no sign of movement nor any life within or atop the structure.

He stared for a time at the high gates, visible behind the drawbridge. They seemed to be a pair of narrow doors, rising together to a point. Before those doors stood the tall, plank roadway of the drawbridge, now raised almost to a vertical elevation by chains that emerged from slits in the tower's wall, forty feet above the entrance.

As Ariakas studied the place, his hand came to rest against his chin, and he explored the deep scar that remained from the slice of the kender's knife. No mirror allowed him to inspect the cut, yet his fingers had told him many times in the past week that the wound was wide, gaping from the ridge of his chin into his lower lip. He could press his tongue between the two halves of that cut, and though the injury had healed without infection, it created difficulties in eating and drinking. His imagination told him that the raw flesh in the cut glared angry and red.

Since his encounter with the kender, Ariakas had spent many hours reflecting on his carelessness. He felt bitter shame for his loss of control, knowing that—if he'd kept his wits about him—he could have avoided that slashing blade. Why had the bitch been so foolishly self-destructive? He wrestled with the question for the thousandth time. Surely she knew she had no chance against his sword. Or had she really felt that he'd lose complete control, enabling her to strike a killing blow?

An unusual sense of disquiet permeated the warrior's thoughts. His confidence sorely waned with the memory of his last challenge—a simple retrieval of his locket, an operation that left him maimed. Was that failing the factor that brought him now to this formidable tower, contemplating this mad task? Or was it, perhaps, the ogres? He bore no love for the beasts, and the murder of his father, plus a thousand other outrages, had given him ample desire for vengeance. Did rank hatred propel him into this suicidal course?

He knew that he was driven by more than this. Unconsciously, he reached his hand into the pouch at his side and curled it around the solid box of the locket. Then, as always, his imagination completed for him the image of a woman—*the* woman, she had become.

As always, he was amazed at the clarity, the consistency of his mental image. Of course, he had the likeness of the tiny picture to begin with, but a full array of additional details had been added by his mind. Only the woman's clothing ever changed—now in his thoughts she wore a flowing dress of powdery blue, whereas this morning his imagination had pictured her in a filmy gown of silky white. Her shoulders were bare, for the dress was cut low, and her long, ink-black hair was coiled upon her scalp with queenly majesty.

Her face was long, sculpted in a beauty too serene for words. Her dark eyes alternately flashed and wept, and her sweeping neck was adorned with glittering jewels. Graceful fingers rose to her face, as if she felt his intrusive presence. But, too, it was an intrusion that he sensed she wanted, for her breasts rose and fell with the increased tempo of her breathing, her lips parted, moist, in silence that he took as invitation.

Why did he feel compelled to reach her? The "lady" in the tower, she had been to the kender. . . . She was rich, a princess, perhaps. Ariakas liked money, had felt the draw of wealth throughout his life—had even known the pleasures of extravagance, when coins had flowed from his fingers like water over a dam. It was a grand feeling—wealth—and a powerful summons.

But it was not the thing that drew him now.

Night pulled in its shutters, and the tower disappeared from view—except for one high window, where a yellow light broke the stygian darkness like a solitary star. Clouds lowered, and flurries of snow eddied around Ariakas, but still that light gleamed like a beacon, calling him onward and upward.

He rested through the night, sleeping little. When he did close his eyes, the image of the lady grew and burned in his mind. After a few moments of this, he would awaken and stare at the tower, at the lone light that still flamed in the sky, even as dawn began to color the eastern horizon.

Despite his restless night, he crawled from his bedroll with a sense of vigor and purpose. The mist had burned away, and the tower stood out in stark black outline against the clear sky. The sun sent its first probing rays from beyond the horizon, and these illuminated the highest peaks—and, soon, the tower. Yet when sunlight struck the dark walls, it seemed that the brightness vanished into the black stone surfaces.

His observation was interrupted then by a strange sound—the first noise he'd heard in many days other than the moaning of the wind or the splashing of a mountain rivulet. It was the unmistakable clink of metal against metal, and in a few moments Ariakas discerned the measured beat of footsteps.

Pulling down behind the security of the twin boulders, he studied the pathway below. Shortly a large metal-clad figure came into view, swaggering up the trail. It took Ariakas less than a second to recognize the brute as an ogre. A great, toothy mouth gaped wide below a blunt snout, and twin tusks, yellowed with age, jutted upward from the corners of the jaw. The creature stood fully eight feet tall, with a barrel-sized chest and two huge, stumpy legs. As it marched it cast wicked eyes to the left and right, diligently searching the slope above the trail.

Ariakas crouched and froze, listening as the brute trundled past. By then he could hear the sounds of other marchers, grunting, groaning, and cursing under some strain. Risking another look, the man saw that the lead ogre had disappeared around the next bend in the trail. Immediately below, a pair of ogres labored under the weight of a heavy log, precariously balanced across their broad shoulders. Others came into view, each hauling a tree trunk destined, Ariakas speculated, for the fireplaces of the lofty keep.

Finally the band of ogres worked its way around the bend, but still Ariakas held his position, waiting and watching the trail. Minutes passed. The sounds of the grumbling ogres faded up the trail. Still the warrior waited.

A man came into sight, walking slowly and carefully up the path. Like the ogre who had led the column, he scanned the slopes above the trail with diligence and caution. His hand rested on the hilt of a long sword, and the weapon swung at the strange warrior's side with a grace that spoke of long familiarity.

More significant was the man's armor. Ariakas allowed his face to twist into a scar-split smile when he saw the metal helm—it included a visor lowered to cover the warrior's face. He was a large fellow, well-muscled and long of leg. Like the fully masked helm, these facts also met with the approval of the figure concealed above the trail.

Ariakas took a quick glance up the path, checking that the ogres remained out of sight. He then hefted a small stone, nestling the oblong shape in his palm as he watched the lone rear guard pass his place of conceal-ment. The blank mask of the helmet faced upward, and Ariakas froze while the gaze swept past his niche. Fortu-nately, as he had expected, the narrow vantage point and the surrounding shadows concealed him.

Then, as the rear guard looked farther up the trail,

Sholem Aquatic Center   Clerk: 061
Date: 06/13/2007   Time: 13:18:15

Daily Sale

          Description   Ext Price
_____

Pool Daily NR Admiss   7.50
Pool Daily NR Admiss   7.50
Pool Daily NR Admiss   7.50
Pool Daily NR Admiss   7.50

Rcpt#   166564 Sub-Total: 30.00
                Sales Tax: 0.00
                Total Due: 30.00

                Tot Paid: 30.00

CASH Payment of: 30.00

Rcpt# 166564

Ariakas pitched the stone through the air, watching as it fell perfectly—about ten feet on the other side of the warrior, *down* the slope.

The fellow would have been inhuman if he had ignored the sudden rattle of sound. The man's sword was in his hand in a flickering instant, instinctively slashing the air behind him. Only then did he hear the sounds above.

Whirling, the warrior raised his long sword to face Ariakas, who plunged his broadsword downward with both hands. The guard staggered backward, then dropped his blade, and for a sickening instant Ariakas feared that he would plummet over the edge of the steep trail. But the man caught his balance, and his faceless helm dipped downward for a fraction of a second as he looked for his weapon. That splinter of time was enough—Ariakas thrust sharply, aiming for the gap between the man's helm and his breastplate. The sword slipped through the niche, and the guard groaned once, an exhalation of shock and surprise. Then he slumped to the ground, dead.

Now Ariakas had to work fast. Glancing up at the lofty tower, he saw no movement, no sign of any reaction at all. All he could do was hope that he remained unobserved. Swiftly he tore off his own leather armor, replacing it with the dead man's plate mail and helm. Discarding his knapsack, he took the locket, his dagger, and—after only a moment's hesitation—the flask of lavarum and stuffed them into his small belt pouch.

Slipping the helmet over his head, he dropped the faceplate to conceal his features. After cleaning and sheathing his own sword, he started up the trail. As he jogged along, he slipped the shoulder plates over his arms and pulled the gauntlets onto his hands.

With the faceplate down, he knew he presented a reasonable facsimile of the man he had slain. How long he could maintain the charade he didn't dare to guess.

Instead, he concentrated on closing the distance that separated him from the ogres and their heavy load of firewood.

The trail twisted and wound on its way up the narrow crag adjacent to the ogres' tower. Ariakas's lungs struggled for air as he lumbered ahead, dragged down by the unfamiliar weight of metal armor. Finally he came around a bend and caught a glimpse of the steep upward slope before him. The brutes had apparently been waiting, for some of the ogres lolled on the ground around their great logs while others stamped their feet impatiently and glared back down the trail.

As soon as Ariakas came into sight, the sitting ogres lurched to their feet, though with some visible reluctance to resume their labors. One of them gave him a casual wave, which the warrior returned, while the others heaved the logs to their shoulders and started the march.

Now Ariakas tried to assume the mantle of his new role. He inspected the heights and the back-trail just as he'd seen the dead man do, ensuring that no one followed the party back to its lair. The trail entered a series of steep, narrow switchbacks, and he was acutely conscious of the ogres marching along the face directly overhead. He paid them little obvious attention, reasoning that their human rear guard would be more concerned with any unknown threats lurking to the sides of the trail.

Eventually the path opened onto the narrow summit of the crag, and the party moved onto the crest. Ariakas guessed that they approached the lowered drawbridge, and he hastened up the slope below. His plan depended on him reaching that portal before the crossing was raised again—he didn't want to risk calling out for the guards to lower it. After all, he didn't even know what language they'd speak within the forbidding tower.

He crested the ridge to see the drawbridge resting across the chasm, the double gates of the tower just swinging outward as he approached. The keep soared to the sky before him, looming upward like an extension of the solid, craggy peak. Several of the outer towers extended toward Ariakas, giving the impression that the entire keep leaned forward, ready to fall upon him. Huge squares of dark granite intermeshed perfectly to form the high, sweeping wall. Except for the six outer towers, no external features interrupted the curved wall. Smooth palisades thrust upward to meet the overhanging lip of the cone-shaped roof, far overhead.

The ogres lumbered forward, trudging across the long drawbridge and disappearing through the gates into the tower. Ariakas hastened to follow. Risking an upward glance, he studied the tower as he reached the edge of the bridge. Narrow windows slit the walls in many places, and he imagined numerous eyes upon him. He could see no movement in the darkness within, however, and soon even the ogres before him had vanished into the dark maw of the gates.

Stepping onto the bridge, Ariakas was struck by an overwhelming realization of the immense drop yawning below him. The gorge lay more than a thousand feet below the bridge, and a sensation of dizziness overtook him. Gritting his teeth, he strode resolutely forward.

Passing between the open gates, he saw shadowy outlines of the winch and gear mechanisms that operated the doors. Two ogres, grunting impatiently, cranked a capstan and wheeled the huge portals shut with surprising speed. At the same time, the rattling of chain overhead informed Ariakas that the drawbridge mechanism had also been engaged. The gates slammed shut behind him, and he knew his course was set.

"Here, Erastmut—saved you a glop!" grunted one of the ogres, holding out a slime-streaked bottle. Ariakas took the flask, at first feeling a measure of relief that the ogre spoke in Common. At the same time, he knew he couldn't afford to raise his visor in the presence of someone who knew Erastmut.

Silently nodding his thanks, Ariakas took the bottle and reached for his faceplate. An acrid stink, mingling cheap whiskey and ogre drool, nearly sickened him as he lifted the bottle. Then, as if remembering a great secret, he held up his palm and gestured toward his belt pouch. He reached inside and pulled out his prized flask of lavarum. Setting the ogre's bottle down, he passed the flask over to the brute.

"Good!" grunted the ogre, sniffing at the neck appreciatively. He raised it and took a long gurgle.

Ariakas grimaced at the sight of the precious stuff running down the monster's chin, but still he dared not speak. By then the other ogre gatekeeper had stepped over to them, and Ariakas gestured for him to take a drink as well. The first one scowled and shook his head. "No—din't get a good taste that time." Again he hoisted the flask and guzzled.

"Hey—save some!" barked the second, reaching out with a massive paw. Predictably, the first ogre pulled the bottle away, sneering at his companion in the sublime superiority of one who holds a winning hand of cards and doesn't care who knows the fact.

"Gimme!" insisted the second, his temper aroused by his companion's air.

The drinker cuffed his fellow's grasping fist away, lumbering a few steps to hold the flask out of reach. The thirsty ogre snorted and lunged in pursuit.

Ariakas took the opportunity to slip down the entry corridor. The high-ceilinged passage was bracketed by stone walls, with a bare floor of crushed rock. Many doors and passages opened to the sides, most of them dark and silent though an occasional glimmer of torch or candlelight showed beneath a portal. He reached a side passage where he had seen some ogres disappear to the left, and here he veered right. The corridor continued a short distance and then branched. The telltale ammonia stench from the left branch told him that it led to a latrine, so he continued right.

At last he was out of sight and hearing of the door. Though he desperately missed the ability to see and hear freely, he still did not dare to remove the constricting helmet. He had no idea how many humans might be quartered in this tower. He also realized that the scar on his face made him a rather memorable figure, and he feared that even among the dull-brained ogres his appearance would draw attention.

The corridor Ariakas followed turned a corner and terminated at the foot of a wide, straight staircase. His heart flamed into hope—the kender had said the lady was imprisoned at the top of the tower. Abruptly he heard the tromp of bootsteps coming down the passageway. Without hesitation he leapt to the stairs, climbing them four steps in a bound. His heart pounding, he vanished into the upper shadows just before the marching ogres emerged into the corridor below.

Chapter 4
The Light at the Top of the Tower

Concealed from the threat below, Ariakas slowed his pace on the stairway and listened for activity. The bootsteps below faded, though he heard rumbles of laughter and short bursts of squabbling from many places on the ground floor. Above him, all remained silent. Torches flickered from wall sconces at the top of the stairs, which climbed straight up at least forty feet in total. Ariakas cursed the narrow field of vision provided by the slits in his helmet, but he dared not remove his disguise.

Carefully climbing the remaining steps, he began for the first time to consider the grandeur of this isolated fortress. The stairs were dark hardwood, though the walls within the keep seemed to be the same granite as the outer faces. Many tapestries draped the walls of the stairway, torches flared and sputtered within elaborate wire cages, and smooth, elegantly carved handrails were mounted on the wall to either side.

Obviously, this place had not been built by brutish humanoids. Ariakas wondered about the mysterious ogre warlord Oberon, questioning for the first time if the fellow were really an ogre. The relatively decent maintenance here suggested otherwise. After all, he had plundered enough ogre lairs to well remember the pervasive stench of urine and collected refuse that had characterized them all. Here, however, someone had either cleaned up after them, or compelled them to clean up after themselves. These ogres even used regular latrines, as he had sensed below.

The second floor encircled a wide hall in the center of the keep. The stairway reached one end of this hall while another series of wide steps led upward from the opposite side. A dozen torches flared on the walls, showing Ariakas that the room was empty of ogres. Several dark hallways gaped around the room's periphery, and here too the walls were lined with ornate tapestries.

Without wasting time in further inspection, Ariakas hastened across the room and up the next stairway. The memory of that beacon in the night burned in his mind, drawing him toward the top of this lofty keep.

The next floor proved to have a much smaller central hallway, with many more corridors branching from it. From some of the side passages muted torchlight spilled outward, while from others emerged the basso rumbling of ogre snores. Here, too, the stairway narrowed to a mere ten feet width; apparently the ceremonial portion of the fortress was below.

Stealthily, the warrior crossed the short distance to the next flight of stairs, moving upward to another floor similar to the one he had just passed. The fourth floor, however, showed evidence of being completely deserted—no torches or snores disturbed the stale, musty air.

Quickening his pace, Ariakas bounded upward. He soon reached the fifth floor, where the very vastness of the room brought him to a cautious halt. Fading daylight showed through the slit windows on three sides, so he knew the room was as wide as the keep itself. On the fourth side, facing the neighboring mountain, a small room blocked a portion of the outer wall. His upward goal still urged him on, but Ariakas felt suspicion about this level. As silently as possible, he crossed to the flat wall of the small room. A heavy door, banded with iron and equipped with brackets to hold a sturdy bar, stood slightly ajar.

Cautiously he peered around the door. With a pleased sense of confirmation he recognized the huge capstans and large coils of chain that could only be the drawbridge machinery. From the weight of the chain and the bridge, he assumed that dozens of ogres were required to raise the platform. Lowering it, he thought with a smile that tugged at his split lip, would be another matter entirely.

Hastily he turned back to the stairway. The next floors he reached were all the same—huge, circular halls that filled the entire width of the keep. Concentric rings of stone columns circled a large, central post, which gave these vast chambers the appearance of a dark, petrified forest. The last beams of sunlight, spilling horizontally in the western windows, added to this eerie effect like late afternoon rays intruding onto the shady woodland floor.

These levels he passed quickly, taking no more than a cursory look for ogres. Finally the stairs embarked on a long ascent, uninterrupted by interceding floors. They angled upward to a horizontal landing, then zig-zagged back to another. Torches were placed at each landing, though much of the expanse between was lost in shadows.

After four of these landings, Ariakas began to realize that, though surrounded by the walls of the stairway and the bulk of the castle, he was nevertheless very high above the rest of Krynn. His lungs labored for breath in the thin mountain air. The dark metal helmet seemed to close around him, and the scar on his chin and lip burned in the confinement.

His caution banished all these concerns as—halfway up from the fourth landing—he heard measured, tromping footsteps overhead. Flattening himself against a railing, he tried to vanish into the shadows.

A huge shape hulked into view, marching on the floor above, looming in the torchlight at the top of the stairs and then continuing past, out of sight. Ariakas heard the footsteps cease and then, following a slight shuffle, turn back toward the stairs. Remaining immobile, Ariakas watched the ogre guard again trundle across his line of vision, and then heard him halt and return. The cadence continued, with less than half a minute between each of the ogre's passes.

Cursing under his breath, Ariakas analyzed the formidable foe. This was the first diligent ogre he had encountered in the castle. Clearly the beast was guarding something of great value. Hope flared within Ariakas—hope so strong that it acted as its own confirmation. There, just beyond the ogre guard, he knew he would find the lady!

Carefully, Ariakas crept up the stairs, one step each time the ogre passed. He was thankful that the shadows remained thick near the railing, and also that the ogre showed no inclination to look down. Instead, the brute kept its eyes to the front as it paced back and forth, its repetitive path forming the crosspiece to the **T** of the stairway.

Finally, Ariakas reached the edge of the shadows, about five steps from the top. Once again the ogre passed, marching to the warrior's right, and now Ariakas drew his sword and gathered his feet below him. His mind vividly imagined the charge—a low rush from the darkness, his sword darting upward into the flab-rolled neck. A sure strike into the brain would bring instant death . . . the slicing of the jugular slightly slower, but no less certain.

Still tense, Ariakas suddenly realized that the ogre should be returning. Instead, he heard the guard's steps clomp some distance away. Abruptly the steps halted, and the warrior heard a telltale gush of water.

Springing upward, he quickly reached the corridor at the top of the stairs, mentally thanking whoever had compelled these ogres to use latrines. Ariakas first looked for another stairway leading up, but there wasn't one. Since the ogre was off to the right, he darted left. A gleam of torchlight spilled from a side corridor. Instead of sooty smoke, a scent like flowered incense washed outward with the light. The lady.

His heart thundered from more than lack of air as he turned down the lighted corridor. He burst through a doorway, gasping for breath and blinking in the bright light. At first he thought that the entire room glowed, but then he quickly narrowed his focus to three lanterns suspended from the ceiling. Fumes of foggy scent billowed around these lights. Beyond the chamber's lone window, black night hung. Ariakas knew that this was the aperture he had studied from the windswept mountain below—the beacon that had glowed seductively throughout the long night.

Then all other details fell into insignificance as *she* stirred. The lady lay upon a huge bed beside one wall, and now she shifted her head to look at him.

Ariakas's knees turned to jelly, and he staggered from the impact of her beauty. She was the mirrored reflection of the black-haired figure who had haunted his dreams . . . the image etched into the platinum of the precious locket.

Without thinking—perhaps it was the weakness that suddenly permeated his legs—he dropped to one knee before her and removed his helm. He bowed his head, seeking to hide the deep scar on his chin and neck. For the first time he felt its true grotesqueness. Reverently he knelt, consumed by ecstacy tinged with a kind of terror. Who was she? It didn't matter.

"Rise, warrior, and approach me."

He shivered, her voice piercing him with exquisite joy, and slowly he stood. His legs still felt wobbly beneath him, but he was pleased that he could walk steadily, taking three firm steps. Daring to look at her, he finally let his eyes absorb the beauty that had already suffused his spirit. He no longer cared about the deep, disfiguring scar on his face.

Then, for the first time, he noticed the cruel iron collar that encircled her neck. Outrage exploded as he saw the heavy, dark chain, the sturdy bracket bolted to the wall beside the bed. His voice choked with anguish, he could utter no words to express his grief at this indignity.

Her body was long, he noticed—certainly she would stand as tall as he. Her face formed a perfect oval of sculpted allure, with high cheekbones framing black eyes that seemed to smolder with promise . . . or danger. Her cheeks tapered to a strong chin. Lips like the dark crimson of a royal robe parted slightly, glistening from the moisture that, he imagined, was left by her darting tongue. Her neck was long and supple, angling gently into narrow shoulders and a straight back. A gossamer gown of blue silk did little to conceal the full outlines of her breasts, her trim hips, or her long, graceful legs.

Only her feet altered slightly the image of his imagination. In his mind they should have been tiny, and clad in immaculate slippers of some suitably ornamental material. Yet she was barefoot, and the skin of her toes was cracked and calloused.

Her captors had not allowed her the decency of footwear. Fury formed a film across his vision, and his hands clenched unknowingly into fists as he imagined the vengeance he would wreak in her name. But then she smiled, and all thoughts of violence and bloodshed vanished from his mind.

"You have come for me . . . I thank you," she said, and her words were the silken tones of music that had nearly held him spellbound before. There was no hint of question in her words—she *knew* why he was here.

"What—what is your command, Lady?"

"Take me from this place, warrior!"

The weakness in his legs disappeared, replaced by a steely determination that—almost—told him that he could slash his way through an army of ogres.

"Yes—that's why I've come. How many ogres are there in the tower, do you know?" he asked.

"I suspect there are several score—perhaps half a hundred."

"I thought so, too," he agreed. Crossing to the window, he peered from the opening, suppressing a sense of vertigo as the extreme height of his vantage opened before him. There would be no escape that way—the tower wall plunged downward for hundreds of feet, and then it met the mountainside itself, which was nearly as steep. Even the darkness couldn't conceal the vast scope of the fall.

"Do they know you're in the tower?" she asked softly.

"No—we have that going for us, at least." He gestured miserably to the chain and iron collar. "But how do we get you out of *that*?"

She sighed, and sank back on the bed. "Oberon is a cautious lord—it will not be easy."

"Do you know Oberon?"

There was a bitter tint to her smile. "Would that I didn't," she replied. "But it is Oberon who keeps me here, like this." She gestured to their surroundings.

For the first time Ariakas noticed the true splendor of the lady's apartment. Soft draperies lined the walls. Deep, plush couches and gleaming tables of marble and teak rested on the floor. Indeed, except for the iron collar and chain, he might have entered the formal chambers of some countess, even a princess or queen.

Sight of that confining chain brought raw hatred to Ariakas's heart. He wanted to meet Oberon, to plunge his sword into the villain's breast with a sneer of triumph on his face. And even that, Ariakas knew, would be insufficient to right this grievous wrong.

"With your permission . . ." He reached for the chain, and the lady nodded. Seizing it in his powerful fists, he first tried to bend the links, and then to pull the bracket from the wall. Though the veins stood out on his forehead and a film of red crept across his vision, he could not so much as bend the solid metal.

"I was a prisoner in a dungeon cell before Oberon brought me here. I know that he keeps a master key ring there, in the catacombs below," the lady offered. "The chief warden—he's a big brute of an ogre—keeps it on his belt. You'll usually find him sleeping on a bench right outside the main guard room."

Ariakas sank on the bed, heavy with despair. "*Below* the castle? I am willing, but I must warn you the chances of my capture are great."

"There's another way. Often Oberon visits me by the secret stairway, avoiding the main part of the castle. It's concealed in the outer wall, and will take you all the way down."

New hope infused the warrior. He rose to his feet eagerly. "Where—where is this passage?"

She pointed to a heavy curtain of pale blue velvet. "Draw that aside. Then push on one of those stones above your head—as high as you can reach."

He soon found the catch-stone, and a panel of wall soundlessly slid sideways to reveal a small landing and a tight, narrow stairway curving downward to the left. His sword held before him, he turned toward the concealed passage.

Then, in a moment of decision, he turned and crossed

back to the bed, kneeling again beside her. The lady's face invited him, only a few inches away. Her lips were still parted slightly, shining with excitement or desire.

Without hesitation, he seized her and kissed her. She melted into his arms, and met his mouth with a fiery force of her own, a force that set the blood to racing in his veins. Even his scar was forgotten.

A fierce grin lit his face as he turned back to the secret door. He felt that he could face any adversary, any challenge, if only to win the chance to hold her again.

Chapter 5
Ferros Windchisel

Reaching upward, Ariakas again found the catch-stone for the door. When he released it the portal slipped quietly shut behind him—and plunged the entire landing into utter darkness.

His sword sheathed, Ariakas felt for the top step with his foot while he balanced with his hands against the walls. Finding the edge of the landing, he took a step downward, and another. The stairs circled through a regular spiral, so he soon found that he could move fairly rapidly even through the darkness. He knew that if he came to a missing step or some other obstacle, he ran the risk of injury, but he couldn't bear the thought of the lady remaining a prisoner any longer than absolutely necessary.

For a long time the stairs circled steadily downward. Ariakas noticed several narrow, slitted windows that served to admit such gleams of starlight as spilled from the night sky. Nevertheless, as his eyes grew accustomed to the gloom, he found that even this dim illumination gave him the ability to speed his descent.

After some time he came to another small landing. A quick investigation showed him a concealed door leading into the interior of the keep. He decided to risk opening the portal to learn all he could about their prospective escape route.

True to his suspicions, the door opened into one of the huge, column-studded rooms that lay below the lady's chamber. Quickly he closed the door and started downward again. He passed several other landings, mentally ticking off the floors, and then he stopped to open another door.

This time the portal slid aside to reveal a masking tapestry. Ariakas was about to pull the curtain aside when he heard the muted grumbling of ogre voices. Cautiously, he peered around the edge of the cloth. He had reached the small room containing the drawbridge machinery. Two ogres stood beside a tall window, where the great winch-chain fed outward to the bridge. The main door to the room still hung ajar, only a few paces from the secret entrance. Ariakas grimaced in thought; certainly these two guards created an obstacle.

He silently continued down the stairway, passing several more levels, until his memory told him he had reached the main entry hall of the tower. Where Ariakas had left two ogres bickering at the gate, he now heard raucous sounds of ogre merriment, ranging from bellowed curses to hearty, stone-shaking laughter. Quite a party, it seemed, had developed around the main gates.

He turned away from the ribald ogres and descended farther, through several long spirals with no sign of any alcove or landing. The passage now was completely dark, and—frustrated by the enforced slowness of his pace—Ariakas felt a need for caution. He groped with his toe for each step, all the while keeping hands on the side walls to ensure balance.

Finally he felt a space to his right, and at the same time the air took on a dank, claustrophobic character that told him he had entered a region some distance underground. Feeling his way out of the stairwell, he moved carefully along a narrow corridor. The passageway abruptly veered to the right, and a faint glimmer of light rounded a corner before him. The intensity of the illumination rose and fell as if it came from a flickering torch. Impatient, Ariakas forced himself to remain still and listen.

The light before him continued to brighten and dim, though he could hear no sound of flame. Gradually, however, he discerned a deep, rhythmic noise. The sound resembled a low growl, drawn out for a long time before it ceased. Then, after a similar interval, the growl came again. . . . Snoring! The depth of the tone suggested a large nose and deep, resonant chest. It didn't take much imagination for Ariakas to picture an ogre guard slumbering beside the torch, just out of his sight. Could this be the chief warden the lady had described?

Gradually he became aware of other features of his surroundings. The corridor before him was narrow, but not so tight as the stairwell. Darkened niches stood at regular intervals along the walls, and in them stood the doors of countless cells. Apparently only one guard kept watch, and not very well at that.

Creeping forward, Ariakas encountered something the dim light had not revealed: a cluster of rubble on the floor, through which his foot scuffed loudly. The noise echoed like thunder through the dungeon hallway, but Ariakas heard no disruption in the vast snoring. Carefully, he worked his way along the hall. A few steps carried him past several heavy cell doors to an intersection with the side corridor.

Around the corner, an obese ogre slumbered on a long wooden bench, a torch in a wall sconce flickering and flaming above him. Beyond another row of shadowy cells, the corridor ended in an open door, and another flight of stairs led upward.

He took a step around the corner, taking care to move as silently as possibly. He would have to tiptoe right up to the ogre to get the keys, but he was willing to take that chance.

"*Ssssst!* Hey, *you* out there!"

The whispered voice froze his feet to their tracks. Whipping his head around, he saw no sign of anyone in the corridor with him.

"Help me—I need your help!"

Again the words, which might have emerged from the ether for as much as Ariakas could discern their source. Angrily he stepped back around the corner, out of the slumbering ogre's line of sight.

"Who is that?" he hissed.

"In here," replied the whispering voice—more a croak, now that Ariakas listened carefully. It seemed to emerge from the cell door he had just passed.

"What do you want?" he demanded.

"Water . . . need water," came the voice.

"I can't help you," Ariakas replied. "Be silent!"

"Help me—or I'll make more noise than you can believe."

Seething, Ariakas looked at the door to the cell. The portal was solid iron, with a small hatch over a narrow opening—barely space enough to slide in a cup or a bowl. Pressing his face to the opening, he saw nothing more than darkness beyond.

"Who are you?" he demanded again. The prisoner was obviously an enemy of the ogres, but that was no guarantee Ariakas would find him to be a friend.

"My name is Ferros Windchisel—and all I ask is a cup of water!"

The name sounded dwarven. Ariakas had fought and drunk beside dwarves, and he respected their prowess in both categories, but had never befriended one. Nor did he have any intention of doing so now.

"You seek to gain this water by threat?" hissed Ariakas. "What good is it to you to reveal my presence here?"

"No good to me," replied Ferros conversationally. "But even less so to you. Call it a threat if you will—I call it a reasonable price to pay for my silence."

"Where is this water?"

"The guard keeps a bucket beside his bench—but be careful. He's a light sleeper."

Ariakas didn't like the suggestion or the threat, but one thing he remembered about dwarves was their gods-cursed stubbornness. He had no doubt that Ferros Windchisel would make quite a racket if he refused his request.

"I'll get your damned water," he snapped.

"Come in and get my cup, then," rasped the dwarf.

Surprised, Ariakas tested the cell door. It was bolted on the outside, but not locked. At first he thought it a careless arrangement, but when he pressed the bolt aside and entered the cell, he saw that the ogres were taking no chances.

A thin reflection of torchlight spilled through the door, revealing a short, bearded figure sitting against the far wall of the small cell. Ferros Windchisel reached out, the movement making a pronounced rattle. He was chained by the neck to a solid bracket in the wall—a situation identical to that of the lady, save for the bleak surroundings.

"Thanks, friend," said the dwarf, extending a filthy tin cup toward the warrior.

"How do you know I won't kill you right now to make my job easier?" demanded Ariakas.

"I hadn't thought of that," replied the dwarf. "I suppose you could do that before I could make too much noise." He reflected ruefully on the prospect, his dark eyes glaring reflectively up at the large human.

"Ah—to the Abyss with it!" grunted Ariakas, even more irritated. He reached out and snatched the cup from the dwarf's hand. Quietly he left the cell, turned the corner, and shielded his eyes from the direct torchlight. Stealthily approaching the slumbering ogre, he saw the bucket of water, half-full, beside the stout bench. The beast slumbered unsuspectingly as Ariakas dipped the cup through the film atop the liquid, scooping out a drink for the dwarf.

Hastily retracing his steps, he stalked into the cell and extended the cup. "Here you are—and make no mistake! If you don't stick to our bargain, I'll get back here before the ogres catch me. You'll die before me!"

"Bargain?" The dwarf, whose face was streaked with grime, managed to look mildly perplexed. "Oh, you mean not to wake the guard?"

"What else would I mean?" growled Ariakas.

Ferros took a deep drink and looked sheepish. "Actually, I exaggerated about the guard being a light sleeper. That slug could nap through an earthquake and never miss a snore—you didn't have anything to worry about from me."

The first flush of Ariakas's rage was replaced by an astonishing desire to laugh. He shook his head in mute surprise.

"I don't suppose I could get you to spring this lock?" inquired Ferros hopefully. "The key's on the big ring he wears at his belt. My Hylar cousins would be grateful."

"No." Ariakas shook his head. "The last thing I need's a hue and cry getting started over an escaped prisoner. Sorry, dwarf."

Surprising himself, Ariakas actually *did* feel sorry for the dwarf. There was something very capable, even important, about Ferros Windchisel that struck a chord of sympathy in the man. Still, it was not enough to overrule his own objectives of rescue and escape.

Ferros slumped backward, apparently not surprised. "I suppose you're here about the lady?" he ventured.

Ariakas felt a shock. "What do you know about the lady?" he barked.

"Lots of fellows like you have come through here. Some of 'em died right down the hall from here, after the Painmaster finished his stuff."

"And yet it would seem that none has succeeded in rescuing her," Ariakas pressed.

"Well, no—if that's how you look at it."

The warrior didn't waste time pondering the dwarf's unusual phrasing. "How many ogres and human warriors are there in this tower?" Ariakas asked.

"Ogres?" Ferros shrugged. "Too many, that's all I know. I've only seen one human, though. He was wearing a breastplate a lot like yours."

"No humans, then," Ariakas noted grimly, half to himself. Then, with a rekindling of his anger, he remembered Oberon.

He turned to go. As a last thought, he spoke to the dwarf from the entrance to the cell. "I'll leave the catch on your door released. If you can get that collar off your neck, then I wish you good luck."

"Farewell—for now," said the dwarf cheerfully as Ariakas pulled the portal shut. True to his word, the warrior drew the catch-bolt slightly short of its socket. He didn't think that the dwarf could manage to escape, and this way the position of the bolt was so subtly altered that he suspected the guard would notice nothing amiss when next he brought Ferros Windchisel his water or food. Ariakas didn't speculate as to how long that might be.

The guarding ogre slumbered in blissful ignorance as the human crept past. Ariakas thought for a moment of slicing the great, blubber-ringed neck, but he quickly discarded the idea. All he needed was the ogre's replacement tromping down the steps to discover his cohort in a pool of fresh blood. No, he would take his chances with one more ogre in the tower.

The key ring hung from a clip at the ogre's huge belt. Dozens of metal keys arced around the heavy circlet of iron, but the warrior was elated to see that they were supported by a thin strip of leather. A quick flick of his dagger brought the keys into Ariakas's hand, without a disturbance in the slumbering ogre's snores.

Hefting the ring, careful to avoid jangling, Ariakas turned back into the dungeon. He crept silently past Ferros Windchisel's cell, through the corridor, and back to the foot of the secret stairway.

Chapter 6
The Pride of the Hylar

Creeping silently upward, Ariakas felt a mental weight dragging at his footsteps. His pace slowed, and finally he stopped altogether, no more than a dozen steps from the bottom of the secret stairway.

The urge to rescue the lady still drew him forward, but with the keys in his hands, he began to consider the prospects of a realistic plan. How would he get her through the keep and over the drawbridge with a castle full of ogres watching over them? The more he thought, the more he decided that some sort of diversion was essential to their chances of success.

Decision made, he turned and descended the stairs again, stealthily advancing into the dungeon to the door he had left partially unlatched. Sliding the catch-bolt quietly to the side, he stepped within.

"Is that you, warrior?" The voice rasped from the lightless cell. The dwarf's eyes were far more attuned to the darkness than were Ariakas's.

"I've come back to give you that chance at freedom," he announced without preamble. "You still want to escape?"

"More than anything—but why give me a chance now?" The dwarf's voice was tinged with skepticism; this stout Hylar would not be fooled by any tale of philanthropy. Ariakas's adjusting eyes showed him a look of shrewd appraisal on Ferros Windchisel's dirt-streaked face.

"I'm going to make my own escape, with the la— another prisoner. The more of us who get away, the more confusion we'll cause the ogres."

"Diversion, huh?" Ferros Windchisel digested this information with the pragmatism he had displayed all along. "Can you get me a weapon?"

Ariakas cursed sarcastically.

"The guard's dagger would do," Ferros offered helpfully. "You'll have to get the key for this collar off of him anyway."

"I've already got the key," Ariakas whispered, raising the ring.

Ferros nodded and took the iron circlet. He worked his way through four or five keys before he found one that fit. Then, with a satisfying *click*, the ring sprang open, and the dwarf was free. He immediately turned to the chain and collar that had held him close to the wall. As Ariakas had noted before, a second lock connected the chain to a bracket in the wall. Fumbling for a few moments, Ferros found the key to release that catch, and he turned back to the warrior. In one hand he now swung a five foot length of chain that terminated in the heavy collar.

"Not the ideal weapon," Ferros allowed, "but better than nothing."

Ariakas had to agree. He led the dwarf back to the secret stair and started climbing to the ground level. "I heard a bunch of 'em in the main entry," he told the dwarf. "Hopefully they'll have gone on to other things by now."

His heart fell as they reached the first exit, however, and plainly heard the boisterous shouting of ogres beyond the door. He slumped against the wall, memories of the lady dancing through his mind. Fleetingly he thought of pushing the dwarf into the hall of ogres, but he knew that would create no useful diversion whatsoever. He had to get Ferros out of the tower, get the ogres to chase him in pursuit.

"Have you seen where the drawbridge mechanism is?" asked Ferros Windchisel.

"Yes—the stairway goes right past the winch room."

"Well, if you feel like taking a chance, I'm willing to take a bigger one," offered the dwarf. "Let's go have a look at it."

Wondering what the stocky fellow had in mind, Ariakas led him up the three spirals to the drawbridge room. "Last time I checked," the human warned in a strained whisper, "I saw two ogres standing guard in there."

"*Only* two?" replied Ferros Windchisel brightly. "That shouldn't be much of a problem."

Ariakas, in spite of himself, liked the hearty dwarf. "How'd a resourceful fellow such as yourself get tangled up with these scum buckets?" he asked.

"I had a que—some important business that brought me into the Khalkists," Ferros explained. "And then I didn't pay enough attention to routine precautions. Bastards took me prisoner while I was sleeping," he admitted ruefully.

Soon they reached the alcove leading to the drawbridge room, and Ariakas carefully opened the concealed door and pressed aside the tapestry.

The two ogres remained. One looked out a slot in the wall where a supporting chain ran to the raised draw-bridge; the other was grumbling and pacing across the small floor space. The shadows and pillars obscured the rest of the room from view. The heavy door connecting the room to the rest of the tower stood open, but they could hear no sounds of other ogres on this level.

Drawing back the tapestry, the human lowered his voice to a faint whisper. "You close and bolt the door—that'll keep the rest of 'em from joining in. I'll try to get one ogre in the first rush. We can both finish the second one off."

Ferros nodded. They pulled the tapestry aside again, and signaling his advance by a touch on the dwarf's shoulder, Ariakas charged into the room. His sword drawn, he raced toward the ogre who looked out the wall opening.

The dwarf darted to the door, and Ariakas heard it slam, then *thunk* as the catch-bar fell into place. The human then cursed as his own plan went awry.

The pacing ogre uttered a grunt of astonishment at the first sign of attack, and the sound was enough of a warning to the warrior's intended target. That brutish creature whirled from the window and brought up a knotted club. Ariakas snarled as his blade bit deep into the tough wood, his blow effectively, if crudely, parried. So much for the surprise attack.

He heard a growl of rage as the second ogre moved up behind him, but he could spare no attention for this new attack.

The ogre in front of him yanked its club free of the sword and raised the weapon menacingly. Ariakas watched the club begin a plummeting descent toward his skull. Only when the monster had committed all of its muscle-power to the attack did the man dart to the side. The weapon struck the floor with a shattering of flagstones just a few inches to the side of the lunging warrior.

The ogre emitted a strangled grunt as Ariakas drove his sword deep into the monster's sagging belly. The beast then howled in outrage and pain, staggering backward, but the warrior kept up the attack. Withdrawing the gore-streaked blade, he thrust again, piercing the ogre's thigh and felling the monster like a toppling tree trunk. One quick thrust to the neck finished the job.

Whirling, he raised his weapon to face the second ogre, only to gape in surprise at the sight before him. The great beast lay on its back on the floor, kicking and flailing with its massive arms and legs. There was no sign of Ferros Windchisel, and Ariakas wondered momentarily if the dwarf had fled, cowardlike, back into the stairwell. At least Ferros had slammed and bolted the door. But what could be choking the ogre, he wondered.

Then he noted the necklace of iron links drawn tight around the ogre's throat. The bloated face grew purple and quickly darkened to a deep blue. The creature's eyes bulged out, and a dark blue tongue protruded pathetically, a fetid wheeze coming from the throat. The huge body was racked by an involuntary shudder. Finally it collapsed, dead.

"Hey—move this son-of-a-musk-ox off me, will you?" came a grunting voice.

Grinning in relief and amazement, Ariakas pulled on one of the strangled ogre's tree-trunk legs.

Ferros Windchisel, lying on his back underneath the ogre, pushed with his powerful arms and quickly scrambled free. He unwrapped his chain from the ogre's neck and looked at it reflectively.

"It's an old dwarven tradition," he announced with a smug grin. "If we don't have a weapon, we make a weapon out of whatever we have."

"That one worked damned well," Ariakas allowed, impressed.

They took a moment to listen at the door, and were relieved to discover that their brief fight had apparently passed without notice from the rest of the tower. Then both turned to the chains and gears linked to the massive bridge.

"Here's my idea," said Ferros, completing an inspection of the device and nodding. "You want a diversion, and I want to escape. It won't do either of us any good if they catch me a hundred feet from the gate, will it?"

"Go on," Ariakas said warily.

Ferros crossed to the strangled ogre and pulled the brute's weapon from its belt. The two-foot blade had served as a giant dagger to the monster, but for the dwarf it would be a serviceable sword. Next Ferros hoisted the length of chain, with its ring still attached. He gestured out the narrow window, and Ariakas saw that the drawbridge support chain emerged from the window to be secured by a heavy eye-bolt near the very end of the bridge.

"I'll hook this ring around that bolt—*before* you start to lower the drawbridge," the dwarf explained. "That way I can hang onto the chain, on the far side of the bridge, and they won't see me go down—at least, not right away."

"Perhaps they won't see you at all," Ariakas countered. "What kind of a diversion is that?"

"You *are* the suspicious type! But wait 'til I finish. When you get the bridge down most of the way, those buggers will try to climb out on it—if I know ogres, and I do. You've got to give me a few minutes. Hold the bridge above the ground, too far for an ogre to leap. I'll swing that chain back and forth and get me a jump that'll carry me to the far side. The ogres're sure to see me then—and even if they don't, I'll give a yell after a couple of minutes. At that point, you can let the drawbridge down all the way, and I guarantee they'll come after me for all they're worth."

"How do you know they won't send a couple after you and leave the rest here to keep an eye on me?" demanded Ariakas, immediately distrustful of the dwarf's plan. "How do I know you'll shout—what's to prevent you from disappearing into the dark and leaving me here with a tower full of ogres?"

"You have my *word*. I'll call out," replied Ferros, stiffly. He scowled at Ariakas, apparently for the first time wondering if *he* should trust the human. "And as for the former, I told you—I *know* ogres. There's no love lost between their folk and mine. If they suspect they're about to be humiliated by a dwarf, they'll do everything they can to stop him—me."

Ariakas pretended to study the chain, the drawbridge, and the winches, but all the time his mind was racing through the convolutions of the plan. He *didn't* like it. Once the dwarf was dangling within reach of the far precipice, Ariakas lost control of events, and he was forced to place his trust in this stranger. True, the dwarves he'd known had generally been a forthright lot. But that was no guarantee as to the veracity of this particular individual. And Ariakas hated a plan that depended upon someone else.

"Look—you can always lower the drawbridge right away. *I've* got a helluva lot more to lose than you do," stated Ferros bluntly. "We have to do *something*, and quick! You got a better idea?" he concluded, with terminal logic.

Ariakas admitted that he didn't. At the same time, the burning memory of the lady in the upper chamber stirred within him, and he yearned to get back to her. For the moment, he just wanted to see, to touch her—whether or not they escaped almost paled into a secondary consideration.

"All right," he agreed tersely. "Let's give it a try."

"*That's* more like it," Ferros snapped. "After all, *I'm* the one sticking my head into a noose!"

"I'm not going to draw it tight," Ariakas promised, half joking. In truth, if the dwarf had shown any signs of betraying him, the warrior would have tossed him to the ogres without a second thought. But for now, the plan on the table, which required the dwarf to be alive, seemed to be the only one they had.

Ferros tucked the short sword into his waistband and wrapped the chain around his shoulder and chest. He turned, once, to regard Ariakas with a faintly appraising eye. "You know how the drawbridge works?" he asked.

"This latchpin is the release—these coils hold tension on the chain to let the bridge down slowly," Ariakas explained with confidence.

"I'm glad I asked," Ferros replied tartly. "Unless you engage this friction bar, those coils won't hold up a thing. You'd have squashed me into a hearthcake!"

"Oh, the friction bar," Ariakas said sheepishly. It was a simple lever, and he pushed it into its engaged position—a detail he would have forgotten on his own.

"Wish me luck," said Ferros rhetorically. He sprang into the narrow window and tested the tension on the chain.

With remarkable agility, the dwarf scrambled along the chain, dangling beneath it and supporting himself with broad, long-fingered hands. The muscles in his shoulders tightened from the strain, but he quickly worked his way to the great eye-bolt in the drawbridge's end plank. Beyond him yawned full darkness, with just the snow patches on the surrounding peaks visible in the faint starlight.

Heaving himself up to the edge of the bridge, Ferros straddled the end beam for a moment while he manipulated the ring, latching it around the same eye-bolt that supported the drawbridge chain. Then, with a quick wave, he dropped out of sight behind the stout wooden barrier.

Immediately Ariakas turned to the winch mechanism to reassure himself that the friction bar remained engaged. He released the latchpin, and—true to Ferros's prediction—the weight of the bridge began to draw out the chain with a slow, deliberate rattle.

The low drone of ogre voices that Ariakas had heard throughout the keep changed in timbre. First came a slight pause, and he pictured the brutes reacting with shock to the lowering of their drawbridge. Then, as he expected, he heard cries of alarm and footsteps thundering up the stairs.

A quick glance showed him that the bridge still had a long way to go, so he ran to the stout door and checked to see that the bar was firmly placed. In the next instant he heard a booming smash against that barrier, and then another. Gruff, growling voices snapped and barked at him from the other side. The words were unintelligible but the outrage came through clearly.

Good—at least the first part of their plan had taken the enemy by surprise. He ran back to the window, careful to avoid the chain that steadily clanked outward and down. The drawbridge had reached its halfway point. Although the darkness of the mountains closed in, he could make out enough of the shadowy platform to judge its distance from the ground. As it fell farther away from the main hall, sputtering torches in the entryway cast their illumination outward, an orange glow creeping slowly up the planks.

The ogres continued to pound at the door to the room, but the beam was stout and showed no signs of splintering. The drawbridge dropped lower, and Ariakas tried to imagine Ferros's situation. He knew the dwarf must be swinging back and forth from his short chain during the entire descent. The warrior pictured that terrifying gorge, yawning nearly bottomless below the Hylar's feet, and vertigo tightened his gut. He admitted to himself that Ferros Windchisel was nothing if not courageous.

Finally he saw ogres scrambling up the sloping surface of the descending bridge—the dwarf knew his ogres—and Ariakas quickly jammed the latchpin into the winch. Immediately the drawbridge ceased its descent, poised a distance that he hoped was within the dwarf's swinging range above the opposite lip of the chasm.

The bridge lurched, and as Ariakas leapt back to the window, he saw one of the scrambling ogres stumble and fall, surprised by the sudden cessation of movement. The monster rolled from the edge of the bridge, screaming frantically at his companions—two of whom, in a surprising display of courageous loyalty, dived to catch their cohort's hands.

But the ogre's hold was too precarious, his weight too ponderous for any such dramatic rescue. Slowly, inexorably, the grip of clutching fingers weakened until at last he fell free. The wriggling form swiftly vanished into the darkness below, but the echoes of his terrified scream lingered long afterward, ringing from the surrounding crags.

Had Ferros Windchisel made his leap? Ariakas had no way of knowing, for it was fully black beyond the end of the drawbridge. How long should he wait before dropping it the rest of the way? What if the dwarf chose to escape silently, failing to draw any of the ogres after him?

A long, ululating cry rose from the darkness, well beyond the lip of the drawbridge. Ferros was as good as his word! Immediately the ogres fell silent, almost as if the dwarf's taunting call had touched some deep, primal instinct within them. Then their howling grew to a maddening frenzy, and those on the drawbridge scrambled desperately outward, as if hoping that their weight alone would be enough to drop the bridge the rest of the way.

Now was the time. Ariakas started back to the latch-pin, but then paused for an instant. A cruel grin split his scarred lip, and he disengaged the friction bar. Only then did he release the latch.

Chain whizzed past him with a high-pitched scream, unrolling as fast as the unrestricted gears could turn. With a shuddering crash the drawbridge smashed onto the far side of the chasm, bouncing sharply upward before it came to rest again. At least two ogres tumbled off the sides—there may have been more, but Ariakas didn't see them. In any event, terrified howls added to the din as the unfortunate beasts tumbled thousands of feet to their deaths.

But now the drawbridge was down and then, once more, that strangely musical howl rose from the darkness. The ogres thundered out of the tower in a stampede, bellowing their outrage and fury as the entire band rumbled toward the echoes of the dwarf's unearthly cry.

Ariakas listened a moment, satisfaction growing within him. Even the ogres who had been pounding at his door rushed down the stairs to join in the stampede. The fools! He crowed to himself, allowing his pleasure to grow into a kind of elation.

Quickly he pulled aside the tapestry and raced around the dizzying spirals toward the top level, his breath drawn in gasping pants by the time he reached the next landing. Struggling for air, he pounded higher, lumbering through the darkness of the secret stair. He passed another landing, and then another.

A few steps above that landing Ariakas crashed headlong onto a solid grate of iron bars. The shock of the impact knocked him off his feet, sprawling to his back with a clatter of armor and sword.

As the echoes of his fall rang through the darkness,

he reached forward to confirm with his fingers what his intuition already told him: Someone had closed an iron grate, completely blocking further ascent up the secret stairway.

Chapter 7
Three Ways to Die

Climbing to his feet, sword in hand, Ariakas pulled against the grate and found it securely locked. His senses tingled in alarm, and his eyes strained to penetrate the blackness. Had anyone heard his crash? He waited, but after a few seconds his immediate tension eased. The delay would prove fatal for whoever had blocked his path; certainly Ariakas himself would have wasted no time in slaying an enemy who so carelessly announced his presence.

He descended to the first landing and found the catch for the secret door. If his memory were correct—and he knew it was—the room beyond the door was one of the upper tower levels. He remembered the circular chamber, with its rings of stone columns. Even in daylight there would be plenty of places to hide. At night, it could be full of ogres concealed so effectively that he wouldn't be able to see any one of them.

Still, he had nowhere else to go if he wanted to continue back to the lady's chamber. Slowly, as silently as possible, he pushed open the door. Peering cautiously outward, his eyes strained to penetrate the shadows of the large room.

The moons had risen, providing the only illumination. The red light of Lunitari spilled through the eastern windows, and the pale wash of Solinari glowed to the north. The multitude of columns in the circular room again gave him the impression of towering tree trunks and a smooth forest floor.

He felt keenly certain that there were ogres in the room. Why else bar the secret stair? For an unsettling moment he wrestled with a new thought—how did the ogres *know* about the secret stair? The lady had told him it was used only by Oberon himself. Could it be that none other than the great warlord awaited him within? Ariakas had no choice but to find out.

Beyond the tower the sounds of ogre pursuit had gradually faded into the night. Ariakas deduced that the monsters had finally separated, since the noise of their raucous chase had soon expanded to resound from many of the nearby heights. There had been no bellowed crow of triumph, so it seemed that Ferros Windchisel had not been caught—yet. Ariakas found himself hoping that the dwarf would complete his escape, and not only because a longer chase would make for a more successful diversion. The courageous fellow *deserved* his freedom, the warrior told himself, surprised at the strength of his sentiment.

For long moments he held still, listening and looking. His eyes, already adapted to darkness, searched every shadow, every darkened archway between the pillars. Soon he saw the first ogre near the center of the room, waiting to the side of the main stairway. The hulking brute crouched in the darkness below the stairs, a long club or sword held across his knees, eyes staring fixedly upward.

The second ogre identified itself by a dull cough that rattled from the darkness, not terribly far from the alcove of the secret stairway. The warrior shifted slightly, but he couldn't see any sign of the creature. Still, judging from the sound, he guessed it to be hiding behind a pillar three or four columns away from his own location.

Ariakas continued his observations for many minutes. He saw no other ogres, nor was the telltale cough repeated—for all he knew the second ogre could have stealthily changed position since then. Yet, with the grate blocking the secret stair, he had no alternative but to advance into the room.

He decided to do so with aggressive stealth. Keeping as quiet as possible, he pulled the door open just enough to allow him to emerge, and then stalked quickly to the place where he had heard the ogre cough.

A shadow darker than the surrounding blackness rose before him, uttering a grunt of surprise. Ariakas stabbed, and the rude sound became a bellow of outrage as the ogre twisted away from the attack. A noise whooshed and the warrior ducked, shivering as a heavy club smashed into the column beside him.

Ariakas thrust from his crouch and again felt the steel tip of his sword strike flesh. The ogre groaned, a deep and agonized sound, and the man pressed forward, driving the sword home with all of his strength. With a strangled, gurgling moan, the monster slumped to the floor, kicking weakly, unable to rise.

Another bellow jerked Ariakas's attention back to the main stairway. The ogre he had seen in the shadows was charging. Abandoning his wounded opponent, Ariakas raised his blade to meet this lumbering onslaught. Metal clanged sharply against his own sword, and the human staggered into a pillar, stunned by the force of the ogre's blow. The brute's weapon was a sword of immense proportions.

The monster's blade whistled again, and the human rolled to the side, just beneath an explosion of sparks where sword smashed column. Ariakas sprang upward and drove his blade toward the brute's chest, but the ogre deflected the attack as a man might swipe away an annoying mosquito. Once again that massive sword chopped, and this time the sparks flashed along the floor, barely two inches from the warrior's foot.

Frantically dodging, Ariakas darted behind one of the pillars and then rolled to another, the ogre barely a step or two behind. He bounced back to his feet and thrust again, but once more the monster parried the blow, preparatory to another crushing attack of his own.

Dancing through the wash of red moonlight, Ariakas fell steadily back. The ogre moved through the same illumination, and the warrior saw the dull glint of steel on his enemy's sword—this monster bore no blade of corroded bronze!

A slight movement in his peripheral vision whirled Ariakas around, just in time to see a shadow loom toward him. A third ogre! The beast had remained hidden until the warrior was fully engaged—only the vagaries of moonlight saved Ariakas. The man dived forward, rolling between the two ogres and barely avoiding the chopping of that deadly sword and the bashing of a heavy club.

Whirling to his right, Ariakas came around a pillar and drove his sword into the flank of the club-wielding ogre. The monster howled, twisting so sharply away from the wound that he almost tore the weapon from the man's hand. Ripping the blood-streaked blade free, Ariakas again lunged to the side, feeling the *thunk* of the other ogre's sword chopping a piece from the heel of his boot.

Now the two monsters separated, advancing carefully with a row of pillars between them. Ariakas had no choice but to fall back, since the beasts effectively blocked any sideways attempt at escape. He feinted toward the deadly sword but was quickly driven back by a vicious slash—a slash that would have decapitated him if he'd pressed his advance.

In the darkness, the third ogre, badly wounded but not killed, groaned piteously. The warrior took advantage of the sound to scuttle past the club-wielder. Once more Ariakas slashed with his broadsword into the sagging belly. Warm blood splashed onto his hand as the beast barked in sharp agony, but even that wound didn't prevent the ogre from swinging its heavy club.

The gnarled wood smashed Ariakas in the shoulder, driving him into one of the pillars, where he stumbled to the ground.

He sensed both ogres lumbering toward him, but for a precious instant, his body refused to move. With concentrated effort Ariakas propelled himself into flight, scrambling crablike to avoid the sword. The ogre's blade again drew sparks from the bare floor, but the man cursed in pain as the club smashed onto his left arm. He heard bones snap in his wrist, and in the next second searing agony shot through his shoulder and side.

Furiously he rose to one knee and drove his broadsword upward, piercing the soft flesh of the ogre's stomach and driving the blade all the way to the hilt. The monster's howl of agony shook the rafters of the ceiling as he doubled over in mortal pain. When the great body tumbled to the ground Ariakas could only dive away to avoid being crushed, cursing as he was forced to release his sword—and then shouting in anguish as he stumbled and tried to catch himself on his broken arm. Instead, he tumbled headlong to the floor. He executed a desperate roll as the surviving ogre pressed his advantage.

A film of agony grew taut around Ariakas's eyes, the

sensation pounding at his brain, driving him toward oblivion. All his determination could barely hold blissful unconsciousness at bay—but, by dint of his will, he refused to yield.

The heavy sword flashed again, and this time Ariakas shouted from the fiery pain in his leg. Warm liquid sprayed across the floor, and he idly knew that this was his own blood. Instinct seized him then as, rolling and scrambling, he squirmed away from the ogre's repeated thrusts, though not before the keen edge also put a slice into his left shoulder. Finally he darted back, feinting right, and then tumbling over his wounded arm to collapse with his back against a column. The ogre, in the full momentum of his charge, lunged after the feint and then lost his balance, crashing to the floor.

Unarmed and maimed, Ariakas clawed his way to his feet and stumbled past several of the stone pillars. The booming footsteps of the ogre reverberated behind him as he ducked this way, dodged that. The ogre was fast, but not nimble, and at last Ariakas leaned against a stone pillar, gasping for breath and trying to suppress the shrieking pain of his wounds. The ogre groped through the darkness some distance away.

Where could he get a weapon? The slain ogre had effectively pinned Ariakas's sword in the death-wound. The wounded ogre flailed weakly on the floor, nearly dead, but the only weapon he'd carried was that great club—a wooden tree limb that the human would have been hard-pressed to hoist with both hands. Now, his arm smashed and his body fatigued, the knobbed stick was useless to him.

Finally his thoughts fell on the long dagger, still buried in his belt pouch. It was hard to imagine the twelve-inch blade inflicting a killing wound on the huge, flab-fleshed ogre, but Ariakas grasped the slender steel weapon—his best, his only, hope. Still listening to the thumping pursuit of the sword-wielder, who had temporarily lost his quarry, Ariakas unsnapped the pouch's buckles with his good hand.

The sounds of the clasps brought the ogre thundering toward him. Ariakas darted around columns, nearly slipping on the blood of the dead ogre, and then back-tracked through the shadows until once again his clumsy pursuer had fallen behind. Only then could the man thrust his hand inside the pouch. He pulled the dagger free just before the snarling humanoid reached him.

Leaping over the dead ogre, Ariakas once more tried to stumble away. The pursuing beast tripped over the corpse, sprawling heavily to the floor. The monster caught itself with its great paws, gasping for a moment while it peered through the darkness with bloodshot eyes.

Sensing his opportunity, Ariakas lunged at the ogre's head. The monster's mighty sword came up, but Ariakas fell to the side, then slashed inward with the dagger. The knife seemed hot in his hand, thirsty for blood as he drove toward that bulging neck. The keen blade sliced through skin and muscle as if the ogre's flesh were nothing more than a down pillow.

Shrieking in pain, the monster twisted away, dropping the heavy sword. As the weapon clanged to the stones, the ogre plunged toward it, but Ariakas's quick kick spun the blade out of the monster's reach.

Before the ogre could recover its balance, the man had leapt on the dropped weapon, and though it required all of his strength to raise it in one hand, Ariakas leveled the huge sword at a point between the ogre's bulging eyes.

"Wait," croaked the monster. "Don't kill!"

"You won't bargain for your life with me!" snarled Ariakas, drawing back his hand for the fatal blow.

"Let me talk!" spit the ogre, cringing away from the blow that didn't fall . . . yet.

"What do you want to say?" Ariakas gestured with the blade for the ogre to continue.

"This tower—it's trap for you! The lady, she's our captain—she orders us to whump you, warns us that you pretty good."

"Liar! How dare you—" A flush rose to Ariakas's face, and once again he steadied his aim.

"She tell us to goes after dwarf—all buts us. We gets to kill you," blurted the ogre.

"Why kill me? What would be your reward?"

"You big test—kill you, and I gets to keeps my sword." The beast nodded at the weapon Ariakas still held leveled before the brutish face.

A wave of nausea swept upward through the warrior's body, and he suddenly felt dangerously light-headed. The ogre, too, sensed his weakness—the beast pulled his legs beneath him, readying for a powerful spring.

"Liar!" repeated Ariakas, driving the blade forward, piercing the ogre's throat even as the monster broke to the side. Fatally cut, it fell, kicked several times, and died.

Groaning, Ariakas slumped to the floor. His arm throbbed, and his lungs struggled for breath. Even as he labored to retain consciousness, he listened for sounds of danger—and he heard nothing. All three ogres had expired, and the rasping in his own throat was the only sound in the large room. As his heart settled, he realized that the entire tower was silent, and then his mind shifted back to the lady who awaited him above.

The ogre was lying! This conviction rose to reassure him, but then the fog of his pain played silly games with the truth. How had the ogres known of the secret stair? Why had the lady told him exactly where to find the keys? But of course—if she'd wanted him to fail, she'd never have told him about that key ring!

Still, contradictory assumptions and suspicions whirled through his mind, heightened by the rising obfuscation of physical pain. Blood flowed from a multitude of wounds, and his broken wrist throbbed. He must go to the lady! There he would learn the truth.

He considered trying to retrieve his sword and immediately discarded the idea. Instead, he clutched the ogre's huge sword in his good hand. Before he started toward the stairs, he reeled against one of the pillars as a wave of pain and nausea threatened to drag him down. Grimly he shook off the feeling, like a wounded bear might shrug away the pestering bites of a wolf pack.

Lurching from pillar to pillar, using his sword hand to support him against each, he staggered toward the landing of the tower's main stairway. For the last five steps there were no columns to lean against, and he stumbled forward to fall at the foot of the stairs. He looked upward, vaguely remembering the many flights leading upward to the lady's chamber.

Slowly, with gritty determination, he clumped upward, one step at a time. A filmy haze, blood red in color, drifted across his eyes, but he shook that off as he had earlier banished the creeping unconsciousness. Instead of weakening, he seemed to grow stronger as he climbed, striding firm and steady past the first and second landings.

Upward he marched, past the third, and finally around the fourth landing. Now his memory burned clear, and he knew he climbed the last flight before the lady's chamber.

Then, with a nauseating wave of weakness and despair, he heard the sounds of marching overhead. Only then did he remember the guard posted at the top of the stairs, and the prospect of another fight sapped the little blood he had left in his veins. But he had come too far—the prize was too great—for him to turn back. Blundering up the stairs, he abandoned stealth in favor of speed, seeking the flickering torch that illuminated the top.

True to pattern, the ogre sentry clumped past shortly, marching to the man's left, apparently unaware of the threat ascending from below. As soon as the ogre passed the stairway, Ariakas lurched upward with all his remaining strength. The creaking of his boots betrayed him, but the ogre merely hesitated in his monotonous patrol, the great head cocked to one side as if to hear better. The huge sword drove like an arrow toward the monster's blunt neck.

Some dull premonition spurred the ogre to spin with remarkable dexterity. Ariakas snapped a curse as his blade merely gouged the flab rolls around the hefty neck. Eyes widening in surprise, the ogre drew its own weapon —a huge, bronze-tipped hammer.

Once again Ariakas struck, desperate to slay this last obstacle. This time the sword plowed deep into the bulging abdomen, and the ogre grunted as a jet of blood spurted from the wound.

The great jaws gaped, and the hammer flailed outward. A glancing blow to the man's broken arm brought a cry of pain from Ariakas. Gasping in agony, he pulled his blade back slightly, and then drove it forward, again aiming for that fat-protected neck.

"Unghhh!" The monster uttered the beginning of a word, but then the cold steel sliced through his larynx, his jugular, and finally his spine. Collapsing like a sack of potatoes, the beast crashed to the floor at the top of the stairs. The hammer clattered to the flagstones, poised at the rim of the steps, and then bounced downward, clanging and ringing toward the landing below.

His mind a fog of pain, Ariakas instinctively turned down the corridor toward that bright room, that ephemeral beauty. Before he made it halfway, however, the wave of sickness swept upward again, seizing him and swirling a cloak of unconsciousness around his brain.

Then she was there, appearing to him in sudden clarity. She was strong, this lady, and she knew more about him than he dared to believe about himself. In that instant of understanding, he knew that the ogre had spoken the truth.

He was not aware of the impact as his body went suddenly limp and crashed to the floor.

Chapter 8
The Lady of Light

Ariakas opened his eyes, but immediately closed them again as the full brightness of the sun seared his vision. He didn't know where he was, though his body felt as though it floated upon a mattress of air, or drifted in bathwater of perfect warmth. He tried to see again, this time cautiously parting his eyelids a bare slit, recoiling slightly from the intense glow that washed over him. Only slowly did he realize that the light did not come from the sun after all.

Instead, it was the lady herself who glowed. She extended a bright hand to his leg, and he felt her fingers probe the edges of the near mortal sword wound. Miraculously, there was no pain in her touch. Then, even more astonishingly, the pain from his wound ceased entirely.

With wonder, he reached a hand downward, touching his skin through the long tear in his leggings. Everywhere he touched, his flesh was firm. There was no hint of the cut, no lingering sensation of the wound—it was as if the ogre had never struck him. Beside him he felt the edges of a cushion, and guessed that he lay upon the mattress in the lady's room. How had he gotten here? Surely she hadn't carried him.

Yet, when he turned his head, Ariakas saw a trail of blood leading to this place. The wound had not been a fantasy, a trick of his fevered imagination. It had been real, and nearly fatal—yet now it was gone.

He raised his hands to touch her, and only then noticed that the bones in his left arm were whole and strong, as if they had never been broken.

Her hands rested on his, and he opened his mouth to speak, feeling the dry skin of his scarred lip crack from the effort.

She silenced him with a kiss, and he allowed himself to collapse against the mattress, warm and secure in her embrace. When finally she raised her lips from his, he touched his hand to his mouth.

With a profound sense of wonder, he found that his split lip, his brutally scarred chin, had become whole.

Finally, as if he were watching the scene from somewhere very far away, he began to recall their dangerous circumstance. The ogres might be gone for now, chasing after the diversion of Ferros Windchisel, but whether they caught him or not they would be back before long! But wait . . . his mind struggled with a vague recollection . . . there was the thing the ogre had told him. Did she mock him, now, with this kindness and caring?

He could not believe that she did.

Ariakas struggled to sit, and though his muscles were fit and his body free of pain, he fought against a languorous ease that threatened to hold him as firmly as any paralysis. It took him a full minute to muster the words to speak.

"The ogres, Lady . . . we must flee before they return!" The warning seemed to take all of the energy he possessed, yet he felt profound satisfaction in having spoken the words. Again he relaxed, bathing in the warmth of her smile.

"We're safe," she whispered to him. "There's no need for you to worry."

"Did you . . . did you order them away from here?" he asked, his voice sounding very far away.

She pulled her head back from his and regarded him with a shrewd narrowing of her eyes. "Yes," she said after a pause. "I did."

"Oberon . . . ?"

"There is no Oberon," she replied quietly. "Or, if you prefer, I am he."

He was able to digest this answer with a minimum of surprise. "Why, Lady—why did you have me fight the ogres?"

"It was a necessary thing . . . a test," she said quietly. He detected a trace of sadness in her voice, but he sensed that the glow he saw in her eyes came from desire.

"A test for what?"

"To see if you were the one . . . the one whom I have been placed here to welcome."

"The 'one'? What one is that?"

"Hush, now," she whispered, as if he were a small child. Oddly, he didn't feel like arguing. "You have to stop asking questions. . . . Some things you must accept as they are."

She leaned over and kissed him again, and all trace of suspicion left him.

"I accept!" Ariakas pledged solemnly, unaware of any irony in her smile.

"Now, warrior, you must tell me your name."

It seemed to him that she had become suddenly grave, and he responded with equal seriousness. "I am Duulket Ariakas, scion of Kortel." The thought continued to its logical conclusion. "And how, Lady, are you called?" he asked.

Again he thought he detected a hint of sadness in her deep eyes. "My name is . . . unimportant," she explained after a pause. "It would please me if you should still call me 'Lady'." He did not view her request as strange, but her next words brought him a sense of discomfort. "Come, Lord Ariakas," she said. "Allow me to bathe you."

For the first time, he noticed that the air in the room was moist, filled with steam that billowed from a grand, tile-lined tub on the other side of the chamber. How she had heated the water, he couldn't imagine, but the thought of easing his muscles in the bath overcame his initial modesty.

Somehow, she had removed his leather overshirt while he pondered the question. His breeches and blouse followed, and then he blissfully immersed himself in the nearly scalding water.

For a time he floated at the edge of dreaming, his body suffused with health and vitality, his mind wondering at the splendor of . . . splendor of what? The feelings were somehow greater than he had ever known before, yet at the same time distant, remote. It was as though he had left his weary flesh behind.

Then, when finally he emerged from the bath and the lady took him to her bed, the dream transcended rapture and carried him to an ethereal height. Still there seemed a gap between his body and his surroundings, as if he looked down upon himself from a lofty perch. Yet when the mysterious lady welcomed him with her arms, all thought of that distance vanished, and the immediacy, the ecstasy, of the moment seized him full in its implacable grasp.

* * * * *

They slept for many hours, and for Ariakas it was a slumber of utmost insentience. If his mind ventured on further journeys, it went to places that he could not recall in the morning. As daylight poured through the eastern window, he awakened, fully invigorated.

Leaping from the bed, he crossed to the window, where the shutter stood open to admit a chill breeze. He saw flakes of snow wafting past, and though he could see the neighboring mountain, the more distant peaks of the range had vanished in the flurry. Already snow had gathered along the narrow trail leading from the drawbridge.

"Snow's covered the trail—we're trapped," he said without preamble, but also without bitterness.

"No matter," she said, astonishing him with the cheerfulness of her tone. "We've food enough for a long time —a *very* long time—and we're quite safe in here."

"Hot baths . . . food?" observed Ariakas. "How do you do all this?"

"Stop asking so many questions," she demurred, casting the coverlet of bearskin aside. At the sight of her body, further interrogations vanished from his mind. . . .

Afterward she rose and disappeared into a small alcove of the room. Shortly she emerged with a full plate of boiled eggs, a loaf of bread apparently fresh from an oven, small roasted sausages, and fresh cow's milk. Again, when he asked her about the source of this wondrous meal, she turned his questions away, and he did not protest at her change of topics. He was too hungry to.

By afternoon the room began to grow chill, and she told him where—on the second level of the tower—a great supply of peat and firewood had been stashed. Ariakas spent several hours hauling bundles of the fuel to the upper chambers that were his lady's apartments.

Already he had forgotten that he had ever viewed it as a cell, so commodious were the arrangements she made there for both of them. Indeed, after his labors with the fuels, while the fire crackled at the hearth, she drew him another bath, and when he emerged from the water she presented him with a roast hen, packed with spices and an assortment of potatoes and peppers. Again she offered bread, and cheese with the sharp tang that spoke of expert aging.

"Tell me, Lady, about this 'test' that brings me here," he ventured as they sat beside the fire and enjoyed a clear wine.

"It is too soon," she replied. "You have barely begun to enjoy the rewards of your success."

"My 'rewards'? Do you mean this splendid repast?" he inquired, half in jest—though out of curiosity he watched her eyes to see if she took offense.

Instead, her eyes twinkled with amusement. "The food . . . and *other* things," she said coquettishly. She showed not the slightest hint of embarrassment at the notion that she, herself, was somehow his reward.

"My wounds," he said, trying a different tack. "How did you heal them so quickly—so well? It seems like a secret of the gods themselves!"

"Perhaps it is," she noted, surprisingly coy.

"But everyone knows the gods deserted Krynn at the time of the Cataclysm!" Ariakas protested. "How can you claim differently?"

"Perhaps the gods *are* there, for those who will listen. If not all of them, perhaps one—perhaps a very significant goddess survives and rewards her faithful followers with powers."

She had become very serious, and Ariakas listened with a kind of awe. This test, these rewards—surely they were not some scheme of an immortal!

"Those who would serve her, who would *obey* her," continued the lady, her eyes glowing with a fervent light, "those shall know *power* the like of which the world hasn't seen for centuries."

"Power," he inquired with an ironic cock of his eyebrow, "and 'rewards'?"

Her robe slid to the floor.

"Yes," she said as she came to him. "And . . . 'rewards'."

* * * * *

For several days they rested, feasted, and reveled in physical pleasure. The lady would do anything to enhance the luxury, the ease of Ariakas's life. The food she prepared from the secret alcove was always splendid, always hot and fresh—and never did she duplicate a dish that she had already served. To his questions about the source of the food she simply smiled and place a finger to her lips, or to his.

The second day he removed the ogre bodies from the tower, winching them through windows and watching them tumble into the deep chasm. Though he lacked the strength to raise the drawbridge, he closed and barred the gates. Yet he failed to see any sign of the ogres beyond the tower. Those pursuing Ferros seemed to have lost themselves in the wintry Khalkists.

On his third day in the keep the lady sent him to the dungeon to retrieve a heavy, foot-powered whetstone. She instructed him to sharpen the great, two-handed sword he had removed from the last ogre he'd slain. He spent many hours honing the weapon to a deadly sheen, and at the same time was very impressed by the blade's quality and obvious durability.

More snow squalls spread through the heights, but Ariakas ceased to worry. He spent long hours by the opened window, watching avalanches tumble from the surrounding peaks, hearing the thundering power of the destructive slides from the safety of the lofty tower. One day it occurred to him that the passes would be closed, now, for the duration of the winter, and he greeted the realization with nothing more than a simple shrug of his shoulders.

Indeed, he began to wonder why he would ever *want* to leave this tower.

He remained strong, every day spending hours carting fuel up the stairs for the several fireplaces throughout their chambers. The tower made a perfectly comfortable home, and he gradually familiarized himself with every aspect of its passages and chambers. He found secret corridors and concealed doors, and when he showed them to the lady she clapped her hands in delight and praised his ingenuity.

Eventually he found the doors that led upward to the six spires surrounding the great central keep, and hesitantly he ventured into those perches. The bases of these slender towers were cantilevered into the keep, so that they stood freely outside the walls, nothing but a yawning chasm underneath.

At first Ariakas's vertigo threatened to produce panic, even hysteria, when he ventured into these places, but he forced himself to explore, unable to bear the thought of shame in *her* eyes. Soon he stood unconcerned on the outer parapets of these towers, and even allowed his mind to float free. He imagined that the tower was flying, and for a time his mind drifted in idle fancy, picturing the potent, unstoppable military machine such a soaring citadel would create.

Further explorations revealed a concealed door on the level with the drawbridge mechanism. For several days he worried at the lock, using every key he could find, and even bits of wire, broken daggers, and eating utensils. When he finally sprang the catch, he stepped into a tiny room and gasped in shock. He was surrounded by piles of gemstones and coins in all conceivable sizes, shapes, and denominations. The stones included diamonds, emeralds, garnets, bloodstones, and rubies, among small mountains of lesser pieces such as jade and turquoise.

When he raced up the stairs to report his find to the lady, she smiled and told him that the treasure was theirs—though she also reminded him that such baubles had no value to a pair of humans with every imaginable luxury at their fingertips.

Once in a while for their dinner, the lady presented him with a bottle of fine wine—even an occasional decanter of potent lavarum—and it seemed to Ariakas that never had wine tasted so sweet, or rum so satisfactorily biting.

The nights grew longer, the cold more intense, but by diligent chopping and hauling, Ariakas kept the rooms of their apartments warm. As always, the lady continued to delight his palate with an array of exquisite foods, apparently produced out of thin air.

Plush furs kept their bed snug against the bitter cold, and a seemingly limitless supply of candles provided as much light as they needed or desired. If anything, the cold weather heightened the intensity of their love-making. Ariakas estimated that they spent days at a time huddled under the mountain of thick furs, sharing delights too intense, too serene to be the province of mortal man.

During all this time, though he asked her often, she never told him her name. Her background and future plans remained as vague and enigmatic as her smile, and yet she had a way of making these things seem like trifling details, barely worth the attentions of a man like Ariakas.

He had deduced that the food she gave him was a product of the same clerical powers that had allowed her to heal his wounds. But what god gave her such powers? The woman welcomed his new understanding, but when he pressed her for further details, she always counseled his patience.

"One day you will know all that you seek," she chided. "But for now, can you not wait a little more?"

"I'll wait as long as you command, Lady," he pledged. "I only hope that the bond we form here, now, will grow even stronger with the telling."

"It will. . . . It will become as steel," she promised softly. "But before you can be prepared to receive it, I must ask your word on something."

"Anything!" he declared in a loud voice and with a flourish. "You have but to name it, and it shall be my command!"

"This is not a command," she replied. "But a pledge that you give freely, and now."

He nodded, and waited for her to continue.

"You must promise me, Lord Ariakas, that at a time in the future, when I shall give you a single command, you must perform it immediately and without question. Will you make this promise?"

"With all my heart, Lady—when you name the task, I shall perform it straightaway, asking no questions. It is my solemn pledge to you and to the gods!"

"I thank you," she said softly, and he saw that her eyes were wet with tears. Then she nestled at his side, and for once she just wanted him to hold her, which he did for the remainder of that unusually dark night.

It seemed to Ariakas that his strength must atrophy during the long hibernation, but here she was adamant: he must perform the rigorous hauling of wood and peat every day, working until his body ached and his brow slicked with sweat. Never mind that sometimes they built the fires to raging blazes, throwing open all the doors and windows of the tower to gain the cooling benefit of the icy breeze.

All the time he kept the two-handed sword honed to a razor's edge, caressing the fine piece of steel with all the care in his veteran swordsman's hands. And always, after the food and the drink and the baths and the work, there was that great, soft bed. When he looked back on the tower in his later years, it would seem to Ariakas that he had spent most of that winter underneath the warm bearskin of the lady's quilts.

Chapter 9
The Price of a Vow

Ariakas stayed with the lady for all of that long, cold winter. Vaguely he remembered his intention to make his way to Sanction, to purchase a palatial residence with the jeweled locket, and then . . . then, what? He couldn't imagine anything that would make a finer life than he had right here.

Spring came with wet storms and flooding streams, slowly stripping the snow from the peaks. Ariakas watched the rebirth of the mountains, and gradually a new yearning grew within him. He did not want to leave the lady, but the tower itself began to seem too constrictive, too confining, now that the weather melted the walls of their icebound prison.

New summer came to the Khalkists. The slopes around the isolated keep, which Ariakas had thought the abode only of granite and quartz, exploded in a profusion of wildflowers. Soaring hawks and eagles swooped past the ramparts of the tower, while sheep and goats scampered onto the surrounding heights.

As the mountain fastness reluctantly opened its snow-bound gates to the rest of Krynn, Ariakas knew for certain that his time in the tower was drawing to a close. A life in one place, however luxurious, would not content him—he needed more freedom than he could find here. And with the lady at his side, Ariakas knew he could be happy anywhere he journeyed.

On one remarkably warm day, the first day that could truly be called summerlike, he sought his lady in her chambers, after he had finished his fuel-hauling labor—labor that had not lightened in any way, despite the coming of spring.

"Lady, will you come away with me—to Sanction?" he asked when he found her resting on the soft divan.

She rose to a sitting position and regarded him with an expression akin to sadness.

"Do you really want to leave?" she inquired, a curious catch in her throat.

Ariakas fell to one knee. "My time with you has shown me the true value of life," he declared. "And if it meant leaving you behind, I would stay here with you forever. But think of it—you and I, together in that city of fierce splendor."

She sighed and lowered her eyes to the floor.

"I have money," he assured her, afraid that worries of poverty brought her hesitant response. "We could live like nobles there! And there's the treasure in the room below—if we took just a few of the largest stones we could trade them for another fortune! We could have all the wealth and power of monarchs!"

"But pray, Ariakas," she retorted. "Is that not how we

live here, now? Is there a king or a queen on all of Krynn who shares the freedoms, the pleasures and joys, that are our daily fare?"

"It *is* the matter of freedom," Ariakas admitted. "This tower has become our palace, but it has also become our prison! Don't you yearn, just a little bit, for the sounds of civilization, the press of a crowd or the bustle of a great marketplace?"

She shook her head, and he was startled at the raw honesty of the gesture. "No," she replied, "I don't. But I see now that you do, and that is what is important . . . to us both."

"What do you mean?"

"I mean that it is time for you to remember your promise—do you?"

"Of course." His pledge, to perform a single task for her without question, remained fresh and vivid in his mind. "It's a pledge that I shall honor! Is it your command that I remain here with you?" Though Sanction had begun to loom in his imagination, he would not have been heartbroken to agree.

"No—if only it could be that simple!"

Now he studied her in surprise, for he sensed that she was on the verge of tears. "What is it, Lady—what is your command?" he pressed. For the first time he felt a vague but growing disquiet. "Tell me, and it shall be done!"

"Tomorrow will be soon enough," she said, and there *were* tears welling in the corners of her eyes. "For now, tonight, you must hold me and love me."

That night passed, and with the dawn Ariakas remembered her words. "Now tell me," he begged. "What is your command? Tell me so that I can demonstrate my love!"

She rose and went to the great sword—the two-handed weapon he had claimed from the ogre he had slain his first night in the tower. After months of tender care, the blade was as keen as any on Krynn, the weight sufficient to crush bone. Bringing the weapon to him, she extended the hilt toward his hand.

"My command to you, Lord Ariakas," she told him somberly, "is this: You are to take this blade, and with it you must slay me."

For a moment he reeled backward, certain that his ears had deceived him. The determined look in her eyes—it was no longer sadness, but instead a kind of grim acceptance—told him that he had heard correctly.

"But—*why?* How can you ask this—the one thing I can't do!" he protested.

"You *can,* and you will!" she retorted. "*Take* it!"

Dumbly he took hold of the hilt, and she pulled the long scabbard away with a jerk of her hand. "Now, *kill* me!" she cried.

"No—tell me *why!*" he demanded.

"Because *she* commands it!"

"She? *Who?*" His temper exploded into fury.

"My mistress! She who has given me the power to heal, to feed—even to *love* you," she cried. "It is the price she exacts, now."

"Tell me the mistress you serve!" Ariakas demanded furiously.

"You will know soon," the lady said. "But it is not for me to tell you. Now, I command you—in the name of your promise to me—*kill* me! It was a promise you made freely, and remember, Lord Ariakas—you pledged that you would carry it out *without question!*"

"Wait," he said, his own tone softening, grasping for some shred of sanity. "Forget that I suggested we go to Sanction. We'll stay here all summer—for all the summers to come, and we'll be happy. I . . . I *can't* do what you ask!"

"You must!" she insisted. Almost scornfully she tore the bodice from her dress, exposing her breasts in a brazen challenge. "I *command* you, Lord Ariakas—in the name of the pledge you have made! *Slay* me!"

A furious passion took possession of him then, lowering a kind of blood-fog over his mind, numbing the sensations of grief that nevertheless racked him. He knew that she was right; he had made his pledge, and he would honor his word.

He stabbed her through the heart, his blow powerful and true, the blade penetrating her rib cage and emerging from her back in a shower of blood. With an agonizing yank, he pulled the weapon free, and waited for her to fall.

Thick liquid spurted from the wound, splashing onto Ariakas's boots and quickly pooling onto the floor. He reeled in shock; the blood that spilled down her belly was verdant green in color. It pooled between her legs, a surreal puddle of false paint. Ariakas gagged in shock and revulsion.

The lady kept her dark eyes upon him, and he stared into them with anguish in his heart, waiting for his victim's vision to glaze with the fog of death he had seen so many times before.

But she didn't fall!

"Again!" she commanded, her voice as strong as ever. Sickened, he thrust once more, chopping at her throat and releasing another shower—but this time the liquid was bright blue. Unquestioningly he hefted the blade, thrusting it through the center of her torso in another surely fatal blow. This time crimson blood showered forth, quickly gushing into a pool on the floor. His next thrust cut her deeply across the stomach, and blood of pure, midnight black spilled forth.

"Die! Why don't you *die?*" he choked.

He attacked again, slashing wildly with the great sword, chopping her head from her shoulders with one brutal slice. The bright white liquid erupting from the wound like thick milk was a final, grotesque horror. Overcome, he turned away and retched the contents of his stomach over the floor.

Yet still, as her head thudded to the flagstones and his heart broke within him, her body did not fall. Instead, it seemed to shrink, as if the multicolored blood had inflated her skin, as if the very stuff of her body flowed outward from the gaping wounds.

Ariakas stumbled backward, noticing that the blood flowing around her was no longer liquid, no longer collecting in sticky pools on the floor. Instead, it became like smoke, swirling upward into the air, forming serpentine columns, coiling into five great snakes. Each slinking form was the color of one shade of her blood.

The sword fell from his nerveless fingers as the snakelike shapes writhed, spreading and encircling him in their coils. He saw wicked heads take shape at the end of each snake, each with a pair of eyes that glittered wisely at him. Five horrific mouths gaped, and the smoky snakes thickened in the air until they seemed solid and real. Yet he sensed in the depths of his soul that these things were not real, that he beheld a presence that came from beyond Krynn. It was only the sacrifice of his lady that allowed this grim creature to appear, to reach out and speak to him.

"Tell me, Lord Ariakas," commanded one of the snakes—the red one—in a voice that was sibilant and heavy with might and power. "Do you know, yet, whom you serve?"

He could only shake his head.

"Take up your sword, warrior," commanded the crimson serpent.

Numbly, he reached down and raised the weapon. He noticed, with distant surprise, that the blade was a clear, unblemished white in color.

"Do you know that I have been with you for many years, Lord Ariakas?"

He nodded, believing it. "When I woke in the night and knew someone had been through my camp . . . had stolen the locket . . . ?"

"Yes, it was *I* who awakened you," hissed all the dragon heads. "And I have been testing you for years, and you have measured full to my standard."

"*Testing?*" demanded the human boldly. He gestured to the place where the lady had finally fallen. "This . . . this was *butchery!*"

"This was the final test, warrior—and once again, you passed. Know this, Ariakas: I shall give you power beyond your dreams . . . make you strong, stronger than you have ever imagined! You shall have women—all the women you want or desire! And you shall serve me well for all the years of your life."

Ariakas listened mutely, holding the great sword against the ground.

The voice took on an iron edge. "But remember, warrior—you were to obey *without question!*"

Racking pain seized Ariakas by the bowels, constricting his insides into an agonized mass of tortured flesh. With a cry of pain he slumped to the floor, sobbing and thrashing as the pain worked its way through his veins, upward into his neck, pounding like a great warhammer against the inside of his head. He knew that he was dying—no man could hope to survive such pain. And then, as quickly as it had begun, the agony ceased.

"Remember well, Lord Ariakas, the cost of disobedience."

He nodded weakly, gasping as he climbed to his hands and knees. The pain was gone, but sweat still rimmed his head, and the memory of the punishment was nearly enough to send him cringing to the floor.

"Now rise," she continued. Her tone was no longer harsh, and, slowly, he obeyed.

"Take that blade as *my* talisman," continued the voice. "You have passed my tests and proven yourself worthy. For many months you have known the wealth of my beneficence—and now, today, you have learned the depths of my determination."

He could only listen, his heart pounding in overwhelming awe.

"You will go to Sanction, and there you will work in my name. You will be my servant, as this woman was my servant—as the moneychanger Habbar-Akuk is my servant, and a thousand others who are my agents.

"And you, of them all, shall sit at my right, Lord Ariakas—this I know, and I pledge."

"But—why did she die? Why did you make me kill her?"

"Fool!" The fury of the retort sent him reeling backward, flailing for balance. "She was a *tool*—her purpose was to find you and to begin your training. Know this, Lord Ariakas: for as long as you live, as the gift of my generosity and the price of my favor, you shall have any woman you want—but each woman who gives herself to you shall perish within the year! As with this lady—her purpose will be done, her time past. But for you, Lord Ariakas—your time is just beginning!"

Ariakas tried not to succumb to his awe. His mind reeled between dark visions of horror, and wild fantasies of erotic fulfillment. She would offer him one and make the other her price . . . and yet, he knew that he would be willing to pay.

"Why do you send me to Sanction? What do you expect of me?"

"In that great city you shall go to my highest temple. They will know you there, and teach you. . . . In time, you shall become my exalted—first among my highlords! But you have much to learn first, and they will teach you in the temple."

"They already expect me?" wondered the warrior in disbelief.

"You carry my talisman in that sword," replied the five-headed serpent with a hint of rebuke. "That blade will be the key to your teachings and the tool of your success. It shall serve you as faithfully as you serve me."

Ariakas looked at the pure white blade, impressed in spite of himself with the flawless perfection of the sheen. "This talisman . . . what does it do?"

"You shall find out when you need it," the vision replied. "But remember this command, Lord Ariakas—and keep it close to your heart, lest in the end you fail me." Here the words took on a deep and rhythmic tone, and the force of the command riveted Ariakas to the spot. "This sword is my symbol, and with it you shall rule over vast hosts! But remember this thing, if you would achieve your lasting glory: *Hold the blue blade, warrior—for in the heart of the world it shall set fire to the sky!*"

His mind reeled with the import of the words, though they mystified him—and he dared not ask for explanation. Instead he bowed in humble acceptance.

"Tell me, then," he inquired instead, forcing every measure of his courage into the words. "Who are you—*whom* do I serve?"

"I am known by many names . . . but when I have made my return, I will choose to share the one by which all Krynn shall know me. You, noble warrior, will pave the path of that return!"

"But *what is your name?*" demanded Ariakas.

"You shall call me Takhisis," hissed the crimson serpent while the four other heads chortled in agreement. "But within your lifetime all Krynn shall tremble before me! And the masses will know and fear me everywhere as the Queen of Darkness!"

PART TWO

CORRUPTION

Chapter 10
City of Smoke and Fire

Perhaps because it stood on the brink of destruction, Sanction was a city more vibrant, more *alive*, than any place Aria-kas had ever been. As he sat on a bench in his garden, slightly uphill of his sprawling, many-roomed house, he looked at the volcanic Lords of Doom and felt a great sense of awe . . . and destiny.

Below him, Sanction filled the steep-sided valley that lay between the three great volcanoes and a steaming, lava-scarred harbor. The waterfront faced a finger of the Newsea that dared to probe into the forbidding Doom-range. The fiery mountains smoked and rumbled, dormant only to the extent that they did not now spew flame and rock into the sky.

Great cracks on the face of the northeastern summit emitted twin rivers of slow, remorseless lava into the valley. The widest of these streams was joined by flaming spillage from the southern mountain, creating the great Lavaflow River. Dull crimson, the molten rock seethed and bubbled through the heart of the city. The flow was spanned in several places by wide stone bridges. At night, Ariakas found the massive, inexorable river strangely compelling. Then its radiance reflected from the glowering cloud cover—an ever-present mix of sea mist and volcanic ash, casting the city in an eerie and pervasive light.

The waterfront was a steamy, stinking collection of buildings smashed shoulder to shoulder like patrons pushing into a crowded tavern. Numerous small ships filled the wharves and docks, the lot nestled between two natural breakwaters formed of hardened lava. Beyond the breakwaters to either side sprawled flat, steaming deltas of fiery fury, boiling water hissing away from contact with the slowly expanding shelf of liquid rock.

Around this sweltering waterfront sprawled alleys and courtyards, great manor houses and teeming slums. Even the marketplace of Khuri-Khan paled in comparison to several of the thriving bazaars in Sanction. As the only natural harbor in the entire eastern expanse of the Newsea, Sanction drew restless souls like a magnet. It also stood at the terminus of the only road through the Khalkist Mountains. This wide valley opened onto a pass between Sanction and cities to the north and east— productive mercantile centers such as Neraka and Kalaman. This valley and port linked to form the only connection between eastern and western Ansalon.

The population of Sanction was far and away the most diverse gathering Ariakas had ever seen. Tall plainsmen from Abanasinia traveled with painted Kagonesti elves, while humans from Solamnia sold all manner of goods to merchants from places as far as Neraka and Balifor, or even bartered with minotaurs, Kayolin dwarves, and an occasional, regal Silvanesti elf. The scampering kender were ubiquitous. Other short folk—smaller even than kender or dwarves—went about the city cloaked in dark robes. Ariakas noticed that many citizens gave these robed midgets a wide berth.

From a distance, most of the buildings of Sanction blended into a melange of brown, black, and gray blocks. A great plaza sprawled along the riverbank, rended by steaming fissures and chasms. Several noble manors stood on higher slopes, crowning the city's skyline. One of these now belonged to Ariakas: in Sanction, nobility was purely a matter of wealth, and Ariakas was a very wealthy man indeed. In fact, after only three days in this metropolis, the warrior had gained for himself all the trappings of nobility, most obviously symbolized by this splendid manor on the southern heights of Sanction valley.

Three structures in the city loomed proud and solitary over even the great villas and mansions, bowing only to the mighty volcanoes themselves. These were the Great Temples, of which Ariakas had heard a little. Built at the time of the Cataclysm on the lower slopes of each Lord of Doom, the temples consisted of walls, buildings, and subterranean chambers. Each was an impregnable fortress, and each held commanding position over a great section of the city. The mightiest, the Temple of Luerkhisis, stood to the northeast.

Upon entering Sanction, however, Ariakas had been strangely reluctant to approach the great temple. Instead, he immediately sought the moneychangers, several of whom bid frantically for the locket and gems. By nightfall of his first day he had been a rich man, and by the next day he had purchased a grand house.

The stone-walled residence consisted of two dozen large, airy rooms gathered around a teak-lined great hall, the whole ringed by a perimeter of balconies and columns. Outside, a wide courtyard encircled two sides, with a large stable in another direction and the once-lush garden to the rear. The fountains in the courtyards had been dry for years, and the hedges reduced to tinder-brush and thistle, but Ariakas had plans to restore the place to its former glory. And still the garden offered wide walkways and several good views, overlooking much of the lava-ravaged city.

After settling his house purchase with the formerly impoverished seller, Ariakas had enough money left over to purchase several fine horses, and then to hire a dozen servants, contracting them through the year. Tonight he had eaten a splendid meal cooked in his own kitchen, and then he retired to the garden for a stroll. For the first time since leaving the tower, the frantic pace of his travels had eased, and he found himself with no clear task before him. At the same time he felt profoundly restless, agitated. Looking across the valley to the highest temple, he knew without question the source of his discomfort.

Takhisis, Queen of Darkness, awaited him.

At times he had come close to convincing himself that his sojourn in the tower—and especially the memories of his last hours there—were the products of some delusionary dream. Of course he knew the truth, but a part of him had urged during the long hike to Sanction that he abandon the calling cast his way. He hadn't chosen any test—and why should the plans of others matter to him?

Yet never could he rationally embrace this urge. The events in the tower had been branded into his mind and his soul. He had made the vow and slain the lady, had witnessed the vision of a goddess he'd thought long dead. A destiny had been laid upon him there, and it was a fate he could not think of avoiding.

He felt he deserved a certain sense of pleasure and accomplishment after his arrival in this great city. His brief forays had shown him taverns, casinos, brothels, and smoking dens aplenty. Yet now he was completely disinterested in such common entertainment.

Still, across the wide valley loomed the Temple of Luerkhisis. It was positioned on a gentle slope, a commanding yet contained presence. Resembling the half-submerged head of a crocodile, the structure leered from the heights like a huge, monstrous reptile, its serpentine snout pointed straight at Ariakas. Two vast cave-nostrils led into entry halls, and round temple buildings perched like bulging eyes on the ridge above the maw. On dusks such as this one, the rays of the sun penetrated the ash cloud, illuminating the sinister bulk of the temple with a surrealistic glow.

Ariakas stood, and again his memory drifted back to the tower . . . to the lady. He missed her still, though not so much as he had during the long, bleak trek to Sanction. While climbing among the peaks, he had recalled each detail of her perfect body . . . every smell, every nuance of each meal she had served. Gradually the memories had faded into a sort of gentle background, pleasant to recall but irrelevant to the matters at hand.

Now, when he saw that great temple on the mountainside, staring down at him like some gargantuan dragon regarding an ant, the full force of the Dark Queen's will stormed within him. He knew an awful sense of failure, of abject unworthiness to serve her. Ariakas staggered backward, falling against the brittle branches of a withered yew. Cursing the sharp pain, he bit back his complaints, bowing to the rekindled awe he felt before the Queen of Darkness.

As if it had lain dormant like these steaming volcanoes, the full force of her will swept through him. He would serve her! He already bore the talisman, the white-bladed sword, and now he would go to her temple and take up service in her name. What kind of greeting to expect, he didn't know, but that concern meant less than nothing. All thoughts of freedom vanished. The desires of his goddess now known to him, he left his house, hurrying through the streets of Sanction to reach her temple.

With sunset, the city came to life around him. Streets that had been empty an hour earlier thronged with people, and he pushed his way through crowds to approach the great stone bridge in the city center. He wore his sword visibly. Since the huge blade was too long to wear at his waist, it rested in a scabbard strapped to his back, with the two-handed hilt jutting upward over his left shoulder. The sight of the weapon encouraged even armed men to give way.

Tavern keepers threw open their doors and numerous customers quickly gathered, further blocking the streets where Ariakas tried to pass. Most of these hearty socializers seemed to be seasoned mercenaries like himself. Curious, he wondered who they served. He had seen no standard of any army posted around the city, and as a free trade center Sanction had little need for its own militia. The uncommon number of men-at-arms, he presumed, were drawn to the city by its numerous exotic delights, and the great value of imported coins.

The road opened into the Fireplaza, where the crowd thinned. Ariakas looked across the broad courtyard, intrigued by the strange monument at the far end: three stone ships, appearing to float some distance off the ground. It had caught his eye before, but he had yet to find out what it was. Now, however, he was too intent on reaching the temple to detour for a closer inspection.

As Ariakas climbed the gentle lower slope of the mountain, the activity of the streets fell away behind him. He moved over a broad, flat shoulder of the massif. It was an empty space, but his soldier's mind suggested that it would be a perfect site to marshal a huge army. The location, he noted, offered the protection of the lava rivers to the east, south, and west.

Even this broad plateau fell behind, and the twin entrances to the temple loomed overhead, resembling even more the nostrils of some great, half-submerged reptile. The roadway opened onto a broad plaza below the arched temple entrances. Ariakas was alone as he walked across the wide, smoothly paved yard. Before him, the entrances yawned ink-black, but orange lamplight gleamed overhead from the two great windows that served as the 'eyes' of the colossal beast. He had the feeling that something watched him from within those sinister chambers, though he could see no silhouette, nor sign of movement. He knew beyond doubt—*this* was where he belonged. Youthlike vigor infused him, and unconsciously the pace of his walking increased.

Pure darkness screened each of the twin approaches, like a film of ink laid across the air itself. Quickly he advanced to the left arch. Passing through, Ariakas was swallowed by utter blackness, and immediately embraced by a sense of warmth. Breezes wafted against his face, and he realized that some vent in the bowels of the volcano brought hot air swelling upward, creating this comfortable warmth.

"Lord Ariakas . . . welcome to the Temple of Luerkhisis." The female voice, spoken with a pleasant, adolescent tone, reached his ears through the impenetrable blackness.

"Who is that?" the warrior demanded, surprised that anyone could be so close without his sensing her presence.

He took another step forward and suddenly emerged into light. A huge chamber opened around him, and though he had passed through no physical obstacle the boundary between the darkened anteroom and this brightly lit chamber broke as clearly as if it had been a velvet curtain.

The girl who had welcomed him knelt and bowed deeply at his feet. He guessed her to be no more than fourteen, yet she carried herself with the serenity of a well-trained priestess. Her long hair was black and diligently combed. She wore a silken dress of deep blue, and carefully kept her eyes lowered from his as she stood. Ariakas noticed that a white leather collar encircled her slender neck.

All around spread a huge chamber, rectangular in shape, occupied by many small pockets of conversing people. The vast hall stretched for a length of at least two hundred feet, and was half that in width. Dozens of oil lanterns hung from wall sconces, creating the bright light that washed every corner of the marble walls—except for the magical screening darkness of the entryways.

He noticed other young priests and priestesses in the hall. Some gathered around gray-haired elders, males and females both. Others sat in solitary and silent meditation, surrounded by a wide circle of emptiness on the floor. The priests young and old wore a variety of garments, including trousers, robes, and skirts. Many of these garments were white, but he saw others of red, green, black, and blue. These priests also wore collars, mostly of white, though the tutors more often displayed leather bands of black or blue.

"If it pleases my lord to accompany me . . . ?" the young priestess said humbly, gesturing to the far side of the large hall.

The girl led him through an open doorway, and he followed her down a long, marble-walled hall. He watched her walk, noting in particular the way her tiny feet glided across the floor—as if she didn't so much walk as skate. Soon she reached an open doorway, from which bright lamplight spilled. She bowed again, then gracefully retreated, gesturing for him to enter.

Ariakas stepped to the doorway and peered within, not at all certain what to expect. He found the fact that this girl had known his name profoundly unsettling. Now, apparently, she knew right where to take him, and that made him wonder if he were walking into some kind of trap. Instead, he saw a welcoming smile on the face of an elder priest seated beyond a great marble slab of a desk. The fellow rose and came toward Ariakas, bowing politely—but without the obeisance shown by the girl.

The priest regarded the warrior with intense, searching eyes of dark brown. Long and full brown hair grayed at his temples and swept back from his face. He had a swelling belly and a careworn face, creased not so much by age as by maturity. In his hand he carried a short wooden object, more decorative than a club—perhaps a scepter, thought Ariakas. At the tip of the shaft was a metal star with five points—one tine in each of the five colors he'd observed in the temple. A striped silken mantle framed the priest's robe of shimmering black. He, too, wore a collar around his neck, though the band was crimson in color.

"My Lord Ariakas, welcome! Welcome to our temple! We have long been expecting you, but now that you are here the occasion transcends mere words! I trust your journey to Sanction was, er, without major mishap? One could can hardly expect to call it 'pleasant,' I suppose."

The bombardment of words took the warrior by surprise, but he saw nothing beyond honest welcome in the man's round, guileless face.

"Forgive me," the fellow continued. "I am Wryllish Parkane, High Priest of the temple. I will personally see to the majority of your studies . . . though of course you will have the freedom of all the specialists, as need arises. We have a personal chamber ready for you, beyond the audience hall, where you entered. Perhaps you would like to freshen up a bit before I give you a tour of the temple?"

Stubbornly Ariakas shook his head, stunned by the extent of the priest's knowledge, and his plans. He felt a sudden reluctance to immerse himself in his new role, though he knew it was too late to change his mind. "That won't be necessary," declared Ariakas, determined to retrieve some momentum. "I have quarters in the city where I will live, and I came here from there. As to the tour, however, I'm ready for that as soon as we can begin."

"Of course—of course!" If the high priest were distressed by Ariakas's news, he gave no indication. Instead, he hurried around the huge desk and placed a firm hand on the warrior's arm.

Ariakas's sense of reluctance gave way to a certain satisfaction. Obviously, he was not to be treated as some kind of apprentice or lackey. They had expected him—and Takhisis herself had told him that he would sit at her right! Smiling tightly, the warrior allowed the priest to escort him from the room.

In the hallway the young priestess awaited further commands, her posture rigid, her eyes still downcast. "That will be all, Heraleel," commanded the high priest. "You may await me in my chambers."

"Yes, Lord Patriarch," replied the girl before gliding silently away.

Wryllish noticed the warrior's gaze, and chortled softly. "We have numerous young apprentices," he said. "I will be certain to have one appointed to you—immediately."

Flashes of memory came to Ariakas of the warmth he had shared with the lady in the tower. The memories vanished, replaced by a yearning ache that brought real temptation. Then he recalled the Dark Queen's words and her warning—any such liaison would cost the young woman her life within the year. "Not at the present," he said quietly.

"Now, these are the chambers of our novices," explained Wryllish Parkane, leading Ariakas past a long row of open, well-lighted chambers. In the first they saw a number of young men learning the art of swordplay and parry from a grizzled veteran. Several pairs of youths banged away at each other with mock savagery while a group of students formed a circle around the thunder-voiced teacher.

"They show skill," Ariakas admitted, watching the subtle use of feint and misdirection.

"Ours is a faith that does not disdain the use of force wielded righteously," Wryllish explained. "Some faiths of the ancient gods disdain bloodletting weapons. . . . Our mistress takes a more practical approach."

"I respect practicality," Ariakas remarked.

The patriarch nodded. "Indeed, before the crowning of our queen it will be necessary for a great host to take up arms in her name." Here the priest looked at Ariakas shrewdly, as if measuring his worth for a role in that master scheme. The warrior, in turn, recalled the masses of leaderless men in Sanction—could they be marshaled to the Dark Queen's banner?

"This is our unarmed combat training," Wryllish Parkane next declared. They had come to an arenalike chamber where a slender woman spoke sternly to several younger students. Barefoot, she wore a blue collar and a silken blouse and trousers. The gauzy material outlined her supple, muscular body.

Abruptly she swung her foot upward, lashing at one student's face before lunging forward to seize another by the crotch and neck. With a quick flip, she threw the struggling young man across the platform.

"Very impressive," Ariakas observed.

"Lyrelee is one of the best instructors we have. The temple is fortunate she chose to become a priestess."

They moved through many long corridors, past other rooms, some light, some dark. Ariakas heard sounds of intense, sometimes confrontational, conversation. Some noises were unintelligible, while others—groans and cries—suggested activities causing either pain or ecstasy.

Eventually Parkane led Ariakas to a high arch. A pair of green-collared men-at-arms, each dressed in red livery and carrying swords and shields of immaculate steel, flanked the opening. Just beyond, a wide stone stairway descended into the depths below the temple. The two guards snapped their weapons to attention and stepped back as the priest and warrior approached.

"But here, milord—*here* is where you see the true glory of our mistress's plan!" whispered Wryllish, his voice cracking with excitement. "These are the Sanctified Catacombs. Only the most trusted of her servants are allowed here—those of the blue or red collars. Of course, sometimes we have brought prisoners here as well, but they haven't emerged."

"Why me, then? I wear no collar," the warrior pointed out as they passed the sentries and started down the stairs.

"Why, my lord," the priest said, surprised. "Of course you are the natural exception to this rule.

Ariakas nodded, as if the response were expected. His stony features in fact masked fierce elation that he would have the freedom of the entire temple. He felt tingling anticipation as they descended toward the catacombs. The two guards were the only watchmen he'd seen, and given the deserted appearance of the dark stairway, he decided that these passages must be a well-kept secret to the outside world.

"Tell me," Ariakas pressed as they descended beyond earshot of the two guards. "How did you know I was coming? That I would be here tonight?"

Wryllish shrugged modestly. "We *didn't* know it would be tonight . . . but as to your eventual arrival, *she* told me, of course."

"Do you *speak* to her?"

"Oh, no—not while I'm awake. But often she comes to me in my dreams, and regarding you she was quite specific. I am to train you in the highest calling of the priesthood, though I am assured that as a warrior you are already eminently capable."

"I *am* a warrior!" Ariakas growled. "I never gave any thought to becoming a priest, and I don't plan to now!"

Wryllish Parkane looked at him in some surprise. "Indeed? But that's not what I . . . well, no matter. Come along down here, won't you?"

The priest's assumptions, if anything, made Ariakas even more curious, so he continued to follow him down the straight, seemingly interminable stairway. The torches in the wall were very far apart, and darkness filled the gaps between them. Ariakas was about to suggest they take one of the brands with them when the priest astonished him by muttering a few indistinguishable words, causing a bright light to flare into life atop his short scepter. The metal star glowed with a cool but surprisingly extensive illumination.

"The power of our mistress is a wondrous thing," noted the long-haired priest. His strides increased in tempo as the long subterranean corridor continued.

Ariakas kept pace easily, trying to take note of their surroundings as they advanced. He saw several yawning cave-mouths branching to the right and left from the main passage, all of them utterly dark and lifeless. In several cases he felt certain—based on dust and spiderwebs—that the passages led to completely unvisited regions below the temple.

Still, perhaps it was only the priest's light that made their current path seem different. Ariakas noticed several chambers outlined in stalactites and stalagmites—natural caves in the ancient limestone bed of the Khalkists. The newer lava and basalt of the Lords of Doom frequently overlapped and buried the bedrock, but in places the two surfaces met. The temple of Luerkhisis was obviously one such juncture.

"Tell me," inquired the high priest conversationally. "What do you know of dragons?"

"Dragons?" Ariakas pondered the surprising question. "As much as anyone else, I suppose. They were the scourge of Krynn in the Age of Might, until they were bested by humans and the knights in the great dragon war. That was some thirteen centuries ago, and they've been gone from Krynn ever since."

"That *is* the common perception," noted Wryllish vaguely. "You, of course, have never seen one?"

"As I said," Ariakas retorted, somewhat sharply, "there have been no dragons for more than a thousand years—how could I have seen one?"

"Quite. As a matter of fact, I haven't seen one either." The priest stopped suddenly, and turned to face Ariakas. Wryllish scrutinized the warrior, an expression of reflective curiosity on his face. "Tell me, Lord Ariakas—have you ever seen the birth of rain in the clouds overhead?"

"Of course not!" snapped the warrior, irritated with the ludicrous question.

"Ah!" declared Wryllish, ignoring his companion's agitation. "But that does not mean such a birth does not take place, does it?"

"How should I know? The rain falls on the ground— that's good enough for me!"

"Of course . . . of course. But my point is this: does the fact of your not having seen something constitute evidence that that thing does not exist?"

"In that case, no. If you're speaking about dragons, however, I would say that the combined experience of the population of Krynn would give some basis for making the assumption that they don't exist." In spite of himself, Ariakas found himself enjoying the verbal sparring. The priest, he noted, reflected on his response seriously before beginning his reply.

"Even in that case, dispute is possible," Wryllish ventured. "For in our discussion thus far we have neglected the matter of faith."

"Faith? In dragons?" Ariakas countered.

"Faith in our *goddess*," the priest corrected gently. "And if it is the will of Takhisis that we believe in dragons, then how can one who has faith in the goddess not believe, implicitly, in dragons?"

"Has the goddess made this claim—that dragons exist?" demanded Ariakas.

"No—not in so many words," replied the serene cleric. "Yet, I suspect that soon she will."

"You *suspect?*" Ariakas was unable to keep the scorn from his voice. "But you don't know—have not been told this?"

"I leave it at this," said Wryllish, enjoying the sight of the warrior's agitation. "I believe this is the will of our mistress: Before many more years have passed, dragons will once again be known and feared upon Krynn. And when they return, they will do so not as a scourge, nor a menace. . . they will come as our *allies!*"

"Some would call you mad," the warrior said bluntly. "Is that the way of this temple—the insistence that some extinct lizards are going to return and bring us to glory?"

Despite Ariakas's hostile tone, Wryllish Parkane refused to be riled. He merely smiled smugly, and indicated the corridor before them.

"Pray, continue," he said with elaborate politeness, "I wonder if you'll think the same in a few moments."

Chapter 11
Deep Treasure

The Sanctified Catacombs twisted, mazelike, through the vast darkness below the temple of Luerkhisis. Several times the passage branched into smaller routes, and Wryllish unhesitatingly made his choice, leading Ariakas what seemed like miles under the ground. For a while after their discussion of dragons, the priest remained silent, and the warrior walked beside him, intrigued.

"Are all these tunnels the province of the temple?" Ariakas asked abruptly.

"Yes—each temple, actually. It is rumored that these passages run underneath Sanction and connect all the temples secretly."

"All three temples are dedicated to Takhisis?"

"Now, finally, they are. Her presence has ruled in Luerkhisis for many decades, but the Temples of Duerghast and Huerzyd across the valley had been dedicated to false gods of the post-Cataclysm."

"The tunnels are reached only through the temples?"

"As far as we know," the priest admitted. "Though there are passages that have never been explored. It's true there are rumors . . . tales of some mysterious tunnel-dwellers, the 'shadowpeople,' and so forth. . . ." Wryllish's tone made it clear he put no stock in such stories.

"Where are we going?" inquired Ariakas after several minutes of silent, fast-paced walking.

"I will show you the thing that most proves the glory of our mistress . . . our queen. When you behold it, you will know the absolute truth of our destiny!"

The priest paused before a heavy wooden door set into a stone frame in the cavern wall. With a flourish, he produced a small key and slipped it into the lock. "This is a secret chamber," he whispered. "Only the elders— and you—know of its existence. But when the time is right . . . !"

His speculation trailed into silence as the latch clicked, and the door swung slowly, silently open. Quickly Wryllish darted inside, gesturing for Ariakas to follow. The warrior complied, ducking from the light of the priest's glowing scepter. When he looked around the room, he could not suppress a gasp of astonishment.

At first he thought they had entered a chamber of huge, perfect nuggets of pure gold and silver. Each was a sphere too large for him to wrap his arms around, gleaming metallic in hue. They were piled against the walls of the large room in stacks that reached twice as high as the warrior's head. Each massive nugget shone like freshly burnished metal of the highest quality. The wealth represented by the hoard astounded him. It was hard to believe that this much gold and silver existed on all of

Krynn! He looked closely at the nearest of the gilded spheres, impressed by the shiny regularity of its outer surface, as if a pure film of liquid gold had been poured over a smooth, rounded surface.

"Impressive, is it not?" asked the priest, quietly.

"Very. Where did all this gold come from? Are they solid, or is it a coating?"

Here Wryllish smiled in a condescending way that irritated Ariakas. "You could say that it's a coating . . . but I still don't think you fully understand."

"Understand what? Explain."

"These are part of the proof," replied the high priest. "Here, touch the surface."

Gently, hesitantly, Ariakas ran his hand over the smooth surface of the nearest sphere. Though not so hot as his flesh, it was surprisingly warm—far warmer than the surrounding air of the underground chamber. Too, the material did not feel like metal. There was a very slight sense of *give* to it, as if the metallic surface were only a sheen over a tough, leathery hide.

The truth came to him in a flash, and he stepped backward instinctively before he spoke. He looked with awe at the mountain of spheres, and then allowed his gaze to drift back to Wryllish. Ariakas narrowed his eyes, and the priest nodded, as if pleased with his pupil's perspicacity.

"They're . . . *eggs*, aren't they? *Dragon* eggs?"

The high priest smiled, the expression growing to spread across his face. "Very astute, my lord."

"But—*where* did they come from?"

"A place very far away, where some of the dragons have dwelled in exile since the Third Dragon War—the war of Huma and the lance, of which you spoke earlier."

"Then—then dragons *are* real?" the warrior murmured, beginning to consider the prospects for good or ill.

"Oh, yes, very real. Some of them will serve our

mistress, presumably with the same devotion shown by you or me. Others are her mortal enemies, sworn to drive her from the world and to hold her at bay throughout the centuries."

"And they wage war, now—unsuspected by men?"

"No—there is no war at the present. But they will come again. Dragons of red and blue, of black, green, and white. All the children of Takhisis will once more take to the skies in her name!"

"And these dragons of metal will be their enemies?"

"Yes!" Wryllish exclaimed. "The dragons who, with the same arrogance that brought the Cataclysm, call themselves the 'good' dragons." The high priest's voice was heavy with scorn. "In their righteous blindness they invite the same kind of disaster on themselves. And to think, they would call us 'evil'."

"How do you—do *we*—come to have these eggs here?" asked the warrior.

The priest was positively beaming. "The Queen's agents have brought them here, into this temple. Come, allow me. . . ."

Wryllish led Ariakas from the chamber, still holding his glowing scepter high. They came to another door and the priest unlocked it. The warrior stepped inside to see another mountain of metallic eggs, these a shining copper color that was only slightly less brilliant than the gold.

"Eggs from all the clans of dragons who stood against our queen are now held in her temple!" crowed the high priest. "We have the ultimate weapon against our enemies—for we hold the fate of their children in our hands."

"It is indeed a commanding leverage," Ariakas allowed. He shook his head and turned to the priest. "Given the evidence of the eggs, you force me to admit the existence of dragons. Still, what assurance do we have that they will fight as our allies?"

"It is by her command." Wryllish talked as he led Ariakas onward, showing him a room full of eggs in a deep, bronze hue, and finally to a chamber that contained more eggs than any of the others he had seen. "The brass dragons—most common of all the enemy wyrms, and thus they have given us the greatest number of eggs."

"But the dragons of color, those called 'evil'—they, too, exist still?"

"More than exist!" Wryllish replied. "They are present on Krynn, only awaiting the commands of our mistress. And when they surge forth, all the world will tremble in fear."

The priest nodded meaningfully at Ariakas's huge sword, which jutted upward over his shoulder. A small swatch of the white blade showed above the scabbard. "I see," Wryllish Parkane said, significantly, "that you have already been blessed by a gift from our lady."

Ariakas was jolted by the word. "Our 'queen', you called her. I don't think of her as my lady!"

The cleric seemed surprised by his vehemence, shrugging the distinction away as if it were a little thing. "You will," was all he said.

"What did you mean about my sword?" Ariakas pressed, returning to the priest's observation. "As a gift from . . . the queen?"

"It has been blessed, very powerfully," Wryllish explained. "Soon, I'm sure, the fact will be clear to your eyes as well. If you should call on her name in a cause that pleases her, the great fury of her vengeance will be revealed in your hand."

Ariakas vividly recalled the transformation of the huge sword, the weapon he had sharpened and honed over the long winter. With each blow against his lady, it had changed color—color to match the blood flowing from the wound. It had become this pristine white, and he had assumed that the blade was permanently marked. It hadn't in any sense lost its sharpness or strength, but neither had it gained any obvious property or power. Yet now this priest repeated the words of Takhisis herself. What shape would the blessing of the Dark Queen take? He was not entirely sure that he wanted to find out.

"But all these rooms are just introductory," said Parkane, "to the place I truly wanted you to see."

"Lead on," said Ariakas.

Wryllish Parkane turned down a narrow corridor, a natural stone passage that had been hewn into more or less rectangular proportions. Still, the passageway snaked this way and that, so that the cleric's light was often reflected from walls twisting before and behind them. Ariakas sensed a slight descent in the floor beneath his feet, though the sharp turns of the hall made it hard to see any distance to the front or rear.

They reached another door, similar to the portals to the various egg rooms, but smaller, and remote from those chambers. Wryllish removed his key ring, but then paused before inserting a key into the lock.

"This was merely a small overflow chamber," the priest explained, taking a deep breath. "There were too many brass eggs to fit in the storage room, so some of them were brought down here."

Still the priest hesitated. He turned to Ariakas and looked the warrior directly in the eye. "What I am about to show you is known to only two other persons . . . myself and a wizard of the black robes named Dracart, whom we consulted for advice. The very knowledge of this room's existence would be enough to cost a novice his life."

"Open the door!" Ariakas snapped, growing tired of the priest's hesitation. He was gratified to see that Wryllish hastened to obey, inserting the tiny key into a metal keyhole and twisting. The latch clicked, and the door swung inward a crack.

Ariakas reached out, ready to push the portal all the way, when the stench emerging from the room struck him like a physical blow. A sickening odor flooded the air, swarming almost visibly around him, suggesting corpses long dead or food that had been given over to mold. He gagged and stepped backward, turning to spit the pungent film from his tongue.

"What in the name of the Abyss is *in* there?" he demanded, throwing his hand over his nose and mouth in an inadequate attempt to filter the air.

"You'll have to see for yourself," replied the cleric.

"*Tell* me, damn it!"

"The truth is, Lord Ariakas, that I *can't* tell you, because I don't know. You'll really have to see for yourself." Raising the light over his head, the priest overcame his hesitation, pushed the door open, and stepped boldly into the room beyond.

Ariakas followed, pausing at the door to draw a deep breath. What he saw within the room sickened him almost as much as the scent of its air. The floor seethed with small, lizardlike creatures, squirming and wriggling pathetically over each other. The longest were nearly three feet from nose to tail, and many of them displayed razor-sharp teeth along ridged and bony jaws. As he watched, one of the lizards chomped down on another, crushing its body. While the killer began to chew on its cannibalistic prey, an even larger lizard bit the predator on the head and then tried to swallow both of the corpses.

In other places the tiny serpents butted against the wall, or tried to claw their way through each other. The presence of Wryllish's light didn't seem to affect them in any way, though the priest kicked several of the creatures away from his feet. Only then did Ariakas realize that the miserable serpents were blind. He noted, too, that several were missing their rear legs, and others bore webbed, batlike stubs of flesh that might have been wings if they had been allowed to develop fully.

In a far corner of the room, more of the slithering

creatures caught his attention. A bundle of them—perhaps a dozen or more—all squirmed outward from one leathery egg. The shell was slit and withered along several openings, and the little reptiles, their bodies coated with a thick, oily film, twisted and clawed their way free of the ragged sphere. All around the room were the fragments of these great eggs, though the metallic sheen had corroded so much that Ariakas never would have been able to discern the original color.

"Are these . . . dragons?" inquired Ariakas. He couldn't believe that something he'd always pictured as power and nobility personified could begin life in this pathetic state.

"Most assuredly *not!*" Wryllish Parkane confirmed. "They are *corruptions* of dragons, which so far have occurred only in this room."

"Brass dragon eggs, these were?" Ariakas wondered. After a few moments in the room, the stench had lessened to an unpleasant, if pervasive, aura.

"Yes. But their origin, we think, has little to do with this grotesque mutation."

"Has something happened to these eggs—something unique?" asked the warrior.

In answer, Wryllish Parkane nodded and smiled. "Perhaps it would be more . . . comfortable, were we to speak outside?" he suggested, raising his eyebrows in question.

Ariakas readily agreed, and they stepped back through the doorway into the deep cavern passage. Even with the door shut the warrior imagined that potent stench clinging to his clothes, hair, skin.

"Have you ever heard of the Zhakar?" inquired the cleric, surprising Ariakas with the apparently irrelevant question.

"The name means little to me," the warrior admitted. "In Khuri-Khan it was rumored to be a kingdom in the Khalkists—mountain savages who ruthlessly kill any intruders. No one knows where it is, though speculation puts it on the border of Bloten." Ariakas shrugged, remembering another fact. "I traveled well to the north of its supposed locations when I came to Sanction. There are enough tales of folk who've disappeared there to give the legends some credence."

"You were wise," remarked the priest. "Zhakar is a real place, and deadly to those who intrude. Only in one detail do your eastern legends miss the truth."

Ariakas remained silent, waiting for the explanation.

"Zhakar, you see, is a nation of *dwarves*," Wryllish Parkane explained. "They are the only remnant of the mighty kingdom of Thoradin, which was destroyed by the Cataclysm."

"Okay, so it's a bunch of savage dwarves," Ariakas retorted. "What does it have to do with these eggs?"

"Oh, there is more you need to know," cautioned the priest. "After the Cataclysm, Zhakar was afflicted by a horrible plague, borne by the mold that grew in the vast food warrens underneath the city. Many of the dwarves died; those who lived became terribly afflicted with disfiguring disease. Their skin rots away, their hair turns to mold and crumbles. . . . It's not a pretty thing to see."

"I imagine not," Ariakas murmured.

"In any event, some of these dwarves have come to Sanction to live and to trade. They offer high-quality steel and gems in exchange for all kinds of things. They also practice thievery, with varying degrees of skill, and are generally an unpleasant lot to be around. They go about robed to conceal their repugnant appearance."

"I remember them—fully cloaked, shorter than a mountain or hill dwarf, but still stocky. They looked very sturdy."

"Those are the Zhakar," agreed Wryllish Parkane. "Now, some months ago, a Zhakar thief was caught in our temple. Guards pursued him into the catacombs, and found him hiding in this very room. At that time, the room contained nothing more than a hundred or so brass dragon eggs. He was caught, and we interrogated him. Unfortunately, we were able to learn little more than the name of his lord. Finally, justice was done to him. Barely a week afterward, however, two apprentices discovered that one of the eggs in there had begun to . . . well, do what they're *all* doing, now."

"Two apprentices? I thought you said only one other person besides us knows about this."

"Yes." The priest looked a little distressed. "The secret was judged too important . . . the apprentices have gone to an early meeting with the Dark Queen."

"I see." Ariakas was impressed to learn that this priest was capable of ruthless action when necessary. "Now, tell me why you've shown all this to me."

"Well, it's because of the Zhakar, you see," Wryllish explained. "We believe that some aspect of the mold plague has caused the corruption of these eggs. We scrubbed them clean, but apparently it was too late to remove the corruption. Naturally, we want to learn more about it. Who knows? It might even prove to be a useful discovery."

Privately, Ariakas didn't know what good a bunch of blind, cannibalistic lizards were going to be to anybody, but he didn't interrupt the priest's explanation.

"It's possible—quite conceivable, actually—that the Zhakar would be willing to trade some of the fungus if it proves to be useful. But as it stands right now, we know little about them. They have resisted all attempts of our clerical agents to meet with them."

"You want me to affect a meeting," guessed Ariakas.

"You seem like a very logical choice," the cleric hurriedly encouraged. "You're so much more, well, *worldly* than those of us who spend our time in the temple. If you could meet with Tale Splintersteel and make the arrangements, you would do the mistress a great service —a *very* great service!"

"Who is Tale Splintersteel?"

"He's the richest Zhakar in Sanction. He seems to be an unofficial chieftain for them, and he arranges all the large commercial deals. He's a prosperous merchant lord in his own right, one of the wealthiest people in Sanction. He's also the lord of the Zhakar thief we caught—the one who reputedly sent the cutpurse on his mission."

"Do you know where this Zhakar, Splintersteel, is?" Ariakas inquired.

"He lives in the slum, somewhere—no one knows exactly where. However, he frequents a tavern owned by another Zhakar, near the West Bridge. The place is called the Fungus Mug, and chances are good that you will be able to find him there."

"Very well," said Ariakas. "I'll seek him there tomorrow."

Without further exchange, they departed the Sanctified Catacombs, Ariakas walking in silent reflection. He bade farewell to the high priest and emerged from the darkened cavern of the temple to stroll reflectively down the mountainside, under the glowing crimson clouds of Sanction at night.

He reached his house very close to dawn, and when he slept his dreams were filled with squirming lizard creatures, spawn of the metal dragon eggs. Yet the images of the grotesque creatures, he was surprised to find, gave him not horror, but hope.

Chapter 12
The Fungus Mug

After sleeping for most of the day, Ariakas awakened to a steaming bath followed by a massage from his valet, Kandart. The man was a middle-aged Nerakan mute, completely attentive. Deciding that he enjoyed the life of nobility, the warrior followed his relaxation with a meal of tender roast lamb, and by the time he had briefly honed his white sword, it was time to set out once again into the streets of Sanction.

Ariakas had some difficulty finding the Fungus Mug; the bar occupied a street of seedy taverns in a district composed exclusively, so far as he could tell, of seedy taverns. His only clue was the West Bridge, and after an hour of fruitless searching he concluded that 'around the

West Bridge' could serve as a direction to something like a thousand saloons and taverns.

And none of these thousand was a place called the Fungus Mug. He tried asking passersby and received replies varying from completely uninformative to downright hostile. He began the second hour of his search along a dingy row of alleyways that ran perpendicular to the busy Bridge Road. Pedestrians hurried through these alleys, keeping their heads low and their ears alert. Here, too, flopped the destitute, the drunken, the losers at gambling . . . and anyone else temporarily bereft of lodging and funds. Sometimes these pathetic wretches begged for alms—pleas that Ariakas inevitably ignored, or responded to with a kick of his heavy boot. Occasionally one would wait until he'd passed, and then slip toward the warrior's back. Ariakas whirled several times, half-drawing his huge sword; always the culprit scurried away.

In the third alleyway, he felt a glimmer of optimism. Several stocky characters trumped along in front of him, and though they were heavily cloaked, they looked like dwarves. Then, too, there was a scent on the air here that actually suggested mold and mildew, like a cellar that was flooded and left closed. In time, he saw the small sign, chiseled stone set in a wooden frame. Beneath a carved image of a stout drinking glass Ariakas made out the words: "The Fungus Mug." The stonecarver had added a curious detail to the mug: it seemed to be puffing out gentle clouds of steam, as if the contents were very hot.

Pushing through a low doorway, Ariakas was forced to duck his head. He remained stooped within, for the ceiling support beams were exactly the height of his forehead. His first sensation was the overpowering smell he had detected in the alley—it was as if he had *entered* that cellar he had earlier imagined. The next thing he noticed was the nearly complete darkness of the inn. He could

hear sounds of laughter and angry words exchanged in a
variety of languages. Somewhere a glass broke, and a
female voice joined the cacophony.

Ariakas bumped into a stone ceiling support and muttered in vexation. He massaged his forehead and groped
his way past the obstacle. A huge fireplace stood in the
far wall, and within the vast hearth the remains of a coal-
fire smoldered. The embers did not cast much light, but
slowly Ariakas made out vague details of his surroundings.

There were many tables between him and the fireplace, and most of them seemed to be occupied. The
laughing and bickering immediately around him ceased,
and he suddenly felt very self-conscious. A long, low bar
stood along one wall, and small oil flames glimmered in
several places behind the bar. Hunched silhouettes
showed Ariakas where the customers were, and by
avoiding these he found a seat facing the barkeeper.

Sitting, he now got a good look at the little flames.
Each flared beneath a copper kettle, and from these con-
tainers steady clouds of steam escaped. He watched the
bartender fetch several empty mugs from dwarven customers and refill them from the steaming pot. A waft of
steam floated past his nose, and he realized that the
warm liquid was the stuff he had smelled even out in the
alleyway.

"What'll it be—I ain't got all night!"

The cantankerous voice drew his attention down, and
he saw the shadowy outline of a dwarven barmaid, fists
planted firmly on her hips, face upturned. Though he
couldn't see details of her features, the irritation in her
voice blended well with the other sounds of debate and
disagreement in this place.

"An ale, cold as you've got it," he replied curtly.

"Don't get your hopes up," she retorted, ducking
behind the bar. She drew a mug from a tap, and brought
the stuff over to Ariakas.

The warrior flipped her a silver piece, declaring he'd be ready for another in a few minutes. When she marched off, presumably to harass a few more customers, he turned and slumped his elbows on the bar, wondering how to go about finding Tale Splintersteel. Tasting the brew, he found it palatable, if a bit more bitter than the grainy eastern ales he was used to—but nowhere near as bad as he had already decided the steaming stuff in the pots must be.

Looking up and down the bar, his eyes grew further accustomed to the gloom. The warrior observed several other humans, but most of the customers had the short, stocky outline of dwarves. He noticed, with curiosity, that the dwarven figures were universally cloaked in dark cloth, often with garments wound so tightly as to expose only eyes and mouth. Others had their faces free, but hid their features within deep hoods. Though the dwarves used their hands frequently, both for drinking and for communicating, they all wore gloves. Often they gestured with clenched fist right in the face of a comrade, and he saw several dwarves shoving each other back and forth brutally. Among humans, he would have expected such duels to explode into fights, but the dwarves seemed able to settle their differences thus, with one or the other finally conceding and the whole group sitting back down.

"Well, drink up if you want another—like I said, I ain't got all night!" The barmaid barked at him, appearing suddenly out of the darkness. Her face glowered at him from the depths of her hood. The dwarf woman's skin seemed pocked and rough, though Ariakas could see no details in the dim illumination.

He drained his mug, and when she returned with the refill, he asked a question. "That stuff in the pots . . . what is it?"

"Tea," she explained brusquely.

Ariakas grabbed her shoulder as she turned to go.

"What's it made from?"

She looked at him fiercely, apparently torn between bashing him on the jaw and answering his question. "Mushrooms. Zhakar mushrooms," she answered, jerking free of his grasp and starting through the darkness again.

He regarded the pungent scent critically. So the Zhakar dwarves liked 'mushroom tea,' he reflected with a grimace—quite a difference from the other dwarves he had known, all of whom preferred drink of a much stronger nature.

His curiosity grew. What horrid plague effects caused them to cloak themselves so heavily? And if the argumentative atmosphere in the bar were any indication, they were more hostile and unpleasant than any other dwarves he'd encountered—and that included a fair number who lacked social grace.

At this point he didn't even try to solve the problem of meeting Tale Splintersteel. He could barely get two words out of the barmaid who worked here—he could imagine the reaction he'd get if he asked to meet the most important Zhakar in Sanction. His reflections were interrupted by a startling clap on his shoulder. Ariakas reached instinctively for his sword, then held his hand at the sound of a familiar voice.

"So, warrior—our schemes bring us together again in Sanction!" Ferros Windchisel's hearty words sent a surprising jolt of pleasure through Ariakas.

"Your escape was successful I see. Congratulations!" The man pumped the dwarf's hand as the Hylar slumped onto the seat adjacent to Ariakas. He felt a warm flush of friendship; the presence of Ferros brought back the memories of his stay in the tower.

"And you, too—though I began to wonder. I kept my eyes on that drawbridge for a couple of days and didn't see any sign of you coming out."

"No—as it was, storms closed in before we could

leave. I was trapped there for the winter," Ariakas said softly. He couldn't bring himself to tell Ferros that it had all been a test, and that his reward had been the 'prisoner' in the top level of the tower. "I didn't get to Sanction until a few days ago."

"You did *what*?" sputtered Ferros Windchisel. "What about the ogres?"

"You did a great job of leading them away," Ariakas said with a grin. "The snow was so deep after the first storm that they couldn't get close to the mountain."

"By the way, you're looking good," Ferros noted. "Your face isn't in two pieces anymore."

Ariakas scowled, annoyed by the reminder of his encounter with the two kender. "It healed over the winter," he explained tersely.

Ferros squinted at the human and then shook his head with a rueful grin. "Pretty gutsy, that—to live in an ogre den."

Ariakas squirmed uneasily, uncomfortable with the knowledge that, like himself, Ferros Windchisel had been a pawn in the Dark Queen's test.

"I wish *I'd* had that luxury," the dwarf continued, grumbling good-naturedly. He shook his head. "One night I had to kick a bear out of a cave just to get a place to sleep. And those ogres weren't any too pleased with me, either. Had to bop a couple of 'em when they kept following me too close."

"Did you winter in the mountains?"

"Nope—made it into the lower valleys before the heaviest snows hit, then I was able to clomp down into Sanction by mid-Cold-Rust. You'd be surprised how warm it stays around here, what with these mountains smoking and belching all the time."

"You've been here all that time?" inquired Ariakas, surprised. "I thought you had some pressing business to attend to."

"I *do!*" Ferros agreed, subconsciously lowering his

voice and looking furtively around. All the nearby dwarves argued and bickered with their comrades, paying the two companions no attention whatsoever.

"You knew about my quest?"

"Only that you had a reason for exploring the Khalkists," said Ariakas. "You never told me about it."

"I came here looking for dwarves," Ferros Windchisel explained without preamble. "All the way from Thorbardin—on the trail four years before I got captured by ogres."

"Thorbardin?" Ariakas had heard of the place. The name conjured pictures of dwarven legions gathered under the banner of the mountain dwarf king. When considered from his own eastern homeland, Thorbardin was impossibly distant, so far removed that it might have been located on another world.

"Aye. What I wouldn't give for a smooth ferry-ride across the Urkhan Sea," Ferros mused. "Thorbardin's a wonder, you know—I'm amazed that I ever got around to leaving."

"Why *did* you leave?" Ariakas asked. "If you were looking for dwarves, I'd have thought you were in the right place before you started."

Ferros chuckled. "That I was. But, see, I *know* about the dwarves in Thorbardin—we all do. I'm looking for signs of dwarves that we've lost touch with. Several of my Hylar clansmen have set out on this quest in the last decades. We look for kingdoms around the whole of the continent that, since the Cataclysm, have been closed off from one another."

"And you believe that one of those kingdoms is in the Khalkists?"

"I *did* believe—now I *know!*" hissed the Hylar, his voice confirming the triumph of his discovery.

"You've heard, then, of Zhakar?" asked Ariakas.

Ferros looked somewhat deflated. "So, someone told you already, huh? Yup, that's the place."

"Good luck," the warrior noted wryly. "I've heard they kill anyone who even gets close to their borders. No one even knows where it lies!"

"Except for the Zhakar themselves," said Ferros, gesturing to the dwarves crowded around them.

"That's why you're here? To get directions?"

"An invitation would be even better. I've learned they have a head honcho here in Sanction. I figure if I could talk to him, tell him why I'm looking for Zhakar . . . well, that'll be someplace to start, at least."

"You're looking for Tale Splintersteel, I take it?" Ariakas asked.

Ferros managed to look crestfallen and indignant at the same time. "Do you know *everything* about these guys?" he groused. "Here you get to town yesterday and already you've learned what I've scraped together in the last three months!"

"Cheer up," Ariakas said. "I'm sure there's something you know that I don't."

"I don't even know what brings *you* into this tea-dive," Ferros complained.

"As a matter of fact, I'm looking to meet Tale Splintersteel myself."

"So you know him, then?"

"I don't even know what he looks like," the warrior admitted.

"*There* I've got you!" crowed Ferros. "I not only know what he looks like, I know where he's sitting!"

Ariakas nodded, impressed. "Care to share that information?"

Ferros made a pretense of considering his request, then grinned good-naturedly. He nodded toward the darkest corner of the bar, where Ariakas discerned nothing more than indistinct shadows gathered around an unusually long table.

"Splintersteel's the one at the head of the table," Ferros explained. "The only dwarf I've seen in here who doesn't get a lot of lip."

"Well, let's go talk to him," suggested Ariakas, rising to his feet. At first he wondered if Ferros were about to object, but then the Hylar shrugged and stood beside him. The human warrior pushed his way through the Zhakar huddled at the various tables, working toward that darkened alcove.

Gradually the bar fell silent around them. The dwarven customers suspiciously watched the pair.

"Watch my back," the warrior hissed as quietly as he could, and he felt Ferros clap him on the shoulder to signify that he'd heard.

By the time they reached the long table, the Fungus Mug had fallen silent as a still winter night. This close, he could see perhaps a dozen dwarves seated along the sides of the table, and each of them seemed to have his hands out of sight. The warrior readily imagined that each held a weapon—they could easily leap to their leader's defense if Ariakas should make any suspicious move.

Stiffly, he bowed to the dwarf, who was still half-buried in shadows, the man's eyes shifting back and forth between the bodyguards to either side of the table. "Tale Splintersteel?" he inquired. "I request the honor of an interview . . . regarding a business matter that may yield considerable profit."

"Impossible!" snapped the dark figure at the table.

When he didn't elaborate, Ariakas pressed, his tone hard. "Why is it impossible?"

"Your companion . . ." replied Tale Splintersteel. "His very presence is an affront to me and my people. He should have the decency to remove himself from my sight."

"Hey, you're no pretty boy yourself!" snapped Ferros Windchisel. "Talking about affronts—"

"Perhaps you could wait over there," Ariakas said softly provoking a sputter of indignation.

"I will grant you your interview, human," noted Tale Splintersteel, "if you will first grant me a small entertainment."

"I'm no harpist," growled Ariakas.

"Not *that* kind of entertainment—but something that falls well within your obvious skills."

"What do you have in mind?" Ariakas felt an ominous sense of suspicion.

"Kill the mountain dwarf. We shall discuss your business over his bleeding remains," suggested Tale Splintersteel conversationally.

"Hey—get your hands off me!" demanded Ferros Windchisel. Ariakas whirled to see three or four Zhakar bearing the Hylar to the floor, though Ferros kicked and punched, throwing two of the Khalkist dwarves off.

In that split second, Ariakas made his decision. His hands grasped the sword hilt over his left shoulder, and with one whistling slice the white blade flew from the scabbard, whipped through the air, and cut a deep gouge in the shoulder of the Zhakar holding Ferros's arm. With a cry, the wounded dwarf dropped to the ground, and the entire bar exploded into uproar. Ferros cursed and drew a small axe from his belt, forcefully chopping his other captor.

"Kill them both!" howled Tale Splintersteel, leaping to his feet and gesturing his followers forward. Even in the confusion, Ariakas was surprised to note that the influential Zhakar was little more than three feet tall—a foot shorter than Ferros Windchisel.

Then armed dwarves surged at them from all sides. "Back to back!" the warrior shouted, and the Hylar pivoted to match his own maneuver. The two fighters fended off a press of Zhakar dwarves, Ariakas driving his white blade over and over into the crowd of shadowy figures.

"Hold, you fools!" Tale's voice rose to hysterical levels, and the chaotic crowd of attackers paused for a moment.

"Form ranks!"

"Quick—over here!" grunted Ferros, darting toward the wall of the large room. Ariakas followed, realizing that their slim chances improved if they could get solid cover at their backs.

"After them!" cried Tale Splintersteel. The horde of howling Zhakar must have numbered a hundred or more, and as Ariakas killed the first two it seemed that ten—twenty!—more leapt in to take their places. He grunted as a steel blade bit into his arm, and then cursed as another cut gouged his knee—even as both attackers fell dead from the lightning-fast back-and-forth of his counterblows.

"I'm down!" gasped Ferros Windchisel, collapsing back against the wall, pierced by a Zhakar sword.

Ariakas stepped to the side, straddling the body of his friend as the rabid dwarves lunged closer, driven to fury by the prospect of victory. The slashing of that white blade couldn't hold them at bay for long. His weapon seemed to be the only brightness in the place, gleaming like ivory as it rose and fell. What was it about that sword?

Call on her name in a cause that pleases her, and the great fury of her vengeance will be revealed in your hand.

"Well, Queen," he muttered. "If ever I've had a dire need, this is it!" He brandished the sword, not sure what to expect. A sneaking Zhakar hacked a deep cut into his thigh, and he shouted in pain. Blood trickled down his leg, and Ariakas wanted to slump back to the wall. Only the knowledge of Ferros Windchisel's inevitable fate kept him on his feet.

Snarling his frustration, Ariakas swung the weapon hard enough to decapitate the Zhakar who had wounded him. "Please, Mistress!" he cried, in real desperation. "In the name of Takhisis, all-powerful Queen of Darkness, *please* come to my aid!"

The hilt trembled in his hand, groaning with a sound

reminiscent of the crushing avalanches he had heard throughout the winter. A deep rumbling shook the very foundations of the inn. Even the Zhakar sensed the disturbance, ceasing their attacks and falling silent in suspicion and fear.

Abruptly, a blast of cold air slashed him in the face, and a noise like a howling blizzard shrieked through the Fungus Mug. Wind eddied and swirled, driving stinging needles of ice against Ariakas—but that was nothing compared to the fate of those who stood at the other end of his sword. An explosive cone of murderous frost swept outward, freezing flesh and blood, slaying dozens of shocked, terrified Zhakar in the instant of its assault. Whirlwinds gusted through the room, sweeping over tables and chairs, frosting clothing and skin into brittle sheets of ice. Across the room, shutters erupted outward, and the howling of wind rose.

In panic, the surviving Zhakar ran screaming away from this nightmarish warrior and his deadly weapon. Ariakas looked for Tale Splintersteel in the crush, but he could see no sign of the dwarven merchant-lord. Their business was not concluded yet.

As a wide circle opened around him, Ariakas seized Ferros under one shoulder and roughly lifted the Hylar to his feet. Supporting his injured companion in one hand and brandishing the blade in the other, the man slowly dragged them both from the Fungus Mug. During his deliberate advance to the door, none of the Zhakar made a move against him, perhaps because fully a quarter of the bar was filled with frozen dwarf statues, mute reminders of the price of resistance. The rest had been frozen by fear.

Finally, the pair tumbled across the threshold and into the alleyway beyond. A crowd had gathered, but these humans and Zhakar quickly parted as Ariakas, growling as he breathed, half carried Ferros away from the Fungus Mug. He stopped for a moment, realizing that he still bore his sword. As he moved to resheath the weapon, Ariakas looked at his sword and nearly dropped the dwarf in his astonishment.

The gleaming blade, once pure white, had changed to an absolutely unblemished sheen of darkest, inky black.

Chapter 13
The Way of the Temple

Ariakas supported Ferros as they stumbled down the alley, but the dwarf quickly slumped, a dead weight. The human lost his balance, and the pair tumbled into the wet gutter, blood from their wounds mingling with the effluence of the street.

"Thanks, warrior," grunted the dwarf, each word pushed forth with audible effort.

"Shut up," Ariakas groaned back. "Save your strength —I'm not gonna have you die after I went to all that trouble on your behalf."

" 'Fraid you're outta luck—that bastard stuck me pretty good." Ferros lifted his hands from his belly. Both palms were smeared with dark, sticky blood.

"Hang on," Ariakas commanded him. Pushing himself upward with his hands he reached his knees, and then laboriously climbed to his feet. His left leg and both arms throbbed from nasty wounds, though the bleeding had subsided somewhat.

Reaching for the dwarf, he hoisted Ferros to a sitting position. "Hold that wound tight," he instructed.

"What d'you think yer doing?" demanded Ferros, with spirit.

"Shut up," Ariakas repeated. Kneeling, he grasped the dwarf and hoisted him over his back. Ferros grunted in irritated surprise, but kept his hands tightly pressed to the hole in his belly.

Stumbling like a drunkard, Ariakas struggled to retain his balance. He knew that if he were to fall he would never get up again—at least, not with Ferros on his back. Slowly at first, then with greater steadiness and deliberation, the human carried the dwarf to the end of the alley and turned onto Bridge Road. He didn't make for his house, however. Instead, his steps carried him up the long, climbing road to the temple of Luerkhisis.

He had no recollection of how long it took him to make that long hike, which had winded him the previous night when he walked it uninjured and unburdened. In the lower, crowded portions of the city, bystanders took one look at the lines of furious determination etched in the warrior's face, and hastened to get out of the way.

He reached the lonely stretch of road and made his way under the early glow of crimson Lunitari, which had just risen over the shoulder of the volcano. Still he plodded forward, his mind blank, a trance of exertion propelling him through the repetitive steps.

Only when he at last reached the vast, dark snout of the temple did his awareness return. He didn't hesitate at all, marching right into one of the veils of blackness. Suppressing a shudder as the magical dark engulfed him, he continued resolutely forward until he emerged into the great, lamplit central hall.

Novices and priestesses hurried toward him from all directions as he gently lowered Ferros Windchisel to the floor. The dwarf's eyes were closed, and his skin—where it showed between beard and scalp hair—had faded to a pasty gray. Still, the warrior felt a trace of a heartbeat, and the Hylar held his hands clenched determinedly over his wound.

"Lord Ariakas! What's the matter?"

Ariakas looked up, grateful to hear his name. He recognized one of the mature young priestesses from his tour of the temple—she was a green-collar who had been leading a discussion class.

"We need the high priest! Show me to a private chamber, and get this dwarf carried there—but go easy on him! It's bad. And send someone for Wryllish Parkane—*immediately*!"

He felt a jolt of cruel satisfaction at the fear that flickered across the young woman's face. "Take them to the meditation rooms!" she barked at the novices, then turned and bowed to Ariakas with full composure. "I'll get the high priest myself!" She spun and raced off through the hall.

Six strapping novices gingerly lifted the dwarf and carried him through a door at one end of the great hall. Ariakas, unaware any longer of his own weariness or pain, followed them into a hallway leading to many smaller rooms. The young priests carried Ferros into one of these, laying him carefully onto a low bed against one wall.

Before the warrior could kneel beside the dwarf, Wryllish Parkane hurried into the room, still tying the knot on his belt. Gesturing the novices to leave, the high priest turned to Ariakas.

"I came as soon as I could—you brought a dwarf, Derillyth said!"

"He's badly wounded," Ariakas said peremptorily. "Help him!"

The priest approached Ferros Windchisel doubtfully. "He doesn't look like a Zhakar. . . ."

"By the *Abyss*, man—he's *not* Zhakar! Who said he was? Just help him, before it's too late!"

"Look here, my good Lord Ariakas," objected Wryllish. "You were to investigate the *Zhakar*. And when I heard you'd brought a dwarf here, I naturally thought—"

"*Damn* your thoughts!" snarled the warrior. "I went to those accursed dwarves and this is the result of my attempts! The Zhakar are the nastiest, most murderous bunch of little swamp leeches I've ever seen in my life!"

"You *antagonized* them?" inquired Wryllish Parkane, disapprovingly. "But we *need*—"

"Listen to me." Ariakas lowered his voice, but his grim determination carried through the level tones. "If you let this dwarf die, his won't be the only corpse I leave behind when I depart this temple. Now, get busy."

Shock was replaced by fear in the high priest's eyes, and again Ariakas felt that fire of satisfaction. Good, he thought, the man knows where I stand.

Wryllish Parkane took a deep breath. The momentary terror that had flickered in his face quickly vanished, replaced by serene confidence. "I shall not heal him," Wryllish began.

Ariakas suppressed the urge to draw his sword or repeat his demand. He sensed that the cleric had more to say. Nevertheless, Parkane's next words took the warrior by complete surprise.

"*You* will," concluded the high priest.

Ariakas opened his mouth to object, but held his tongue at the sight of Parkane's upraised hand.

"You do not think you can do this—but you can," he explained. "Now, kneel beside the wounded one."

Mutely, Ariakas did as he was told.

This close, he was shocked by the deathly pale cast to

Ferros Windchisel's features. Even more disturbing, the warrior saw that the dwarf's hands had relaxed, and though they had fallen away from the puncture, no fresh blood emerged.

"Place your hands over the wound," instructed Wryllish Parkane.

Ariakas lowered his palms to the bloody, sticky hole in Ferros Windchisel's tunic.

"Now, pray—*pray* to the Dark Queen that she grant your miserable request! Call upon mighty Takhisis, warrior, and beg that she grant you her favor!"

Wryllish Parkane's voice had taken on a hard edge, and Ariakas flinched under the onslaught of the words. It took all of his self-control to keep calm, to hold his hands on the dwarf's belly and try to shake off his frustration and rage.

Slowly, he focused his thoughts on his companion. He recalled the Hylar's loyalty, his courage. Parkane's ranting continued unabated, but Ariakas pushed it to the far recesses of his mind. Instead, his thoughts returned to the sinuous, five-headed being that had appeared before him in the tower. He sensed that the Queen of Darkness could slay him any of a dozen ways, with no more effort than Ariakas would use to kill a mosquito; this was a power that he could respect. He pleaded with her to heal Ferros, begging her to mend his flesh, to restore the dwarf's blood to his body and the hearty color to his skin. And gradually, in the depths of his prayer, he felt himself surrender. Yielding up to the swelling knowledge within him, he granted that he would be the Dark Queen's tool . . . her agent for whatever tasks she wanted him to perform.

In return, all he demanded was *power*.

Not knowing whether he spoke aloud or only within the anguished passages of his mind, he groveled, he professed his loyalty, he promised to always obey her will. He offered up his past in its entirety as a wretched waste of time and years—for it had not been dedicated to labors in *her* name.

Despite his prayers, her power hovered yet beyond the grasp of his mind, his being. How long he knelt there, tears streaming down his face, he did not know. It did not matter. At some point during the long darkness of the night, his professions of faith passed from the conscious to the unconscious realm. He slept, but his dreams continued on the winding trail begun by his thoughts. Takhisis appeared in those dreams, and he would never recall the things that she told him, the pledges he made to her. When he awakened, all he would remember was that she was pleased.

* * * * *

Sunlight streamed through a window Ariakas had not even noticed on the previous night. The warrior lay slumped on the floor. He stretched and turned, gradually recognizing the still form of Ferros Windchisel.

Suddenly the dwarf gave a snort and sat up, blinking in confusion. He saw Ariakas, seated on the floor beside his bed, and his eyes widened in shock.

"What are *you* doing here?" he demanded, embarrassed. Then he blinked and looked around. "Well, maybe first you can tell me *where* we are."

"The temple," explained the warrior. As Ariakas spoke he saw Ferros scowl, obviously settling the events of the previous evening into place in his mind.

"Wait a minute!" Ferros inspected the hole, crusted with dried blood, that had ruined his tunic. Gingerly, his fingers explored the skin underneath. "This is . . . strange," he said softly.

For the first time Ariakas noticed that his own numerous wounds were gone. He held out his arm, looking for the especially deep gash over his biceps, but found no sign of even the faintest scar.

"All right," spat Ferros Windchisel, his face locked into a fierce scowl. "What happened? How come I'm not dead?"

"Is that what you wanted?" retorted Ariakas sourly. "I went to a lot of trouble—"

"Yeah, sorry," Ferros interrupted sheepishly. "It's just, well, kind of a shock. So tell me, why aren't we both full of holes?"

"There is power here," Ariakas said cautiously. He was not prepared to take Ferros, or anyone, into his confidence regarding the trancelike experience of the night before. "One of the old gods, I should say. I think the priests used that power to heal us."

"How did I *get* here?"

"I carried you."

The Hylar's eyes widened, and he appraised Ariakas. "Thanks," he offered gruffly. "I owe you my—"

"The account's even," Ariakas interrupted. "Remember the ogre in the drawbridge room?"

Ferros shook his head. "That was different. If you had died, my chances of escaping would have died with you. Here, you could have left me in the bar or outside, and saved yourself a lot of trouble. I mean it—I owe you."

"Those were quite ornery buggers—your cousins," noted Ariakas. "Are you glad you found them?"

"I'm not done yet," Ferros Windchisel said grimly. "Did you see if Tale Splintersteel got frosted with the rest of 'em?"

Ariakas shook his head. "As far as I know, he skipped out the back way. Not that it would be much use going to talk to him, anyway," he reflected ruefully, remembering the high priest's disappointment.

"It's not *him* I want to find," Ferros said, sitting up. Ariakas noticed that clean clothes had been provided for himself and the dwarf, and the two dressed while the Hylar explained. "I want to find the kingdom itself. I won't be going back to Thorbardin until I can learn more about them."

"Last night didn't tell you enough?"

Ferros scowled stubbornly. "I can't assume that one tavern represents the attitudes of an entire nation. And, too, when one dwarven nation is in trouble, even unfriendly dwarves can make good allies."

"You sound like you think there's going to be some kind of war," noted Ariakas, raising his eyebrows. He started to shave, using his dagger and cold water. "Does Thorbardin face invasion?"

"Nobody knows for sure. But it's not just us, or me," Ferros declared. "There's a lot of talk of trouble—the elves of Qualinesti patrol like there's a threat on every border. And surely," Ferros added, studying the human carefully, "you've noticed the troops here in Sanction. I think *someone* is getting ready for war—and when one army gets ready, all the rest have to prepare."

"I had noticed the numbers. But I don't think they're in service right now. You don't see any unit standards or barracks."

"How much of the city have you really *seen?*" pressed the Hylar. "All the alleys and buildings? Who knows what goes on in them?"

Ariakas shrugged. "As for me, when there's war, there's work. Not that I'm looking for either."

He told the dwarf where he lived, and when he learned that Ferros was quartered in a noisy waterfront inn he invited the Hylar to be his guest. Ferros agreed to bring his things over later in the afternoon, and Ariakas led him through the great hall of the temple to the door. "I'm going to talk to the high priest," the warrior told the dwarf.

Ferros gruffly repeated his thanks, then ducked through the curtain of darkness and disappeared.

"You were going to speak to me?"

Ariakas whirled in surprise as Wryllish Parkane silently stepped up behind him. Flushing, he nodded.

"We'll talk later," said the high priest. "Right now,

Patriarch Fendis is beginning a lesson—historical studies I think you will find quite interesting. It's as good a place as any to begin your tutorship."

"My *tutorship?*" Ariakas glowered at the unperturbed priest.

"Forgive me. Doubtless there are many important matters requiring your immediate attention. Just remember," Wryllish said, "it is not for me, nor for yourself that you now make your choices—it is for *her*."

The meaning of the priest's words hit Ariakas like a blow. For a moment he had to suppress an urge to kneel, to beg his queen's forgiveness. He spoke to her mutely in supplication, knowing he was right not to display weakness before the high priest.

"Where is the patriarch holding forth?" he asked.

Wryllish Parkane smiled slightly and led the warrior to one of the many small rooms off the great hall. He saw several novices, and two gray-haired priests, blue collars, all seated on the floor. One of the elders was speaking, which he continued to do without pause as Ariakas entered and sat on the opposite side of the room from the circle.

"The Kingpriest of Istar epitomizes the arrogance of faiths who claim the mantle of 'goodness'," Patriarch Fendis was explaining. "At first, that ignoble ruler hurled his hatred at everything he branded as 'evil,' and even in the beginning he forged his branding irons with his own convenience in mind."

Ariakas was in fact immediately interested. His travels had taken him around the fringes of the Blood Sea, and he had marveled at the thought of the mighty nation that lay buried by the crimson maelstrom. The power to rack a land like that, he had often reflected, was the ultimate attainment of mastery.

The cleric continued through the morning, presenting an insightful description of the ebb and flow of god-power that had culminated in the Cataclysm. Ariakas learned that Takhisis had remained aloof and uninvolved in that celestial conspiracy. Alone among the gods of great power, she watched Reorx, Paladine, Gilean, and the lesser deities hurl flaming wrath from the heavens.

Yet in the wake of the godswrath, when humans declared themselves bereft of immortal leadership, Takhisis had been cast aside with the rest of the pantheon. Now she worked slowly to spread word of her existence, and her destiny—the destiny of greatness that would be shared by all her faithful.

The pictures woven by the patriarch's words brought to Ariakas's mind images of huge armies, powerful war machines, and vast, stone-walled fortresses. And, vividly imagining, Ariakas saw that he rode in the thick of battle—he *commanded*, wielding the power of his queen like a mighty sabre over the field.

* * * * *

In the following weeks, Ariakas attended regular studies at the temple. Though every instinct told him that Tale Splintersteel must be punished for his treachery, Ariakas somehow found the serenity to delay his revenge until the future.

As the days passed, he delved into mountains of information on topics to which he'd never before devoted much attention. In addition to history, he was exposed to the poetry of the ancient bards, the Public Tomes of Astinus, the elven histories by Quivalin Sath, dwarven epics by Chisel Loremaster, and an assortment of legends and mythologies from across the width and breadth of Ansalon.

He also learned of the profusion of cults, all worshiping false gods, that had sprung into existence since the Cataclysm. Many of the warriors who had served him had professed great allegiance to one or another of these deities. It amused him to think that their prayers had been directed to nothing more than an uncaring cosmos.

And he learned that, of the true gods of Krynn, Takhisis was the being meant to inherit mastery of all. Mortals and immortals together would one day worship at her altar, each and every one of them owing existence itself to her pleasure. For now her favored clerics were marked with leather collars to display their status in her service—with red reserved for the high priest and blue for his chief lieutenants. Declining through black and then green, the white collars denoted the many young novices.

Of the dragons, his teachers said much. He learned of the mighty scarlet wyrm, the red dragon whose breath burned like the flame of an infernal furnace, and the white, whose exhalation exploded like a blast of arctic frost. When Fendis described this serpent, the warrior vividly recalled the frigid eruption from the white blade of his sword. Then he learned of the black wyrm and—mindful of his midnight blade—he listened avidly to the description of this dragon's caustic acid breath. Spit in a long stream, the liquid could rot flesh, wood, or metal with ease. Neither were the green and blue dragons excepted. The former's expulsion of poisonous gas, a seeping, seething cloud of noxious fumes, brought insidious and horrifying death. The latter's lightning bolt could sear enemies with explosive force, or pulse through metal with sizzling heat, melting even steel bars in a way that mere fireballs could not. And these five attacks comprised only the breath attacks of the colored dragons. The creatures also possessed claws that could rend an ox and jaws that could crush a small house.

Many dragons, he learned, stood so high in the favor of their goddess that the Dark Queen granted them spells with which to further her aims. And it was with the discussion of these spells that another fascinating phase of his training began.

Fendis and Parkane worked with Ariakas alone, drawing forth from him the memory of the power that had possessed him when he had cured Ferros Windchisel's wounds, and his own. For long hours the clerics instructed him on the rituals of prayer that allowed mortals to tap into immortal power.

Ariakas showed a remarkable aptitude in these studies. Soon he could call into existence a globe of light such as Parkane had used in the Sanctified Catacombs, or weave an enchantment to create a fine meal—or to corrupt and decay a large stockpile of food. A useful spell allowed him to neutralize a poisonous meal even before it was ingested, or to cure the effects of toxin afterward.

He learned chants that could increase his effectiveness in battle, and others that could reveal the presence of traps and snares in his path. The two elder priests were astonished at the rapid pace of his progress, and for a time it seemed that every day added a new magical incantation to the warrior's repertoire.

Not all of his studies consisted of these lessons in history, magic, destiny, and power. The temple encouraged well-rounded training, and Ariakas joined a class taught by the priestess Lyrelee in bare-handed combat. When he first observed her, he was fascinated by her skill in the unique hand-fighting technique, and greatly attracted by her feline power and beauty. He welcomed the opportunity to join her class. In his initial lesson he watched her throw several young and obviously inexperienced novices onto the floor, deflecting their attacks with clever feints and crisp, well-practiced maneuvers.

When he stood up for his turn, he all but swaggered over to her, determined to show the youngsters what a real warrior could do when faced with such fancy footwork—and incidentally ensuring that he earned this woman's respect. Several seconds later, from his position flat on the floor, he reflected that perhaps the lightning-quick woman could teach him a thing or two.

Wryllish Parkane himself instructed Ariakas on the techniques of meditation, which the high priest assured him would greatly facilitate the communication between man and goddess. Wryllish sat for hours, motionless, and—though at first the monotony threatened to drive Ariakas mad—the warrior swiftly developed the patience to match his teacher. He found that these sessions really did liberate his mind, allowing his imagination to drift into places usually reserved for his dreams.

This is not to say that Ariakas became a monk. In fact, though he visited the temple for at least a short time every day, he returned to his house on most nights. Ferros Windchisel had wasted no time in making himself at home there, and when Ariakas remained in the temple for several days at a time the warrior was glad to know that someone was keeping watch over his property.

When Ariakas did come home, the dwarf and the human often made a long evening of it, exploring the inns and taverns of Sanction. Often they got roaring drunk, occasionally they found—and won—a fight, and always Ariakas felt in the dwarf a kindred spirit. He reflected that a true warrior is a warrior foremost, be he dwarf or human.

The Hylar spent his days seeking information on the Zhakar, a task that had become exceedingly difficult in the weeks following their confrontation at the Fungus Mug. The mysterious dwarves might have all gone underground, for as much information as Ferros could garner.

Growing increasingly irritable as time passed without success, Ferros Windchisel began to complain about life in Sanction. His favorite gripe was a claim that the place was infested by tiny, biting firebugs. Showing Ariakas raw, itching wounds on his arms, the dwarf insisted that vile insects took nocturnal snippets from his skin. Ariakas suffered no bites himself, but he could not dispute the reality of the dwarf's suffering.

The best that Ferros could do about his quest to find Zhakar was to get a secondhand description of a convoluted trail from an old ship's captain. The man claimed he'd once hired a Zhakar mate who had divulged a few details about his homeland. These the captain related to Ferros—in exchange for the two barrels of beer consumed during the discussion.

Of all Ariakas's activities, inside the temple and out, he found that the combat lessons with Lyrelee were the most appealing and invigorating. The woman knew a tremendous amount, and was eager to share her knowledge. Ariakas, in turn, began to instruct Lyrelee and some novices in the use of the sword, dagger and bow—the three weapons with which he was most comfortable.

He continued to find the priestess to be an alluring female, and for the first time since his stay in the tower he began to consider the delightful prospect of intimate physical joy. He had routinely hired harlots since his arrival in the city, but regarded time spent with them as little more than fleeting and impersonal entertainment.

Ariakas spent time talking to Lyrelee after the other students had departed the class, and the warrior sensed that she, too, felt a kindling of desire. He remembered the warning of Takhisis regarding his women, but sometimes he tried to convince himself that it couldn't truly apply to the lithe priestess. Certainly a woman who labored so diligently in the Dark Queen's service could not be made a scapegoat for her punishment!

These were the thoughts that occupied his mind as he made his way home, long after dark, one late-summer night. He had just crossed the Grand Bridge, which was still crowded even at this late hour, and had begun to meander up the hill toward his palatial house.

A scurrying form moved through the shadows of an alley, and Ariakas spun, reaching for his black-bladed sword—though he didn't draw the weapon.

Cloaked in dark robes, a short figure shuffled toward

DRAGONLANCE Villains

him, stopping ten feet away. He could make out no details beneath the deep cowl.

"Tale Splintersteel wants to see you," hissed the figure. "He will meet you tomorrow night, alone. Be in the center of the Fireplaza at midnight."

Before Ariakas could respond, the hunched figure darted into the shadows and disappeared.

Chapter 14
Plaza of Fire

"I'm going with you!" Ferros insisted after Ariakas told him about the mysterious summons. The two sat in the estate's great room, with glowing embers in the fireplace and tumblers of lavarum near to hand. The house was silent around them, though Ariakas knew that mute Kandart watched and waited in the shadows, ready for the moment when the glasses were empty.

"I don't think that's a good idea," the warrior disagreed. "I was told to come alone—and besides, you know what your presence did to him last time."

"By Reorx, man—I didn't mean I'd walk right out there and shake his *hand!* But when you go to see that treacherous little weasel, I intend to be hiding in the background, someplace where I can get a good view."

The dwarf patted the heavy crossbow he had recently acquired, and Ariakas reflected that Ferros could provide him with a measure of security. After all, the warrior wasn't certain *what* the Zhakar wanted, but he'd learned enough from their first meeting to go into the rendezvous with full preparation and alertness.

"I don't think he'll try anything," Ariakas noted. "After all, he had a good taste of my sword last time. Still, it would be good to have you there to keep an eye on things."

"Yeah—I smell a trap," groused Ferros. The dwarf stood, furiously scratching at the rash along his arms, chest, and belly. "Damned firebugs!" he snarled. "Worse than ever last night!"

Ariakas chuckled sympathetically. "I still haven't had any in my bed—maybe they like your smell!"

"Humpf! So, you going to be ready for this?"

"I will be by midnight," Ariakas replied, grimly confident.

The warrior had decided not to tell anyone at the temple about the upcoming meeting. If it turned out well, Ariakas could bring Tale Splintersteel to Wryllish Parkane and show the high priest that his efforts had in fact met with success. If nothing—or, even worse, something disastrous—came of the meeting, there would be no need for his temple-mates to learn of the failure.

Ferros spent several hours honing to razor-sharpness the heads of his bolts. He had a full quiver of the steel-shafted missiles, and proudly informed Ariakas that the arrows could punch through plate mail at a hundred paces.

The human warrior, meanwhile, went to his dry garden and sat on a stone bench in the brittle bower.

Before him spread the valley. Today, with its eternal shroud of haze hanging unusually low, Sanction had a tight, enclosed feeling. Ariakas felt power tingling in the air, believed with certainty that things of great portent were in the works. He took his sword and laid the naked blade across his lap. The perfect blackness of the steel mirrored his own spirit to an infinite depth.

Gradually his mind filled with a sensation of falling— but very gently, as if wings had sprouted from his shoulders and now carried him easily toward Krynn from a great height. For nearly two hours he sat on the bench, his heart and lungs slowing their pace as his mind drifted on the currents of the Dark Queen. It was after sunset when he emerged from the trance, and he felt his body tingling with power and energy. He crossed through the courtyard into the main room of his house, and there he found Ferros Windchisel.

"I'm going to head down there early—get a look around," announced the Hylar. "It'll give me time to lie low before you show up."

"How will you contact me if there's trouble?" asked Ariakas.

"I'll figure something out—just stay alert," assured the dwarf. Ferros slung his crossbow over his right shoulder, where he could raise it and shoot in an instant. He wore a colorful plaid cape that served to conceal the short sword at his waist.

The dwarf made his way into the dusk, and Ariakas settled his nerves with a meal. His current chef was a domineering old matron who had held the job for two months, much longer than either of her two predecessors. Now she presented him with a light, delicious supper—as always, she performed splendidly. Finally, an hour before midnight, he left.

Ariakas wore his huge sword on his back. He had purchased a new scabbard of unadorned but sleek doeskin that completely hid the long blade. He could draw the sword with either hand, and if he gripped it with both he could bring it forward in a powerful, skull-crushing blow. Despite his fast progress in Lyrelee's unarmed fighting classes, he was grateful for the security offered by the weapon.

Approaching the Fireplaza obliquely, Ariakas crossed down to the Lavaflow River and started toward the center of the city. The right side of his body warmed to the radiance of the deep, crimson stream beside him. In the distance, he saw the Grand Bridge, the gray stone arcing upward through the darkness. The underside of the bridge glowed with its own light, heated, ovenlike, by the volcanic fury of the river.

The Fireplaza sprawled along a great section of this river, with the huge bridge connecting to the far end. Tall, stone-walled buildings surrounded the expanse. Several wide fissures gaped across the plaza's stone surface, and many of these belched forth clouds of steam, gas, or flame. At the opposite end stood Sanction's only public decoration—the War Monument.

This unique memorial consisted of the raised replicas of three sailing ships, supported by three clumps of stone columns. The three ships were clustered in close formation, and from across the plaza, they looked as though they sailed through the air. The monument was dedicated to the fallen who perished during a brief fracas several decades earlier—one column had been raised for each of the one hundred and two men who had lost their lives.

During his months in the city, Ariakas had gleaned the tale of the structure, whose appearance had so puzzled him at first. The war had been a campaign against nearby Saltcove, reputedly a den of pirates and freebooters. The battle was Sanction's only claim to military glory, and the veterans of the conflict—all of whom had been well-paid by the city's merchants—had been able to extort the memorial's costs from their former employers.

From a reputable bartender Ariakas had learned the true story of the commemorated hostilities, which were grandiloquently entitled the 'Saltcove War.' The campaign was in actuality a single battle and had involved a boisterous, liquor-sodden expedition against the nearby fishing village, where several small-scale pirate captains had in fact maintained their strongholds. The town fell in the first rush, with several of the pirates fleeing to the hills with their henchmen. A few resisted, and four of Sanction's men perished in actual combat. The other ninety-eight fatalities had occurred when two of the overloaded invasion ships, both piloted by drunken captains, collided at the entrance to Saltcove's harbor. The warriors aboard, armed and girded for battle, went down like stones as the ships broke apart around them.

It often surprised Ariakas that a city with such a surplus of warlike men could not boast of a more glorious military history. Still, a story of hearty, courageous men cursed with bad leadership was not unique in the history of Krynn. He speculated on what the armies of Sanction could accomplish if they were only leashed to a single goal. These men might even subdue Bloten, he believed —remembering all of the undersized expeditions he'd been forced to lead from Khur and Flotsam.

Ariakas passed between the monument and the Lava-flow River, picking his way between two of the long fissures. The gaps were only ten or twelve feet wide, but zigged and zagged for several hundred feet across the plaza. In a few places they were crossed by bridges, but the width of the chasms constantly shifted, so these crossings were short lived at best.

Several folk were about, including a few vendors of fruit, trinkets, cheese, and bread—all of whom had blankets spread on the ground, or small two-wheeled carts to display their wares. Somewhere a minstrel strolled, singing a bawdy song to laughter and jeers.

Ariakas veered to avoid the hustling approach of an old beggar woman, but the hag fairly leapt toward him, tugging at his sleeve and glaring up at him with one penetrating eye. The lid of the other was sewn shut, the seam vanishing in a maze other wrinkles lining her bony, angular face.

"Alms for an old woman, warrior?" she asked, glaring slyly at him. "Mayhaps in trade for your fortune told? This one old eye sees very clearly, mark my word!"

"Get away with you!" barked Ariakas, checking for danger as he raised a hand, ready to swat.

"One best listen to one's future," she said, ominously. "Even a Hylar dwarf knows that much!"

Ariakas froze, and then lowered his hand into his belt pouch. He passed the woman a steel piece, hoping that no other beggar in the vast square saw the transaction.

"Did you tell the fortune of a Hylar tonight?"

"I've seen the futures of *everyone* tonight," she retorted. "And who I tell is my business. But for you, warrior. . . ." She lowered her voice portentously. "Look you toward the pillars of the Saltcove War—danger lurks in the shadows. Danger small in size, but great in number—danger going cloaked, hidden from the light."

Nodding his thanks, Ariakas surveyed the plaza in light of this new information. He reached for another coin, but the old woman shook her head and gave him a knowing smile. "The Hylar are not as stingy as some would say," she declared, cackling softly to herself as she hobbled away.

He turned his back on the flow of molten rock, moving into the center of the plaza and keeping the War Monument to his left, a good two hundred paces away. He knew that at that distance, he was safe from any bow shot out of concealment.

But how was he to find Tale Splintersteel? Never before had he realized just how *big* the Fireplaza actually was. And where was Ferros Windchisel? He scanned the space, seeking the familiar dwarven silhouette, but was disappointed. Though he could see several hundred individuals within the plaza, many remained eclipsed by vendors' carts, the great monument, or knots of people.

As he searched, a fissure near him spit a great spume

of steam into the sky. The eruption lasted for several seconds, and even after the blast ceased, a huge, white cloud drifted across the plaza, floating toward the river —where the radiant heat of the lava would quickly burn it away.

Then he saw a figure striding forward, emerging from the mist, and for a moment he wondered if this were Ferros. But the fog cleared slightly, and he saw someone considerably shorter than the Hylar, and yet equally broad in the shoulder and chest. The newcomer, fully wrapped in a cloak of fine embroidered silk, swaggered to Ariakas's right. The warrior pivoted to face the fellow obliquely, maintaining a watch from the corner of his eye on the multiple and shadowy columns of the memorial.

"Hello, warrior."

Ariakas recognized the same cold arrogance that had characterized Tale Splintersteel's voice in the Fungus Mug. Again that black cloth concealed most of his face, leaving only a thin slit where the two glittering eyes peered forth.

"Greetings, Zhakar Splintersteel," the human replied. "I am glad to see that you are well."

"That was not the impression I received when you massacred two score of my fellows," Tale snarled. He continued to approach Ariakas, and the warrior was forced to turn his back fully to the monument. Ariakas stepped to the side, however, to place a wide fissure behind him, protection against attack from the rear.

"I was merely defending myself," Ariakas retorted without rancor. "I should think you could understand my reasons perfectly." His voice masked his own surprise that the weapon had erupted with killing frost.

Tale Splintersteel shrugged. If he was terribly distraught about the loss of his henchmen, he hid the fact very well. "When you approached me in the tavern that night, you intimated there was a matter you wished to discuss—a matter of mutual profit."

Ariakas nodded, noncommittally. "That is what I said—*then*," he concluded pointedly.

Now it was Tale's turn to nod, which he did as if he understood the human's position completely. "Perhaps I acted with too much haste during our previous meeting. . . . I offer my apology. Understand: our antipathy was not directed against *you*."

"Why Ferros Windchisel, then?" demanded Ariakas. "You called him an 'affront' to you! He was ready to greet you with friendship, and you ordered us killed!"

"That is a matter between dwarves," Splintersteel said. "I offer my apologies that you were involved."

"Your apology is accepted," Ariakas added. "With the notation that I won't hesitate to use my sword if you try anything treacherous."

"Ah, that sword," mused the Zhakar. Ariakas thought the eyes flashed heatedly in the depths of that robe. "I have spent my life around weapons—making them, selling them. Even, upon occasion, using them. Yet never have I seen a blade as potent as that."

"It serves me well," Ariakas allowed, suspiciously. He cast a quick glance behind and saw that nothing moved among the shadows below the War Monument. "I hope you didn't ask for this meeting to talk about my sword," he added.

"Only in part. As I told you, I'm an admirer of splendid weapons—and yours is the most magnificent I have ever seen. It is natural to desire another look at it. However, as you suggest," the Zhakar merchant continued, "that is only secondary to the true purpose for this meeting. What is the nature of the business transaction you wished to discuss?"

"It concerns a . . . henchman of yours. He was caught as a thief within the temple of Luerkhisis. It seems that he had something with him—something the priests could not recover, like a dust or powder of some sort. Do you know what it was that he carried?"

"Perhaps. Why? Has this 'dust' some sort of value?"

"I am asking as an agent for the temple—the priests are interested," Ariakas replied vaguely. He didn't want to reveal important negotiating information any more than did Tale Splintersteel. "But before we can discuss this I need to have some assurance that you know what we're talking about."

"Indeed, I do," replied the robed dwarf. Something in his posture appeared to slump, as if the knowledge set a heavy load upon the Zhakar's shoulders. "Why don't you ask this 'henchman' for an explanation?"

"He proved very close-mouthed," Ariakas said wryly. "Even though the priests can be quite . . . inventive with persuasion. The only thing they could get out of him was that he'd gone on your behalf."

Tale Splintersteel shrugged. As with the henchmen in the bar, if the fate of his agent troubled him in any way, he concealed the fact from Ariakas.

"What did he carry?" asked the human bluntly.

"Now *that* I am not prepared to tell you, unless you tell me why it's of interest to you."

"Suffice to say that the priesthood might create a market for you—a very lucrative one."

"Then why does the priest not come and talk to me himself?" demanded the Zhakar.

"Your reputation does not encourage friendly overtures," Ariakas replied pointedly. "I came because I can take care of myself—or you, if necessary." Ariakas nodded slightly toward the sword to emphasize his point. Once more he cast a quick glance to the rear, ensuring that the monument was quiet.

He turned back, startled to see that Tale Splintersteel had raised his right hand. Reacting to the threat of attack, Ariakas started to reach for his sword, but realized that the Zhakar's hand was empty.

"What are you doing?" the warrior asked suspiciously.

The sound of Tale Splintersteel's voice—distant and

removed, but full of subdued power—suddenly told him. The wretched dwarf had cast a spell.

Ariakas lunged toward the Zhakar, when abruptly the entire plaza vanished around him, swallowed by complete blackness. Dizzy, he whirled away from an imagined attack, realizing that he'd been rendered completely blind. He heard Tale Splintersteel's voice some distance away, and sprinted toward the sound—when, with equal suddenness, that clue ceased. Every noise in that bustling city halted abruptly, and he was left in a world of utter blackness and silence.

The warrior reeled, completely deaf, totally blind. Turning his face, he could feel the river by the heat radiating onto his skin, but he could see no sign of the brightly glowing lava. His feet scraping across the flagstones made no sound—and, most sinister of all, neither did the treacherous Zhakar.

Ariakas remembered the chasm he had carefully placed to his back—now it yawned as a deadly threat an unknown distance away. Instinctively he reached for his sword—he could draw the weapon and flail blindly, at the very least! His hands closed around the hilt and in that instant his vision and hearing returned, bombarding his senses with light and noise. The pommel of the weapon tingled in his hand, and he felt there the power that had broken the Zhakar's spells.

He saw Tale Splintersteel creep toward him, no more than a dozen paces away. The Zhakar carried a hooklike sword that could be used to stab, slash, or grasp an opponent. As Ariakas's huge sword came free from its scabbard the dwarf's eyes stared madly through the narrow slit in his robe.

Pretending that his senses were still obscured, Ariakas staggered through a circle, waving the weapon as if he had no idea where his enemy stood. His heartbeat quickened as his gaze swept past the War Monument—scores of dark shapes now scurried forward. Obviously they had lurked among the shadowy columns until Splinter-steel had given them some kind of signal.

Ariakas finished his circle, pausing in a fighting crouch but holding his blade at an awkward angle, as if expecting the Zhakar to be some distance away. Out of the corner of his eye, Ariakas saw the dwarf resume his advance. Those glittering eyes held steady on the massive sword in the warrior's hands.

Although Ariakas could have leapt toward the dwarf and slain him with a quick, sudden blow, he judged that this was not fitting retribution. The man wanted Tale Splintersteel alive—the Zhakar would learn the folly of betraying the queen's champion!

Wheeling through a circle again, Ariakas raised the black blade toward the figures scuttling toward him across the broad Fireplaza. Tale Splintersteel froze, watching carefully—and ready at an instant's notice to dive away from that death-dealing sword.

Ariakas called upon the power of Takhisis. The plea was easier this time, a natural surrender to power much greater than his own. Energy thrummed through the sword blade, and the warrior pointed it toward the approaching dwarves. A gout of black liquid hissed outward, flying in a long stream across the plaza. Ariakas directed the stream against a clump of charging Zhakar. Searing, caustic acid showered across them, bubbling through their garments and quickly dissolving skin and flesh. When the liquid struck, the dwarves screamed and tumbled to the ground, writhing for several seconds before they grew still.

Ariakas shifted his aim, splashing the corrosive stuff across another group, and these uttered screams of terror and pain as the acid sizzled through their bodies. With a quick glance, Ariakas saw Tale Splintersteel darting away, but then another group attacked, coming around the end of the chasm he had used to guard his back. Again Ariakas shifted his aim, and the black acid arced through a showering trajectory, bringing the final Zhakar charge to a horrific halt. Slowly, the warrior lowered his sword, but he froze when a flash of color caught his eye. He gaped with astonishment, seeing that the steely blade had turned bright, crimson red! As with the white and black, the red color was pure and unblemished, a perfect hue that extended from the tip to the base of the metal surface.

Wonderingly, Ariakas turned through a circle. The dwarves who had been missed or mildly injured by the spray scrambled or limped back toward the War Monument. The warrior let them go and turned back to find their master.

But Tale Splintersteel had disappeared. Whirling this way and that, squinting through the darkness, the warrior tried to discover where the devious merchant had gone. He saw a flash of movement in one direction, then spat an oath—just a thieving urchin fleeing from a fruit vendor.

A sharp cry of pain ripped through the darkness, very near. He rushed over to the chasm and there he saw the huddled figure of the Zhakar. Splintersteel had climbed down the steep side, intent on concealing himself within the gorge, when something had arrested his flight. Ariakas saw the steel bolt that had punched through the Zhakar's forearm, driven deep into the rock wall of the chasm. Tale Splintersteel screamed in agony, twisting and dangling from the missile that pinned him to the wall.

Ferros Windchisel swaggered to the lip of the precipice. He held the reloaded crossbow ready in his hands. Despite his confident gait, the Hylar's eyes flicked across the wide plaza, looking for danger in every direction.

"Help me!" shrieked the Zhakar.

"I'm in no hurry to do that," Ariakas remarked casually. He strolled to the top of the chasm and looked down. Tale Splintersteel was pinned to the wall perhaps ten feet down. The Zhakar clawed at the steel bolt with his good hand, but couldn't break it free from the porous bedrock. Far below, the shadows of the bottom ebbed and swirled with faint tufts of steam.

"Tell me—what was it that the Zhakar took into the temple?" demanded the warrior.

"I don't know—I lied!"

"I think you're lying now," Ariakas retorted, keeping his voice level and calm. "Nice shot," he added with a grin directed at Ferros.

"I figured this little worm was up to something. Never woulda thought he'd try to make a getaway down to the lava pits, though." The Hylar smiled wickedly, enjoying the plight of the Zhakar.

"Help!" pleaded Tale Splintersteel again.

"You were just about to tell me something," Ariakas said. "What was it? Oh, yes—the stuff that the Zhakar carried into the temple! Come on, now—I think you know what it was."

"Mold," gasped the Zhakar, his voice contorted with audible pain. "It was the dust of the plague mold . . . not carried . . . it's with him, *on* him—on *all* of us!"

"Now we're getting somewhere," Ariakas declared. "Where can we get some of that mold?"

"Get me up—I'll tell you!" groaned Splintersteel, his tone thinned by pain. "Just, please, *help* me!"

"You'll have to forgive me if I don't trust you," the warrior gently chided. "Do better than promise."

"What do you want me to do? By the gods, man—I'm bleeding to death here!"

Indeed, a dark, slick streak ran down the chasm wall below the struggling Zhakar. His protestations had grown weaker until his voice faded to a rasping croak. Splintersteel slumped, as if resigned to fate.

Ferros Windchisel came around the crevasse to clap Ariakas on the arm. "I thought of looking in there for him because I'd been using one of these cracks as a hiding place for the whole night. It worked swell, too—except for a few funny looks from folks who strolled past the edge."

"Good service, my friend," Ariakas acknowledged with a nod at the trapped Zhakar.

The Hylar removed a long, supple rope from a coil around his waist. He fastened an iron clip around his belt and ran the loop through. He extended the other end of the rope toward Ariakas. "Here—take hold of this and lower me down. I'll bring him up here to talk, if you promise not to make him too comfortable."

"Don't worry. He's a stubborn bastard—I think we'll have to do a lot of persuading to get what we want out of him." The human wrapped the rope around his waist and set his feet. Paying out line, he watched Ferros descend over the brink of the crevasse.

The Hylar rappeled nimbly down the wall until he was just above the Zhakar. Taking no chances, Ferros held a slim dagger ready as he dropped the last few feet until the rope supported him directly beside Splintersteel. With a quick lash, loop, and knot, Ferros took the slack line hanging below him and secured the rope underneath the other dwarf's arms. The wounded merchant lord seemed dazed and listless, taking little note of the activity.

Next, Ferros grasped the steel bolt he had shot through Tale Splintersteel's arm. The loose material of the Zhakar's robe flapped around it, so the Hylar tore it away. Sinews tightening in his arm, Ferros pulled slowly and steadily. The straining power in his stocky body was obvious to Ariakas, who realized that the missile must have driven very deeply into the hardened lava.

Finally the shaft wiggled slightly, and with a grunt Ferros pulled it free, drawing a sharp outcry of pain from the formerly motionless Tale Splintersteel.

"Haul away!" the Hylar called up to Ariakas. The

warrior immediately began pulling in the line, aided by Ferros walking up the wall. The dead weight of the Zhakar increased the load dramatically, but the pair finally heaved the injured dwarf over the lip of the chasm, where he sprawled, groaning, onto the plaza.

Ariakas gave Splintersteel a sharp kick on his wounded arm. "I should kill you right now," the warrior snarled. "Two times over you've earned death for your treachery!"

"Let's have a look at his face," suggested Ferros. "I can't figure why he's got to mask himself—unless he's even uglier than I can imagine." The Hylar reached down and roughly tore away the cowled robe that covered Tale Splintersteel's head. As the Zhakar's hate-filled visage was revealed, the Hylar gasped in surprise and instinctively stepped back

"He *is* uglier than you can imagine," Ariakas remarked, trying to keep his tone droll as his stomach surged upward in revulsion.

Tale Splintersteel's two black eyes flashed vitriol from the middle of a mass of decayed, encrusted flesh. The dwarf's scalp, cheeks, and much of his chin had rotted away, replaced by a greenish layer of some kind of fungus. His hair was gone, except for small patches struggling to survive on the back of his head, and a few tufts of beard that managed to emerge around the scabrous growths on his face. The mouth looked like nothing so much as a moist sore, gaping open and then clapping angrily shut.

"Please!" groaned the Zhakar, reaching pathetically for his torn hood. Without a word Ferros tossed the rag back to Splintersteel, and the hideously afflicted dwarf hastily drew it back over his features.

"Are you *all* like this?" demanded Ariakas, remembering that every Zhakar he'd seen in Sanction had gone about cloaked and robed.

"More or less," replied the dwarf, with a resigned

shrug. He no longer seemed menacing, nor even sinister—instead, he was just pitiful.

"That's all very interesting," Ferros interrupted, "but don't we have something to do?"

"Right," agreed Ariakas. He yanked the Zhakar to his feet. "This mold dust? Where can we get some?"

"You *can't*!" groaned the Zhakar. "It grows only in two places—within the fungus warrens of Zhakar, and on the skin of dwarves who suffer the plague!"

"On *your* skin?" asked Ariakas cautiously.

"Yes," grunted Splintersteel.

"Give me some, then—scrape it into a pouch," demanded the human, suppressing a shudder.

"It dies within minutes of removal," the afflicted dwarf retorted. "It won't do you any good."

Ariakas reflected on that information. Meanwhile, Ferros lashed the dwarf's hands behind his back, and by then the warrior had made his decision.

"Come on, Tale Splintersteel," announced the warrior. "We're going to make a call on the temple."

Chapter 15
The Ways of Shadow

"Patriarch Parkane is in High Communion," Lyrelee explained. "He won't emerge before dawn."

Ariakas and the two dwarves stood before the priestess in the great hall of the temple. Tale Splintersteel, hands still bound, sagged weakly against a pillar while Ariakas pondered the news. A crude bandage around the Zhakar's arm stanched the flow of blood.

"We can't wait that long," he decided. Ariakas turned toward Ferros Windchisel. "I'm taking him into the deepest part of the temple. It's sanctified territory, and I can't bring you with me."

"What?" sputtered the Hylar. He pointed accusingly at the Zhakar. "What about Fungus-Face, here—it can't be *too* sanctified with the likes of him around!"

Ariakas shrugged, unmoved. "He's a prisoner—it's a completely different issue."

"Yeah, he's a prisoner—he's *my* prisoner! And a damned treacherous one, too. How do you know he's not faking? That he won't pop right up and stick you when you least expect it?"

"I'll come with you," Lyrelee offered.

Ferros looked at the priestess skeptically.

"She's been training me in combat for the last few weeks," Ariakas announced smoothly. "I'll be glad of your company."

"I don't like this!" warned the Hylar, furiously scratching his arm. "That dwarf is my ticket to Zhakar."

"And I thought you were just trying to help," Ariakas replied.

"I'm waiting right here, damn it!"

"If you want—but you'll have a long stay." Ariakas, impatient, turned to Lyrelee. "Let's go."

Leaving the fuming Ferros Windchisel, Ariakas and Lyrelee prodded Tale Splintersteel into the great hall. In silence they stalked through the inner corridors, past the red-coated guards at the gates of the Sanctified Catacombs, and started down the long, straight stairway.

Ariakas employed a technique he had developed during previous forays into the darkness: he cast a light spell on a gem set in his helmet's front. Illumination spread through a wide arc before him, and naturally swiveled with his head whenever he looked around.

The Zhakar shuffled along ahead of them, head held down, hands lashed together at his back. Occasionally he stumbled, and once he fell. Ariakas then lifted him by the scruff of the neck, the man's stomach churning at the thought of the festering skin beneath the robe.

"Where are we going?" grunted Tale Splintersteel eventually. Abruptly the Zhakar stopped, and Ariakas almost tumbled into him. "At least tell me that much, if you want me to keep walking."

"We're going to the place where the Zhakar thief I told you about . . . the one who claimed he was your agent . . . was caught."

"I see." Splintersteel resumed his plodding pace, a little more firmness in his step.

Lyrelee, meanwhile, crept quietly ahead. The lithe young woman moved like a cat, thought Ariakas—and fought like one too, armed only with the weapons nature had given her. He found himself again studying the outlines of her body through the filmy trousers and blouse. She darted ahead and whirled into the shadows of a side passage, vanishing for several seconds before reappearing and flitting across the corridor to the next branching hall.

His first impressions of her, as an exceedingly effective fighter, had become softened by a haze of allure. Now as she scouted these tunnels, the warrior's mind focused instead on the slim curve of her breast, or the tight sinew of her leg. His awakening desire burned low, but with a steady heat that must eventually consume. Ariakas fully accepted his growing passion, feeling it move him toward an imminent plan of action. As soon as they had finished with the Zhakar, he resolved, he would take her in his arms and declare his feelings. He had little doubt as to the affirmation of her reply.

Only then did it occur to him that Lyrelee was acting rather strangely, considering that they moved through the inviolate reaches of their own temple. She scouted the next passage ahead of them before striding back in long, silent steps.

"What is it?" Ariakas asked, seeing the concern etched on her narrow face.

"I don't know," she replied, glancing quickly behind her. "It's just—something *feels* wrong."

"What threat could be down here?" pressed the warrior, disappointed in her reply. "What do you mean:

'feels wrong'?"

She confronted Ariakas frankly, while Tale Splintersteel's hood followed the back-and-forth of conversation. "I've noticed it a few times before . . . a sensation of being watched, spied on."

"You've never seen anything suspicious down here—signs of an intruder?"

"None of us has," replied the priestess. "But even the high priest has had the same feeling—that there are *eyes* in the darkness, watching . . . waiting."

The warrior was irritated. The high priest had certainly not indicated any such disquiet in his presence. *Ariakas* certainly didn't feel any strange sensation, and his acute sense of danger had saved his life many times.

"Let's go," he commanded. "If there *is* a threat, the worst thing we can do is stand still and gape at our surroundings."

She flashed him a look of surprise and, perhaps, hurt. But Lyrelee turned unquestioningly toward the deep tunnels, leading them on through the maze that Ariakas only vaguely remembered from earlier treks with Parkane. Lyrelee turned into another passage while the warrior and prisoner, about ten paces behind, continued forward. Ariakas watched the intersection expectantly, but the priestess did not emerge.

Tale Splintersteel halted, and Ariakas went around the Zhakar, the great sword held in both hands. The warrior cast a quick glance at the prisoner, seeing that the robed figure remained bound and still, though the hooded eyes watched his advance with interest.

Tension tingled through every nerve in the warrior's body. He silently cursed the woman, suspecting that nothing more than her unease affected him. Still, when she had not returned for a space of ten heartbeats, he began to feel real concern. Ariakas, nearly to the corridor, looked back. The dwarf hadn't moved.

The warrior whirled around the corner, sword raised

for battle. The light from his helmet-gem spilled down a winding, narrow passage. He saw no sign of Lyrelee. Then, something moved at the limit of his vision, a shadowy flicker partially concealed by the curving walls of the naturally eroded cavern. Ariakas leapt forward, feet pounding along the floor as he raced to investigate.

He didn't see the net until it had fallen from the ceiling, wrapping him from the tip of his sword to the soles of his boots. Ariakas tumbled to the floor, and then something jerked on a line, contracting the strands around him. His helmet toppled off of his head, tipping in the net so that the gleaming gem shone directly in his eyes. Everything beyond the tight enclosure was pure blackness.

And silence.

His attackers moved with uncanny stealth, passing through the darkness like a soft breeze. After an initial second of thrashing, Ariakas lay still, trying to ascertain something, *anything*, about the ambushers. He caught a scent of pungent, wet fur, like a hound's after the dog has run through a brackish fen. Strong hands tugged on the ropes securing the net, and Ariakas felt it constrict even more tightly. Trying to move, he found that he could barely even kick his feet.

"What?"

He heard the word, spat indignantly by the voice of Tale Splintersteel. In the next instant the Zhakar cursed, and then his voice was muffled. Mutely Ariakas raged— so close to success, and now to be thwarted!

Straining to penetrate the silence, he heard a pattern of low, deliberate breaths, and recognized the cadence of one of his training exercises from the temple. Lyrelee! Judging from the sound, the priestess was nearby, though she was obviously reluctant to call out. He heard scraping on the floor, and deduced that she, too, had been ensnared in the folds of a net.

Gradually he twisted his helmet around, casting the

illumination of the gem away from himself. True to his deduction, the gleaming light revealed Lyrelee, trussed like a rolled roast of meat in folds and coils of netting. Her own eyes met his for a moment before she turned away from the light and resumed her silent, deliberate struggle to escape.

Ariakas no longer heard anything from Tale Splintersteel or their captors. They were gone. Judging from the captive's exclamation of surprise, the Zhakar hadn't exactly been rescued. But if not, why had he and Lyrelee not been taken? Or harmed, for that matter? The two had simply been trussed up, with embarrassing ease, and left to squirm to freedom—long after Tale Splintersteel had been spirited away.

Ariakas seized the hilt of his sword and began to saw the blade back and forth over several of the cords in the net. The material proved surprisingly tough, resisting the razor-sharp blade for the better part of a minute before Ariakas severed the first strand. Cursing silently at the time-consuming task, he started on the second strand, and then the third, and the fourth.

By this time his muscles had begun to cramp up, and sharp pain racked his spine because of the uncomfortable position in which he found himself. He paused in his struggles, leaning around to get a look at Lyrelee—and was surprised to see that the priestess had almost broken free. Somehow, by flexing her arms around to her back, she squirmed through the coils. Ariakas gave up his own nearly fruitless struggles in the hopes that soon she could help him.

Her hands emerged from the top of the net, and then the collar of coils slipped down her forearms, past her elbows, and tangled around her head. With a few twists of her neck, the priestess drove her forehead out of the narrow aperture. The rest of her supple body followed quickly.

As soon as she was free, she sprang to her feet and

then dropped into a crouch, looking back and forth through the corridor. Seeing nothing, she darted to Ariakas's side and began working at the net with deft fingers. Within a few minutes she had loosened the knots, and he was able to pull slack line through the constricted mouth. Careful not to scrape the edge of his sword on the floor, Ariakas crawled forth and stood, his body creaking in pain and stiffness.

"Well done, priestess," he said, impressed.

"Did you see who attacked us?" she asked.

He shook his head. "Just some movement in the shadows—and a smell. Something like wet fur."

"I saw even less," Lyrelee admitted ruefully. "Though I, too, remember the smell." The priestess fell silent for a moment, obviously reflecting. "Have you ever heard of the shadowpeople?" she asked, finally.

"Only the word itself. Wryllish Parkane seems to think they don't exist. I assume they have something to do with this attack?"

"Only speculation," she said. "They're said to lurk in caverns and caves throughout the Khalkists. Very reclusive folk, though reputedly harmless. They'll go to great lengths to avoid being seen."

"What makes you think of them now?" he inquired.

"Only this," she responded. "They're supposed to be covered with fur."

Ariakas reflected on that news for a moment. "Do you know of anyone who fights with nets?" He was still amazed at how effectively they had both been neutralized by the meshwork ambush.

"That's new to me," she admitted. She looked at one of the tightly webbed objects. "I don't even know what it's made out of—look, it's not hemp."

Ariakas saw long fibers woven into a tight spiral. The material was smoother than either hempen rope or wool. When he pulled at one of the narrow strands, the material dug into the flesh of his hands, but absolutely refused to break. "It's plenty strong, whatever it is. I'll take this one back with us as a sample. But first, to business."

"Which way do you think they went?" asked the priestess.

"Splintersteel squirmed when they hit him, and then the sounds ceased. I don't think it's likely they carried him past us. Let's try checking out our back-trail."

They started along the corridor, walking as quietly as possible. Ariakas held his sword ready before him, while Lyrelee frequently whirled and scrutinized the shadows behind them. After a few minutes they came to the first branching corridor, and here they paused. Turning his face toward the floor, Ariakas brought the gem to bear on the blank stone. If there was any clue as to the direction of their quarry, it was beyond their skills to find.

"I have an idea," Lyrelee said, indicating the main passage. "Let's go a little farther."

Ariakas agreed and followed the priestess for another hundred paces. They came to a three-way branch, with corridors leading forward, to the right, and left. Once again there was no visible spoor to tell them which path to follow.

"Down there are the water warrens," Lyrelee announced, pointing left. "They're surplus overflow, mostly, for the temple's cisterns. But they go quite a long way, and both of us smelled something wet."

"I can't argue with your logic," replied the warrior. "We're reduced to guesswork any way you shake it!"

The passage proved to be more finished than many of the other tunnels in the catacomb network. Ariakas saw evidence of bricklaying to reinforce many walls, and soon they came to a well-chiseled flight of stairs, leading downward. As soon as they began the descent the warrior noticed the air growing damp around him, and he felt the dank mustiness of the walls. His light spell cast illumination about two dozen steps down, and for a long time it seemed as though this stairway must descend into the very heart of the world. He lost count of the individual stairs, though the number certainly passed a hundred.

Then, finally, the light reflected against a smooth, dark surface—liquid. Soon he saw the stairs end at a subterranean wharf. The stone pier, sprouting from a narrow landing, extended onto a surface of still water. The light spell swept over several tall posts placed, presumably, for the hitching of boats.

When they reached the bottom Ariakas saw that one long-hulled craft did in fact bob at a mooring, far out at the end of the pier.

"Is the boat usually here?" he asked.

"In the past there've always been two of them," Lyrelee replied. "The priests use the boats for fishing, for patrols . . . but not very often."

Ariakas stalked onto the pier. The light reflected from dark and still waters stretching beyond—*far* beyond its illumination.

"Where does it lead?" he asked, gesturing to the placid lake.

"Well, nowhere in particular, I guess," the priestess replied tentatively. "I've only been this far—but Wryllish Parkane indicated that it's just a watery portion of the Sanctified Catacombs. I assume that some of the passages go pretty far."

In the space between their words, the silence yawned around them, wider and darker than any quietude of the upper world. It was a silence that brought things like heartbeats into the audible range, made a gasp of breath seem like a shriek of alarm.

In this background of stillness, they heard a noise, a brief splashing of water. They waited breathlessly, but the sound was not repeated.

"That way." Ariakas pointed into the darkness to the left of the pier, utterly certain of his bearing across the black water.

Lyrelee untied the boat swiftly, and Ariakas stepped

into the low hull. The seats were narrow, six of them lined across the beam at four-foot intervals from bow to stern. The craft bobbed slightly as the priestess also entered. She sat at a middle bench, hoisted the oars, and propelled them cleanly out across the lake. Ariakas stepped to the bow, allowed his glowing gem to sweep the water before him like a beacon.

And then he saw them: ripples, almost imperceptible, rolling toward the starboard bow in an arc so broad it was almost a straight line. Only the utter placidity of the water allowed him to discern the effect, and that just for an instant, before the ripples were cleanly split by the gentle bow-wave of the boat.

"Bear to my right," Ariakas hissed, and Lyrelee smoothly swung the bow through a gentle curve.

She rowed for several minutes, steady strokes of the oars propelling the sleek boat through the water. Then, with shocking suddenness, a solid surface jutted into the scope of the warrior's light.

"Stop!" he hissed, dropping to the seat just before the priestess dug the oars into the water. The lake swirled and churned, but Lyrelee slowed the boat to a gentle bump by the time they reached the barrier.

The wall seemed to be the shore of the lake. Since the lake was contained by a cavern, however, this shore rose in a vertical barrier of moisture-streaked stone, extending upward and then, perhaps twice the height of Ariakas's head, leaning above their heads to begin its vast dome over the water. Turning to each direction, Ariakas couldn't see any clue as to how someone or something could have left the lake.

"Bear right," he commanded again, guided by a nameless instinct.

Dipping the oars with silent power, Lyrelee started them slowly along the shore. She hadn't taken more than five strokes when his intuition was rewarded. Breaking the solid wall of the lake shore was a narrow crack. At first glance, Ariakas thought the opening too small to allow the passage of a boat.

Then his eyes fastened on an irregularity in the surface, just outside of the crack. He stared, and in a moment made an identification—it was an oar.

"There—into the crack," he ordered, and the priestess turned the prow toward the gap.

The boat slipped between two slick walls of rock. They found the route tight, but passable, and in another moment it opened around them.

"Here's a landing," announced Ariakas, satisfied to see a platform of rock that sloped right down to the water's edge. Beyond the platform a dark hole promised at least the beginning of a passageway. Even more significant, drifting several feet away from the slab was a boat that was the twin of their own.

Lyrelee cast a look over her shoulder and glided the craft on a perfect course toward the landing. Ariakas looked around, and several facts confirmed his conviction. First, he saw streaks of water on the sloping stone floor, some of which still trickled back to the lake. Whatever had dripped onto the stone, he guessed, had done so not terribly long ago.

As the bow nudged the ramp, Ariakas stepped onto the shore, his sword held one-handed, pointed up the passageway beyond, the bowline grasped by his other hand. With a solid tug, he brought the first third of the boat up the ramp—enough, he felt certain, to prevent their transportation from drifting away.

Lyrelee stepped lightly beside him as they started up the passage. He winced inwardly at the thought of his bright light, which clearly revealed their position to anyone who lay in wait for them. Still, without it they would be handicapped even more.

Abruptly the priestess halted. "Let me walk behind you," she whispered, her voice barely audible.

He agreed with a nod, realizing that Lyrelee would at

least be able to conceal herself from any observers in the shadows. Now Ariakas made a point of checking the ceiling, remembering the net that had swooped down, unobserved, costing him his prisoner. The warrior saw no threat above, nor did he see anything amiss in the shadows to the front. The passageway twisted and climbed, narrower and more roughly hewn than any of the catacombs Ariakas had seen before.

One wall, in particular, struck him as unusual. The stonework was natural, ancient limestone that had been buried for ages, but a curious grid pattern had somehow been scored into the rock. As they walked they were forced close to the strange wall by a tight passageway.

Then the grid flew outward, muffling the curse exploding from Ariakas's throat. This time the net struck him with such force that it knocked his sword from his hands before tightly rolling Ariakas and Lyrelee into a compact, completely immobile bundle.

Chapter 16
Vallenswade

Ariakas struggled to turn his head, but once again a net bound him too effectively to allow even minimal movement. Lyrelee breathed heavily, pressed by their bonds against the armor of his back. He felt her wriggle, but the net restrained them so tightly that she could do little more than move her fingers.

"You are persistent, humans." The well-modulated voice emerged from the shadows, the tone cool but not unimpressed. "I would have thought we lost you back in the catacombs."

Again Ariakas tried to turn, to bring his light to bear on the speaker, but he could not. Something tall and lanky moved through the shadows beside him, and then that supple form squatted on the floor.

Ariakas cursed, recoiling involuntarily from an ape-like visage that suddenly dropped into his line of sight. The creature's face was covered with fur, and it had a protruding muzzle flanked by two yellow eyes centered with dark, slitted pupils. Those huge eyes blinked, presumably in reaction to the light, and then a wide mouth gaped open, revealing several sharp fangs.

"Who are you?" demanded Ariakas.

"I am called Vallenswade. Like you, I am a warrior," replied the ape creature, lips and tongue articulating in a very humanlike fashion. In fact, this bizarre-looking fellow seemed better spoken than a good number of the men and women Ariakas had known. "And you, two—how are you called?"

The warrior bit his lip, refusing to answer, anticipating a kick or some other prodding persuasion. Instead, Vallenswade simply rose to his feet and turned away. The man saw a bare foot, also furred, equipped with a large toe that reached to the side like a thumb, before the creature was swallowed by the darkness.

Sudden panic infused Ariakas. "Wait!" he cried, cursing the tension that thrummed in his voice. "I am called Ariakas—I am a warrior with the temple that stands above our heads. Tell me, Vallenswade," he pressed, his voice sounding more relaxed. "What manner of creature are you? Do you live here, in the Sanctified Catacombs?"

He heard a dry, rustling chuckle. "I am one of a very old race—as old as the ogres, we are. We are the *Shilo-Thahn*—you humans, I believe, know us as the shadowpeople."

"Only by repute," Ariakas said with a grunt. His position became increasingly uncomfortable. "Do you suppose you could loosen this net a bit?" he asked.

"Will you give your word that you will not attack me or my people?"

"Yes—I give my word," Ariakas said hastily. "I just want to talk."

"Of course," Vallenswade agreed. He barked some commands in a strange tongue, and the warrior immediately felt the strands loosen around them. Lyrelee rolled free, gasping for breath and rubbing her chafed arms.

Ariakas sat up, looking out the corner of his eye for his sword. He saw a flash of red in the darkness, and sensed that one of the shadowpeople had picked it up and whisked it away.

"My apologies, Warrior Ariakas," said Vallenswade. Surprisingly, he really did sound rather sad. "I know you have given your word, but it would make us feel more secure if we retain custody of your weapon—for the time being, of course."

Ariakas nodded silently, surprised far more by his captor's politeness than by the loss of his weapon. The shadowpeople had already shown him more courtesy than he would be likely to extend to any prisoner.

"Why did you attack us?" the warrior asked bluntly.

Vallenswade blinked those huge yellow eyes. "Well, I didn't really think of it as an attack," he said softly. "After all, we simply immobilized you long enough to accomplish our task. If we had wanted to harm you, we could have done so." He gestured dismissively, and for the first time the human noticed a long, thin membrane of skin hanging from the Shilo-Thahn's wrist, attaching at his waist and ankle.

"I know," Ariakas admitted. "But why did you snatch my prisoner?"

"Your prisoner?" Vallenswade seemed puzzled. "But I thought—well, it doesn't matter why he came down here. The important thing is that he was stopped."

"What does that matter to you?" demanded the warrior, intrigued by the shadowperson's assertion.

But Vallenswade was not about to elaborate. "Come," he invited, though the invitation was more of a command. "I would be honored if the two of you would accompany me through the catacombs."

Lyrelee looked to Ariakas for a response, and the warrior bowed his head politely. "The pleasure will be ours," he replied.

The shadowarrior's simian face split into a grotesque baring of teeth, which Ariakas took to be a smile. He was vaguely aware of several other shadowy figures falling into step behind them, and he could see at least four of them—including the one who carried his red-bladed sword—walking in front of Vallenswade.

"I must compliment you on your ambushes," Ariakas admitted honestly. "You caught us neatly, twice—and that was a thing I would have sworn could not be done."

Vallenswade flipped his hand in a deprecating gesture. "Do not feel shame—we are at home in the darkness, and know how to use it for our ends. Doubtless, were we on the surface, the advantage would have been yours."

They walked for a long distance through a winding, natural passage in the rock. Ariakas tried to memorize the route back to the lake, but he soon became lost in the maze of crossing corridors, branching pathways, and ascending and descending ramps. Too, he began to develop the conviction that the shadowpeople followed a very roundabout pathway, designed to throw off their direction sense. They passed an unusual stalagmite, and since the unique markings on its surface seemed familiar to him, he judged that they had come this way at least once before.

The warrior reflected in silence for a time. He had been a prisoner once, of ogres, and though he had eventually escaped, he had been very roughly treated. Many other times, he and his men had taken prisoners, and their fate, too, had not been pleasant. He found it astonishing that Vallenswade would treat them with such deferential politeness, almost as if they were honored guests.

What would be their fate? Although he didn't fear immediate execution, he wondered whether the shadowpeople would ever be inclined to let them go. He suspected not, and he didn't look forward to a life spent in this sunless dungeon—regardless of how friendly and polite his captors were.

"My . . . companion," Ariakas asked after this long silence. He didn't want to reaffirm that Tale Splintersteel was more like an enemy. "Is he alive?"

Vallenswade looked at him reprovingly. "Of course. We are not butchers. Even though he did kick one of my warriors quite ignobly, breaking his knee, we see no point in vengeful retribution."

"May I see him?" pressed the human warrior.

Now the shadowarrior sighed. "That, I'm afraid, will not be so easily arranged. Indeed, I could not allow it. Only the councilors could permit such a thing."

"Who are the councilors?" asked Ariakas. "Are you taking us to them?"

"I have been summoned," Vallenswade replied, as if there were no more to the question than that.

Ariakas flashed a look at the priestess, seeing that Lyrelee remained alert to their surroundings. She studied every side passage, every branching corridor, and the warrior could only hope that her memory proved better than his.

"Do you know that you dwell in the Sanctified Catacombs of a mighty temple?" asked Ariakas, changing the tack of his conversation.

"We know that some humans think as you say. However, we have lived here longer than the temple has stood, and if these corridors are sanctified in the name of your goddess, she has not made the fact known to us."

Ariakas wanted to threaten or bluster, but he sensed that any declarations of imminent vengeance would fall on deaf ears. Even if the high priest sent a well-armed expedition after them, it seemed unlikely that priests and warriors would be able to follow the path of the shadow-people . . . unless someone thought to check the wharf, as they had! The thought gave him a flash of renewed hope,

until he heard soggy footsteps sloshing in the corridor
behind them.

A soaked shadowarrior approached Vallenswade and
spoke to him in long, guttural phrases. The chief warrior
nodded and turned to Ariakas. "We have taken the precaution of returning the two boats to the temple wharf.
After all, we have no need of them—it was only your . . .
companion, the dwarf, who had difficulty with the
water."

"I see," replied Ariakas, hoping disappointment didn't
show on his face.

"But come," invited Vallenswade. "There is more that
I would show you."

The two prisoners followed the great, shaggy warrior
until the Shilo-Thahn stopped and raised his face to the
ceiling. His voice rippled through a long, wailing cry—a
sound that sent shivers down the warrior's spine.

Immediately afterward a panel of apparently solid
rock in the corridor wall slid silently outward. Following
Vallenswade, Ariakas passed through the door, with
Lyrelee and their guards following.

The first sensation to strike the warrior was the moist,
verdant fertility of the air, like garden soil freshly turned
after a rain. The chamber was huge, swiftly swallowing
the feeble emanations of his magical light. Nearby he
saw clumps of fungi, gathered artistically around
smoothly paved paths. The Shilo-Thahn warrior started
along one of these walkways, leading the prisoners into
the huge cavern. As they walked, Ariakas was astounded
at the lush beds of huge fungi around them. The plants
grew in amazing variety, pale and dark, bulbous and
gangly. In clusters they sprouted from all parts of the
cavern. Many of them towered higher than his head, and
these seemed to be the source of the meaty, rich scent in
the air.

Occasionally he saw bright eyes reflecting from the
darkness, and he guessed that numerous shadowpeople

were scattered about this huge cavern. Probably their lair, he decided. He tried to estimate the number of the ape creatures around him, but couldn't come up with a realistic approximation.

Vallenswade halted. In the illumination of his gemstone, Ariakas saw that they had reached a large, circular clearing. None of the cavern walls were visible around him, and when he tipped his head back the ceiling was swallowed by the darkness as well. Stone benches formed a pair of concentric rings around the clearing, which was surrounded by a virtual wall of the tall fungus clumps.

Several other shadowpeople sat on the benches, and as he cast the light around, Ariakas was able to form a generalized impression of these strange creatures. All of them were covered with fur. They seemed to average about seven feet in height, though the lightness to their frames suggested even the large males probably weighed less than Ariakas. Their protruding muzzles and overhanging brows gave them a simian appearance, but the warrior saw many differences in shading, facial features, posture, and mannerism.

He noticed that all the shadowpeople seemed to have the long, loose membrane connecting their arms and wrists to their legs and hips. The skin was a smooth, supple surface that folded neatly against the creature's side, except when the hand was extended. Then the flap swung loose, an elegant wing draped like the regal robe of an imperial monarch.

"These are the councilors," Vallenswade said as Ariakas and Lyrelee followed him into the center of the circled benches. The warrior saw perhaps a dozen shadowpeople seated around them. As a rule, these looked slighter, a trifle more frail perhaps, than the warriors who had captured them. He saw several with fringes of gray whiskers, and at least one who stooped forward in his seat like a very old man. The seated Shilo-Thahn each regarded

Ariakas with intense concentration, but if the dark-furred faces betrayed any hint of emotion, the warrior couldn't tell. Still, he felt an intimidating sense of power in these councilors.

His reaction was to stand straight, slowly letting his eyes meet those of the gathered audience. At the same time he noted Vallenswade taking a seat on the closest bench, while the other warriors stood at the outside of the circle. Ariakas made careful note of the Shilo-Thahn who held his crimson-bladed sword.

Why do you bring the dwarf here, Human?

The question hit him with shocking force. He knew that he hadn't *heard* anything, yet the interrogative could not have been more clearly enunciated. He frowned at Lyrelee, but she returned his stare with a curious lift to her eyebrows—obviously the message had reached him alone.

The mute probe into his mind unsettled him more than he wanted to admit, and so he planted his hands on his hips and met the expressionless faces of the councilors with what he hoped was his own look of stubborn noncommunication.

Do you understand the risks?

Again a question, and this time he took a single step backward, literally knocked off balance by the mental probe.

"Who interrogates me?" he demanded, glaring around the ring of Shilo-Thahn elders.

We are the councilors, came the unnecessary reply. *We ask again—do you understand the risks?*

"The only risks I've suffered have been at the hands of your warrior," he said, indicating Vallenswade. The Shilo-Thahn grimaced, stung by the inference that he had placed the human in danger.

"Who are you talking to?" hissed Lyrelee, regarding him as if he had lost his mind.

He shrugged off the question, indicating the gathered

ring of councilors without elaborating.

You were taking the dwarf and his disease into the treasure chamber. The phrases were heavy with accusation and tinged with confusion. *Did you not realize the corruption that could occur?*

"What concern is it of yours?" retorted the warrior.

It is the concern of everyone, came the response, a trifle mystified in tone. *Don't you understand what could happen?*

"The treasure that you talk about—it doesn't belong to you, does it?" Ariakas challenged.

Of course not—how could the eggs 'belong' to anyone except the mighty beings who gave them life? The councilors were completely puzzled now.

"There are those who claim the eggs—and are prepared to defend that claim," Ariakas retorted.

We know—but the eggs were brought to the catacombs with the understanding that they were to be protected. It is too dangerous to allow the dwarf to go near them.

"What do you fear?" demanded the human.

Our people have been to Zhakar. . . we know the horrors that can result from the spread of the plague. It must not be allowed to touch the eggs.

"Is that why you attacked us? To abduct the dwarf? How do I know you've even kept him alive?"

We are not killers—of course he lives. But we have taken him to a place of safety, away from the treasure.

"Why should I believe you? Produce the Zhakar and then we can talk. Until then, I'll assume that your plans for us involve the same kind of fate as you might have already given to the dwarf!"

Ariakas fixed the front row of councilors with a belligerent glare. He didn't really believe that the shadow-people would kill Tale Splintersteel—he had seen enough of them to decide that they weren't violent or vengeful—but he didn't want his own conclusion to reach them. Could they hear his thoughts as well as speak directly into his mind? He wished he knew. Angrily he tried to direct his thoughts through rambling, unfocused pathways.

Surprisingly, the shadowpeople seemed a trifle set back by his bluff. The councilors exchanged glances that might have been hesitation or confusion. Abruptly Vallenswade stood up. He faced Ariakas directly.

"I have told you that the dwarf lives—now, the councilors have told you the same thing. Why do you not believe us?"

"Where I come from, captors have been known to lie to their captives—and enemies lie to each other as a matter of course," he replied bluntly.

"We are not your enemies!" insisted Vallenswade, his simian muzzle barking out the words with force.

"Then give me proof!" demanded Ariakas fiercely. "Produce the dwarf! Show me that he lives!"

Vallenswade slumped back in resignation. The faces of the councilors reflected their confusion, but then the message came.

Very well. We will bring in the dwarf.

"Come with me," announced Vallenswade with the first trace of ill manner Ariakas had seen in the Shilo-Thahn warrior. The lanky creature led Lyrelee and Ariakas to a clump of the tall, mushroom-shaped fungus. The stems of the plants had grown together so thickly that they created a solid wall of tough, spongy tissue. Vallenswade removed a bar that ran through a pair of supports on the solid barrier of woodlike plants. Pushing forward, he propelled a large, wedge-shaped plug into the enclosure Ariakas saw within.

The Shilo-Thahn warrior preceded the two prisoners through the hole, then turned and gestured for Ariakas and Lyrelee. The warriors behind the pair pressed closer, emphasizing the fact—though the one who held Ariakas's sword maintained a careful distance. With no choice, the two followed Vallenswade into the hole.

The ring of mushrooms surrounded a small, circular corral, no more than twenty feet across. The top of the wall was at least that high above their heads, however, and the caps of the mushrooms overhung the trunks by a good distance, making climbing out an apparent impossibility. The only access to the outer cavern came through the thick, wedged gate-plug.

"You will remain here until we get the dwarf," Vallenswade explained.

"Why? How far away is he?" demanded Ariakas.

The Shilo-Thahn sighed. "He was taken to a different part of the warrens . . . until we could determine whether or not it was safe to bring him here."

"Safe? For him—or for you?" pressed the human.

"I wish you would answer half as many questions as you ask," replied Vallenswade resignedly. "Safe for us, of course. Because of his condition, we took great care so as to not risk introducing a contagion into our colony." With that, the tall creature bent low to exit the lower door, turning to pull the gate into its socket behind him. Ariakas heard the bar drop into place on the outer wall, and though he tugged furiously, the thing wouldn't budge. Because of the plug's wedge shape, he knew that pushing on it would only jam it more tightly into its socket.

"Damn!" He couldn't stifle the frustration. It galled him to feel so completely at the mercy of his captors.

Lyrelee regarded him silently. When he settled himself on the floor, his back against the mushroom wall, she sat beside him. Only then did she speak, and she held her voice to a mere breathy whisper.

"They know what we think," she said.

"What do you mean?" Ariakas whispered, though he was too irritated to hold his voice down to her barely audible level. "I *told* them what we think!"

"No, I mean about our actions . . . our intents."

Now the warrior fell silent, giving her his full attention.

"I observed the two warriors who followed me," Lyrelee explained. "If I decided to move over to the right while I walked, one of them sidled over to that direction—*before* I did anything! Merely the thought, the intent, was enough to cause him to take action!"

"Could it be a coincidence?" Ariakas questioned skeptically. Nevertheless, the memory of that eerie questioning, of the words entering his mind with no audible sound, nagged at him, and he feared that Lyrelee was right.

"I don't think so. Do you remember the one who held the big hook—he was the central rear guard?"

Ariakas nodded. The distinctive-looking weapon, which consisted of a steel head and a carved wooden shaft, had been slung from a strap over the Shilo-Thahn's shoulder.

"Well, as an experiment, I began to think about turning around and snatching it from him. When I looked, he'd placed both hands on the shaft—it's the only time he touched it during the whole time he guarded us."

"Any ideas what we can do about it?" he asked.

"I think we have to act on the spur of the moment," she suggested. "If we don't know what we're going to do until we do it, then they can't know either."

"So far that hasn't been a problem," Ariakas chafed. "They've kept too close a watch for us to do *anything*!"

"I know—but consider," Lyrelee replied. "Does it seem to you that these are natural warriors? Or are they simply folk who've been cast into weapon-bearing roles?"

"I think the latter," Ariakas confirmed. "They don't seem to have the killer instinct."

"No. It's almost like they're innately *gentle*. It might be that our own battle sense, at the moment of truth, will be stronger than theirs."

"It's a hope," Ariakas admitted, none too encouraged. "I guess it's as good as we've got. I don't feel like waiting around here until they let us go."

"When they take us out of here, I'll watch you," the priestess said. "Give no warning—but if you see a chance to escape, take it! I'll be ready."

"That's our best shot, I guess," Ariakas conceded. But how was he to look for a chance to escape without thinking about escaping? Indeed, perhaps the range of Shilo-Thahn senses was enough that the creatures already knew about these plans! They lapsed into silence. The warrior felt an acute vulnerability, unlike anything he had known before. He tried not to think about escape or combat.

"Do you think they can 'hear' us through these walls?" he asked, after a few minutes of fruitlessly attempting to stifle his mind.

Lyrelee shrugged. "I'm guessing that there are some real limits to their power. After all, they're not the masters of Krynn—which they could be if they were able to read everybody's thoughts."

"Maybe they don't *want* to be conquerors," noted Ariakas. The prospect of a creature having access to incredible power, yet choosing not to exercise that power, was a strange one to the warrior. Yet Lyrelee was right—there was something inherently nonaggressive in the apelike humanoids.

Shortly thereafter the light spell that had been steadily illuminating the gem on Ariakas's helm faded into blackness. The full cloaking of subterranean dark closed around them, and the warrior shifted his position uneasily. Still, when Lyrelee—who also possessed the clerical power of light creation—asked if he wanted her to re-illuminate the gem he told her no.

"If they come to get us, *then* we'll want some light," he suggested. "For all we know, they'll keep us here for six or eight more hours—it won't do any good to have your spell used up before then."

Although the warrior knew that diligent prayer to the

Dark Queen would grant him a return of the light spell he had expended, he couldn't bring himself to make such a prayer in this place. Perhaps it was the ignominy of being a prisoner, or, more likely, simple discomfort at the fear that even his prayer might not remain private. In any event, he wanted to escape this predicament on his own, without having to beseech his goddess for help.

They heard a shuffling on the outer wall of the corral, and then Ariakas felt the plug slide into the enclosure beside him. Lyrelee muttered a quick word, and his gem flared into light, revealing the blinking visage of Vallens-wade.

"Come," said the Shilo-Thahn in his ponderous, dignified tones. "I will take you to the dwarf."

Chapter 17
Darkwatch

Again Vallenswade and a half-dozen of his comrades formed the escorting party. Ariakas saw that one of these still carried his red-bladed sword, and the human felt a flash of elation, then chagrin when—as if in reaction to his hopefulness—the weapon-bearer fell back from the rest of the party.

On the smoothly paved walkways, they passed through the large cavern. As they approached the mouth of one of the smaller connecting passages, Ariakas realized that the shadowpeople had not in fact brought the Zhakar dwarf into their warren. Instead, they were taking the two prisoners out to meet him.

"We have brought him to another place, near here,"

offered Vallenswade, causing Ariakas to wonder if his captor had in fact been reading his thoughts.

The warrior tried to concentrate on *not* thinking about escape, but that only seemed to bring the matter to the forefront of his awareness. Around him the guards shifted, and he saw several of them regarding him with narrowed, watchful gazes.

Vallenswade led them down the twisting, narrow corridor. The route finally branched into a side passage and proceeded to climb a very long flight of stairs—at least a hundred steps. Puffing slightly from the exertion, the warrior plodded along, noting with disgust that neither the shadowpeople nor his fellow prisoner seemed to have any difficulty with the ascent.

At the top, they reached a landing, followed by more mazelike passages. Ariakas forced his mind to wander, tried to remember pleasant nights spent drinking with Ferros Windchisel. He thought of the woman beside him, imagining Lyrelee in the throes of passion, and found the image enticing. This train of thought occupied him for a long time, until he realized that Vallenswade had stopped.

"We are holding him in here," said the Shilo-Thahn, gesturing to a low, arched doorway in the cavern wall. The portal stood open, and in the light of the gem Ariakas could see a wall no more than twelve feet in from the doorway.

Stooping, Vallenswade led Ariakas and Lyrelee into what proved to be a long, albeit narrow, room. A dark figure lay on the ground at one end of the chamber, while a lanky shadowarrior squatted beside the prone shape. That shape, Ariakas quickly deduced from the once-splendid robes, was Tale Splintersteel.

"He lives," Vallenswade said, again startling Ariakas with the answer to an unspoken question.

The shapeless bundle stirred, and now the warrior saw the cloaked face, with the split in the mask revealing the dark, hateful eyes.

"I might have known you'd be back," said the dwarf bitterly. "Come to gloat over me now?"

"I'm here because I demanded proof that you still lived," replied Ariakas.

Vallenswade, meanwhile, looked sharply between them. "Are you two bitter enemies?" he demanded.

"Give me that hook there, and I'll rip his guts out," Tale Splintersteel offered pleasantly. "That's how good of friends we are."

Ariakas, meanwhile, narrowed his eyes; Vallenswade's question indicated to him that the shadow-people's skills stopped far short of complete mind reading. Even if they could anticipate reactions on a moment-to-moment basis, he felt it unlikely that the shaggy warriors knew anything detailed about his and Lyrelee's intentions.

"Then why did you press so hard to see the dwarf?" the Shilo-Thahn queried Ariakas.

"Ask him," the human replied, flipping a scornful gesture to the huddled Zhakar. His response meant nothing —it was merely a stall for time. To his surprise, Vallenswade whirled, ready to confront Tale Splintersteel with the question.

Ariakas cast a quick glance behind him, seeing that two of the simian warriors—not, alas, the one with his sword—had followed them into the room. Already, at his sideways glance, those two stiffened, reaching for the hooks that swung from their shoulder straps.

The human warrior moved even as the idea entered his head, lunging for one of the Shilo-Thahn, sensing Lyrelee leaping immediately behind him. His victim pulled the great hook free, but Ariakas batted it away with his forearm, and then bore the fur-covered warrior to the floor. The pair rolled over and over, grappling for advantage. The shadowperson was nimble, but the human had greater strength. Slowly, deliberately,

Ariakas wrestled the squirming creature into a pin.

He heard Lyrelee shout behind him, recognizing her harsh battle cry. The sound was followed by the snapping of bone, and a sharp bark of pain as another Shilo-Thahn went down.

Ariakas punched with all his fury, driving his fist into the apelike face of his foe. The shadowperson's head cracked backward onto the floor, and the yellow eyes drooped shut as the body went limp. Ariakas leapt to his feet and turned his light toward the door.

The other two Shilo-Thahn guards lunged into the room, one wielding his great hook and the other, more clumsily, brandishing Ariakas's red-bladed sword. Lyrelee and Vallenswade were somewhere behind him—Ariakas had to hope that the priestess could immobilize the leader.

Reflexively Ariakas backed up a few steps, looking toward the creature with his sword—but, as if they understood his intentions, the simian warrior bearing the hook charged him from the left. Ariakas ducked under a vicious cut, or at least, he thought he did. At the last second, however, the apelike warrior reversed the direction of his blow, and the curved metal head jerked around the human's arm. The Shilo-Thahn pulled, and Ariakas lurched off his feet.

Tucking his head, the man somersaulted between the two attackers, determined to attack the one who had felled him—but with a flash of insight he changed his mind, springing headlong at the warrior holding the great, two-handed sword.

Obviously the fellow had never wielded such a blade before. He swung it broadly, and Ariakas feinted, waiting for the slashing blade to swing past his face. The heavy weight pulled the Shilo-Thahn around in an off-balance follow-through, and the human lowered his head, slamming his skull into the warrior's furry gut.

The creature went down with a great exhalation of breath, and the human's heart leapt at the sound of his blade clanging loosely to the floor. He broke from his gasping opponent and snatched up the sword as the second warrior reached toward him with that gleaming hook.

But now Ariakas was armed. The red blade whipped upward, then flicked to the side, parrying the shadowarrior's attack with a ringing clang. Next Ariakas thrust, driving the blade through the creature's chest. The apelike body proved surprisingly frail, a leather bag filled with sticks and straw, and the human's single stab was immediately fatal. In the follow-through motion he swung back and killed the warrior on the floor.

Whirling about, Ariakas saw that, with the skillful use of his long hook, Vallenswade had driven Lyrelee into a corner. Of the guards, two writhed on the floor, legs broken by Lyrelee's kicks; three more were still.

Ariakas sprinted down the long room. Vallenswade heard him coming and turned from Lyrelee, ducking away from her leaping kick as if he had eyes in the rear of his skull. The hook came up, but once again the crimson blade smashed the weapon aside. Vallenswade barely parried an otherwise fatal thrust, but when he lashed out with the hook again, Ariakas bashed it so hard that the weapon fell from the simian hands. Unarmed, he stood before the human with his hands at his sides. Then, with rigid dignity, he bowed.

"You have reversed our positions," Vallenswade said calmly. "I offer my congratulations."

"The amazing thing is, I think you *mean* it!" Ariakas mused, shaking his head.

Lyrelee, in the meantime, jerked Tale Splintersteel to his feet. The Zhakar's robes were a mess, covered with mud, dust, and crusted blood, but he stood steadily, blinking impassively behind his black-cloaked mask.

"I want you to lead us out of here," Ariakas declared,

raising the blade slightly to emphasize his determination.

With a shrug, Vallenswade refused. "It would be far better if you did not escape," he said.

"I hate to disagree with you, friend—but I think it would be far, *far* better if I *did* escape," Ariakas retorted with amusement. Then he grew serious. "Lead us out of here, or I'll be forced to kill you."

Vallenswade blinked, as if considering the bleak prospect, but he did not reply—nor did he move.

"Do you understand?" demanded Ariakas, suddenly conscious of precious time slipping away. How long before more shadowpeople—a dozen, a score, even more —arrived to help?

"I understand. My refusal means my death," replied Vallenswade simply. "I had hoped to live somewhat longer than this," he admitted.

Ariakas glared at him. "Show us the way out of here, and you'll be spared!"

"I thought I made it clear that you should not escape. . . . It would be bad."

For a moment Ariakas quivered at the edge of murder, raising the blade toward Vallenswade's unprotected neck. Finally he spun away in disgust. His eyes fell on the two wounded shadowpeople, both of whom still groaned and quivered on the floor. Turning back, he fixed his captive with a deadly stare.

"Show us the way out of here—or I'll kill *them!*" he threatened, gesturing to the wounded pair.

Vallenswade flinched, lowering his brows in an unhappy frown. "Why?" he demanded. "Why must you kill three of us? Their deaths gain you nothing."

"I don't *want* their deaths!" fumed the warrior. "I want to get out of here!"

"Then kill us and go," retorted Vallenswade. He looked away, as if bored with the conversation.

The murderous force built within Ariakas, but suddenly it dissipated, and he was left with a feeling of emptiness and despair. He and Lyrelee would have to make their way through this maze on their own, and whether or not Vallenswade was alive or dead behind them didn't seem to make much difference.

He cast his eyes over the wounded shadowarriors, noting that one bore the tight bundle of a net on his back. That would do just as well.

"Tie them up," he told Lyrelee. "All three of them. And hurry—it's time we're out of here."

* * * * *

"Which way?" asked Ariakas when they reached the first intersection. The chamber where they had found Tale Splintersteel—and left a securely trussed Vallenswade and his two companions—lay some distance behind them along the winding tunnel.

"Here," Lyrelee indicated unhesitatingly.

Prodding the muttering Zhakar dwarf ahead of him, Ariakas turned into the passage. His gem light illuminated the path before them, and the priestess walked slightly behind in order to gain the benefit of the illumination—and to remain concealed from any watchers in the shadows.

They followed the new corridor for some time, and then the priestess indicated another branch that they should take. For some time they made their way through the maze, and the young woman's memory produced a firm recommendation at every fork.

Finally, however, they came into a large chamber that neither of them recognized. No less than six different tunnels led, in various directions, through the subterranean darkness.

"*Now* where do we go?" Ariakas asked, but Lyrelee could only shake her head.

"I don't know," she admitted. "I know we didn't come this way before."

Abruptly Ariakas stiffened. His senses tingled. The five-pointed star, holy symbol of Takhisis, winked at him from its pendant at Lyrelee's neck. He reached out and snatched it, ignoring her shout of surprise.

"*Look!*" he said, holding the star flat in his hand. Extending his arm, he displayed the holy symbol. The centermost tine of the star, the point that lined up with the passage across the chamber, glowed slightly. Ariakas looked at Lyrelee, his eyes narrowed shrewdly, and she nodded.

"I see it, too," the priestess whispered.

"What? See what?" demanded Tale Splintersteel.

"Shut up," Ariakas barked, roughly pushing the Zhakar forward.

They proceeded farther, coming to several more branches. Each time Lyrelee and Ariakas both observed that one point of the star glowed until they had made their decision. Thus guided, they moved very quickly through the maze of the catacombs. With each crossroads the star seemed to grow a little bit brighter.

Around them the air grew moist, and then the corridor they followed opened into a large cavern. The illumination from the gem light was swallowed by darkness above and to the sides—even below. A narrow, flat ramp extended like a bridge from the entrance, but to either side of the ramp yawned nothing but an apparently infinite blackness.

Vertigo rose to rebel in Ariakas's stomach, but he roughly forced aside the hesitation and, prodding Tale Splintersteel before him, boldly stepped onto the bridge. The priestess followed, and they moved cautiously outward.

No sound except their own breathing and footsteps disturbed the vast cavern. A scattering of loose gravel covered several patches of the bridge. Wary of a trap, Ariakas prodded some of the stones with his boot, and as they swept off the path he heard them splash into water some distance below.

"The lake," Lyrelee said softly. "We're crossing it."

Ariakas nodded, his attention riveted to the bound dwarf in front of him. If Tale decided to try and escape, this bridge would make a good place. Though the human felt he could deflect an attack, he warily wondered if the Zhakar might hurl himself into the darkness.

"Remember the long stairway down to the wharf?" Lyrelee asked. "We're way above that, now—maybe even as high as the main catacombs."

They reached the end of the bridge without mishap—apparently the Zhakar valued his miserable life too much to make a suicidal escape attempt. Once more, stone walls enclosed them, and they picked up the pace of their march.

"It won't be far, now—I *know* it!" Ariakas replied.

A few more passages brought them into sight of a distant, pale source of illumination. Then a figure—a *human* figure—came into view, hurrying toward them followed by several other men.

"Lord Ariakas! Thank the queen you're alive!" Wryllish Parkane swept his arms outward to clap Ariakas on the shoulder, ignoring the woman and the dwarf. The warrior saw that the priest carried a holy symbol, the match of Lyrelee's, in his hand. "When I emerged from High Communion and heard that you'd come down here, I was elated," the patriarch gushed. "Then, of course, when it seemed you were missing, we were terribly worried! But you felt my summons?"

"If that's what is was, it worked," the warrior agreed, handing the medallion back to Lyrelee.

"And you're safe. Did you encounter difficulties?"

"Your Sanctified Catacombs aren't as sacred as you think," Ariakas replied. "We've got a source of trouble down here, but I'll tell you about that later."

For the first time Ariakas looked at those who accompanied Parkane: Patriarch Fendis, two other blue collars he recognized from the temple, and a lone figure who stood some distance back from the rest. That gaunt, dark-haired man wore a black robe, and had the most piercing blue eyes Ariakas had ever seen.

Noting his attention, the patriarch stepped back to make introductions. "Allow me to present Harrawell Dracart—of the Black Tower," he added unnecessarily. The wizard's robe clearly indicated Dracart's allegiance.

"This way. Let us go to the treasure chamber immediately!" proclaimed Wryllish Parkane. He led them a short distance along a wide, straight passage. They saw no sign of the shadowpeople, though Ariakas warned them all to remain vigilant.

Soon they stood outside the door to a small room, one Wryllish explained had been set aside for the test. It contained a single brass dragon egg, raised upon a stone table.

"The mold dust will live for some minutes, you told me," Ariakas said to Tale Splintersteel. "Now is the time to give it to me—you will remain out here."

The Zhakar's eyes flashed stubbornly from the depths of his hood. "I will be present," he insisted. "Your alternative, I know, is to kill me and make your test. Then, if you want this mold, you'll have no source. Or you can bring me in, and I'll be the key that will unlock the vaults of Zhakar!"

Ariakas had come to despise the wretched creature, and the temptation to kill the Zhakar was great. He had spoken the truth before—twice already Splintersteel had earned his death! Yet pragmatic considerations won out. The dwarf was right—if the mold dust proved valuable, they would need an agent with access to the source. Tale Splintersteel, as odious as the thought was, would be the ideal choice.

All eyes remained on Ariakas as the warrior nodded. "Very well—you'll go in there with us."

Wryllish Parkane used the tiny key, and they stepped

into the room, forming a circle around the gleaming egg. It lay like a metal-coated boulder on the low platform and reflected the light from its glossy surface.

"Quickly—let's not delay!" For the first time the wizard Dracart spoke, licking his lips with a bright red tongue as his eyes gleamed hotly.

"Come, then—scatter the mold onto the egg!" urged Wryllish Parkane.

Ariakas remembered that scarred, tormented skin, and his stomach heaved as Tale Splintersteel stepped up to the egg. The dwarf held out his hands, and as the scabrous flesh emerged from the sleeves of his robe, several of the priests gasped and stepped backward. Ignoring the reaction, the Zhakar rubbed his palms together above the egg.

A fine dust powdered downward like snow, sprinkling over the surface of the egg. The stuff glistened in the gem light, almost as if each speck were a multifaceted diamond. Ariakas found it strangely pleasant that out of such astounding corruption could come an impression of such remarkable beauty.

"O Mighty Takhisis—all-powerful Queen of Darkness!" began Wryllish Parkane, his voice taut with suppressed anticipation. "Grant us thy will and thy power! Give to us thy tools, and make them from the children of our arrogant, metal-skinned foes!"

Immediately the sphere pulsed, small ripples flowing across its surface. The shining brass shell began to corrode, decaying to grimy scum in a matter of seconds. The orb shivered in steady contractions, wrinkling and bulging all across its surface.

The high priest raised his voice in a mighty prayer to the Dark Queen. The wizard muttered an incantation of his own, and from Dracart's fingers, pulses of blue magic flickered outward, wrapping the egg in a cocoon of sorcery. Then the surface of the corroded sphere split apart, ripping in several directions like the jagged, expanding tracks of an earthquake. The tearing crackled loudly though the air, and a pervasive, putrefying stench filled the room.

Creatures slithered forth, dripping with ooze—but these were not the blind, malformed creations of the earlier corruption. At least ten distinct lizard beings were visible, snapping and clawing at each other. Rising upon powerful hind legs, they stood as tall as men. Talon-studded forepaws wiped the mucus from reptilian eyes, and baleful glares fastened upon the humans and dwarf in the room. The scaly humanoids advanced, forked tongues flicking from fang-studded mouths. Leathery wings, still sticky from the egg, stretched awkwardly from the shoulders of each of the monsters.

"These are not *dragons!*" hissed Tale Splintersteel, in awe and disbelief.

"No—not dragons," replied Ariakas, now seeing the potential of these creatures with astounding clarity. The others stood silent, waiting for him to continue, instinctively trusting him to lead.

"Not dragons—but the spawn of dragonkind." Ariakas suddenly knew what these things were, what they would be called—and how they would serve him. "They are draconians."

He acted then, snatching the star of Takhisis from the patriarch's hand. Fastening his eyes onto the hideous faces of the monsters, he projected his will, his mastery, toward them. The lizard beasts stopped at the sight of the medallion, hissing and bobbing uncertainly. "Kneel, wretches!" Ariakas commanded. "Kneel before the symbol of your mistress—your *queen!*"

And when he raised the symbol overhead, all ten of the draconians collapsed, groveling, onto the floor.

PART THREE
TRIUMPH AND TREACHERY

Chapter 18
Zhakar Road

Ariakas stood in a vast, cavelike chamber, surrounded by a horde of scaly draconians. Beyond them ranked legion upon legion of heavy infantry, horsemen, archers, and spearmen. All of them stood silently at attention, awaiting his command. But he couldn't make a sound. This mighty host stood on the brink of conquest, and yet he could not send it forth—could not so much as utter a stammering word.

At his back was his great sword, and he instinctively drew the weapon, raising the gleaming steel into the air. The army shouted, its collective voice a growing roar, swelling until the noise pounded him from all sides. Yet now the sword was frozen, even as was his voice. As if some powerful, invisible fist had seized the blade, gripping it with immortal strength, the silvery steel weapon hung in the air before his face. Heaving mightily, Ariakas could not lower it, could not even wiggle it from side to side.

He snarled, frustration growing within him, and the silvery blade turned white. Snow and ice swirled around him then, masking the troops and the draconians, sending shivers of inhuman cold piercing through his body.

Abruptly the sword became black. Still Ariakas could not twist it free from the invisible grip of the air, and as he struggled, a rich, full darkness surrounded him, cloaking vision in every direction—though the cheering of the troops continued to bombard him.

The darkness fell away, and the blade of his sword glowed blood red. The metal bore a shining gleam on its surface that actually looked wet, as if the weapon had just been immersed to the hilt in some fresh, gory wound. Yet still he could not move the sword, though he tugged and pulled and wrenched at its long grip. Fire rose around him, a great circle of crackling, hissing flame, surging upward higher than his head. He cried out, not from pain so much as outrage, and immediately the flames died away.

Ariakas sensed great creatures around him, then, lurking in the depths of the vast chamber, beyond the reach of his vision. Towering in height, serpentine in shape, they skulked unseen in the shadows, their presence tingling with portent and power.

Suddenly he was surrounded by a cool, blue light, and Ariakas could see that the illumination emanated from his blade. Slowly, reverently, he took the hilt and pulled, gently drawing the sword to him. The force that had imprisoned the weapon gave way easily.

Once again Ariakas was the master of his sword, and his fate. Holding the blue blade upraised before him, he turned this way and that, allowing his troops to shout their adulation. For many minutes they roared, and his heart swelled with martial pride.

When he sheathed the sword, the cheering continued, but now it had faded to a background noise, mere accompaniment to the ringing knowledge that had begun to grow in his mind.

The blue blade! He remembered the prophecy in the tower, spoken what seemed like a lifetime ago: *Hold the blue blade, warrior—for in the heart of the world it shall set fire to the sky!* Only now did he begin to sense the meaning. And as he walked the pathway that opened before him amid the ranks of his troops, he understood it would be the blue blade that would give him the might to command, to rule.

As he marched onward, he realized that the pathway was no longer an aisle, but a bridge. On one side he saw a bright landscape, stretching to the infinite horizon, lined with columns of troops—all of them trundling forward under his command. In an awestruck moment, he beheld the skies overhead, filled with vast formations of huge dragons, winging outward to expand the Dark Queen's domain. All of this mighty host marched away toward the far points of Krynn.

But then Ariakas shifted his eyes to the other side of the bridge, and he could not help but cower away in reeling terror. Below him, beginning at the very toes of his feet, fell away an abyssal chasm, plummeting all the way to the midnight heavens.

Yet within that darkness was no cheery glimmer of a constellation, nor even a lone evening star. Instead, the place was a well of nothing, yawning hungrily forever, promising only pain and blood, darkness and dissolution . . . without even the eventual respite of death.

* * * * *

Ariakas awakened with a start. A chilly film of sweat clung to his skin. The heavens *did* yawn overhead, but these were the familiar skies of Ansalon, with a gentle haze of dawn light already filling in the space of the eastern valleys.

So it had been a dream. He exhaled, feeling Lyrelee stir beside him under the bedroll. The experience had been so vivid, so real, that he actually felt as though he had commanded that mighty army. Then he remembered the horror of that black chasm, and the chill shook him again.

For a moment he thought of the woman, so warm beside him. But this was not a problem for which she could bring him any comfort. Irritated, he rose into the dawn and looked around their small camp. Ferros Windchisel would be near, he knew, hiding in the shadows while alertly maintaining the last watch of their night's bivouac.

Tale Splintersteel still slept, which did not surprise Ariakas. Ever since their little group had departed Sanction, the Zhakar had been the deepest sleeper of the four. Just as well, Ariakas thought, since Splintersteel could not be trusted on watch duty. That seemed all well and proper to the moldy dwarf because—as he had loudly pointed out—*he* was the one who was taking them to Zhakar.

In that role, at least, the merchant lord had wholeheartedly embraced their endeavor. As broker of the mold that had suddenly developed value, Tale Splintersteel stood to make himself very rich—*if* they could get into Zhakar alive.

Ariakas cast another look at the sky, seeing that sunrise was still nearly an hour away. He decided not to roust the others, choosing instead to stroll the dim twilight until he found Ferros Windchisel. Mindful of the trackless Khalkist wilderness around them, he strapped his sword to his back before he walked away from the dying fire.

"Over here, warrior," came the hoarse whisper, making his job that much easier. He found the Hylar nestled in a niche between a great boulder and a sturdy fir tree.

"Another quiet night," remarked Ariakas, settling himself atop the boulder.

"That makes twelve now," Ferros agreed. "By the Zhakar's reckoning, we don't have much farther to go." The Hylar leaned back, then shifted awkwardly to rub at an itch behind his left knee. "Damned firebugs followed me out here!" he griped. "If anything, the little scuts are worse than ever! Can't stop scratching. It about makes me crazy."

Ariakas barely listened—the Hylar's complaint had become a regular morning litany. The human's mind instead drifted into solitary meditation.

Twelve days on the road, and Tale Splintersteel had suggested it would take two or three weeks to reach Zhakar. Despite the rugged Khalkists, to date the trek had not been physically grueling. It surprised the warrior to realize how much, after the bustle and crowds of Sanction, he enjoyed the solitude and silence of the mountain heights. For the first part of the journey, he had been concerned with threats in the rock-bound fastness around them. Ogres were the traditional foes in the Khalkists, but now they had gotten beyond ogre country. The land between Bloten and Zhakar, where Splintersteel's vile-tempered cousins dwelt, had seemed to offer few threats. Of course, even with Tale accompanying them, he wasn't certain they would be received with open arms when they reached the dwarven realm.

The Zhakar merchant had told them a little about his homeland. Though the realm itself was extensive, including numerous crags and the valleys between, the dwarven population was concentrated in the subterranean city of Zhakar. The only part of that metropolis exposed to the light of day was a great, five-sided keep, which stood proudly on the rising slope above a mountain torrent called the Stonecrusher River. Though the keep itself was a respectable castle in size, Tale Splintersteel had told them that it was nothing compared to the vast network of delvings and warrens concealed underneath. It was those warrens that their expedition hoped to reach. That was where the plague mold grew, and that was where they could gather enough of the dust to corrupt vast numbers of the metallic dragon eggs.

Ariakas smiled privately as he remembered the results of the first hatching of draconians. The lizard beings that emerged from the brass egg had proven strong and hardy, albeit rather stupid. They could not fly, but they were fast and readily used their fangs and claws for battle. Three of them had already been slain in the tests they had conducted in the temple, but Ariakas had become convinced that these draconians would form the backbone of a huge and capable army.

". . . far today?" Ferros concluded his question, looking at Ariakas expectantly.

"Sorry," the human replied. "What did you say?"

"Forget it," groused the dwarf, reaching around to scratch an itch behind his back. "Just making conversation—wondered how many of these ridges we'll have to cross today."

"However many it is, you'll find us the passes, my friend," Ariakas said warmly. Indeed, the mountain dwarf had proven adept at guiding them along the best routes. Sheer granite barriers rose in seemingly endless succession across their path, and Splintersteel had told them that no regular overland route existed between Sanction and Zhakar. Each dwarven trading caravan, laden with weapons and coinage, apparently sought its own path to the port city.

"This isn't turning out like I figured it would," Ferros observed after a few moments' silence. "When I set out to find the dwarven kingdom in the Khalkists, I pictured a place like Thorbardin. Sure, there's bickering 'tween the clans, but by and large it's a prosperous, thriving place. Mountain and hill dwarf don't get along too well, but at least the hatchet's been buried for a few centuries, now.

"But here!" the Hylar continued, his tone growing exasperated. "Can you imagine a whole nation of dwarves like that little weasel over there? I tell you, it makes my skin crawl—and not just because of the way they look on the outside."

"They're not your run-of-the-mill dwarves, I'll grant you," Ariakas said good-naturedly. "Still, without Splintersteel we wouldn't have a chance on Krynn of reaching their kingdom." The warrior looked at the dwarf shrewdly. "Why are *you* so determined to find this place? I'd have thought you'd given up on the Zhakar as allies, by now."

Ferros shrugged. "I suppose I have . . . but there's something more. What *made* them into such hateful little snipes? Even if they'll never be allies of Thorbardin, *I* have to know. . . . I guess that's why I'm here."

"Do you think they can be changed—that *you* can change them?"

"I *know* the answer to that," Ferros sighed with a shake of his head. "At least, I think I do—and it's not hopeful."

"Nobody made you come along," Ariakas reminded him.

"True enough." Ferros went back to grousing. "Still, if you two had been left alone with Fungus-Cheeks, who knows what he might have done? And you!" The Hylar's tone grew accusing. "Bringing a woman along on a trip like this? What's the matter, didn't you get enough in the tower?"

Ariakas flushed. "It's *different* from the tower, damn it!" he snapped. "I thought you understood that!"

Ferros blinked, taken aback. Then he shook his head stubbornly. "You might call it different, but it looks to me like this one's got you hopping through the rings right in order."

"Never mind about her," the warrior replied, rising to

his feet. Suddenly he was in a foul humor, anxious to get moving. He saw that the sunrise had already brightened most of the sky.

"Come on," he said peremptorily. "Daylight's wasting."

While the Hylar, grumbling, rose from his sheltered niche, Ariakas went to wake Lyrelee and Tale Splintersteel. In neither case was he particularly gentle, and soon all four of them had dressed and hoisted their packs for another day on the trail.

This day, as on all the others, they climbed a steep ridge only to see from its crest the rolling ranks of the Khalkists, stretching before and behind them like breakers on a vast, restless sea. Still, after all this time on the trail their muscles were hardened and their endurance great. The four travelers barely paused to catch their breath at the first summit before Ferros began picking out a route into the narrow valley below.

Tale Splintersteel followed directly on the heels of Ferros Windchisel. Always robed from head to toe, the Zhakar dwarf nevertheless made good time on his stocky legs. He seemed to have great freedom of movement even within the confines of his garment, leaping nimbly from rock to rock or scampering from ledge to shelf down a steep defile, and he often demonstrated real strength in his arms and shoulders when called upon to perform a belay or to hoist himself up or down a rope.

Lyrelee came next. Though the priestess was garbed in traveling leathers instead of the silken pants and blouse that she normally wore, Ariakas still saw in her the cat-like grace of movement that had first attracted him. Now, as he watched her climb, his mind often wandered over the delightful and sensual experiences they had shared in the past weeks.

Their intimacy had begun in Sanction, immediately following the creation of the first draconians. The combination of the dangers they had shared and the thrill of opportunity present in the corruption ritual had infused them both with an animal passion that the time since had done very little to diminish.

Only after their first, exhaustive embrace had Ariakas recalled Takhisis's warning regarding women. Since then he had tried to rationalize the state of affairs, almost convincing himself that the goddess would not claim the life of one such faithful and capable priestess.

At first, when Tale had agreed to take Ariakas to Zhakar, neither the priestess nor the Hylar had struck the warrior as likely traveling companions. Ferros Windchisel remained determined to investigate the dwarven kingdom, however, and Ariakas had not tried hard to dissuade him from making the journey. Strangely, now that he knew the true nature of the Zhakar, Ferros had pursued his quest with more conviction than ever. The mountain dwarf's skills proved such an asset that even Tale Splintersteel had been forced to lay aside his prejudices.

Lyrelee had joined them immediately before their departure. Wryllish Parkane had complained that the expedition was not powerful enough to impress the innately hostile Zhakar. Though the high priest had envisioned a fully armed company of troops as an escort, Ariakas had demurred, insisting that the ability to travel fast and light would more than make up for the lack of numbers. He had also pointed out that his crimson-bladed sword was more powerful than a full complement of men-at-arms.

Tale Splintersteel had offered to provide an escort of two dozen Zhakar, but Ariakas had immediately rejected that suggestion. He would not appear to these dwarves as a prisoner, nor as an escorted guest. He intended to dictate terms as strongly as any potential conqueror. As a compromise, and with very little persuasion necessary, the lord had offered to take Lyrelee as an additional fighter.

For a week following the corruption of the eggs, Ariakas had trained diligently under the high priest himself, learning new spells that might help their mission. He could now cure many types of wounds, as well as diseases and poisonings—and, too, he could cause the same kinds of injuries to his enemies as he could heal in his friends.

Other spells opened wider paths of communication between him and his goddess. These he often employed in the still of the night, ensuring that the Zhakar did not lead them into treachery or ambush—especially since, after his experience with the Shilo-Thahn, he was a lot less willing to trust his own instincts to protect them against surprise attack.

Ariakas knew that the greed driving Tale Splintersteel was a powerful motive, but he was not entirely certain it would overcome the dwarf's inherent hatred and spitefulness. Thus far, apparently, avarice had won out. At the same time, Ariakas had not forgotten the measure of revenge due the treacherous Zhakar.

The real keystone of their defense rode on Ariakas's broad back. The two-handed sword that had blown frost and spewed acid remained a perfect red, and the warrior could barely begin to imagine the strength of the firestorm that would swirl forth from it upon his command. The breath of the red dragon was, in many ways, the most terrifying of any serpent's attack. When the time was right, he felt certain that the red blade would serve very well to bring the Zhakar to heel.

The trail meandered onto a broad, grassy slope, and for a time they were able to walk abreast, conversing with more ease than was usually possible on the trail. As they often did in such instances, the companions continued to question Tale Splintersteel about his homeland.

"You said that you Zhakar are ruled by a king—not a thane?" Ferros asked.

"Aye—the king of Zhakar. A chief as grand as any

mountain dwarf king, I assure you."

"Interesting. In Thorbardin, the heads of the various clans are called thanes. The king represents a uniting of the Theiwar, Daewar, Hylar, and all the rest. I would think that in a nation composed of one clan . . ."

"We are all we are," the Zhakar said stubbornly.

"Who is your king—do you know him?" Ariakas inquired.

"I wish I didn't," said the dwarf sourly. "When I was dispatched to Sanction, I was a trusted cousin of the king. Since then, my cousin was killed. A dwarf named Rackas Ironcog took over the throne. He's treated me as an enemy ever since."

"Could he have you replaced? Is your position in Sanction official?" asked the human.

"It is—and he would, if he could. I've been far enough away to handle my own problems. He's sent a number of agents to try and remove me." Tale's voice broke into a bitter bark of a laugh. "None of them, so far as I know, has survived the rigors of the trip home."

"So we face a political problem as well," mused Ariakas. "Do you have friends in Zhakar—dwarves you can count on?"

"I think so. There's another cousin of mine—distant, but we've worked together before. Whez Lavastone's his name. He's got designs on the throne, I'm sure."

"Perhaps we can use him. Can you think of any particular threats that we have to worry about once we're in the city?"

"You mean, assuming they don't kill us on sight?" asked Ferros dryly.

Ariakas didn't reply—he merely pointed to his sword.

"Do you know about the savants?" the Zhakar inquired. When Ariakas shook his head, the dwarf continued. "A few of our people have some magical power. These study under the masters, and can use their powers for treachery or concealment. A savant can often blind or deafen his target just by the use of his spells."

The warrior vividly remembered the encounter in the Fireplaza. "You didn't mention that *you're* a savant," he observed.

"Must have slipped my mind," Tale Splintersteel said with a dismissive shrug.

Ariakas noted the information, but then his mind wandered back to one of his favorite topics lately: considering the military potential of the draconians. The wizard Dracart, as well as Wryllish Parkane, had been certain that the number and the capabilities of the lizards could be improved upon. Perhaps a dozen, or a score, or even more draconians would eventually be yielded by the corruption of a single egg.

What an army they would make! He imagined the host, snapping and growling restlessly, spreading across the battlefield. What human force would stand before them? Ariakas felt, with a fierce and exultant confidence, that even steady veterans—even troops like ogres and elves—would be sorely pressed to hold firm against a rushing horde of draconians.

There was no doubt in his mind but that he was meant to command these beasts. Now his destiny seemed clear to him. The reasons for the testing in the tower, the warm reception he had received in the temple, all these curious things made sense in light of this manifest for action.

Where would they campaign? For now, the targets of the war seemed secondary to him. In truth, he felt that all of Ansalon might be his eventual target. Certainly, with savage troops like these, he could choose anywhere he wanted for his first onslaughts. Backed by the might of the Dark Queen, they would be an army such as Krynn hadn't seen in a thousand years!

Propelled by thoughts and ambitions, Ariakas barely noticed the miles falling behind them. When he finally took note of their surroundings, they had reached the knife-edge summit of a tall ridge—one of the highest they had yet climbed.

"There," Tale Splintersteel said, pointing at a cone-shaped peak in the middle distance. "That's Mount Horn. It stands above Zhakar Keep and marks the spot well."

Ariakas estimated another two days' march would be needed to reach the mountain, crossing no less than a half dozen lesser ridges he could see between them. Still, he found it very heartening that they were so close to their destination.

The others, too, gained new vigor from the knowledge. They started down the slope on the other side of the ridge, moving quickly, even sliding in the midst of small, gravelly avalanches that were triggered by their descent. The ridge slope was steep, scored by numerous parallel ravines from top to bottom as if it had been raked by the claws of some monstrous beast. As before, Ferros Windchisel led the way, while Tale, Lyrelee, and Ariakas followed in line. They moved down one of the ravines, which promised a straight route all the way to the stream at the valley floor.

A shout from the priestess attracted Ariakas, and in surprise he looked toward Lyrelee. She threw her hands into the air and then toppled forward, slipping and tumbling down the slope of the ravine. Only when she flipped onto her back did Ariakas see the bent shaft of a crossbow bolt, jutting out from her rib cage. Then battle cries arose from the surrounding rocks, and at least a hundred stunted, warlike figures broke from cover, swarming to the attack.

Chapter 19
Fire on the Mountain

Lyrelee lay still where she had fallen, nearly a hundred feet down the steeply sloping ravine from her companions. Ariakas saw the twisted missile in her body but then was forced to forget about the priestess as he and the two dwarves faced a howling onslaught. The trenchlike walls of the narrow gully gave them some protection from the crossbows, but as he crouched there and studied the attackers, Ariakas realized they had walked into a well-planned ambush.

The attackers were Zhakar, judging by their stature and the heavy cloaks covering them. Their next volley of bolts ripped savagely toward all three of the travelers; these dwarves apparently cared nothing for their kinsman. Indeed, several carefully aimed their small crossbows at Tale Splintersteel, and it was only the merchant lord's quick reflexes that saved him.

A bolt ricocheted from a rock beside Ariakas, and the warrior ducked as another grazed his shoulder. His sword was in his hands, though he had no memory of drawing it. He looked around, frantically trying to form a plan of defense. They were surrounded. Looking upward, he saw a rank of cloaked dwarves surging down the gully from the crest of the ridge.

Below, Lyrelee lay motionless, and the Zhakar ignored her body as they spilled into the gully and began to charge upward. Ferros Windchisel, in the lead, met the first of the attackers. The cloaked dwarves, disadvantaged by attacking uphill, quickly fell back before the Hylar. Ferros sent a pair of them tumbling, skulls split by his keen battle-axe.

"Your *sword!*" Tale Splintersteel's voice cracked with terror. Cowering in the bottom of the narrow gully, he frantically gestured Ariakas forward.

Sneering in disgust, the human was about to leave the Zhakar to his own defenses when he remembered that, without Splintersteel, their chances of getting an audience with the dwarven king would be virtually nonexistent.

"Fight, damn you!" Ariakas barked. "Unless you think you can talk them out of this attack!"

Leaping from rock to rock, the nearest Zhakar now loomed beside them. Apparently without fear, the stocky fighter launched himself through space, howling madly as he flailed toward the human warrior. Ariakas stuck him with the red blade, dumping the body off to the side with the force of the dwarf's own momentum before whirling to deflect the diving attacks of the next two Zhakar.

By this time Tale Splintersteel had drawn his own hook-bladed short sword, though he continued to jabber at Ariakas, pleading with the man to use his potent blade.

For his part, Ariakas fully intended to incinerate a bunch of Zhakar in the red blade's fireball. The attackers, however, were spread thinly across four directions of the steep slope, and the dragon-breath attack would only scour a part of one of those approaches. If he didn't want to waste the attack—and he didn't—he'd have to wait until his targets were more tightly packed.

The three of them fought for their lives. The Khalkist dwarves set aside their crossbows and brandished swords, whooping and screaming as they attacked in furious waves. The companions kicked rocks and stones to tumble free against the attackers below. The narrow gully gave them a little cover, and also served to channel the downslope attackers straight into the Hylar's axe.

Ariakas killed two dwarves at the edge of the ravine, then spun and drove back the attackers on the other side. Skidding noises warned him to look upward, and the warrior's sword swiftly gored another pair of Zhakar that had charged straight down from the ridge crest.

Ferros gave a shout as the loose rock beneath his feet broke free and he slid down the slope. Falling to his back, the Hylar skidded on the tumbling scree, kicking a Zhakar full in the face when the cloaked figure tried to slash him with a hook-sword.

"After him!" shouted Ariakas. He seized the squirming Tale Splintersteel by the scruff of his collar and pushed him down the ridge. The merchant dwarf slipped and bounced, but kept his feet as he plunged after the careening Ferros Windchisel.

The human warrior brought up the rear, taking long strides to keep up with the dwarves. After five steps Ariakas stopped, planted his feet, and whirled to face upward. A half-dozen shrieking Zhakar rushed in pursuit along the steep gully. The first of these leapt at Ariakas, and he knocked the dwarf to his right with a sweeping blow of his sword. He bashed the second one on his backswing and repeated the maneuver back and forth until all six, gouged and bleeding, had been sent rolling down the ridge.

Turning in the momentary lull, Ariakas plunged downward again, nearly losing his balance as the gully floor dropped through a steplike progression of three-foot cliffs. A Zhakar leapt at him from the right, and he chopped the dwarf almost in two, barely breaking stride. Another one rushed to the left edge of the ravine, but then ducked away when he raised the sword.

Ferros Windchisel finally arrested the momentum of his slide, though not before he had reached Lyrelee's motionless body. His rapid descent had carried him through the bulk of the attacking Zhakar. Tale Splintersteel joined them a moment later, and finally Ariakas reached the group. The Zhakar pursuers, for the moment, had been left behind and above them—though several skipped nimbly down the slope, closing fast. Again crossbow bolts bombarded them, but here the gully walls rose high and the runty dwarves could not find clear targets.

Ariakas saw with relief that the priestess was alive. Lyrelee's eyes were opened, and her parted lips revealed tightly clenched teeth. Her chest rose and fell rapidly from the staccato beat of her gasping breaths.

"Look out!" warned Ferros, and Ariakas looked upward in time to hack a charging Zhakar and drive back two more with lightning slashes of the crimson blade.

"Come *on*—let's run!" cried Tale Splintersteel, starting to lunge past Ferros and flee down the ridge.

Ariakas again grasped the Zhakar by the scruff of his neck, jerking him back none too gently. He bent downward, confronting the terrified eyes behind the cloak with his own grimly determined glare.

"Help her!" he snarled, releasing Splintersteel.

"Your sword!" begged the Zhakar. "Use it! Kill them!"

Angrily Ariakas shook off the suggestion. The attackers were still too scattered for him to slay more than a few, and he wasn't about to squander the precious power.

Lyrelee, still unspeaking, sat up; her face was pale and her eyes were dim, unfocused. Tale Splintersteel, muttering, reached for her arm and roughly helped her to her feet.

Now several Zhakar closed in from each side. Ferros and Ariakas did their best to hold them at bay while Tale and Lyrelee hobbled slowly down the gully. The mountain dwarf's axe blade was spattered with blood and bits of Zhakar robes, and streams of sweat ran down his bearded face while he whirled to face each new attack.

Ariakas maintained his position as rear guard, where an increasing number of the attackers came at him. Soon the companions had dropped well below the area of the ambush, and Ferros—freed of the necessity to hack his way through dwarves—aided Tale in helping Lyrelee. Their pace picked up considerably, Ariakas falling back to hold the pursuing dwarves at bay.

The Zhakar displayed a healthy respect for his crimson blade, gradually becoming reluctant to press close. They held back, launching bolts from their crossbows whenever Ariakas turned to hurry after his companions. One of these stuck him in the shoulder, inflicting a painful wound, and when he spun to do battle, another missile lodged in his breastplate.

Numerous dwarven bodies littered the bottom and sides of the ravine, and many other dwarves moaned piteously where they had fallen. A number of these had been injured when tumbling down the rocky slope, so that all told the ranks of the attackers had been sorely depleted.

Still, by the time they reached the bottom of the long slope, Ariakas could see many dozens of the stunted dwarves creeping down the ridge in their wake. A desultory rain of crossbow quarrels arced downward, and one of these scraped the Hylar's hand, producing a growl of anger from Ferros. Still, the barrage lacked the intensity of the opening volley, and the companions broke from the shelter of the ravine across the narrow valley floor.

A thin stream splashed through the steep-sided vale at the foot of the ridge, while another slope—it could have been a mirror image of the incline they had just descended —stretched toward the sky beyond the brook.

Lyrelee, leaning between the two dwarves, limped toward the streambank, while Ariakas kept his attention riveted on the dwarves above. The Zhakar hastened forward, but now they were too far back to catch the group before the waterway.

At the edge of the water, Tale Splintersteel stopped, though Ferros and Lyrelee stepped right into the stream. The channel was barely two feet deep, which would have been no higher than his chest, but the Zhakar merchant dug in his heels. The attackers surged forward, so Ariakas planted a firm kick in his companion's backside, flinging Tale far from shore before the cursing dwarf splashed into the water.

Ariakas waded after, fetching the spluttering figure up from the current, surprised to see Splintersteel quivering in terror. Desperately the dwarf clutched at the warrior's waist, and in disgust Ariakas carried the wretched figure the few steps to the far side of the stream. Ferros and Lyrelee had already emerged, and the dwarf helped the priestess stumble away from the shore. The Hylar's eyes narrowed thoughtfully as Ariakas tossed the dripping Zhakar onto the bank.

Once out of bow range, the party looked back at their pursuers, gathering along the bank. Ferros Windchisel spoke to the bedraggled Tale Splintersteel.

"Do *all* of you hate the water so much?"

Still muttering, the dwarf gave a surly nod.

"We might have bought ourselves some time," Ferros noted with an appreciative look at the stream. Several slick rocks broke the surface, but anyone trying to cross without getting wet would be in for a real challenge.

They continued away from the stream and toward a steep gully leading up. In moments they had climbed beyond arrow range from the valley floor. Tale Splintersteel's teeth chattered, and he shivered uncontrollably—altogether the picture of extreme misery. True to the companions' deduction, the pursuing Zhakar reached the banks of the stream and began to curse and catcall after them, but made no attempt to wade across.

One of the Zhakar jumped to a rock in the stream, perching awkwardly on the rounded top. When he tried leaping to the next intended stepping stone, however, he slipped and plunged into the water. Shrieking in pain or horror, he frantically splashed back to the shore and crawled out.

Lyrelee groaned and sagged to the ground.

"Keep an eye on that bunch!" Ariakas warned the dwarves, kneeling beside her. The priestess closed her eyes, wincing in pain, and Ariakas saw that the arrow penetrating her side had been jostled and wrenched in its wound. Lyrelee's breathing was shallow, her color pallid.

The man felt a burning determination—*she would not die!* Yet only with the aid of his goddess could he hope to help her.

Everything else vanished into the background as Ariakas remembered his training in the temple. "Takhisis, mighty Queen of Darkness," he uttered softly, "summon forth the healing strength of my faith, and bring it to bear against this woman's hurts!"

He felt the power of the goddess thrumming through his limbs, and—with hands that felt almost detached, as if they belonged to someone else—he first touched the shaft embedded in the wound, and then, very gently, removed it. Lyrelee's eyes flashed open, and she placed a hand over his, drawing strength from the power of the man and the Dark Queen.

Within a few minutes she sat up, and when he helped her to her feet, she stood alone, steadily. The sparkling determination returned to her eyes, and the pale cast of her skin was the only visible reminder of her weakened condition.

"The little beggars are inventive—I'll give them that," noted Ferros Windchisel, indicating the dwarves across the stream.

Ariakas saw that the Zhakar had formed a chain of laborers, passing large rocks from one to the next. The last dwarf in the chain stood at the bank of the stream, pitching the rocks into the water as they reached him. Slowly the line of boulders extended into the water, forming an impromptu jetty, with gaps to allow the water to flow through. Within a few minutes the rudimentary bridge extended most of the way across the stream.

"We'd better get going," Tale Splintersteel urged, his voice tense and agitated. "They'll be after us!"

"You three go on ahead," suggested Ariakas, the beginnings of a plan taking root in his mind. He studied the Zhakar who gathered at the streambank waiting for the completion of the bridge. "I'll stay back—see if I can't give them a little something to remember us by."

Gently carrying the sword with the crimson blade, Ariakas started back down the slope, taking care to remain out of bow range. Several of the cloaked dwarves saw his descent, shouting and jabbering excitedly, pointing toward the warrior and brandishing their weapons in fury.

With a few crashes and splashes, the bridge was finished, and the Zhakar began to pour across, leaping the narrow gaps where water continued to flow. The crowding was so frantic that several of them stumbled from the irregular surface, splashing into the liquid they had tried so hard to avoid. Nevertheless, at least fifty of the runty dwarves surged forward in a mass, infused with blood-lust.

As the tightly packed horde raced toward him, Aria-kas slipped and slid farther down the incline until he had almost reached the level of the valley floor. The nearest Zhakar raised their weapons, no doubt wondering at the folly of this human who accepted such an unequal battle.

The warrior lifted his sword toward the front of the pack, murmuring a plea to his goddess. As before, Takhisis heard, and granted him her favor. The blade began to glow, so brightly that the leading dwarves faltered slightly in their charge, uncertain what would happen next.

They never had time to realize what did. Without a sound, the sword suddenly spit out a searing, brilliant tongue of flame. The fire embraced the leading Zhakar with greedy fingers, devouring flesh and torching robes. Before they could open their mouths or utter any cries of pain, a dozen dwarves had died, blackened to crisp, charred corpses scattered along the valley floor.

Ariakas hefted the blade slightly, allowing the billowing cloud of fire to expand outward and upward. Now the sound of roaring flames rumbled around him, mixed with the pathetic shrieks of Zhakar dwarves who saw death approaching and could do nothing to avoid it. Flames licked across shriveling dwarven skin, and bodies wrapped in fire fell to the ground and writhed, smoking bundles of agony. Billows and sheets of oily flame hissed from one dwarf to the next, seeking, killing.

Those dwarves on the fringes of the assault turned and fled back across the bridge, starkly proving the depth of their water abhorrence. Even in blind flight, the Zhakar crowded onto their impromptu bridge. None of the wretched creatures plunged into the stream, even as the scalding fireball drifted closer.

Finally the swordsman turned the full brunt of the attack against those dwarves who tried to get onto the bridge. The mass of Zhakar disappeared in a howling, smoking inferno, and even when the gouts of fire ceased to belch from the sword, the pile of corpses burned, sending a cloud of black smoke billowing upward into the sky.

Ariakas looked across the valley bottom. He saw a dozen or more Zhakar, still alive, desperately scrambling away from him. Good, he thought. He wanted survivors so that the tale of his might and his brutality would reach the ears of the Zhakar king. Instilling fear within that monarch was a major part of the warrior's plan.

Only then did he look down at the blade. A chill of portent ran through his body as he saw it. When the fires had died and the weapon had performed its deadly work, the steel surface had faded from red, as he had known it would.

Now, however, it became a deep, rich blue.

Chapter 20
The Walls of Zhakar

They rested for a full day after the battle, making their camp in a niche on the leeward side of the tall ridge. There they recovered from the exertion and tended their many wounds—all of which, save Lyrelee's, proved to be minor. Though the priestess had been near death during the fight, the regenerative power of Ariakas's healing magic proved astonishingly effective. By the second night there was no sign that her skin had been punctured.

During this period of rest and recovery, the companions kept a careful watch for attackers. The Zhakar knew where they were, they reasoned, since it would have been impossible for them to effectively hide in the open terrain. Still, they saw not a single sign of the stunted dwarves.

"Did we scare them that well?" Ariakas wondered as the sun set that night.

"It's that sword," Tale Splintersteel offered, pointing to the now-azure blade. "I told you—my people know good weapons, and that is one of the best."

"Know them, sure. But do they really fear this sword *that* much?" The idea that the weapon was all that deterred another attack seemed just a little unsettling to Ariakas. After all, now that the blade had turned blue he was not about to use it for a routine battle demonstration. The Dark Queen's prophecy still resounded through his mind, and he vowed not to employ the power until he understood what she meant.

"In the heart of the world, it will set fire to the sky." he murmured, pondering the gleaming weapon.

"What was that?" asked Lyrelee, reclining near the low fire Ferros had built out of dried brush.

"Nothing—just my mind wandering," Ariakas replied hastily.

She looked at him quickly, a glance that seemed to penetrate right through his lie. Still, she settled back onto her rocky pillow and closed her eyes, apparently unconcerned.

"Keep sharp lookout, tonight," Tale Splintersteel suggested from his bedroll as Ariakas rose to take the first shift of guard duty. "Zhakar eyes are keen in the dark— and my country folk often favor the early morning hours for an attack."

"I'll keep that in mind," Ariakas retorted scornfully. Just the same, he held his blade out of the scabbard as he climbed to a rocky perch above their camp. From here he could see the slope to all sides of them, as well as the valley floor stretching to the right and left and the face of the ridge rising opposite them beyond.

The Zhakar made no appearance even through the

darkest hours of the night, and when dawn found Ferros Windchisel in the watch seat, there had been not the slightest disturbance or intrusion. They ate a cold breakfast and finally returned to the trail, resuming the steep climb that had been interrupted two days before.

Ariakas watched Lyrelee carefully. Though she wore a pack nearly as heavy as his, her steps were firm, her breathing strong. She climbed without speaking, and seemed to show no sign of the nearly fatal wounds she had suffered in the attack.

They crossed three ridges on this day of vigorous marching, and late afternoon found them on a narrow trail that circled the waist of volcanic, looming Mount Horn. Tale Splintersteel had explained that not only did this mountain mark the border of Zhakar's inner realm, it held a watch post garrisoned with a company of dwarven guards.

Ariakas didn't like the looks of the trail. As it scaled the steep sides of the slumbering volcano, it provided room for them to walk only in single file. To the right, the sloping shoulder of the mountain swept downward and away for thousands of feet. It wasn't exactly a precipice, but anyone who fell would certainly roll for a long way before coming to a bruised and battered halt.

Even more nerve-racking was the sight of the mountain's cone-shaped summit rising steeply away to their left. The rocky surface concealed numerous niches and crannies wherein ambushing Zhakar could have concealed themselves by the dozen.

"The watch post's up there," explained Tale Splintersteel, pointing to a notch in the trail before them. Ahead, the slope of the mountain rose into a jagged shoulder, and the steep pathway passed between that shoulder and the main summit. The gap was barely twenty feet wide, with rough cliffs of basalt to either side.

"Can we go around it?" wondered the warrior. Yet even as he asked the question, he looked at the mountainside and realized that the watch post had been well chosen.

Below the rough shoulder, a cliff plunged for at least a thousand feet downward, and below that a jagged tumble of large rocks and loose scree offered a time-consuming nightmare of a crossing. The scree slope spilled all the way to a deep, white-water river scoring a channel along the valley floor.

Above the watch post was a slope that was nearly as steep as the lower cliff, here soaring all the way up to the mountain's sharp, angular summit. Though the place could possibly be circumvented by the upward route, any Zhakar lurking in the notch would have no difficulty moving upward faster than those approaching along the trail.

"They're certain to have already seen us," the dwarven merchant said helpfully. "Might as well march right up there and see what they do—just keep your sword handy," he added to Ariakas.

The warrior nodded, not liking this. The steel blade would provide him no more protection than inherent in its design, he knew, for he would not unleash the magic of the blue blade here.

The companions kept their eyes on the narrow notch as they moved steadily upward. With sunset and the coming of dusk, the wind grew chill, and the stony gap, a half mile away, took on an even more sinister appearance.

"Should we stop here and wait for morning?" asked Ferros Windchisel, mindful of the fading daylight.

"I think we should push on through," Ariakas declared. "This is a damned poor place to sleep, for one thing—no shelter from the wind, no firewood. Not even a flat place to rest besides the trail!" What he didn't say, but knew, was that he couldn't bear the tension of waiting. Whatever fate awaited them at the watch post of Zhakar, he wanted to find out *now*.

"I agree," Lyrelee added. "Even if we don't go any farther tonight—at least up there we'd have a chance for a windbreak.

"Let's go," said Tale Splintersteel with a resigned shrug. "Just make sure they can see that sword," he reminded the human warrior.

They hurried, anxious to reach the notch before darkness surrounded them. The first star had twinkled into sight by the time they made the approach, but the western horizon still shed pale light across the mountain heights.

"Let me go first" suggested Ariakas, moving past the others. The bare blade extended before him, he advanced cautiously toward the gap. The stone walls to the right and left loomed upward, dark and mysterious. Between them, not more than a dozen steps away, the gap opened out again. Even in the darkness Ariakas saw a wide valley beyond, much flatter and more gentle than the terrain they had crossed thus far.

But most of his attention remained on the walls to the right and left. Countless niches and ravines scarred the rough surface, cloaked with shadows his eyes could not penetrate.

His companions waited behind while Ariakas cautiously passed through the notch. He saw no sign of any other occupant, and so he reversed his course, this time closely checking the niches to either side of the path. Nothing there—though several of the cracks were too deep for a foolproof check. For a brief instant he considered casting the light spell, but quickly discarded the idea. Though it would give him the ability to penetrate some of the shadows, it would dramatically outline him and his companions to watchers anywhere in the surrounding valley and heights.

"Seems clear," he reported.

All four of them advanced through the notch, Lyrelee and Splintersteel following Ariakas while Ferros cautiously brought up the rear. Again the passage occurred without incident; for all appearances, the notch had been completed vacated.

"Not bad," Tale Splintersteel murmured, clearly surprised. He nodded at the blue sword. "Word must have gotten around."

Ariakas smiled grimly, his relief immense. They camped in a little swale that provided some protection from the wind. The night passed without incident, and in the first light of dawn they finally got a look at their destination.

Zhakar Keep stood on a slope above the broad valley. The river that circled the base of Mount Horn continued through that vale, widening into a long, narrow lake for part of its length. High, rugged peaks surrounded the two sides of the valley, and the river's outflow dropped out of sight several miles away, suggesting a channel that might be a canyon or a gorge.

The stone-walled keep dominated the entire central section of the valley. Terraced slopes spread downward from the keep to the river, and behind it towering peaks rose toward the sky. The walls were black, as were the squat towers located at various places along those sheer barriers. The place did not resemble a castle so much as a walled compound, for within the walls the companions could see no buildings. Four long, black columns rose upward from the courtyard, and one of these belched a cloud of black smoke. Tale Splintersteel explained that these were the chimneys of the Zhakaran great forge.

"Where are your countrymen?" Ariakas asked, gesturing to the well-tended—but apparently abandoned—vista. Though the terraced fields were obviously devoted to carefully nurtured crops, no one labored there. Like the watch post, now behind them, the valley stood silent, by all appearances completely deserted.

"It's strange," Tale Splintersteel observed. "We must be creating quite a stir—look's as though they're expecting a siege!"

For the better part of the morning they approached the dark fortress. Throughout that time, they saw no sign of the valley's inhabitants, though the keep seemed to grow more ominous and sinister with each step closer. The only sign of life was the black stream of smoke that continued to drift from the chimney.

They approached along a graveled road that led between the fields of the terrace. Ariakas came first, with the naked blade resting casually on his shoulder, gleaming like some surreal but precious metal—liquid turquoise or azure. He made certain that the weapon remained in clear view at all times.

Reaching the double gates, the four companions stood before a wide portal consisting of two solid iron plates mounted on stone hinges. Ariakas knew that each gate must weigh an unimaginable amount. Inwardly, he raised his estimation of Zhakaran skill as craftsmen and builders. Quietly, calmly, he rehearsed the incantation to the spell Wryllish Parkane had taught him. It had been intended to give them access to the keep, but he had never imagined the full scale of the portal that would stand across the path.

"Go away! Strangers are not allowed in Zhakar! Go away, or you will be killed!" A thin, reedy voice came quaveringly over the wall. They could see no speaker, but the words carried clearly to their ears.

"We come in peace—we are a trade mission seeking audience with King Ironcog!" shouted Tale. "Tell him that Splintersteel of Sanction is here!"

"The king is too busy to see you—go back to Sanction!"

"We will see the king!" Ariakas shouted, growing impatient.

"No. Go away! Leave our countryman behind when you depart—he will be punished for bringing you here."

Tale Splintersteel cast wide, fearful eyes at his companions, but they weren't paying any attention to him.

Instead, they stared upward, trying to see any sign of the speaker.

Ariakas decided to proceed. He stepped forward until he stood directly in front of the great, iron gates. Each of the barriers towered upward at least three times his height and was nearly half that in width—dimensions that made him feel very small, indeed. Nevertheless, he murmured a silent prayer to Takhisis and then raised his voice so that it could be clearly heard within.

"I, Highlord Ariakas, command these gates—in the name of a power greater than you can comprehend—to give way before my knock. In the name of majesty and power, I command!"

His heavy fist banged against the gate, once, twice, and again. Booming reverberations echoed around them from the keep and spilled down into the valley beyond.

With a portentous creak, the gates began to swing outward. Ariakas stepped quickly back, brandishing his sword at the ready, studying the slowly expanding crack between the twin doors. Part of him wanted to gape in surprise, astounded that the simple spell had proven so successful. The dominant portion of his mind retained control, however, and his cool, almost bored inspection of the opening gates indicated that he had never expected any result other than this.

He heard gasps of surprise, even cries of panic, coming from the fortress. The gap widened, and he saw a wide, refuse-covered courtyard. Robed Zhakar scattered in all directions from the gates, though several armed with swords, crossbows, and battle-hooks crept hesitantly forward. The gates opened wider, and he saw several dwarves frantically trying to arrest the winch mechanism—but the chain creaked through the gears with automatic, inevitable progression, completely unresponsive to their efforts.

"Peace," said Ariakas, striding forward to meet the dwarven warriors blocking the door. His voice, his posture, betrayed no hint of the doubts and apprehensions he felt. "I offer no harm—and many profits."

Thankfully, the Zhakar backed hastily away from the human warrior, their eyes riveted to the unique weapon in his hands. Lyrelee, Tale Splintersteel, and Ferros Windchisel followed him through the gates, and the four of them confronted the dwarves within as the gates ceased their automatic opening.

"You can close them now," Ariakas announced to the gatesmen, who hastily commenced to crank the portals shut.

Several dozen dark-shawled Zhakar crept toward him, weapons raised, but they didn't look as though they intended to attack. Indeed, Ariakas suspected that a simple flick of his great sword would send them scattering in panic. Many milky, baleful eyes observed him through slits in the faces of the cloaks.

Ariakas looked around the courtyard of Zhakar Keep. The place was like no other fortress or castle that he had ever seen. The high walls were pierced only by the single gate through which the companions had entered.

The ground inside the compound was a chaotic menage of shallow ravines and low ridges, except for one huge, blocklike building in the center of the grounds. From the roof of this structure emerged the four chimneys they had seen in the distance. Otherwise, the many piles and ridges of dirt eclipsed any other features the courtyard might have held.

"Your turn," Ariakas muttered to Tale Splintersteel. "Tell them why we're here."

The Zhakar cleared his throat and stepped forward. Behind the screening masks, the guardsmen's eyes studied him with palpable suspicion and hostility.

"These are not our enemies," began the merchant. "I have brought them here because they can bring great benefits, great prosperity to our realm. That is why it is essential for us to see the king!"

One of the guards stepped cautiously ahead of his fellows, though he cast a quick glance to the rear—as if ensuring that he had a line of escape, if necessary. This ad hoc leader then turned back to the visitors, scowling angrily.

"You know you can't bring outsiders here!" he snapped to Tale Splintersteel. "Did they make you a prisoner? Are you a hostage?"

"No—not exactly," replied the Zhakar merchant, perhaps remembering that at one time he *had* been a prisoner. "They wish to establish trade with us, and they insist on seeing the king themselves."

Next the spokesman turned to Ariakas. "The punishment is death for one of our number who brings outsiders to Zhakar." His tone was tinted with respect, even a little fear. "You must have been very persuasive."

"Have you not heard of the many-colored blade?" demanded Tale Splintersteel in growing exasperation. "This is the man who can slay a hundred dwarves without touching his sword to their flesh!"

The pale eyes widened within the slit of the cloak. "It's true, then—what they said about the valley of the Blackrock? That his sword spit fire, and a whole company perished?"

"Believe every word," urged the merchant sneeringly. "And heed well his sword—lest he use it to bring Zhakar itself crumbling down around your ears!"

Now the eyes widened in definite fear, and Ariakas raised the sword slightly to illustrate the point. The blue blade seemed to float in the air, the most intense color in the courtyard.

"I—I'll go tell the king," said the spokesman finally. "You watch 'em!" he commanded imperiously to his fellows, obviously relieved to have the chance to escape the presence of that awe-inspiring weapon.

The guards who had been assigned to watch them took their job very seriously, though they seemed far more concerned with the blue-bladed sword than with any other aspect of the visitors' appearance. Ariakas took care to brandish the sword so that it could easily be seen. He even whipped the weapon through several training drills, enjoying the sight of the Zhakar nervously backing away—as if they expected the thing to explode at any moment.

"What do you think the king'll say, now?" Ferros inquired of Tale Splintersteel.

Splintersteel shrugged. "That's anyone's guess," he whispered to the others. "Rackas is an old enemy of my family. Still, he's a profiteer first and foremost—he's likely to listen to our proposal."

The warrior nodded noncommittally.

Finally the messenger returned. "The king will consent to an audience," he announced importantly. "The prisoners are to be brought to the Royal Promen—"

"*What* prisoners?" growled Ariakas menacingly. "If you mean us, let the dwarf who will capture me step forward—*now!*"

Predictably, there was no movement among the rank of guards. Two dozen pairs of eyes followed as if hypnotized while the blue blade carved a slow arc through the air.

The messenger stammered and hemmed. "If the, er, emissaries would be so good as to accompany me to the lift station, I will take you to the king."

He led the companions along a winding walkway flanked by mounds of dirt until they reached the wall of the huge stone blockhouse. An iron door opened at their approach, and they entered the structure.

Immediately they were struck by a blast of hot, dry air. Hammers rang against forges, and furnaces roared while bellows pumped fresh air into their fire boxes. The room was shadowy, almost totally dark except for the crimson glow of fires and red-hot metal, which showed hooded forms moving vaguely among hulking forges.

Ariakas murmured a quick magical command, and the gemstone in his helmet immediately flared into brightness. He saw Zhakar cover their eyes and turn hastily away from the illumination, satisfying himself that the light would help him maintain his command in the presence of these miserable creatures. Gradually the sounds of hammering died away, as the strange party was led through a maze of fire pits, anvils, casting pots, winches, and overhead chains.

In the center of the manufactory, they reached a cage consisting of black iron bars surrounding a flat platform. The platform was suspended by a grid of chains, and it swayed slightly as the Zhakar messenger opened the door and stepped onto it.

"How do we know this isn't a trap?" demanded Ariakas, as he and Lyrelee instinctively held back from the strange contraption.

Tale and Ferros, however, passed through the gateway and turned to look at the humans. "It's just a lift," the Hylar said, amused. "We have hundreds like this in Thorbardin. How else would you go up and down— *stairways*?"

Inwardly, Ariakas groused that a stairway would be just fine with him, but he had already shown too much hesitation on the matter. Gruffly he stepped inside, quickly followed by the priestess.

The Zhakar pulled a lever, and immediately the platform lurched below their feet, sinking through the floor into a shaft that had been bored into the rock. Trying to suppress his nervousness, Ariakas watched the stone walls appear to rise around them. He listened uneasily to the clanking of chain overhead.

"This lift is counterbalanced with another one, not too far away," Tale Splintersteel explained. "When this one goes down, that one comes up. If the job is to take something down to the city, then there's no need for any power—our weight does the job, though the chain rolls through several brakes so it doesn't go too fast."

"How can it lift cargo up to the ground level?" asked Lyrelee.

"For that we have the winchmasters," the Zhakar explained. "It doesn't move so quickly, but they can crank a load from the Promenade up to the Keep in a matter of ten minutes or so."

Personally, Ariakas didn't think their descent was any too speedy. His heart pounding, he could not banish the feeling that they had walked into a perfect trap.

Then the lift clanked to rest on a solid stone floor, causing them all to lurch unsteadily. A metal door before them rumbled aside, and they stepped into a vast, dimly lit chamber. A vague, fiery illumination spilled into the place from two yawning cave mouths off to their right. Before them, twin rows of columns towered upward from the floor, vanishing into the darkness overhead.

At the end of the row of pillars, nearly lost in the shadows, the companions saw a pair of immense statues. Carved into the shape of hideous beasts, these figures stood with their backs to the cavern wall. Between the trunklike legs of the statue on the right, they saw a large, stone throne, then noticed a similar seat beneath the statue on the left.

"The King's Promenade," explained the messenger, indicating the wide roadway between the two rows of columns.

Slowly, deliberately, they started down the walk. Ariakas naturally moved into the fore, his bright gem casting a wash of white on the floor before them. The columns to either side and the roadway to the thrones plainly indicated their route. In one of the thrones Ariakas saw a shrouded, shadowy figure. The warrior was amused to see the king shrink into his seat as the party moved closer.

Ferros and Lyrelee flanked the human warrior, a step or two behind, while Tale Splintersteel and the Zhakar messenger brought up the rear. Around them Ariakas sensed a huge number of dark, silent figures. Several forms stood just within range of his light, and the warrior concealed his surprise as he saw Zhakar warriors mounted on four-legged lizards. The animals had a dull, unintelligent look, but the sleek sinew in their shoulders and legs suggested both speed and power. They were no bigger than large hounds, though sharp claws on their forefeet indicated that they could be savage foes in a fight. Yet even these bizarre cavalrymen cringed back when Ariakas swiveled his sword, or let his haughty gaze sweep over them.

His nervousness vanished entirely as he approached the Zhakar king. Ariakas carried the blue blade casually, the weapon unsheathed but resting easily on his shoulder. With a flick of his wrist he could bring it down against a target on any side.

"Kneel when you meet the king!" hissed Tale Splintersteel as they drew closer to the end of the promenade.

Now Ariakas's light fell on the figure seated in one of the huge thrones. The Zhakar was cloaked but unhooded, revealing a face that was scarred by the ravages of the mold plague. The king's beard was mostly gone, though several tufts of hair still sprouted from the skin over his jawbone. He looked bald, though he wore a heavy golden crown that concealed the top of his head.

"King Rackas Ironcog of Zhakar!" proclaimed a dwarf concealed in the shadows off to the sides. "Kneel before the greatness of his royal presence!"

Ferros Windchisel stepped to the warrior's side, and then knelt humbly—a dwarven warrior showing respect to the monarch of another dwarven state. Ariakas nodded to Lyrelee on his other side, and she, too, knelt. Meanwhile Tale Splintersteel all but groveled, prostrating himself on the floor and crawling to the Hylar's side.

Only Ariakas remained standing. He met the flashing eyes of Rackas Ironcog with his own proud stare and then, with regal dignity, leaned forward in a gracious bow. His knees, however, did not bend.

"Who are you?" demanded the king, nonplussed by the display of confidence.

"I am Lord Duulket Ariakas, emissary of a powerful queen—the mightiest monarch on all Krynn," he proclaimed grandly. "I bring salutations and praise to the esteemed lord of Zhakar!"

Somewhat mollified, Rackas Ironcog huffed in his throne. Apparently he was unused to anything even vaguely resembling diplomacy.

For the first time Ariakas noticed another Zhakar, standing in the shadows beside the throne. This one wore a cloak over even his face, which was unusual in the city so far as the human had seen. Also unique was the extensive golden thread embroidered around the fringes of the cloak. The masked dwarf leaned toward the king, apparently whispering something in his ear.

"Welcome to my realm," Rackas Ironcog said grudgingly, after a moment's silence. Ignoring any further pleasantries, he spoke bluntly. "This is the sword that killed one hundred of my finest troops?"

"Aye, Your Majesty," answered Ariakas. Inwardly, he scorned the repulsive monarch, who obviously knew less about court manners than the lowliest pageboy of Khuri-Khan. Still, he would go along with the charade as long as it suited his purpose. "The blade is a gift to me from my queen, and she bid me use it as an instrument of her will."

"She *is* mighty, this queen of yours," replied the king. "Now tell me, human—why does she send you to me?"

"We have come on a peaceful mission of trade," Ariakas responded. "It is a mission that could bring unimagined profits into Your Majesty's treasuries, and at the same time form the basis of an alliance that will greatly benefit both our peoples."

"And you, Tale Splintersteel!" The monarch finally

addressed the merchant lord. "This matter is important enough to cause you to defy ancient tradition, bringing outsiders to the heart of our realm?"

"Indeed, Majesty," replied Tale. "After heartfelt consideration I believe the human's suggestions of profit are based in fact. He who bears the colored sword has proven himself a fighter and negotiator of great strength and determination."

"Strength and determination . . . those are admirable traits." The king nodded, scowling.

"Lord Warrior, will you and your companions accept our hospitality? I shall provide you with chambers in the royal apartments, where you shall have every comfort we can provide. When you have rested, I invite you to attend my table. Tonight, we shall make the arrangements for trade."

"Your hospitality is welcome," Ariakas agreed. "It is a fitting gesture for a meeting that will doubtless result in a long and profitable friendship."

As courtiers led them toward the royal quarters, Ariakas risked a quick look behind. He saw the king's eyes staring at him—but not at the warrior himself, he suddenly realized. Instead, Rackas Ironcog's eyes, glittering with greed, remained fastened to the azure blade in the human warrior's hand.

Chapter 21
To Hold a Throne

The quarters that were given to the companions by Rackas Iron-cog had been hailed by the Zhakar king as the finest ambassadorial apartments in the realm, but to Ariakas they were more reminiscent of a stinking dungeon. Low ceilings forced the warrior into a permanent stoop, while his sleeping chamber gave him barely enough space to turn around. A central anteroom linked their small individual compartments, but the bare stone walls and dank, stale air suggested a place more suited for imprisonment than hospitality. A heavy door barred them from the rest of the royal chambers, and as a precaution, the warrior jabbed a dagger into the frame, ensuring that the portal could not be shut tightly from the outside.

The only concessions to luxury in the sleeping rooms were mattresses of fur-lined stuffing and plush blankets of animal pelts. The companions took advantage of the hours until dinner by resting, though after a little time Ariakas rose and paced in stooped agitation. To the veteran warrior, the situation reeked with disadvantages. He checked the door, making certain it had not been tampered with.

The only illumination in the rooms came from the magical light spells that Ariakas and Lyrelee alternated casting. Of necessity, a few hours had passed in darkness while the two communed with the Dark Queen, replenishing their clerical magics. After he rose from his brief rest, Ariakas perched his helmet with its glowing gemstone in a corner of the main room, where the illumination could spread through the apartments.

Soon Ferros Windchisel emerged from his sleeping room. The Hylar grunted in annoyance as he scratched a patch of red, irritated flesh along his forearm.

"Damned if they don't have firebugs here, too," groused the dwarf. "Too small to see—but I got bites all over my arm." Irritated, the dwarf scratched at a place on the back of his skull.

"I hope we don't have anything worse than bugs to worry about," Ariakas replied wryly. Then he looked at Ferros in sudden concern, seeing as if for the first time the raw skin, the patches of scabs that had began to mar his body. A sickening premonition rose within him.

Ferros scowled thoughtfully. "They have us pretty well boxed in, don't they?"

"I don't like it," Ariakas agreed.

Soon the other two travelers emerged from their chambers, and the four of them gathered in the anteroom to discuss their situation.

They were startled by a knock on the door. Ariakas rose and, after removing his dagger from the jamb, opened the portal to reveal an unusually tall Zhakar male. The dwarf's face was disfigured by the mold plague, but there existed a pride and self-confidence in his posture that struck the warrior as unique.

"I am Whez Lavastone," their visitor informed them, bowing deeply. "Perhaps you will grant me the honor of a private interview?"

Silently Ariakas gestured the fellow into the room, trying not to look at his patchy, disfigured face. The Zhakar squinted away from the glowing gem in the corner and took a seat that left him in silhouetted view to the others.

"Greetings, Merchant Splintersteel," the visitor said, with a formal nod to Tale.

"The same, Lord Lavastone," he replied. Splintersteel turned to his companions, keeping his tone carefully neutral. "Whez Lavastone was a high adviser to Pulc Tenstone, our previous king. There were many, when last I was in Zhakar, who imagined him to be our future ruler."

"There are *still* many," Whez Lavastone asserted. "Though our current monarch is not among them."

"Why do you come here?" interrupted Ariakas.

"Tale Splintersteel served my former lord well, and I wish to reward this service by giving you a warning."

"Go on," said the warrior suspiciously.

"Rackas Ironcog has no intention of opening any trading discussions with you. He desires to kill you and steal your sword—with which he plans to hold onto his throne indefinitely."

"I suspected treachery—though I'm surprised at the bluntness of his approach."

"Ironcog is nothing if not blunt," Tale noted. The Zhakar thought for a moment before speaking to Whez Lavastone. "How stands the support of the new king?"

Their visitor shrugged. "As well, or as poorly, as any king of Zhakar. He holds his throne until someone takes it away from him—and, as always, there are many who desire it."

"One of those, presumably, being you?" inquired Ariakas directly.

"Naturally." Whez accepted the question as perfectly reasonable. "But there are other considerations as well."

"We're listening," Ariakas noted.

"King Ironcog feels that we're already engaged in too much trade with humankind. In fact, since we first observed your approach, he's been using you as an example of the dangers that Zhakar exposes herself to—even through distant Sanction."

"Too *much* trade?" Tale Splintersteel, the merchant lord, was appalled. "I have to fend off demands for swords and shields, for minted coins and arrowheads! I could sell three for every one I get—and at no reduction in price! What madness is this to try and kill the greatest source of income in the realm?"

"It came about during Pulc Tenstone's reign," Whez said with a shrug. "And we all know that you were Pulc's agent. Perhaps if Ironcog had his own minister of trade, he'd feel differently—as it is now, he fears giving too much power to his rivals."

"May we assume, then, that those rivals are more amenable to increased trade?" Ariakas probed.

Whez Lavastone smiled, a grotesque distortion of his plague-pocked face. Even against the glare of the gem Ariakas could see the Zhakar's teeth gleaming between slick, bloody gums. "Witness my presence here," the dwarf noted. "And this warning: take no food at Rackas Ironcog's table, if you would live to see the morning."

"No food!" spluttered Ferros Windchisel. "First we get a dungeon cell to sleep in, and now we're not supposed to eat! This is not dwarven hospitality by *Thorbardin* standards!"

"You're not in Thorbardin," Whez Lavastone retorted, his tone taut with controlled fury—even hatred. "And when Thorbardin abandoned us to our fate, they lost the right to critique our customs!"

"What abandonment?" growled the Hylar. "Why do you think I've come all—"

"This is getting us nowhere," Ariakas interrupted sharply. Ferros Windchisel bit back his objection. "As for the food, I think we can dine safely—and I *do* mean dine," he reassured his companions. "I'll perform a little ceremony before dinner that should see to that."

"Also, beware the king's savant—Tik Deepspeaker. He is ever treacherous, and seeking ways to further himself in his master's eyes," cautioned Whez.

"Was that him in the gold-trimmed robe, standing next to the throne?" asked Ariakas.

Their visitor nodded, and Tale Splintersteel cursed. "I might have known that scoundrel would find his way into royal favor." He turned to Ariakas. "King Tenstone was blinded by a savant before the assassin's knife found his heart. It is widely believed that Deepspeaker was the one who aided in the killing."

"As to this king's reluctance to trade, I'm open to suggestions," Ariakas concluded.

"You could fry him with your sword," suggested Tale Splintersteel. "We could arrange it that the new regime is ready to take over immediately."

"I'm nobody's assassin," Ariakas replied. "If you want him dead, you'll have to do it yourself."

"Very well," said Whez Lavastone, rising to his feet with alacrity. "I didn't expect you to attend to that matter—but at least you know who your enemies are."

"We thank you for the warning," Ariakas acknowledged, standing and nodding his head as the Zhakar headed back to the door. When the visitor had left the human reinserted his dagger in the frame, propping the door open by several inches.

Within an hour they were summoned to dinner, and the four of them were escorted by a rank of Zhakar guards through several long, wide hallways of the Royal Wing. The warrior wore his blue sword on his back, and when the captain of the escorts appeared ready to question him on that point, Ariakas scowled so darkly that the dwarf remained silent.

When they reached the dining hall, the humans were pleased—and surprised—to see that their host had arranged for torches to be placed throughout the large room. In the flickering light, the humans and Ferros would at least be able to see the plates in front of them.

Rackas Ironcog and the gold-robed Tik Deepspeaker were already seated and did not rise as the four guests were ushered to places at the long table. There would be no other diners, apparently.

"Will you join us in tea?" invited the Zhakar king as an attendant approached with a steaming pot. "It is our native beverage, favorite of all our people."

"Please forgive us," Ariakas replied. "But we have, er, *experienced* that tea in Sanction—it does not agree with the nondwarven constitution."

"Aye—nor even the constitution of the foreign dwarf," grunted Ferros Windchisel. The Hylar looked crestfallen, as if he had expected to find a cold mug of ale waiting for him.

Tale Splintersteel examined his cup, apparently expecting something like a poisonous viper to lunge forth. When the scowling king and his masked adviser hoisted their mugs, the merchant followed suit—though Ariakas thought his lips barely touched the steaming liquid.

"Our dinner," murmured the king. He raised a scabrous hand, and a file of servants came forward carrying platters of hot, aromatic food. Most of the breads and pies seemed to have a fungus base, though the Zhakar kitchens also produced a moderately sized haunch of roasted venison.

"Your hospitality is most appreciated," Ariakas said after the platters had been placed on the table. "Perhaps you will allow me the indulgence of a customary honorific?"

"You are my guest," acknowledged the king, though his moldy eyelids lowered suspiciously. He cast a look at Tik Deepspeaker. Within the gold-fringed robe, the savant's eyes glittered evilly at the human.

Ariakas rose. "My Mistress," he said reverently, "we ask your blessing of this meal in full acknowledgment of our host's generous spirit and gracious hospitality. . . ." His voice droned on, reciting a meaningless collection of pleasantries while King Ironcog tapped his fingers impatiently on the table.

As he spoke, the warrior passed his hands over the assembled platters, completing the intricate gestures of a purification spell—an incantation that would remove any toxins from food or drink.

He finished his ritual, and Ariakas smiled pleasantly at the king while he took his seat. They immediately helped themselves to the food, though the warrior noted that the Zhakar monarch and his adviser took only from a few of the platters, ignoring the meat and the pies entirely. With a nod to his companions, Ariakas reached for a helping of everything.

As they ate, Ironcog asked them several idle questions about Sanction, and even managed to speak to Ferros about Thorbardin—though he could not conceal his resentment of that elder realm. At the same time, the monarch scrutinized his guests carefully. Ironcog's eyes glittered as he watched Ariakas raise a large bite of meat to his lips, and then he blinked expectantly while the warrior chewed.

"Delicious," murmured the human truthfully. Indeed, whatever subversive preparations had been done to the food, the Zhakar had cooked a tasty collection of delicacies.

For a time, the king studied Lyrelee, who also ate with gusto, perhaps because—unlike Tale and Ferros—she understood exactly what Ariakas had done to protect them. The two dwarves, meanwhile, picked at their food after they saw the humans eating, but could not entirely mask their unease.

Rackas Ironcog, however, grew increasingly agitated as the meal continued. The king's eyes sought those of the savant, but Tik Deepspeaker kept his own gaze riveted onto his plate, saying nothing during the course of the meal. His mold-encrusted face darkened by a furious scowl, Ironcog's gaze leapt restlessly from guest to guest, searching for some signs of discomfort or weakness. Near the end of the meal, however, with everyone to all appearances well-stuffed, he muttered a curse and, scowling fiercely, made an attempt at conversation.

"You said that you came here to trade," Ironcog said smoothly. "What do you desire that you cannot obtain through our Minister of Trade in Sanction? After all, we have an extensive distribution network of arms and armor, as well as coins and other metal goods, already in operation." The king raised his eyebrows, mutely questioning Tale Splintersteel.

"We seek that which you have never traded," Ariakas began. "It is a thing you have called a curse, but it has a unique application in our temples. It is the fungus of the plague mold, which we understand inhabits the lower catacombs of Zhakar."

"The mold?" Ironcog was clearly surprised and baffled. "In truth, if we could have eradicated the stuff we would have—and now to find you have an interest in it! This is a startling development, indeed."

The king thought for a moment, and then continued. "What would you offer in exchange, should we be willing to part with this unique substance?"

"The agents of the temple have access to many sources of fine gems," Ariakas began. "Diamonds, rubies, emeralds . . . as well as numerous more mundane stones. For a start, we will offer you quarter-weight in gems for all the living mold you can ship to Sanction."

Rackas Ironcog's eyes widened slightly at the generous offer, and for a moment Ariakas wondered if he would give it serious consideration. Then the Zhakar's eyes flicked, unconsciously, to the hilt of the warrior's sword, and the human knew that the dwarven king still desired only one thing out of these negotiations.

"You have spoken of the great warrens of Zhakar," Ariakas noted politely. "Could you possibly arrange for my companions and myself to have a tour of these caverns? It would considerably enhance the negotiations, I assure you."

Rackas seemed on the verge of denying the request, scowling furiously while he apparently tried to think of a good reason for refusing. Nothing came to mind, apparently, for he remained silent for several moments. Beside him Tik Deepspeaker raised his head for the first time in many minutes. The gold threads framed a dark shadow where his face would be, though his bright eyes gleamed within. He looked at Rackas Ironcog and slowly nodded his head.

Only then did the King of Zhakar wrinkle his face into a hideous caricature of a smile, and the glimmer of an idea came to light in his eyes.

"A tour?" he mused, as if discussing a suggestion of profound wisdom. "Very well. You will get a good night's rest, of course—but then, first thing tomorrow, I shall show you the caverns of our fungus warrens."

Chapter 22
Warrens of Plague

Ariakas, sleeping very lightly, heard a noise in the anteroom beyond his chamber. Silently rising, he grasped the reassuring hilt of his sword and stepped through the door into the pitch-dark chamber. His ears strained without success to detect any further sound.

"Oh—hello, warrior." He recognized Ferros Windchisel's voice. The Hylar sounded as though he were in a foul mood.

"Couldn't sleep?" asked Ariakas.

"It's this damned itch," groused the dwarf. Ariakas heard sounds of vigorous scratching accompanied by a muffled series of curses. "It seems to be spreading," added Ferros. His voice now had a serious tenor.

"Firebug bites?" Ariakas did his best to keep his voice casual, but he felt an ominous sense of concern. The Hylar snorted and kept scratching.

Ariakas muttered his incantation, and the gemstone in his helmet—still resting on the floor where it could illuminate the room—flared into light. Ferros slouched against the wall, blinking irritably against the illumination. The warrior was shocked at the appearance of his friend, though he tried to conceal the feeling with a mask of impassivity.

Both of Ferros Windchisel's arms were red, with cracked skin flaking off around his elbows and spreading toward his wrists and shoulders. The Hylar scratched them vigorously. Far more distressing to Ariakas, however, was the new disfigurement of the dwarf's bearded face. Windchisel's right cheek was puffy and distended, with a rough growth of patchy scabs covering all the skin between his eye and his beard. In fact, some of his facial hair had tufted away, leaving the characteristic red, sore wound that Ariakas had seen on many of the faces around him during the past two days.

The warrior met his friend's frank stare, wondering only for a second if the Hylar understood what was happening to him. The bleak despair he saw was tinged with fury, confirming that Ferros Windchisel knew his fate only too well.

"I can't believe I wanted to visit this hell-hole!" snapped the dwarf, awkwardly changing the subject. "It boils my blood just to think that these little degenerates come from the same stock as the clans of Thorbardin! Why, when I see how they treat each other . . . the stupidity and violence. . . ."

The voice trailed off, and Ariakas respected Windchisel's silence. For some time they sat together, each privately recalling the events of their brief but profound friendship. Ariakas wondered about the future—would Ferros try to return to Thorbardin, running the risk of carrying the plague there? He didn't think so. The warrior resolved to himself that, when they returned to Sanction, he would see that the Hylar was given a role in the temple—something suitable to his abilities, that might somehow alleviate the pain of his self-imposed exile.

"It was that damned Fungus Mug!" spat Ferros Windchisel explosively. "That first night—it started then!"

"But you never went back there," reminded Ariakas.

"Seems like it doesn't matter," the dwarf replied. "It's plague—once it sets in, I can't fight it. I'm going to end up like these . . ." His voice trailed off into strangled silence, and for long, excruciating minutes, Ariakas felt his friend's silent pain.

"There might be something I can do . . . a chance, anyway," Ariakas began slowly. "A spell against disease could perhaps reverse the infestation."

"D'you think so?" The Hylar's eyes lit with hope, and Ariakas could only shrug.

The warrior knelt beside his companion. Bowing his head, Ariakas reached out and placed his hands over the sores on Ferros Windchisel's arm. Mouthing the ritual of healing, he called upon his Dark Queen, pleading with Takhisis for the power to heal the scabrous wounds. But the flesh remained moist and weeping beneath Ariakas's palms. Gritting his teeth in an animalistic snarl, Ariakas groped for the power, the faith, to heal the dwarf's cruel affliction. His fingers touched the rotting flesh while his words beseeched Takhisis. And still his goddess did not respond.

At last, exhausted by the effort, the warrior collapsed backward in dismay. Ferros Windchisel leaned his head against the wall, his eyes tightly shut as if in pain—though Ariakas knew it was a spiritual and not a physical hurt that sapped his friend's vitality.

An unknown time later, Lyrelee and Tale Splintersteel awakened. Both of them saw Ferros and, though the priestess's eyes widened in dismay, neither said anything about the Hylar's rapidly advancing affliction. Shortly, a column of Zhakar guards arrived, with the captain informing Ariakas that they would escort the companions to the king. Rackas Ironcog himself would show them the fungus warrens.

"This is one tour I'm not going to take," Tale Splintersteel noted as the others prepared to leave. "I have some old companions I'd like to see. I'll meet you back here before dinner."

"Very well," Ariakas agreed, not displeased to be rid of the wretched dwarf for a few hours.

The monarch of Zhakar met them as they emerged into the Promenade. The fiery glow emanating from the two large side caverns continued to cast the vast hall in a reddish hue, and Ariakas could not help but be impressed by the spectacle of the tall columns stretching up into the midnight distance. The beastlike statue framing the king's throne loomed in the darkness like a living creature, protecting—or menacing—the monarch who sat at its feet. Two ranks of the lizard-mounted cavalry flanked the walk. The beasts bowed their scaly heads in tribute as Ariakas walked past.

Rackas Ironcog sat in his great throne at the feet of the massive statue. The king wore a long, fur-covered robe, and when he rose and advanced toward his guests, the garment trailed onto the floor behind him.

"The guards will escort us," Ironcog informed them. "There are things in the warren that are not always friendly." Without elaborating, the king started toward another large cave mouth extending from the vast cavern. Ariakas noticed that Tik Deepspeaker, too, accompanied them, though the savant remained well in back of the royal party. Ariakas walked beside the king while Lyrelee and Ferros Windchisel followed along behind.

The warrior gestured to the large, smoldering cave mouth across the promenade. "It would seem that you keep large fires burning in your realm," he observed.

Rackas Ironcog nodded. "The passages beyond that cavern extend to the very bowels of Krynn!" he boasted. "From far below, the flames of the great Lavasea itself rise to warm Zhakar."

"A sea—beneath your city?"

"Indeed. That fiery lake is the source of the fire and lava throughout the Khalkists—and we dwell nearest its heart!"

They passed into the small cavern opposite the great, smoldering cave mouth and followed a chiseled stone corridor.

"We have a long descent—though not nearly so far down as the Lavasea," the king informed them as they reached one of the metal cages signifying a lift station. An advance company of the guards, about ten warriors, descended first, and while the group waited for the cage to return, Rackas Ironcog did some explaining.

"The warrens of Zhakar are an extensive network of caves and caverns, mostly dating back before the Cataclysm. The network is divided into three sections, with the nearest of them the lizard warrens. There we raise the creatures you've seen around here."

"They look like good mounts," Ariakas noted. The potential speed and power of the subterranean steeds had indeed struck him as very impressive. If the Zhakar could somehow be allied with his draconian horde, the warrior calculated that a company of lizard riders would make an excellent strike force.

"Good food, too. You've seen the warclaws up here— they're the ones that our most accomplished fighters use. But there are far more of the fastclaws—rarely ridden, but commonly used for meat."

"I see," Ariakas muttered, none too taken with the notion of a reptilian repast.

"The second warren is the water warren," the king continued. "It serves as the great cistern of our kingdom

—a reserve that would last us for many years of drought, should the mountains dry up overhead."

"And then there are the fungus warrens?" guessed the human warrior.

"Aye. They were begun as the primary food source of Zhakar, and many of their chambers still serve as useful farming quadrants. Here, for example, we grow the mushrooms from which we brew our tea. The drink provides the only relief we get from the discomfort caused by the mold plague. But I gather that you are not interested in the fungus we use for food?"

"No—it is the one that has caused your plague that we desire." Still, Ariakas thought, at least that explained why the Zhakar forced themselves to drink the stinking tea he'd first noticed in the Fungus Mug.

If the king had any questions as to why these visitors were interested in such a product, he gave no indication. Instead, when the empty lift cage finally returned to their level, he gestured them forward. Another ten guards waited while the royal party entered. "They'll follow us down," King Ironcog explained.

"If you think it's necessary," Ariakas replied coolly. "Though you'll find that we can take care of ourselves pretty nicely."

The significance of the remark wasn't lost on the Zhakar ruler, who looked meaningfully at the mighty sword worn on the warrior's back. "Of course—of course!" he agreed. "But you must understand—as your host, I simply couldn't allow any threat to be offered to your person while you are the guest of my kingdom."

"Your solicitude is very reassuring," Ariakas said wryly, wondering if the king in fact desired the guards to protect himself from his guests. Of course, the warrior meant what he'd told Whez Lavastone the day before—he was nobody's assassin. He would deal with the monarch of Zhakar and leave it to the dwarves to settle the issue of who their ruler was to be. At the same time, of course, he would not hesitate to respond quickly and violently to any overt treachery on Rackas Ironcog's part.

The cage rattled downward through the shaft in the rock until it finally clanked to a halt on a solid stone floor. Guards outside the lift threw the cage door open, and the four passengers emerged into the warrens.

Immediately Ariakas was struck by the pungent scent in the air. In a way it reminded him of the Fungus Mug back in Sanction, though the stench here was far more overpowering—and yet, somehow, at the same time more *natural*. It was as if the entire cavern had been steeped in the stuff of the bitter Zhakar mushroom tea, yet all the liquid had been poured away, leaving only pervasive and strong-smelling dregs.

In addition to the odor, the air was extremely humid. Somewhere not too far away they heard a gentle lapping of waves against a stone shore, and Ariakas suspected that the water warrens were very nearby. Still, the light from his glowing gem showed nothing more than a surrounding cave of slick, wet rock. Several passages led in different directions.

"This way," said Rackas Ironcog, leading them toward one of the passages. Avoiding the king's trailing robe, Ariakas fell into step beside him, while his companions followed behind. Ironcog paused only long enough to let the file of warriors precede them into the darkness, while the rattling of the lift behind them announced that the Zhakar of the rear guard had arrived in the warrens. The cage door opened and the other warriors emerged and followed.

A steady, rhythmic drumming pulsed in the corridor before them, seeming to come from very near at hand. "What's that?" Ariakas inquired, as soon as he heard the noise.

"Don't worry," the king reassured him. "It's a pair of my drummers in the vanguard. We like to announce our presence so that some of the, er, less cooperative inhabitants of the warrens know we're coming. It gives them the chance to get out of our way, and avoids an unpleasant encounter for all concerned."

"What sort of inhabitants are you talking about?" wondered the human.

The dwarven monarch did not elaborate.

For a long time they marched through the darkness to the steady beat of the drums. Around them dripped stalactites and columns of natural rock. The spires of stalagmites often rose toward the ceiling like gargantuan fangs. Water trickled here and there through these warrens, and the dank, moldy smell continued to grow stronger.

Often they passed large patches of fungus, where mushrooms had sprouted on a surface of wet rock or within the smooth silt of a clear, shallow pool. All in all, this cavern network seemed more *alive* than any subterranean location Ariakas had ever seen—including the lair of the Shilo-Thahn.

Abruptly the drums grew louder, the beat a trifle faster. When Ariakas raised his eyebrows in silent question, the king dismissed his concern with a casual gesture. "We are approaching the growing warrens. This is the place where we have to be most cautious."

The warrior checked the rank of Zhakar before them. The dwarven guards held weapons at the ready, except for the two drummers. Looking behind, he saw that the rear guard, too, marched as if they expected trouble at any minute.

The cavern narrowed and began to twist and wind. The sound of the drums muffled slightly as the foremost dwarves passed around a corner of the cave. Ariakas's senses suddenly tingled in alarm, and he turned to cast a quick look at his companions. Ferros Windchisel scowled suspiciously while Lyrelee returned his look with concern.

Then with a silence as abrupt as a physical blow, the

pounding drumbeats ceased.

"Look out!" shouted Ariakas as he saw sudden movement behind his companions. Shocked, he realized that the words had made no sound—even in his own ears! He yelled another warning—*nothing!*

Tik Deepspeaker, from behind Lyrelee, raised his hands and uttered a short chant, though Ariakas heard no sound. The priestess whirled, stumbling into a stone outcrop, and the warrior realized that the savant had blinded her. Grasping his sword, Ariakas instantly heard the cacophony of battle around him—as in the Fireplaza, the touch of the potent weapon had broken the spell of magical attack.

Before he could strike, Ariakas saw a Zhakar rush toward Lyrelee's exposed back, stabbing brutally. Desperately, the priestess whirled away and lashed with a foot that sent her attacker staggering against the wall. Ariakas touched the hilt of his blade to the priestess's shoulder. She blinked and focused her eyes, once again able to see.

Zhakar rushed from all sides. Ariakas cut down a pair, then lunged toward the king. His blow was brought up short when he glimpsed a Zhakaran spear carrier who darted past him and thrust his weapon into Lyrelee's side. The priestess grunted and staggered. Ariakas chopped downward, splitting the skull of the murderous dwarf. Lyrelee fell forward and lay motionless on the ground amid a growing stain of blood.

Ferros was luckier—he raised an arm and took a treacherous hit on his metal wrist plate. Still, the blow knocked the Hylar backward, where he almost tumbled into Ariakas.

Snarling in fury, the human warrior whirled toward the robed king. The Zhakar monarch shrieked and darted down the passage, but Ariakas chopped savagely, propelling his sword through a vicious overhead swing. The gleaming blue blade chopped through the regal robe and into the shoulder beneath. The terrified Zhakar went down, his left arm hanging uselessly at his side. Vaguely Ariakas sensed the rest of the royal guard fleeing down the corridor, but he focused on the pathetic creature at his feet. The warrior kicked sharply and knocked the wretch over, finally hauling him free of the robe. The mold-encrusted face of a Zhakar stared at him, eyes wide in terror—but Ariakas could not suppress a shout of pure rage.

The dwarf before him was not the king!

In fury Ariakas ran the trembling creature through, casting the dead body aside as if it were an empty flagon of beer. In the seconds before the ambush, he realized, Rackas Ironcog must have arranged for this pathetic fool to take his place, allowing the king to escape with the rest of the dwarves.

Where were they? He suddenly realized that the corridor was empty of Zhakar. The guards before and behind them had vanished into the darkness. Ariakas felt certain he would hear the dwarves if they remained in the same cave. Furious, he realized they must have escaped through a secret passage.

He saw Lyrelee's body, lying facedown in a spreading pool of blood. He knelt and gently turned her over, knowing she was dead—but still, the dull vacancy in her half-opened eyes tore at him like a physical wound.

"Bastards!" he hissed, his eyes searching for a Zhakar—any Zhakar—on whom to vent his fury. He looked at the woman's corpse, thinking of the pleasures that body had given him, before his rage drove him restlessly to his feet.

He heard a groan and turned to the gasping figure of Ferros Windchisel.

"My eyes! They gouged my eyes out!" blurted the dwarf, his voice cracking in despair.

Ariakas looked at his friend, seeing that—though patches of mold already caked his cheeks—the Hylar's eyes were fine. He leaned forward, touching the hilt of the great sword to Ferros Windchisel's chest, breaking the spell of blindness. The Hylar blinked quickly, and groaned.

"Well, okay—they *didn't* gouge my eyes out," he admitted, sitting up and wincing in pain.

"How bad is it?" Ariakas asked.

"Bastard broke my wrist," grunted the Hylar. "Not my axe arm, though."

"Here—I'll help," the human offered. He reached over and placed his hands on the wounded wrist. Closing his eyes, Ariakas tried to conjure up the image of Takhisis, to plead with her for a spell of healing. Instead, that great well of fury opened up. Burned by the rising flames of rage, his faith would not, *could* not, summon the help of his goddess. With a muffled curse, he sat back on his heels, defeated.

"I can still walk!" declared the dwarf.

"Good—we'd better do some of that."

Cursing softly in teeth-gritting pain, Ferros Windchisel rose to his feet. At the sight of Lyrelee's lifeless body he winced, and then looked at the human.

"Can't take her along," Ariakas said coldly. "I think we'll have to fight our way out of here."

"You got that feeling too?" Ferros grunted wryly.

"Still—I don't know *who* we're supposed to fight." Ariakas gestured to the empty tunnels around them.

But Ferros wasn't listening. Instead, the Hylar raised a cautionary hand and concentrated on the passage before them. The human froze, and in the silence Ariakas heard it too: a squishy kind of noise, repeated rhythmically.

Turning his glowing gem toward the approaching sound, Ariakas strained to see the source. His sword felt light, ready in his hands . . . but still he remained stubbornly committed to saving the blue blade. Whatever now approached, they would face it with mortal muscle and keen steel.

Ferros looked questioningly at the weapon, but when Ariakas shook his head the dwarf shrugged and hefted his heavy axe. He wielded the weapon one-handed, whipping it nimbly through a series of arcs and slices.

"By Reorx—what *is* that thing?" demanded the Hylar after a short pause. Ariakas could see nothing beyond the fringes of his light spell.

Then, something moved—something *huge*. A great, bloated shape came into view, advancing by the side-to-side rolling of two massive, trunklike feet. The body swelled into a distended, oblong sphere that was covered all over with scabby patches of mold and fungus.

"It's like some kind of huge *plant!*" gasped Ferros, his eyes wide with amazement.

Lumbering on the huge pads, the bloblike creature continued resolutely forward. The thing seemed to have no limbs other than those blunt, elephantine feet, though its size alone made it a formidable threat. Ariakas advanced, raising the azure blade, aiming a strike at the midpoint of the long body.

Abruptly something hammered into the side of his head, smashing him sideways into the cavern wall. His heart pounded in panic as he heard the clash of his sword clattering loose on the stone floor. Before he could stoop down, another blow struck his head, bashing a deep cut into his chin and hurling him backward, past Ferros Windchisel, to collapse flat on his back.

"What hit you?" asked the Hylar, advancing with his axe raised as Ariakas scrambled to his feet.

Frantically the man looked for the sword, seeing one of the fungus creature's monstrous feet trudge over it. Then he saw the source of the attack. Along the monster's tough skin dangled a series of long, supple tendrils. They blended so well that at first he'd thought they were just part of the body—but now he saw one snap loose with the speed of a whiplash.

The tip of the tentacle was a hardened ball, the size of

a large fist. This blunt end crashed into the side of Ferros Windchisel's thigh, drawing a cry of pain from the normally taciturn fighter. The Hylar went down, his leg jutting sideways at an unnatural angle.

Then the monster stepped past the sword and loomed overhead. Ariakas dived forward, tumbling to the floor and somersaulting around the monster's lumbering feet. He felt immeasurable relief as his hands closed around the hilt of his weapon—but then his consciousness reeled as a smashing blow took him full in the chest. Gasping for air, Ariakas stumbled away from the hulking creature. Ferros Windchisel flailed on the ground as Ariakas lunged forward. A tentacle lashed, and the man chopped with his sword, almost severing the tough, woody limb. Charging past the monster, he whirled and struck again, halting the bloated beast before it could crush the immobilized dwarf.

"Thanks, warrior," grunted the Hylar as Ariakas's whirling slashes and feints drove the creature back a step.

But the shapeless creature held its ground. When Ariakas pressed, it was the human who retreated before dazzling blows—any one of which would have crushed bone, had it landed.

Then they saw another reason for the creature's relentless and dauntless advance—it could be certain of help. In the dim limits of the gem light, but growing closer with each step, came another pair of the resolute plant-monsters. Beyond them, lost in the shadows, advanced the forms of many more.

Chapter 23
Flight of Despair

Ariakas desperately chopped at the monster's encrusted skin, halting the lumbering advance long enough to hoist the Hylar in his arms. Together the pair staggered down the corridor, away from the plodding horrors. The warrior cast a last look at Lyrelee's body, seeing the leading fungus creature kick the corpse aside with its huge foot. Then he ran for all he was worth, his lungs gulping air desperately, his legs pumping to carry them away from the monsters.

It seemed like hours later when he collapsed, falling against the cave wall and slumping to the ground, Ferros tumbling free beside him. The dwarf gasped, too—but not from exhaustion. The pale sheen of sweat across the dwarf's brow and the pallid cast of his skin told Ariakas that his companion was in profound pain. The Hylar scraped listlessly at his skin, which came off in great, flaking clumps.

"What about the sword—can you fry these swamp-muckers with it?" Ferros hissed through teeth clenched with agony.

"No—I can't use the blue blade!" Ariakas retorted, shaking his head in frustration.

The Hylar didn't reply, turning instead to look down the corridor they had used in their flight. Bulky forms moved in the shadows, and he didn't have to see more to know that the pursuers advanced with relentless determination.

"Go on—without me!" gasped the Hylar. "It's the only way you'll get away!"

Ariakas remained silent, watching the nearest of the hulking monsters shamble into the fringe of light from his spell. He couldn't bring himself to look at Ferros Windchisel—perhaps because he knew the dwarf was right.

"Look, warrior—I came in search of a dwarven kingdom in the Khalkists," the Hylar said, his tone growing firm as he banished the pain to some distant part of his awareness. "I wanted to find this place—and now it claims me."

"Their treachery will be avenged," Ariakas promised, surprised at how dull his own voice sounded.

"That's not what I'm talking about!" snapped Ferros, before squeezing his eyes shut as a spasm of pain racked his battered body. "It's this: if you meet a Thorbardin dwarf sometime, get them this word—there *are* no dwarves in the Khalkists! None worthy of the name, at least—none who could ever serve as allies of Thorbardin."

Again Ferros ceased talking, his breath coming in short, rapid pants. Ariakas looked at the grotesque forms of the monsters. The first had halted temporarily, allowing its companions to join it. Then, in a bunched and menacing group, they clumped steadily closer.

The Hylar opened his eyes, and stared fixedly at Ariakas when the human met his gaze. "When Thorbardin meets Zhakar," he growled, his voice taut with fury, "it will be not as allies, but as enemies. And that's a thing I'd just as soon not live to see!"

"Come on," Ariakas said gruffly. His muscles shrieked in protest at the thought, but he rose stiffly to his feet and reached for Ferros.

"No—get going!" shouted the dwarf, holding his axe in his good hand. His smashed leg jutted awkwardly to the side, and a growing pool of blood marked the floor around him. Seated with his back against an outcrop of the cavern wall, Ferros turned to face the advancing monsters—barely a few steps away now.

"*Move!*" cried Ferros Windchisel, his voice shrill with agony and rage. "Don't make my *death* a waste, too!"

With those words ringing in his ears, Ariakas turned and sprinted away. From somewhere his heart and lungs found the energy to fuel his flight. His boots pounded the floor, not loud enough to overwhelm the recrimination ringing in his mind.

He turned down a passageway, blindly lunging in the direction that he thought might take him back to the water warrens. Where had the Zhakar turned from here? Ariakas couldn't remember, so he guessed, still sprinting along the dank, stone-walled passages of the deep warrens.

Another turn, another winding cavern. This one didn't seem familiar—Ariakas sensed that he ran down a gradually descending passage, and he didn't remember doing any climbing on the way in. Still, he couldn't arrest his flight, didn't even want to take the time to see if the monsters still pursued.

Finally he paused, leaning against the stone wall and

gasping for air until his breathing rasped into mere panting. By the time he could hear anything aside from himself, the telltale noise of the fungus creatures' advance reached him down the corridor, urging him once more into flight.

Gradually, as he ran, fatigue settled into the background. He pounded along without noticing the tearing pain in his lungs, the dry hacking of his throat. Instead, his mind focused directly, to the point of obsession, on one thing:

The Zhakar would pay. He would start with the pathetic excuse for a monarch, Rackas Ironcog, but his vengeance would continue long after that lone villain was dead. The savant, Tik Deepspeaker, deserved to die in agony. The entire people, the entire nation, he vowed, would suffer for the treachery with which they had greeted the emissaries of the Dark Queen.

When first he had arrived in the dwarven kingdom, Ariakas had intended to forge a treaty with the Zhakar, to work out an arrangement of trade that would be profitable to both sides. No more. Now he would bargain as master, as conqueror. He would dictate the terms of the agreement, and personally—and gleefully—kill any plague-pocked dwarf who objected to the oppressive conditions!

How he would gain this mastery was a detail that, for the moment, he did not address. It was salve to his spirit merely to make the determination that he *would* have vengeance! Whether it was the weapon in his hand that would smite them, or the force of an army arrayed beneath Ariakas's command, or some other agent of power and destruction, the dwarves of Zhakar would learn the folly of their betrayal.

The grim determination sustained his endurance well beyond the point of exhaustion, and when he at last slowed the frantic pace of his flight, he felt not only physically fresh, but spiritually renewed. He sensed the will of the Dark Queen in the resurgence of his strength, and took the time to pause for a moment.

His fury at Lyrelee's death had already faded; like the lady in the tower, half a lifetime ago, she had now become merely a pleasant memory from his past. At first, the rapid waning of his grief seemed cold and brutal, but soon Ariakas saw with clarity that Takhisis protected, watched over *him!* Any others were extraneous, tools intended to help him work the Dark Queen's will.

Even Ferros Windchisel? Was *he* extraneous? The question insinuated itself into his mind. He twisted the notion this way and that for mere seconds before he knew the answer.

Yes. Even Ferros.

"My Queen, I remain your servant," Ariakas whispered, the words coming from the depths of his soul. "Your tool, your slave—but please, I beg you! Grant me the power to smite these miserable worms!"

With that prayer ringing in his mind, Ariakas became aware that the caverns of Zhakar were absolutely still and silent around him. He had long ago left the realms of the fungus warrens, and though the stone walls near him dripped with moisture, he saw no sign of mushroom or mold. He was thoroughly lost.

Now that he began to piece together the fragmented memories of his long run, Ariakas had a vague sense that he had descended far, far below the original level of the warrens. Perhaps he had chosen the speed of downhill flight, or perhaps he had instinctively fled away from the population of hideous dwarves dwelling in the subterranean city above him.

Whatever the reason, Ariakas knew that he was deeper in the bedrock of Krynn than he had ever been before. He felt a momentary surge of panic when he realized that his light spell had been burning for many hours—but then, like a soothing presence, he felt the aura of his goddess, and the knowledge that she would not let him languish in darkness. At least, not now . . . not when he was so close. . . .

The knowledge struck him like a hammer blow. It was a thing that he sensed in the very air around him, sensed with a certainty that made him angry for not realizing it sooner.

In the heart of the world. . . .

Somewhere nearby, somewhere down in these sunless depths, there was a thing Takhisis wanted him to find—a thing that would . . . *set fire to the sky!* It was *she* who had brought him here, not the mindless urgings of his own panic.

He felt a flood of relief, rising on a tide of determination. She had brought him this far—he would do the rest. Grimly he grasped his sword, starting cautiously through the underground darkness, allowing the clean wash of light from his gemstone to highlight every chiseled stalagmite, every slime-coated rock and mirrorlike pool.

Ariakas moved with the innate caution of the veteran warrior—but he was a warrior on the attack, unafraid to commit himself to a dangerous course. He advanced through the tunnel until he reached a narrow fissure, where erosion had created a steeply sloping channel down and to the left. Without hesitation he turned from the main corridor into this narrow crack, sliding between closely pressed walls of stone, ignoring the knowledge that every step took him farther away from sunlight and fresh air.

Rock pressed close overhead. The ravine formed a long tunnel running downward for a hundred feet. Halfway down it, Ariakas slipped on some sand and slid his battering way along. He almost spilled out the end of the niche before yawning blackness warned him of peril. His hands reached out to the walls on either side, and with his boots already extending from the gaping end of the passage, he arrested his slide.

Carefully he reversed his position, leaning his head outward and allowing the gemstone to illuminate his surroundings. He saw that the ravine terminated on the precipitous side of a vast, lightless cavern. A few pebbles tumbled outward as he shifted his grip, and he heard them bounce and rattle for a long time. Immediately below him, a crack in the wall extended straight down, creating a narrow shaft in the subterranean cliff. He thought that, just maybe, he could descend that chute without tumbling free. The rocky sides were close enough together for him to brace his arms, and numerous boulders seemed to be wedged in its base. These would serve as footholds—presuming, of course, they were wedged securely enough not to break free in a rockslide.

Nevertheless, the compulsion to descend, to move deeper into the realm of rock and fundament, left him no room for alternatives. The winding crack behind led nowhere but up, and Ariakas had no interest in time-consuming detours.

Instead, he reversed his position again, and lowered his feet out of the crack, keeping a grip with his hands until he could kick downward and stand upon one of those wedged boulders. He lowered his body and began to step carefully downward, his hands firmly braced against either side of this narrow chute.

When he looked out into the cavern, his tiny light was swallowed by an apparently infinite expanse of darkness. His footstep knocked a rock free. The stone struck somewhere close below with a sharp *crack*. The echo of the sound did not reach him for several seconds. Then, however, the sound was repeated for a thrumming minute or two, ricocheting back and forth through a vast and resonant space.

Abruptly the rocks beneath his feet slipped away in a clattering cascade, and Ariakas smashed onto his back, skidding madly down the chute. His hands clawed for support, finding only blunt rock. Each foot kicked at the rocks below, but these merely tumbled free and joined the landslide.

Ariakas twisted this way and that, grasping for anything to stop this uncontrolled plunge. A sharp rock jabbed him in the knee, but he managed to grab it as he slid downward. Then another large stone smashed him in the face, drawing blood from his nose and breaking the desperate grip of his fingers.

The sounds of the rockslide grew to a crescendo around him, and Ariakas sensed that the chute grew steeper. For one sickening moment he tumbled into space, free, scrambling to remain upright. Then he smashed with stunning force into a solid surface. Something flat partially supported him, but he felt himself slipping aside. For a second he teetered at the brink of a precipice. Rocks crashed past him, smashing his hands as he tried to grab something, anything. His feet kicked free, followed by his torso, and then his fingers found a crack. Wedging them inward with bone-crushing force, Ariakas at last arrested his fall, though most of his body remained suspended in black, yawning space.

Gasping for breath, the man tried to blink the dust from his eyes. He kicked a foot upward to the side, catching his boot on the lip he clung to by his fingertips. Then, with extreme effort, he scrambled upward to sit on a narrow shelf of rock. His helmet had remained strapped to his head, and now he flashed the gem light around.

Ariakas quickly realized that he was in a very dire predicament. The ledge was narrow—perhaps three feet wide—and only a dozen paces long. Below it, the subterranean cliff plunged away, a sheer descent into darkness, while an equally precipitous wall loomed overhead. Even the chute he had descended became, in the last approach to this ledge, a plummeting chimney that offered no route for climbing back up.

In discouragement, Ariakas turned his light outward,

where it was swallowed in the vastness of dark, subterranean space. He saw nothing beyond this bare cliff, a narrow perch that might let him walk a few steps in either direction. In frustration he kicked at the loose rocks on the ledges, sending them plunging into the depths, listening with awe as the sounds of their fall reached him a long time later.

Suddenly the bedrock shuddered, and the air resounded with a loud *crack*. The ledge shook, and Ariakas fell to his side, madly scrambling for a handhold. Perched on the edge again, he stared downward—then blinked in surprise.

There was *light* down there! A great distance away, something huge seethed and glowed, casting out a dim but steadily growing illumination. The brightness was an ember-red in color, though it seemed to be filtered through some kind of haze.

Quickly he clapped his hand over the glowing gem, completely screening the light—and he could *still* see. In fact, with the gem light covered, he could clearly discern the somber, crimson glow, rising from the depths below. It was as though he stared into a deep well, at the bottom of which smoldered a smoky fire. Thick vapors obscured the air, writhing back and forth, disturbed by currents and updrafts. Within the dense cloud there flamed an unmistakable suggestion of great heat—heat like the Lavaflow River of Sanction, or even the molten hearts of the Lords of Doom.

In the illumination of that hellish fire, as his eyes gradually became accustomed to the vast darkness, Ariakas looked across the cavern. He felt a sense of wonder that rapidly grew into awe. He might have been sitting on the slope of some immense mountain, looking at sister peaks around the range, for all the immensity of the setting— except that these were peaks that leaned inward, coming together far above in a vast dome of rock—a false sky overhead.

Vast, rough surfaces of stone were outlined in the reddish glow, underlit like great, drooping faces gathering around a dim and dying fire. The massive scope of this place made Ariakas feel like a tiny bug, an insignificant insect on the wall of a great castle.

Only after several minutes of awestruck gawking did he realize that something obstructed his view across the expanse. He saw that, midway between himself and the opposite wall of the cylindrical cavern, a shadowy grid structure seemed to float in the air.

His eyes adjusted further, and he saw long, spidery beams, extending outward from the cavern walls to reach the skeletonlike shape.

For a long time Ariakas studied the form, and gradually he discerned that it was a cage. Something huge, impossibly vast, lay within that cage, trapped by iron bars that ringed it on all sides, above and below as well.

Then, with a great stretching of wings and tail, the *thing* moved. It raised a long neck, uncurled huge, talon-studded claws . . . and Ariakas knew beyond doubt that a dragon had returned to Krynn.

Chapter 24
Tombfyre

Ariakas first felt stark, numbing terror—a weakness that penetrated muscle and bone, threatening to turn his legs to jelly. The dragon remained motionless, but its very presence bombarded the man's sensibilities. Suddenly, and for the first time in his adult life, Ariakas felt puny, weak, and insignificant.

Slowly the serpent lowered its head, settling the great wings against its sides. Ariakas studied it for a long time, and finally found himself wondering if it had ever moved at all. Yes, he assured himself—it had.

The immensity of the creature astounded him. The sublime power and grace of the mighty body held him in thrall, so overwhelmed him that he knew nothing other than a vague sense of awe. The fact that the monster was apparently confined in some kind of cage made no difference—it seemed to Ariakas that the wyrm could bend those bars with a tug of its claws, or melt them with a gout of fiery breath.

For a long time—hours, at the very least—Ariakas sat still, enraptured by the magnificent creature before him. After that initial spreading of its wings, the dragon lapsed into repose. It might have been a statue, suspended in that great cage in the center of the vast cavern.

The smoldering light from below continued to grow in intensity—or else Ariakas's eyes developed a dark sense more keen than they had ever previously displayed. In any event, he began to discern details about the huge, serpentine wyrm.

The dragon was covered with a surface of rippling scales, bright red in color. In the reflected glow of the seething fires, the monster's scales gleamed individually, as if illuminated by a thousand pale, internal flames. A huge mane of wiry dark hair encircled the massive head, giving the creature an appearance of great age and supreme wisdom.

Through this inspection the serpent's great eyes remained shut, and Ariakas could discern no movement of the creature's flanks or nostrils—nothing to indicate that it lived. But the memory of that flexing of wings remained with him, the most spectacular gesture he had ever beheld.

Ariakas forgot that he was trapped here, with no apparent means of escape. All of his attention remained rapt on the mighty serpent—the being whose very presence had so terrified and confounded him. Yet as the hours passed and his terror faded, he began to feel empathy for the creature. It was not pity, but more a sense of shared outrage that a noble beast should be so ignobly imprisoned.

The frame of the cage was barely bigger than the huge

wyrm. Ariakas saw now that it did not float in the air. Instead, four girders extended outward from the enclosure to brace it against the walls of the vast chamber. Each of these was a wiry beam more than a thousand feet long. One of these braces connected to the cavern wall several dozen feet to the side of the human's narrow ledge.

No longer fearing the beast, Ariakas studied that beam, wondering if it offered him some avenue off of this ledge. Though he could follow his narrow perch to within thirty feet of the heavy iron structure, the rest of the distance was a sheer surface of slick rock. If it had any slope to it at all, the cliff leaned outward, creating a slight overhang. He had no doubts that if he attempted to reach the girder, any further step would result in a fatal plunge.

Angrily he paced, carefully pivoting on the narrow shelf at either end of the ledge. He could not believe that his destiny had brought him here to starve, or to make this great discovery and then perish before he could share the truth with the world.

Dragons lived! The Dark Queen's legions would again march across Krynn. As the realization sank in, the warrior made a solemn promise to himself—*he*, Highlord Ariakas, would live to ride at their head! In furious determination, he reached over his shoulder and drew the great sword, brandishing it upward in a gesture of determination and defiance.

"I will escape! I will serve my queen!" he cried, his voice surging back and forth in the huge cavern. For long seconds the words came back to him, a staggered series of echoes.

"Who . . . is there?"

The deep, booming question was spoken in a strangely hesitant voice, as if the speaker's lips and tongue had not been used in a considerably long time. Nevertheless, Ariakas had no doubt as to who had spoken.

"It is *I!*" the human boasted to the dragon, watching

the great head rise from its platform. "I am the Highlord Ariakas—loyal champion of Takhisis, and master of the armies that shall march in her name!"

"Impressive, indeed," thrummed the dragon's voice, the tone rich with respect. Now Ariakas saw the gleam of two huge eyes, each a yellow orb tinged with crimson by the infernal fires below. "I am honored to be joined by such an illustrious visitor."

Nothing in the dragon's tone indicated irony, but suddenly Ariakas was struck by the ludicrousness of his own braggadocio. "How are you called, great dragon?" he asked in a tone considerably more humble.

"In the age of the Dragon Wars, I was known as Tombfyre," replied the monster. "Though I suspect that was a very long time ago. In truth, it has been more than an age since I last opened my eyes."

Ariakas's heart quickened. Again he felt that tingling of destiny—a self-assurance that he would not perish, alone and forgotten, in this place.

"Why do you awaken now?" he asked.

The dragon shook his mighty head thoughtfully, the great mane swaying back and forth like a regal robe. "I don't . . . it was the *queen*! She called to me in my sleep, and I obeyed! She has *not* forgotten me!"

"The queen speaks to you—to both of us—through *this*!" Ariakas brandished his sword, and the dragon's sinuous neck raised the great wedge of his head. Clearly interested, Tombfyre regarded the human with new respect.

"Why did you come here, warrior?" inquired the red dragon, his voice a soft hiss.

Suddenly Ariakas knew the answer.

"I came because of this weapon—and the will of our mistress! Because of her prophecy: *In the heart of the world, it will set fire to the sky!*"

Again he raised the sword, and now he began to wonder if he had guessed its purpose, understood now the importance of the blue blade.

"I, too, was given a prophecy," the dragon observed quietly, his deep voice tinged with an incongruous note of awe. "When we were defeated by Huma and his infernal lances, the queen bade us leave Krynn, to languish in exile and banishment beyond the memories of men.

"But when we departed the world," Tombfyre continued, "she made us several promises. Our exile would be long, she warned us—but it would *not* be forever. And as she sent me here, to this lonely prison, she gave a promise for my ears alone."

"What—what did she tell you?" demanded Ariakas, his nerves taut with excitement.

"She said that I had served her well . . . pleased her. When I awakened, she would have a special role for me. When it came time for her call, she would send me the highest of her agents—her champion. Together we would fly, and I would carry him in a blaze of fire through the heavens!"

"Why are you imprisoned, then—held in a cage?" asked the human.

"The champion of Takhisis would release me," claimed the serpent.

"Can't you bend the bars? Melt them with your breath?"

Tombfyre sighed. "I tried, before I slept. These bars are an alloy of copper and iron, too strong even for my muscles. When I breathed, the fire just flowed around the metal—it didn't weaken it."

Suddenly Ariakas remembered a tale from his temple lessons, and in a flash of insight he understood. It *was* the blue blade!

"I ask you for your pledge, Tombfyre Reddragon," Ariakas said solemnly. "When I release you, you will take me from this place and serve me, as we serve the queen who has given us life and power! Will you make this promise?"

"I am not a servile creature," Tombfyre said carefully. "Nor do I see how you might release me from this cage. I will grant you this, should you find a way to break these bars that bind me: I will carry you from this place and aid you in your battles against the enemies of Takhisis. As you command her hosts, I shall command her dragons—and together, we will conquer all who stand in our way!"

"It will not be my power that releases you—it shall be the queen herself," Ariakas countered. "And in that power you will see the destiny that brings us together. No, indeed—you are not a servile creature. You will serve only in the same way as I—in the acknowledgment that in Takhisis we prostrate ourselves before a might that makes puny any power on all this world."

"Agreed, Highlord Ariakas," replied Tombfyre. "I give you my pledge of alliance—if I am released from my cage."

Ariakas stood at the edge of his narrow platform, closest to the place where the metal girder met the cavern wall. Carefully, reverently, he raised the blue blade, utterly confident now of the Dark Queen's will—and of her power, as it would be made manifest by his sword.

"Hear me, O Queen," he murmured. "And show us thy will!"

A brilliant flash exploded in the vast chamber, followed by a sharp clap of sound. The explosion crackled, and Ariakas saw a bolt of energy—like a furious blast of lightning—hiss into the iron strut that spanned the yawning space to the dragon's cage.

The roaring clap of noise created a sustained echo in the cavernous space, but that was nothing compared to the brilliant flare of searing, sputtering fire that took root in the long beam of iron. Where the lightning bolt had struck, the metal began to glow—red, then yellow, and finally a pure white that glared like a desert sun, forcing Ariakas to turn his eyes away.

The light sizzled along the length of the girder in a cascade of smoke and sparks as it streaked toward the caged dragon. Glowing embers trailed from the rippling explosion, and Ariakas smelled a pungent, burned odor in the air all around him.

In an instant the eruption of power reached the cage, and the entire structure of bars stood outlined in glaring, searing light. Within the grid, the huge dragon cringed against the floor, trying to duck away from the fuming, sparking magic surrounding him.

Then, with a burst of sound that swallowed the echoes of the lightning bolt, the metal frame exploded. Pieces of glowing iron showered the vast cavern, some of them landing on the ledge beside Ariakas, while many more tumbled into the smoking depths below. The sound of that destructive explosion boomed deafeningly back and forth, the caverns seeming to growl with the voice of the world. Then slowly the chaos died away.

Ariakas kept his eyes glued to the mighty serpent. Tombfyre tumbled free as the cage shattered. Once again the warrior saw those vast wings unfurl. This time, unconfined, they spread wide, the joints creaking stiffly, and when the serpent struck them downward they swirled a gust of wind that reached Ariakas like a cooling breeze.

The dragon dived, wheeling gracefully to the left and gliding through a full circle in the vast cavern. Then, as he approached the ledge where Ariakas awaited, the dragon craned his neck upward and, with a dip of his tail, swooped up to the narrow shelf of rock, to the very feet of the highlord.

The human held his breath. The dragon had been freed—but would the mighty creature keep his word? Tombfyre turned those huge eyes, now glowing a brilliant sheen of yellow, toward Ariakas. The dragon bellowed, a triumphant, exultant sound of pleasure, power, and promise.

Tombfyre seized the ledge with his front claws, wings beating powerfully as his iron-hard talons cut into the crumbling stone. For a full second Ariakas stared into those huge eyes, seeing the long, slitted irises cutting vertically through the yellow pupils. Then, with just a trace of a mocking smile on the broad, tooth-studded snout, the red dragon dipped his head in a dignified bow.

Ariakas again felt overwhelming awe. He stood still, holding his great sword. Idly, he noticed that the blade was now green—a rich, verdant color like the foliage of a tropical grotto. It was, he reflected, a very beautiful color. Now the weapon seemed more like an icon than a tool, and he gently, reverently, resheathed it.

Again Tombfyre beat his powerful wings, and the human saw the great dragon's sinews tighten in his forearms and shoulders. Too heavy to hover, the creature struggled hard to maintain its position in the air.

Impetuously, Ariakas stepped onto the great, taloned forefoot. The serpentine neck rose to meet him, forming a handrail to his side as he walked along the taut, muscular foreleg, barely conscious of the infinite drop yawning below. Grasping a handful of the dragon's wiry mane, the man slipped around the great shoulder, coming to rest in a natural depression between the roots of the creature's massive wings.

Still holding the tufts of mane, Ariakas smiled grimly when Tombfyre turned his head to meet his rider's gaze. The dragon's mouth, too, split into a cruel grin, and a long, forked tongue snaked from between the reptilian lips.

Then, with a forceful shove, Tombfyre pushed away from the precipitous ledge. For a brief moment Ariakas felt weightless, and only his hands tightly gripping the mane prevented him tumbling into the abyss below. But abruptly the dragon's wings thrust downward, biting into the air and firmly settling the human in his natural saddle.

With another powerful wing beat, the crimson dragon curled them into a fast glide, and then they were climbing higher and higher, spiraling upward . . . ready to set fire to the sky.

Chapter 25
Conquerors

Tombfyre carried Ariakas through a long, laboring climb. Even in the huge chamber the monstrous red dragon had to spiral constantly, striving every moment to increase their altitude. Ariakas stared above them, seeking some sign of the sky—anything that would show them a way out. Yet the higher they climbed, the more clear it became that this massive vault of stone was sealed by a solid dome of rock overhead.

"How did you get in here?" Ariakas asked, as they soared in a circle near the top of the vast space.

"I don't remember," Tombfyre replied with a rippling shrug of his powerful shoulders and sinuous neck. The serpent's tone was bitter. "The queen placed me here after the war—I have no knowledge of occurrences immediately following Huma's victory."

"It may salve your pride to know that Huma died in that battle—your army had its vengeance, at least."

"Vengeance is no substitute for victory," growled the wyrm. Abruptly, he tucked his wings, plummeting into the depths of the vast caverns, toward the smoking, smoldering reaches below. The plunge should have taken Ariakas by surprise, but a warning tingled in his mind a second before the dive—he tightened his hands in the dragon's mane, and when the serpent dived, the human clung securely to his back.

Still spiraling, Tombfyre sped through his long descent. Wind whipped Ariakas's hair back from his face, and his lips clenched into a snarling smile of triumph. The dragon's wheeling path continued downward, circling around the shaft that had held his prison for more than a thousand years.

Smoke stung Ariakas's eyes, and heat began to build oppressively. They plunged ever lower, still faster, and the human began to imagine an inevitable, fiery end to their descent. The smoldering depths became clear, as he saw eddies of cloudy smoke whisking past bright, flaming lava. He pictured an instantaneous finale, life blotted out at the very moment they smashed into the abyssal fires seething within the heart of Krynn.

The light grew brighter, forming a reddish haze of flaming illumination, burning the very air around them. Abruptly, and with a dizzying sense of expansion, the shaft they flew down opened through a hole in the ceiling of an incredibly vast, furiously burning cavern—like a plain of fire, sprawling to the horizons far below the surface of the world.

The dragon pulled out of the dive, and a huge, crimson vista opened before the warrior's astonished eyes. Bubbling lava spread to the limits of vision, smoking, flaming, casting great, liquid gouts upward from the surface of a fiery sea. The shaft where he had found Tombfyre was nothing more than a tall, capped chimney leading upward from this huge, subterranean fire sea.

It seemed to Ariakas that the searing heat should kill him, but though he looked all around, at air shimmering with the scalding effects of fire, those effects did not touch his skin. He rode through the blazes of the inferno as though a bubble of cool, moist air surrounded him.

Great islands of dark stone rose into craggy peaks from the flaming surface, while stalactites funneled downward like inverted mountains from a cavern ceiling that in many places arced a full mile above the violent sea. Bubbling veins of white-hot, molten rock crisscrossed back and forth among the cooler red of the lava, and many of these hot spots spewed geysers of liquid fire.

"Look—there! Smoke's escaping!" Ariakas indicated a vast crack in the cavern's ceiling. They could see shafts of smoke, sometimes accompanied by whirling blasts of flame, surging upward to disappear into the dark hole. "There has to be a vent to the surface!"

Immediately the dragon drove his wings downward, breaking from his glide and striving to gain altitude. The billowing updrafts helped carry them aloft into the crack. Soon stone walls surrounded them, leaving barely room for Tombfyre to wheel through tight circles. Fortunately the rising air gave them just enough lift to maintain the climb.

With a flash of fierce, savage triumph, Ariakas caught a glimpse of the sky overhead—a pale swatch of blue that might have been sunset or dawn. Curiously, the man realized, he had no idea what the time might be on the outside world.

They reached a side cavern in the great shaft, and as the red dragon continued to labor upward Ariakas caught a strong stench of the Zhakar odor—the combination of mold and mushroom tea that had been so pervasive around the runty dwarves. With a flash of inspiration he remembered the tunnels leading into the city from the flaming, volcanic reaches below.

"There—go *there*!" he hissed. "Our vengeance will begin immediately!"

Without hesitating, Tombfyre ducked toward the passage, gaining momentum in the level flight. Cave walls sped past them with dizzying speed, and the smell grew stronger.

In another moment they burst into a large cavern, and immediately Ariakas saw the twin rows of pillars marking the King's Promenade of Zhakar. He heard screaming, observed with cruel glee hundreds of panicked dwarves frantically fleeing from their path. As Tombfyre flew over a group of them, the Zhakar collapsed to the ground, groveling in abject fear.

The serpent dipped a wing and curved with regal majesty, flying directly between the columns, diving straight for the twin thrones and the bestial statues at the far end of the promenade. Below, a full rank of Zhakar lizard riders struggled to control their mounts, but the scaly steeds bucked and pitched frantically, terrified by the soaring wyrm. Their powerful hind legs enabled the creatures to jump very high—perhaps twenty feet straight up—and one by one the riders were thrown roughly to the floor.

The populace scattered amid shrieks and wails of hysterical fear. The bigger dwarves trampled their smaller neighbors in haste to reach the shelter of the huge cavern's corners and niches. As the crowd spread, Ariakas realized that some kind of gathering had been taking place before the great throne of Rackas Ironcog.

Tombfyre dived, skimming the floor in a last rush toward the throne and the cavern wall beyond. Now some Zhakar gaped in frozen horror, abject fear distorting their disfigured faces in clownish exaggeration.

Amid the terror-struck onlookers, Ariakas saw that Tale Splintersteel knelt before the throne of Rackas

Ironcog. The Zhakar merchant was in chains, and a hulking dwarf armed with a broad headsman's axe stood beside Splintersteel, awaiting his monarch's command. The executioner gaped upward, motionless, while Splintersteel threw himself, groveling, onto the floor.

Another prisoner stood a short distance away, and Ariakas recognized the shocked visage of Whez Lavastone. Rackas had apparently wasted no time in rounding up his enemies: guards flanked Lavastone, apparently in the process of clapping chains on his wrists and ankles when the approaching dragon brought activity to an abrupt halt.

Abruptly, Whez Lavastone seemed to shake off the effects of the dragonawe—at least to the point where he twisted free of the two guards holding his arms. Disabling one with a sharp kick, the sturdy Zhakar plucked a dagger from the belt of the second man-at-arms and disemboweled him in the next stroke.

"Stop them! Kill them!" cried Rackas Ironcog, king of Zhakar. The monarch jabbered and gesticulated as the horrifying form swooped straight toward him. In response to his command the royal guards threw down their weapons and fled as fast as their stubby legs could carry them—those, at least, who didn't collapse, paralyzed by terror, to the floor.

Ariakas thought of the green blade on his back, of the hissing cloud of poisonous gas he could send wafting through these chambers. He quickly discarded the thought as an unnecessary extravagance.

Tombfyre spread his broad wings and came to light just before the monarch's great, stone seat. It seemed that a sneer of amusement curled the serpentine lip as the mighty creature looked around at the scene of confusion and fear.

Ariakas saw something move in the shadows behind the second of the great thrones. Several guards crouched there, paralyzed by fear, but one cloaked figure scurried away. The warrior caught a glimpse of the gold fringe on the dark robe, and recognized Tik Deepspeaker.

"Kill him!" Ariakas snarled to his mount, pointing after the fleeing savant.

Tombfyre turned his broad head. Tooth-studded jaws gaped, and a puff of preliminary smoke emerged from the dragon's black nostrils. Then a belch of hellish, oily fire erupted from that horrific maw, spurting outward to hiss and crackle around the second throne, incinerating the guards who had taken shelter there. The greedy fire billowed farther, and in another instant swept around the gold-robed figure.

Even considering the incredible, killing heat of the fiery breath, Tik Deepspeaker managed to scream for a long time. When finally the inferno faded, all that remained was a black chip of charcoal, much smaller than a Zhakar's body.

Rackas Ironcog leapt from his throne and tried to scramble into the narrow niche behind it—a niche that was only wide enough to accommodate his head and shoulders. His terror was both pathetic and gratifying, and he seemed a figure hardly worth Ariakas's or Tombfyre's attention.

Nor was that attention necessary. Whez Lavastone, after killing the second guard, raced toward the king, ignoring the leering dragonhead looming over him. The Zhakar reached his monarch's cowering form, and Lavastone drove his bloody dagger into Rackas Ironcog's back. Withdrawing the weapon with a hysterical cry of triumph, he plunged it downward again, stabbing the dying king through the neck.

"Rackas Ironcog is dead!" cried Lavastone, holding the gory weapon aloft.

Abruptly, Whez Lavastone's eyes met those of Ariakas. The Zhakar's gaze wavered, and the warrior could see the growing fear there—but still, the dwarf did not cower before the awe-inspiring interlopers.

"Swear to me your allegiance, and you and your people will be allowed to live," declared Ariakas. "Falter, and you will join your king in death!"

"I swear!" cried Whez Lavastone, prostrating himself before the dragon and the human. The dwarf quickly rose to his feet and addressed his countrymen.

"I claim the crown of Zhakar!" he shouted. "Is there any here who would face my challenge in the arena?"

For long moments the great hall was silent. The Zhakar continued to slowly creep back toward the soot-blackened thrones, cautiously observing developments.

"Hail King Lavastone!" cried a voice—perhaps that of Tale Splintersteel.

Immediately the call was taken up, and if it wasn't a resounding thunder neither did it possess any note of dissent.

Whez Lavastone turned back to Ariakas and Tomb-fyre. "I realize you seek the mold of the fungus warrens. You shall have as much of it as you desire," he promised.

"I know," Ariakas said with a smug nod.

Tale Splintersteel, meanwhile, cocked a cautious eye upward from the floor, though he still trembled in awe of the monstrous serpent.

"Unchain him," Ariakas commanded, and several attendants crept to obey. The highlord slid down Tomb-fyre's sleek shoulder, striding forward to confront Tale Splintersteel and Whez Lavastone.

"I will take some of the dust to Sanction when I depart," Ariakas continued. Then he turned to the Zhakar merchant. "Your treachery has gone unpunished long enough. You sought to betray me in the Fireplaza of Sanction, and there I swore vengeance—now, accept your retribution."

The green sword flashed, and Tale Splintersteel's head, face locked in an expression of dawning horror, flew from his shoulders and thumped onto the floor.

"This one once served me, but I had no more need of

him." Ariakas turned back to the wary figure of Whez Lavastone. "You will not outlive your usefulness, either.

"Send a caravan to Sanction in my wake. Oh, and you'll want to appoint a new merchant lord—one who meets my approval. I want a hundred barrels of the mold in the first shipment, and that's *only* the beginning."

"B—But what are the terms?" stammered Whez.

"You'll hear the terms when the mold is delivered," snapped the highlord. "Now—*bring me my sample!*"

"Quickly, fools!" yelped Whez Lavastone, crying out to the assembled Zhakar who stood well back from the imposing intruder. "Bring him the dust! Pack saddlebags—*go!*"

Dozens of dwarves hurried to obey. Ariakas and Tombfyre remained alert to activity around them, but felt certain that the Zhakar had been thoroughly cowed.

His mind drifted back to Lyrelee and the delights she had given him. . . . He felt a twinge of regret, but already he saw that there would be other women—as many as he wanted. Perhaps he would choose a young maiden this time, or a wench with a little more flesh on her bones. The problem of their inevitable deaths would only serve to provide variety.

Ariakas's thoughts turned to Ferros Windchisel, and the steadfast friendship that, in the end, had been the Hylar's greatest gift. Together they had shared a road of dangers and delights. Ferros had proven to be a true warrior's companion—a loyal ally willing to live or die as fate decreed. Of the two, he knew that Ferros would be harder to replace.

Ariakas felt a brief sadness for their loss—more so for the dwarf than the woman, he realized. Perhaps Ferros Windchisel had offered him a friendship and loyalty that would be unique in his life.

But then his thoughts turned to the future. As the dwarves carted out great saddlebags of mold dust, he imagined the wealth that treasure would generate in

Sanction—for he intended to charge the temple for his services. With that money, and the power that would come to him by virtue of his new companion, the road to that smoldering city was lined with promise.

Beyond Sanction, Ariakas knew, that pathway would lead him to new heights of conquest and mastery. Legions of draconians would march under his banner! There would be a time—*soon*—when whole nations, when all of Ansalon, would tremble at the mention of his name . . . when, backed by the might of his Dark Queen, he, Highlord Ariakas, would rule the world!

Epilogue

Tombfyre carried his human warrior to Sanction, soaring in one day over mountain ridges that had taken Ariakas and his companions a fortnight to cross. Securely strapped to the dragon's flanks were a pair of saddlebags, stuffed to bulging with the powdered dust of the plague fungus.

Before the pair had departed Zhakar, Ariakas made certain that Whez Lavastone had appointed a new emissary, and that the caravan was ready to march. That Zhakar merchant lord would bring a large load of mold to Sanction very quickly, Ariakas suspected, for only then would the dwarves receive their first payment.

Also during his high-handed negotiations, Ariakas

had demanded that the Zhakar provide him with large companies of foot soldiers and lizard riders. Those would be marching along with the caravan, Whez Lavastone had promised, and the highlord had been inclined to believe him. The troops would join the ranks of the mercenaries he would hire, and the draconians that would soon march forth, in great numbers, from the Temple of Luerkhisis.

The highlord relished the sense of grim satisfaction that could only arise from successful vengeance. Tale Splintersteel and Rackas Ironcog had each paid in full measure the cost of treachery. Justice had been served, and Ariakas reflected that revenge was indeed the sweetest taste.

Flight over the Khalkists was exhilarating, and Ariakas —warmly bundled in furs, ensconced in a deep saddle created by Zhakar leatherworkers—enjoyed the long day of barren, rocky vistas. In flight, Ariakas relished a sense of mastery over even the mountains themselves. He and Tombfyre were alone in the heavens, high above even the soaring eagles. Yet when smoky Sanction hove into view, the human felt fully ready to rejoin humankind. Now, at last, he would do so as master and conqueror—a true highlord!

In the teeming streets people pointed and gawked, and when Tombfyre swooped low overhead they trembled in fear. When the red dragon set to ground before the Temple of Luerkhisis, hundreds of priests ran from the twin gates to prostrate themselves before their emperor and his mighty steed. Soon, Ariakas vowed, he would fly his dragon into the Fireplaza, and there he would gather the squabbling mercenaries of the city to his banner. They didn't know it yet, but those warriors would form the key regiments of an army that would threaten all of Ansalon.

But even that host wouldn't be enough. Already the Zhakar had been enlisted to the cause, and Ariakas had plans to fly to Bloten, threatening the ogres with obliteration if they didn't rally to the Dark Queen's banner. There, as in the city, the highlord felt certain of eventual success—not just because of fear, but because ogres and human warriors both would be unable to resist the picture of victorious battle and rich plunder that Ariakas would use to lure them.

Wryllish Parkane hurried from the temple gates to kneel reverently before both the dragon and the highlord. The high priest quickly rose to his feet, his face serious.

"Apprentices—grab those saddlebags!" barked Ariakas, dismounting and striding to Parkane. "Come on—let's go to the egg rooms."

"The shadowpeople have invaded the Sanctified Catacombs!" burst the high priest. "They've seized the egg chambers, and resisted all of our attempts to drive them out. They say if we bring an army down there they will destroy the eggs!"

"They won't hurt them," Ariakas said with certainty. "But perhaps I can talk to them."

"Indeed—the leading warrior, one called Vallenswade, has asked to speak to you personally."

"Where are they gathered?" asked the highlord.

"They're holed up in a large cavern, where the tunnels all come together. They have all the entrances blocked, and there's no way we can reach the eggs," replied the priest.

"I'll . . . *talk* to them. Bring the mold along quickly—it won't be long before we can get to work," Ariakas said, starting into the tunnels of the Catacombs.

On his back gleamed the emerald-green blade of his sword.

DARK SUN™

The PRISM PENTAD
By Troy Denning

Searing drama in an unforgiving world . . .

The Obsidian Oracle Book Four

Power-hungry Tithian emerges as the new ruler of Tyr. When he pursues his dream of becoming a sorcerer-king, only the nobleman Agis stands between Tithian and his desire: possession of an ancient oracle that will lead to either the salvation of Athas – or its destruction.

Available in June 1993
ISBN 1-56076-603-4
Sug. Retail $4.95/CAN $5.95/£3.99 U.K.

The Cerulean Storm Book Five

Rajaat: The First Sorcerer – the only one who can return Athas to its former splendor – is imprisoned beyond space and time. When Tithian enlists the aid of his former slaves, Rikus, Neeva, and Sadira, to free the sorcerer, does he want to restore the world – or claim it as his own?

Available in September 1993
ISBN 1-56076-642-5
Sug. Retail $4.95/CAN $5.95/£3.99 U.K.

On Sale Now

The Verdant Passage Book One
ISBN 1-56076-121-0
Sug. Retail $4.95/CAN $5.95/£3.99 U.K.

The Amber Enchantress Book Three
ISBN 1-56076-236-5
Sug. Retail $4.95/CAN $5.95/£3.99 U.K.

The Crimson Legion
Book Two
ISBN 1-56076-260-8
Sug. Retail $4.95/
CAN $5.95/£3.99 U.K.

TALES OF GOTHIC HORROR
BEYOND YOUR WILDEST SCREAMS!

Tapestry of Dark Souls
Elaine Bergstrom
ISBN 1-56076-571-2
The monks' hold over the Gathering Cloth, containing some of the vilest evils in Ravenloft, is slipping. The only hope is a strange youth, who will become either the monks' champion . . . or their doom.

Heart of Midnight
J. Robert King
ISBN 1-56076-355-8
Even before he'd drawn his first breath, Casimir had inherited his father's lycanthropic curse. Now the young werewolf must embrace his powers to ward off his own murder and gain revenge.

MORE TALES OF TERROR

Vampire of the Mists
Christie Golden
ISBN 1-56076-155-5

Dance of the Dead
Christie Golden
ISBN 1-56076-352-3

Knight of the Black Rose
James Lowder
ISBN 1-56076-156-3

Available now at book and hobby stores everywhere!

Each $4.95/CAN $5.95/U.K. £3.99

Ravenloft
Books

The Penhaligon Trilogy

If you enjoyed *The Dragon's Tomb*, you'll want to read —

The Fall of Magic   Book Three
A sinister mage unleashes the power of an ancient artifact on Penhaligon, an artifact that drains the world of all magic except his own. In a final, desperate gambit, Johauna and her comrades set out on an impossible quest to stop the arcane assault and save the world of Mystara! *Available in October 1993.*

ISBN 1-56076-663-8
Sug. Retail $4.95/CAN $5.95/£3.99 U.K.

The Tainted Sword
Book One
The once-mighty knight Fain Flinn has forsaken both his pride and his legendary sword, Wyrmblight. Now Penhaligon faces a threat only he can conquer. All seems hopeless until . . . Flinn regains his magical blade. Yet even Wyrmblight may not be powerful enough to quash the dragon! *On sale now.*

ISBN 1-56076-395-7
Sug. Retail $4.95/CAN $5.95/£3.99 U.K.

Novels